FIRST KISS

Conn's hand, which had been caressing her hair, moved down. One of his fingers traced the outline of her lips.

Hayley's trembling started again. "You're cold," Conn said. "Shall I warm you?"

His fingers were rough against the soft skin of her lips. But it was a wonderful kind of roughness. Her lips burned where he touched her. Burned for more of his touch.

His hand slid down to her chin, tilted it upward.

For a long moment, their gazes met and melded.

"Let us proceed with the warming," Conn's husky voice said. Slowly, he lowered his head toward hers.

Hayley's lips parted and she lifted her head to meet his advance. When finally their lips met, a long trembling sigh escaped her. She closed her eyes, letting the intense pleasure of Conn's touch flow over her.

The kiss deepened, became more than a kiss. Gently, Conn pushed her backward onto the grass and lowered himself beside her. . . .

D1521917

Books by Elizabeth Graham

SWEET ENCHANTMENT
COURTING EDEN
MY DARLING KATE
THE HEART'S HAVEN
HAYLEY'S HEART

Published by Zebra Books

HAYLEY'S HEART

Elizabeth Graham

Zebra Books
Kensington Publishing Corp.

http://www.zebrabooks.com

ZEBRA BOOKS are published by

Kensington Publishing Corp.
850 Third Avenue
New York, NY 10022

First Printing: June, 1999
10 9 8 7 6 5 4 3 2

Printed in the United States of America

For three dear friends from the old days in
Missouri and Baltimore:

Jo Baker, Elaine Beilhart and Robin Poe

And for a dear Florida friend, Cathy Golden

PROLOGUE

Philadelphia, Pennsylvania
1762

"Don't leave me, Darryl! Don't go!"

Hayley Armstrong flung herself at her sister. Choking back sobs, she watched the cold, unfeeling man who'd just bought Darryl's bond lead her away.

Hard arms restrained Hayley and jerked her back across the rough wood planks of the platform.

"That'll be enough out o' ye, wench," her own new master muttered.

She felt—and smelled—his reeking breath on the back of her neck. Shuddering, she swiped at her wet cheek and tried to jerk away from him.

His grip held, his fingers painfully digging into her arms.

"Ah, no, ye don't! Ye'll come with me! I've bought your bond right and proper. Paid more than I ought to, no doubt."

He dug his fingers in harder. "Scrawny thing ye are. Probably won't earn your keep. But maybe ye will."

Something in his tone made her jerk her head around. His leering smile made a knot of fear form in her stomach.

She understood what the look meant. All too well. She and Darryl had seen that expression on the faces of many of the ship's crew on the voyage from England.

The last two weeks had been the stuff of nightmares.

First, their parents had died of a fever on board the ship that was carrying them far from their native Suffolk to the Colonies to begin a new life. The same fever had taken other passengers' lives and left her and Darryl weak and thin.

Then they'd discovered their money gone, stolen, they were sure, by the ship's captain, who looked and acted like little better than a pirate.

Their parents had paid all four passages when they left England. When the ship reached Philadelphia, insisting this was the arrangement they'd made for their passage money, the lying captain had sold Hayley and Darryl as bond servants.

Hayley's mouth twisted. The greedy sod had lined his pockets well.

The final blow came when Oscar Pritt bought only Darryl's bond.

And Burle Porter bought Hayley's.

She and Darryl were each other's best friend. Darryl had looked out for her younger sister since childhood.

Burle Porter, her master, her captor, jerked Hayley along as he strode away from the platform toward a farm wagon standing under a tree.

Hayley wrenched her head around, straining for one more glimpse of Darryl. At that exact moment, Darryl did the same.

The sisters exchanged a look. Darryl tossed her head in defiance, mouthing something at Hayley.

Hayley made out the movements of Darryl's lips.

Be brave and strong.

Hayley forced herself to mouth the same words back to her sister.

She *couldn't* stand to be away from Darryl! It would kill her.

Somehow, she'd find out where Darryl was being taken and she'd go to her. Then they'd both run away. Far, far away where no one would ever find them.

Terror gnawed at Hayley's insides. Darryl was the strong one. How could she possibly do what she planned?

From somewhere deep inside, she found courage and resolution.

There was no other choice.

She would do it.

Or die in the attempt.

CHAPTER ONE

Wearily sinking to her knees, Hayley peered out around the big oak tree she hid behind, hoping to catch a glimpse of Darryl somewhere around the many nearby outbuildings. The farm her sister had been sent to was big, like the one Hayley had run away from a week before.

No, they didn't call them farms here in this New World. They were called plantations. Burle Porter, her master, had constantly referred to his many acres as such with boastful pride.

Hayley pushed her straggly hair away from her face, her trembling hand coming away streaked with dirt. Last night she hadn't been able to find a stream to sleep near, to wash at this morning.

"What you doin' there, girl?"

The softly accented voice from behind Hayley erupted into the quiet of the afternoon. Startled, she jerked backward and fell.

Her heart pounding, Hayley gazed up into a brown face. The woman wore coarse work clothes, and a kerchief bound her dark hair.

After a few moments, Hayley's heartbeat slowed. The woman's expression was curious—not hostile.

But that doesn't mean she won't run to her master and tell him about you, Hayley's mind whispered.

And he'll send you straight back to Burle Porter.

"Nothing," Hayley croaked from her suddenly dry throat. She lifted her head and tried to rise. Her head swam, and her empty stomach told her she hadn't eaten in two days. The outside world began to fade, and she started to fall again.

Strong hands caught her, gently laid her back on the grass.

"You ain't nothin' but skin and bones," the brown woman scolded. "What you doin' here?" she asked again.

"I—I'm lost," Hayley muttered, her head clearing a little. If the woman would go away . . . maybe she could find Darryl. . . .

The other woman knelt beside her, still with no trace of hostility in her face, only curiosity now mixed with concern.

"Just let me rest a moment, and I'll be on my way."

"Take more'n any moment 'fore you rested," the woman said. "You skinny as that other chile old Oscar brung in here couple weeks ago. Look a good bit like her, too, now I thinks on it."

Hayley stiffened at those last words—but relief and joy overcame the fear. She felt her lips curving into a smile. Oh, thank God! The nagging terror haunting her that she wouldn't find her sister at the end of this ordeal vanished.

The brown woman's dark brows lifted in surprise. "Why, I bet you *are* that gal's sister. The one she talks and frets 'bout all the time. Says you don' know how to take care of yourself a-tall. Looks of you, she be right."

Hayley's blue-eyed glance met the nearly black one of the woman kneeling over her.

Hayley could dissemble no longer. She was too tired, too hungry. She had to take a chance, throw herself on this woman's mercy.

"Yes, I'm Darryl's sister," Hayley admitted, holding her breath.

The woman nodded. "I knew it. Ain't many gals got such

pale hair and eyes so blue, and that white skin. How on earth you git here all the way from Burle Porter's plantation?''

Hayley shook her head. ''I don't know. I didn't think I could, but I had to. I couldn't stand to be away from Darryl! Burle Porter is a horrible man! He kept following me around, and . . .''

Hayley swallowed, unable to go on.

The woman nodded again, grimly this time. ''Old Oscar ain't no better. He been eyein' your sister ever since he brung her here. I think he 'bout ready to make his move on her.''

Hayley closed her eyes, despair sweeping over her. This place was no better than the one she'd left. Had her terrible journey been for nothing? She tried to take heart. No, she had found Darryl, and she'd known they couldn't stay here long. Darryl wouldn't be able to keep her hidden.

But the thought of running away from here, more days of fighting the woods, scared, dirty and hungry, overwhelmed her. She was so tired. She couldn't do it!

She took a deep, fortifying breath. Yes, she could. They both could. There was no other choice.

''Can you take me to Darryl without anyone seeing us?''

The woman's considering gaze held on Hayley's for a long moment.

Hayley didn't breathe, knowing the other woman would be risking a lot to help her.

Finally, she nodded. ''Yes, and I will. That little girl pinin' away by herself. And you in bad shape.''

Hayley reached down and picked up the cotton drawstring bag that now held only a comb and a shift. She wore her only bodice and skirt, leaving behind the coarse work dress she'd been given at Burle Porter's plantation. She hadn't dared wear it, knowing it would brand her as a runaway bond servant.

Ten minutes later, the woman, who'd said her name was Cilla, opened the door of a small wooden cabin and pulled Hayley inside, quickly closing the door behind them.

The cabin's one room had a bare, rough wood floor, and was sparsely furnished. Cilla half-led Hayley to the nearest of the two blanket-covered cots and gently pushed her down on it.

"This mine and Darryl's cabin. You rest now. I'll go tell your sister you here. Don't you stick your head out the door," she warned.

"I won't," Hayley promised, her eyes closing before Cilla had left the cabin.

"Hayley!"

Darryl's voice penetrated Hayley's stupor. She opened her eyes to see her sister bending over her, joy mixed with fear on her face. Darryl slipped her arms around Hayley's neck and the sisters hugged each other fiercely.

"I couldn't believe it when Cilla told me you were here!"

"I can't believe it, either," Hayley mumbled, sitting up. "I'm so hungry!"

"I know. I brought something from the kitchen." Darryl opened the cloth-wrapped bundle she carried and extended two pieces of thick-sliced bread with a piece of meat between them.

Hayley, her hand trembling, took the proffered food and devoured it. "Nothing ever tasted so good," she said after swallowing the last bite.

"How did you find this place? How did you make a journey like that?" Darryl asked, wonder in her face.

"I had to," Hayley said, simply. "People helped me. One farm woman gave me food for two days and let me sleep in their barn."

Darryl's eyes were still wide with disbelief. "How did you keep from getting lost?"

"I did get lost a time or two. But I went by the stars at night and the sun by day."

The cabin door opened and Cilla slipped in. "You better git back up to the house," she told Darryl. "You be missed in a few minutes."

Darryl rose from the cot, a worried frown on her face. "You stay inside until I come tonight," she told her sister. "Then we'll have to try to figure out what to do. You know what it means if you're caught.''

"Yes. They can add a year or more to my bound time. And to yours for harboring me.''

"We can't let that happen," Darryl said, decisively.

"No," Hayley agreed, quailing inside at the very thought.

"So we won't.''

Hayley sought her sister's glance. "You know what we have to do. We must run away from here.''

Darryl's frown deepened. "But not like you did. We must have time to plan properly. Take enough food with us to survive no matter how long it takes to reach safety.''

"And where will that be? How far will we have to go?''

"I don't know. Neither of us knows this country.''

"You head on south. No one look for you down there in the wilderness," Cilla advised. "They be lookin' up north, toward Philadelphia. They think you go back that way.''

"That's a good idea," Darryl said. "Thank you, Cilla. I'd never have thought of it.''

"No, neither would I," Hayley said. She gave a huge yawn, smothering it with her hand.

"Go to sleep," Darryl said. "You're exhausted. But maybe you'd better put the quilt on the floor behind the cot and sleep there just in case anyone should open the door.''

"All right." Hayley smothered another yawn. "I could sleep for a week.''

But she knew she couldn't. *They* couldn't. They had to get out of here.

As quickly as possible.

But she could sleep for a while. Until Darryl came back . . .

Cilla and Darryl, cleaning up from the evening meal, talked in low voices over the tub of dirty dishes.

"What you goin' to do with your sister while you get ready to run? Somebody sure to see her and tattle to old Oscar.'' Cilla handed Darryl a bowl to dry.

A new stab of fear hit Darryl. "I don't know! What *can* I do except hide her in our cabin?"

Cilla nodded, grimly. "I don't know, neither. I hear bad things 'bout that Burle Porter. You two got to git outta here quick."

"But where can we go with no money? What can we do?" Darryl heard the fear in her voice and firmed her mouth.

She was the strong one, she reminded herself. She had to think of a solution.

"What are you two gossiping about?" Mrs. Whitley's frosty, prim voice said from so close by Darryl jumped.

Not looking at the housekeeper, Darryl swallowed and moved away from Cilla. She reached for another dish in the pan and quickly dried it.

Out of the corner of her eye, Darryl saw Mrs. Whitley, who, it was rumored, shared Oscar's bed on occasion, although she was keeping company with another man, move farther into the room. Her mouth was pursed as if she smelled something bad.

Cilla gave Mrs. Whitley an innocent glance. "We just talkin' about tomorrow's chores."

The woman's thin lips pinched tighter. "I'm sure you were. Both of you are so diligent with your work."

Darryl felt a spurt of anger. Oh, how she detested this woman! Cilla and Darryl *were* good workers, and Mrs. Whitley knew that. It made no difference. She hounded all the household workers, never gave anyone a kind word.

And if she had the slightest suspicion Darryl was hiding Hayley in her cabin, she'd waste no time telling the master.

As if her thoughts had summoned him, Oscar entered the kitchen. His glance at once found Darryl and lingered.

His dark, lustful gaze made Darryl feel dirty. And Mrs. Whitley's face tightened even more as she also caught the look.

"I don't know why you don't sell this useless girl's bond," Mrs. Whitley said, turning to the plantation owner. "It's an everlasting struggle for me to get a day's work out of her."

Maybe that was the solution, Darryl thought, hope leaping

up in her. *Maybe she could behave so outrageously that Oscar would sell her bond.*

And what about Hayley?

Her hope died.

Oscar licked his lips and grinned. He turned to Mrs. Whitley and gave her a derisive look.

"Seems like you're fretting a bit too much over a kitchen girl. What's the matter? Afraid I might assign some of your duties to her?"

His meaning was unmistakable. Darryl heard the housekeeper's shocked intake of breath.

Fear clenched Darryl's stomach. She'd known he wanted to bed her from the moment he saw her, but he'd never before been so open about his intentions.

The plate she held slipped out of her hand. It fell to the floor and shattered. Darryl's fear increased. She hastily knelt and began gathering up the pieces.

"There! See what I mean?" Mrs. Whitley's shrill voice exclaimed. "Useless! Utterly useless and clumsy."

"You're hurting my ears with your racket, woman. Go on, find someone else to harangue." Oscar Pritt's voice had turned frigid.

Mrs. Whitley inhaled sharply again, then left the room, her head held high.

Darryl got to her feet, holding the broken pieces of china. Her glance collided with Cilla's. The older woman gave an almost imperceptible shake of her head.

Be careful, her eyes warned.

As if Darryl didn't know that! But how?

"Cilla, go finish clearing the table," Oscar said, his voice imperious.

Cilla turned to him. "I'm washin' the dishes," she said. "Darryl's been doin' the clearing."

"I give the orders here! Go!"

With one last anxious glance at Darryl, Cilla left the room.

Darryl, still holding the broken pieces of plate, finally looked up at her master.

Oscar's tongue was running over his lips again. A lustful gleam lit his eyes. "Do you think maybe you're ready to take over some of Mrs. Whitley's duties?" he asked, his voice soft.

Darryl's fingers involuntarily clenched on a sharp-edged piece of china. "Oh!" she said, feeling a stab of pain.

She glanced down to see blood oozing out from between her fingers, running over her hand. She released her grip and the broken pieces once more clattered to the floor.

Cilla came running in, her hands full of dishes, which she dumped in the washing pan. "What you done, chile? Here, let me see." She grasped Darryl's wrist, spreading her fingers out.

A deep cut slashed across Darryl's left palm, the blood coming faster now.

Cilla reached for a drying towel and quickly wrapped it around Darryl's hand. "I'm goin' to have to stitch that."

From across the room, Darryl heard Oscar's disgusted snort. He turned and left the room without another word.

Darryl released her held breath in a huge relieved sigh.

Cilla darted her head up. "Did you do that on purpose?"

Darryl shook her head. "No, but I would have if I'd thought of it."

Cilla grimaced. "Me, too, faced with beddin' down with old Oscar. Glad he ain't lookin' my way."

She shook her head. "That hand not goin' to be doin' much for the next week or two."

"But Hayley and I have to get out of here," Darryl protested. "We can't wait that long. Burle Porter probably has men looking for her already. It's a wonder they haven't been here."

"Old Burle and Oscar lose a lot of girls 'cause they go after the pretty ones. Always a bunch of 'dentured folks runnin' around. Some of them get caught. Or die in the woods somewhere."

Darryl's eyes widened at Cilla's words.

Cilla patted her arm. "Don't you worry none about that. Do like I said, you head on south. And I put out the word you done went north, tryin' to get to Philadelphia. That throw 'em off the track."

Darryl's fears eased a tiny bit. "Yes, we'll do that."

"But you better give that hand a chance to heal a little."

Darryl clenched her teeth, then reluctantly nodded. "Only a couple of days. And I'll have Mrs. Whitley after me all the time about not doing my work."

"That better than havin' Oscar after you. You got a breathin' space."

"Yes," Darryl agreed. Oscar would leave her alone for a little while. That would give her and Hayley time to plan their escape.

To where? The thought of trudging through unknown wilderness chilled her to the bone. There was no safe place. But she couldn't stay here, even if she didn't have Hayley to consider. Because eventually—and it wouldn't be too much longer either—she'd have to submit to Oscar's lechery. Share his bed.

A shudder ran through her. Sudden tears sprang to her eyes as she thought of the bright hopes and dreams she and Hayley had shared with her parents when they'd left Suffolk.

A new life in this New World. A chance to own land of their own. Her whole family had worked on a big estate in Suffolk. Somehow they'd saved enough over the years for their passage, with enough left to buy a bit of land for themselves.

All gone now. All the dreams and hopes.

Cilla tugged at her again. "Come on. You dripping blood all over the floor."

Darryl became aware of the throbbing in her palm. "All right."

Her lips firmed. No. She wouldn't accept the end of their hopes. Somehow, she and Hayley would find a solution. Would find a decent life for themselves.

She was the strong one. She'd always taken care of Hayley. And she'd continue to do so.

"Hide!" Darryl rushed into the cabin, closed the door behind her and leaned against it, her blue eyes wide and frightened.

Three days after her injury, the bandage wrapped around her left hand gleamed white in the twilight.

Hayley turned sharply from the hearth, holding a big stirring spoon. "What?"

"Oscar's right behind me. Someone told Mrs. Whitley. Hide quickly!"

Hayley's heart leapt. She looked around the tiny room. "Where?"

"Behind Cilla's cot! Anywhere! Hurry!"

Hayley sped across the floor and dived down along the side of the cot where it sat along the wall, scrunching up as small as she could.

She peered out from under the cot. The door burst open, making Darryl stagger and nearly fall.

Oscar Pritt stood in the doorway, a dark frown on his beefy face. He looked around the tiny room. "Where is she? Where is that sister of yours?"

Hayley held herself as still as possible, taking shallow breaths, hoping Oscar couldn't hear her heart pounding. But how could he not? It beat in her throat, roared in her ears.

"I don't know what you're talking about," Darryl said.

How could her sister's voice sound so firm and unafraid? Hayley marveled. As if she were truly puzzled by her master's demand.

Oscar sneered and moved forward. "That innocent act won't work, little missy." He glanced around the room, walked to Darryl's cot and peered under it.

Fear squeezed Hayley's chest. What could she do? Nothing. Nothing!

Oscar got to his feet. Moved toward the other cot, bent down . . .

Hayley closed her eyes, holding herself rigid as a fence post. Maybe if she didn't even breathe . . .

Oscar let out a roar, jumped to his feet and jerked the small cot from the wall with one heavy arm.

"Got you!" he said, lunging at Hayley. He grabbed her arm and pulled her to her feet.

He glanced from her to Darryl. "Well, what have we here? Two pretty little ladies."

He stroked his fingers along Hayley's arm where her sleeve had moved back.

Hayley couldn't suppress a shudder. She tried to jerk away from him.

"You leave her alone!" Darryl was on him like a wildcat, pounding on his broad back with her small fists.

Oscar let go of Hayley, turned and gripped both of Darryl's wrists in one big hand. He gave her an evil grin. "Go ahead, fight me, you little wildcat. I like my women with some spirit."

Darryl glared defiantly back at him. "You leave my sister alone," she said again.

Oscar's grin widened. He jerked Darryl toward him. "I might consider that if you cooperate. Late spring this year. My bed's feeling mighty cold lately."

"Your bed's not cold. Mrs. Whitley keeps it warm enough," Darryl spat at him.

"Ah, but I'm getting tired of her. I like new partners every so often. Especially when they're young and pretty. Like you and your sister. I'm sure Burle Porter hated to lose her. He'll be delighted to know she turned up here, all ready for him to collect. And maybe add a year or two to her bound time."

Hayley heard Darryl let out her breath. Saw her sag in defeat.

"All right. I'll come willingly to your bed if you promise to leave Hayley alone. And not send her back."

How could Darryl ask that of him? Of course he'd send Hayley back!

Oscar's grin stretched across his wide, florid face. "Now you're being smart," he said, approvingly. "No use fighting when you can't win, is there?"

"No," Darryl agreed, her voice dead.

Hayley couldn't stand to listen to her sister. To let her go with this horrible man. It wouldn't do any good, anyway. He was lying. He'd take his pleasure with Darryl, then send word to Burle Porter he'd found his runaway bond servant.

She launched herself at Oscar's back just as Darryl had done a few moments ago.

He whirled, grabbed her by the waist and flung her down on the cot. He gave her a backhanded slap, then stood over her.

His grin was gone. "If you know what's good for you, you'll stay there and keep your mouth shut."

"Hayley, listen to him," Darryl pleaded, her voice shaking. "I'll be all right."

Oscar laughed, then straightened himself. "You'll be just fine, little girl. Now, come along."

Darryl held Hayley's glance with a pleading one.

Hayley's head swam from Oscar's blow. She couldn't focus her eyes. But she must stop him! She struggled to get up. Oscar pushed her back down. Hit her again. The world grayed out.

"Stop being a fool," she heard him say coldly from what seemed a long distance.

Darryl rushed to him, took his arm. "Come on, let's go!"

"Eager, now, are you? Well, come along and I'll see you don't have to wait too long for your satisfaction. And mine, too."

The grayness surrounding Hayley disappeared as the door slammed. She heard a rasping sound. She staggered to her feet, lurched across the room and lifted the latch, tugged inward.

She beat on it with her fists, but the heavy door wouldn't budge. Oscar had bolted it from outside. There was no window.

There was nothing she could do to save Darryl.

Despair rolled over Hayley in huge waves. She sank down on the floor and let it engulf her while the evening darkened into night.

Rough hands shook her. "Hayley, come on, we have to get out of here, now!"

Hayley staggered to her feet. Darryl knelt beside her, Cilla behind her. Darryl's hair was flying loose on her shoulders, her lips cut and bleeding, her coarse work gown torn down the front.

"What did he do to you? Oh, Darryl!"

Darryl's cut lips pressed together. "I couldn't stand it. I tried to get away and he forced me."

Sickness filled Hayley at the picture her sister's words conjured up.

"How did you get away?"

"I picked up a poker and hit him over the head." She paused and swallowed. "I—I killed him!"

Beside her, Cilla glared. "I like to kill that man myself. He bad clear through."

Hayley pulled Darryl close, held her while wracking sobs shook Darryl's slight body.

Fierce protectiveness filled Hayley.

It was her turn to take care of Darryl now, just as her sister had looked out for her all her life.

"You two gotta get out o' here before someone finds old Oscar," Cilla said, urgently. "I help you git some things together."

She grabbed the drawstring bag Hayley had brought with her, then headed for the food shelf on the wall. Hayley flew to the washstand, wrung out a cloth and cleaned Darryl's cut mouth, helped her into her bodice and skirt.

"Here, take this and git out o' here." Cilla thrust the bag into Hayley's hand. "I tell everyone you headed back north."

"And will they believe you?" Hayley asked.

"Sure, they will. Too rough and wild down south."

Hayley swallowed, fighting down her alarm.

Somehow she'd get them out of here. Keep them from harm. Find them a safe refuge.

She wouldn't fail her sister.

CHAPTER TWO

"I can't walk any farther. Go on without me."

Darryl sank down onto the forest floor, drew her legs up to her chest and closed her eyes.

Cold with fear, Hayley stared at her. Darryl's bodice and skirt were soiled and torn. Her silver-blond hair was dirty and tangled. Hayley knew she must look much the same.

All that wasn't important. She'd survived that and more on her journey to the Pritt plantation. What worried Hayley was that Darryl's cut palm was red, pus oozing from around Cilla's neat stitches. Hayley feared the injury was inflamed.

But worst of all was Darryl's sprained ankle. Darryl had stumbled into a debris-covered hole, former home of some woods animal, two days ago. Now her ankle was swollen and purple because she'd had to walk on it all of yesterday.

Hayley knew Darryl wasn't being dilatory. She truly couldn't go any farther.

But how could they stay here? Their food had run out yesterday. Their water this morning. Last night some animal had stayed just outside their fire's protection. They'd seen its eyes gleaming in the darkness. Not knowing what it was, whether it was only curious or predatory, made their fears worse.

These woods they traversed now were denser, more frightening than any Hayley had encountered during her own solitary flight.

And they had no idea where they were, other than four days away from the Pritt plantation, all of them cloudy, overcast days—playing havoc with their plan to continue south, using the sun as a guide. Their only hope was to put as much distance between them and both plantations as possible.

Hayley crouched beside her sister, putting a comforting hand on Darryl's trembling shoulder. "I know you can't go any farther today. You have to rest so your ankle will heal."

"I'm hungry—and thirsty. My ankle hurts."

Hayley squeezed Darryl's shoulder. "I know. Stop worrying. We'll find some food and water soon."

She grimaced at her lapse into the Suffolk country accent, at her soothing words that even she didn't believe.

How she thought that miracle would happen, she had no idea. She might find a stream, but food was a different matter.

It was too early for wild berries. She'd made a crude spear of a fallen branch, trimmed into a point with the knife she'd taken from Darryl and Cilla's cabin, and tried to ambush a hare.

The hare was much faster than Hayley. So were the next three she stalked. They were country girls, familiar with skinning and eating wild animals. But she'd never had to find any. And her father had used traps, not a handmade spear.

She had to do something. She *would* do something. She'd find a stream and use her spear on a fish or two. Surely that wouldn't be as hard. . . .

She sank down beside Darryl. She was so tired . . . just a moment's rest . . . and then she'd be up and about. . . .

Just before her heavy eyelids closed, she heard a familiar noise . . . like the sound her father's cart made when he went to market day with their old horse pulling it . . .

Her eyes popped open. *A cart.* That must mean someone was close by.

She got to her feet, tilted her head, listened, then began running through the wood, pushing at the undergrowth that snagged her bedraggled skirts and caught at her untidy hair.

Nearing the edge of the wood, she slowed her headlong flight and caught her breath. The rest of the way she must creep slowly, try to determine whether friend or enemy approached.

And how will you do that? her mind asked. *Do you now have your great-grandmam's second sight?*

She ignored the taunting voice and stealthily made her way to the edge of the woods.

A lone man approached, in a wagon, not a cart, pulled by two well-fed-looking horses. He was a young, handsome man, with dark hair and an open face. And he was whistling.

Yes, she could distinctly hear the sound of it, above the noise the wagon made.

He didn't look as if he were out looking for runaway bond servant girls.

But even if he weren't, what if he'd heard about her and Darryl? What if he recognized them? If so, would he turn them in?

The wagon was fast approaching her hiding place. She had to decide. She took a step forward, then stopped.

No, she couldn't ask him for help. It was too dangerous.

And if you don't soon get help, Darryl will die, her mind said. *You have to take the chance this man will befriend you.*

She drew herself up, gritted her teeth, then pushed through the last barrier of bushes.

Conn Merritt urged his horses along the rutted road with encouraging words and snaps of the reins. He shifted his weight on the hard-board seat on the farm wagon.

The tune he whistled died in his throat. Damn, but he wished this trip was over and he was headed home to Holly View! Spring planting was over and everyone was busy taking care of the fledgling crops. The peaches and apples had bloomed well, promising a good fall crop.

He loved his home and farm and ached to be in the middle of everything. Instead of on this journey, which, although admittedly necessary, was not to his liking.

It was damned inconvenient that the bound girl who helped Lavena in the house had recently fulfilled her time and, instead of staying on as a paid worker as they'd expected, had taken her new clothes and the extra pay Conn had insisted on giving her, married a newly free bound man and moved to a neighboring farm where her new husband worked.

Now Conn was heading for Derryville, in the hope of finding someone who'd work for the small wages they could pay after two years of bad crops.

"Wait . . . oh, please wait!"

The sudden cry from the edge of the woods the road skirted startled the horses as much as it did him.

He yanked on the reins, pulling the team and wagon to a lumbering halt just as a woman burst from the shelter of the trees and ran toward him.

She stumbled as she reached the near horse, and for a heart-stopping moment Conn was sure she would fall beneath Royster's huge hooves. She didn't, but instead sprawled so close, Conn flung the reins on the seat and leaped down.

He crouched beside her, noting her soiled and torn gown, her flaxen hair all a-tumble over her shoulders. Where in hell had she come from?

She quickly rolled over and sat up, glancing half-fearfully at him. Her eyes were a startling clear blue, like October skies. Conn saw her swallow as if her throat were dry. Or as if she were nervous about talking to him. He also saw she was young and would be pretty if she were clean and decently dressed.

"What is the trouble, miss?" he asked.

She swallowed again. "My—my sister is in yonder wood. She's hurt and fevered."

The lass had a Suffolk accent, but somewhat educated, Conn noted. Lavena still kept her Suffolk accent, which became stronger when she was angry, although he'd lost most of the old country sound from his own.

"What are you doing here, far from any habitation?" he asked.

She stared at him so long, he began to think she might be simple and hadn't understood his question.

Finally, she said, "Our parents died on ship. We came over to live with kin in Philadelphia, but they were gone. We hadn't much coin and we couldn't find work ... and decided to try to find work on a farm ... but now we're lost."

He frowned as he stared back. Her few halting words didn't begin to explain why she and her sister were here, so obviously fallen on hard times. But the injured sister must be looked after. He'd find out more later.

Later? What did he mean? Was he getting himself involved with this strange woman and her kin?

"Come along, then, show me where she is and I'll take a look." He got to his feet and reached down to help her up.

His hand engulfed her small cold one. An odd feeling went through him as she quickly stood.

Protective ... and something else. He hadn't felt like that since ...

Conn blanked out that burgeoning thought and, after hooking the reins around a plank end, followed the girl toward the woods. Once there, he pushed aside the bushes for her, and in a few moments she'd led him to where another fair-haired female lay curled on her side under a tree, her eyes closed.

Sod and blast! Was the maid dead?

To his great relief, she moaned and moved restlessly and flung a hand up, revealing a soiled bandage wrapped around it. Her gown was ruched up and he saw the swollen, discolored ankle.

There'd be no walking on that foot for a while, and she also had a hand injury. Inwardly, he swore again.

So where did that put him? He knew where. No decent man could leave two helpless females stranded here in these woods. He'd have to take them along with him to Derryville.

The first girl knelt beside her sister. "Wake up," she said, urgently. "I've found help."

Conn's mouth twitched. The girl wasn't slow. She knew he wouldn't leave them here.

The injured girl moaned again; then as her sister gave her shoulder a tiny shake and moved her onto her back, her eyelids fluttered open. Her eyes were the same clear blue as her sister's, but now they were clouded with pain.

Conn's heart stirred. He hated to see any creature, human or beast, in pain. Many a time he'd been laughed at when growing up for what his stern father deemed too soft a heart, which to him meant weakness. Be that as it may, he knew by now he couldn't change that part of him.

He hurried to the maid and smiled at her. "Never fear, everything will be all right."

She stirred, fear coming into her face. "No! Go away! Leave me be!" She tried to rise, then dropped down again with a painful cry.

The sister dropped to her knees beside the injured girl. "Don't fret. This man will help us," she said, her voice low and soothing.

The girl nodded, woodenly, but turned her face away. Her fever must have her near-delirious, Conn thought, dropping to his own knees.

He gently touched her swollen flesh, prodded for signs of broken bones, felt none, then examined the bandaged hand. He didn't like the look of it. Inflammation was setting in if he wasn't mistaken. He laid his palm across her forehead. Warm, too warm.

She twisted under his grasp, and he quickly removed his hand and got up, frowning. The girl was much afraid.

A pitifully small cloth bag, which must contain all their worldly possessions, lay next to the injured girl.

He looked at the first girl. "What are your names and where are you headed?"

The girl who'd flagged him down gave him another of those hesitating looks. She opened her mouth, then closed it again.

Finally, she said, "I'm . . . Jane Johnston and my sister is Anna. We . . . we're looking for farm work. That's why we didn't stop at the towns. We were raised on a farm. Anna and I have done farm work and housework since we were old enough to work."

Again, she hadn't fully answered his questions, and he wondered at her hesitation, but he guessed she and her sister, being comely females, had learned to be wary of men since they'd fallen upon hard luck.

So why is she trusting you? Why did she ask you for help?

Looking around at the deserted countryside, he shrugged. What other choice did she have with her sister in this condition? With their money, and probably food, too, gone?

Another question occurred to him.

"How old are you? You both seem very young."

She shook her head. "Nay. I'm twenty and my sister is twenty-one."

He was relieved at that. They looked younger, but that could be because of their forlorn state. "So you've no family in this country?"

She quickly shook her head. "Nay. Not in this New World nor in Suffolk."

He smiled again. "I pegged you from there. My grandparents came over from that region."

Some of the wariness left her face. She even managed a smile. "Thass good to hear. I thought you were a farmer— planter, from seeing your cart and horses."

His smile widened a bit. "Farmer will do well enough for me. I'll leave the fancy names to others."

He saw the girl's chest expand as she took in a breath, then let it out.

"Do you need some extra help, by any chance? My sister and I are hard workers."

She wobbled a bit on her feet, and Conn instinctively stepped forward. Then she shook her head as if to clear it, straightened, tilted her firm chin and kept her blue gaze steady on him as if defying him to pity her, or disbelieve her words.

He stared back, wondering why he hadn't seen this comin. He opened his mouth to tell her no, he couldn't use her help or that of her sister, then closed it again.

Why not accept her offer? Wasn't his trip for that very purpose?

You know nothing about these two females, his mind told him. *They could steal you blind, murder you in your bed.*

That was true. But it was also true that he had no assurance of these things not happening with any house worker. And he'd never had any serious trouble in the past.

What would be the harm of it? It would be to all their mutual advantages. He'd be spared another day's journey to and from Derryville.

And these two bedraggled wisps of humanity would be spared further hardship.

In any case, he couldn't leave them here.

"As a matter of fact, I do," he heard himself say. "I was on my way to hire another girl to help my sister with the household work."

A light of hope shone in the lass's eyes for a moment, then dimmed.

"But there are two of us," she said, pointing out the obvious fact. "You said you needed only one." The hope lit up those remarkable eyes again. "But I've done farm work. Many a pig have I slopped and many an egg gathered. I've helped with haying, too, and other things. Our whole family worked on a big estate."

Lavena would be sorely displeased if he brought these two waifs back with him, instead of the hearty wench she expected.

He sighed, wishing the cheerful, laughing sister he'd grown up with hadn't changed into a sharp-tongued woman who seldom smiled. But of course she had reason, with her husband dying so young and she and her son losing their farm.

The girl who'd said her name was Jane Johnston smiled at him. Radiantly. He sucked in his breath as her face suddenly became beautiful. He glanced over at the other girl, Anna. That wide-eyed, fearful look was still on her face.

Again, his heart softened.

Lavena would have to get over her displeasure. Because he was going to bring them home with him. And he'd worry about wages for two instead of one later.

"We have no grand estate such as you're accustomed to, but I'm sure I can find enough work for you both."

He bent again and scooped the injured girl into his arms. His heart softened even more. Why, she weighed no more than a feather! These girls needed good food in their bellies, among other things. And that they would get at Holly View.

Neither man nor beast went hungry at his farm. Nor pretty maidens.

"Come along now," he said to the other girl, Jane. Striding toward his patiently waiting team, he glanced down at Anna.

She held her mouth tight, against the pain of movement to her injured ankle. But her eyes remained open, still holding that wary, frightened look.

"I'm sorry," he said, and slowed his pace, holding her a little closer, protectively.

The frightened expression intensified, but she said nothing. Then her eyes fluttered closed. Her long, pale lashes accentuated the dark circles, her unhealthy pallor. He heard the sister close behind.

What had he gotten himself into, taking these waifs under his protection?

He didn't know, and he might regret it later, but as always, when he made up his mind on a course of action to follow, he dismissed the doubts.

He'd see it through, whatever came.

CHAPTER THREE

"Oh!" Darryl cried out as the wagon wheels hit a rut and sent a bone-rattling jolt through the occupants of the wagon.

"All is fine, Da—Anna." Hayley caught her mistake in time, she hoped, darting a glance at the man on the seat in front of her.

Jane. Anna, she repeated half-a-dozen times. *Don't forget again!*

She let out her breath in relief when he didn't turn at her near-lapse.

How was she ever going to remember those false names she'd decided she had to use to try to further protect them?

Her words soothed her feverish sister, and Hayley tried hard to believe them herself. Although the wagon-owner, who'd said his name was Conn Merritt, had eased their predicament, maybe saved their lives, a knot of anxiety still held firm sway deep inside her.

And that's not helped a whit by you noticing he's a fair man to look upon. That black hair and his deep brown eyes . . .

She quickly squelched those disturbing thoughts and turned her mind back to their plight.

Every turn of the wagon's wheels, taking them farther south, away from Oscar Pritt's plantation—and from Burle Porter's—made her feel a little better.

But not enough.

By now, the hue and cry must be raised for Oscar's murderer. How many people on the plantation had seen Oscar take Darryl up to his bedchamber that night? It had been dark—but not black night.

Mrs. Whitley. Whenever her wandering thoughts lit upon that woman, Hayley cringed inwardly. Oh, yes, that woman knew. Even if she didn't, she'd put two and two together soon enough, given Oscar's obvious interest in Darryl since he'd brought her to the plantation.

And the spiteful, jealous housekeeper would like nothing better than to have Darryl accused of murder.

Hayley shuddered, lifting her head just in time to see Conn Merritt's turned head, his gaze full upon her and Darryl.

"How is your sister?" he asked.

Hayley felt sure the concern in his voice was real, else he'd never have bothered taking over their problems. There was something about him that had made her instinctively trust him from those first moments.

More fool you, her mind warned, and she heeded the warning, but still answered back, *We have no choice!*

"Fair," Hayley said, hearing the tremble in her voice. She firmed her mouth and lifted her chin. "I dislike this fever. My feverfew and other herbs were . . . lost on our voyage."

Anger made the knot in her stomach tighten. No, the herbs hadn't been lost. Like all their worldly possessions, they'd been stolen by the blackguard of a ship captain before he'd put Darryl and her off the ship and abandoned them. And in their haste to flee Oscar Pritt's plantation, she'd forgotten to bring the supply in Darryl's cabin.

Conn nodded. "I dislike the fever, too. We'll be stopping at a tavern tonight. The keeper's wife should have a supply."

Tavern? Keeper's wife? Fear shot through Hayley.

No! They couldn't stop anywhere. They needed to hurry on, hurry on south, until they reached Conn Merritt's farm.

Oh, and you think you'll be safe there? her mind jeered. *You'll never be safe anywhere again.*

Hayley turned those bleak thoughts away. All she could cope with now was taking care of Darryl.

She couldn't say anything to raise doubt in this man's mind. Or he might dump them out alongside this rutted road.

Stifling that fear, too, she managed a smile. ''That would be good.''

He smiled back, and his gaze lingered for a moment on hers. An odd feeling stole over her, as if his brown eyes were seeing beneath the surface of her skin, deep into the inside of her, and creating heat everywhere. She felt small prickly sensations up her arms, down her spine. . . .

It was passing strange. She knew, of course, that she and Darryl were comely lasses, and they'd both had their share of male attention. But neither of their hearts had been touched. These were things they'd talked and giggled about in their bedchamber at night. . . .

Along with daydreams about the men they'd someday marry. . . .

Stop your nonsense! she told herself. *Keep your mind on taking care of Darryl and trying to save both your lives.*

Sometime in the afternoon her lack of sleep during the last three nights caught up with her. She relaxed her vigil over Darryl and lay beside her on the wagon floor, covered by a blanket.

The cessation of the everlasting jolting ride woke her. She quickly pressed her palm to Darryl's forehead, frowned at how hot it still felt, then sat up.

Dusk was gathering, and they'd stopped before a big, two-story frame building. A man and woman stood on a wide balcony along the front of the second floor. A sign hung from a post, *White Horse Tavern,* spelled out in bold letters, a picture of a rearing white stallion beneath.

Hayley's stomach clenched. She wanted to slide down beside

Darryl again, beg Conn Merritt, now turning toward her, to drive on.

But she couldn't. She had to face this, pretend they weren't running away, that they had nothing to fear.

She shook her head at his questioning look. No, Darryl wasn't any better. If anything, her fever had risen as the day lengthened toward evening.

As effortlessly as earlier, he lifted Darryl, his big hands careful, muscles tightening beneath his shirt.

Again, Hayley felt that odd, prickly feeling along her nerve ends. Again, appalled, she pushed it aside.

She picked up the drawstring bag that held the hastily gathered items they'd taken from Oscar Pritt's before they fled, and got down from the wagon, flushing as she became newly conscious of her and Darryl's bedraggled appearance.

Bearing Darryl, Conn strode toward the tavern, his bearing confident, as if nothing at all were amiss. As if this were an everyday occurrence for him.

So she followed his example. Ignoring the glances from the couple on the balcony, Hayley straightened her tired back, lifted her chin and followed Conn to the tavern door.

The door swung wide and a pleasant-looking, well-dressed man stood in the opening. He blinked, surprise appearing in his eyes for a moment. Then he smiled and stepped backward.

"Welcome, Mr. Merritt! Good to see you again so soon. Is the young lady ill?"

Conn nodded, walking into a wide hall with a polished wood floor. "Yes, Mr. Warner. I need a room for these two women, and one for me."

The tavern keeper's smile faded, an apologetic expression replacing it. "I'm afraid that won't be possible. We're down to one vacant room. But it has two beds," he hastened to add.

Behind him, Hayley saw Conn Merritt's wide shoulders tense. "All right," he finally said. "This lass needs the attentions of your good wife—and we need baths for both."

Mr. Warner nodded. "Yes, indeed, Mr. Merritt. Come right along."

Passing by the doorway to the taproom on the left and a large, comfortably furnished room on the right, they all went up the stairs and down a hall. The tavern-keeper stopped before a door halfway to the end and opened it with a flourish.

"Here we be," he said.

The room was plainly furnished with two beds and a small chest, with pegs on one section of a wall. But it looked clean, Hayley saw with relief.

Gently, Conn laid Darryl on the first of the beds. She moaned, but didn't open her eyes. Hayley's worry increased.

Darryl's ankle injury shouldn't have caused fever. That must be due to the inflamed cut on her palm.

And what she'd suffered at the hands of Oscar Pritt.

Anger flared in Hayley. She wished the man were here so she could kill him again! A man such as he didn't deserve the gift of life.

And that gift has been taken away by your sister, she reminded herself. *Don't forget that.*

As if she could.

"I'll send Freda right up," Mr. Warner said, and left.

Conn turned to Hayley. "I'll go tend to the team. Will you be all right?

"Yes, and thank you."

Their glances met for a moment. Conn was the first to look away. After another frowning glance at Darryl, he left the room.

Hayley straightened Darryl's skirt and tried to smooth her hair. Darryl moaned again, tossing her head restlessly. A stab of worry hit Hayley. How she longed for her supply of herbs! She'd have Darryl over this by morn.

Another, more worrisome thought hit her. Or would she? Herbs wouldn't help with the other thing that ailed her sister.

"Good evening."

A woman's voice from the door made Hayley jump. She turned.

A plump, middle-aged woman bustled in, carrying a tray, which she placed on the chest next to the bed on which Darryl lay. Then she turned.

Hayley felt her face reddening. The woman's curious glance was taking in every detail of Hayley's and Darryl's slovenly state. Hayley fully expected her to demand Darryl be removed from atop her clean quilt.

Stop it! Hayley told herself. *Never mind what she thinks. You need her to help Darryl.*

Hayley forced a smile. "My sister has hurt her ankle. And is fevered from a cut."

The woman nodded. "Yes, I can see that." Her voice sounded faintly disapproving.

Darryl moaned again, sending another shaft of fear through Hayley. "Will you tend my sister?"

"Of course, of course." The woman moved to the bedside, lifted the bandaged hand and frowned at the deplorable state of its bandage.

"What happened here?" she asked Hayley.

"A bad cut, stitched up. I had no way of cleaning it today."

Hayley paused and decided to say nothing else. Although hating to leave the woman with the impression they were slovenly, she'd best reveal no more than she must.

"It's inflamed for certain," the woman said, easing Darryl's hand back onto the bed. She laid a palm across Darryl's forehead, then withdrew it, shaking her head.

"She's fevered and no wonder, with her hand in that state."

She turned to her tray and took out a steaming pewter mug. "Give her some of this and I'll send up poultices for the hand and ankle and clean rags for a new bandage."

Hayley recognized the smell coming from the mug with relief. Feverfew. That should help and soon. She sat by Darryl and lifted her head. Darryl opened her fever-bright eyes and looked dazedly at the other two women.

"Come on now, take a bit of this," Hayley coaxed, holding out her hand for the mug.

The woman gave it to her, and Hayley held it to Darryl's cracked lips. Darryl shuddered, but obediently opened her mouth and let the hot liquid slide down her throat.

Hayley resettled her on the snowy pillow, and Darryl closed

her eyes again, as though her strength was completely gone. Fright once more filled Hayley. Darryl was very ill!

Tears overflowed Hayley's eyes and started down her cheeks. She furtively swiped at them, not wanting this woman to see her weakness.

A hand patted her shoulder. "There, there, 'tis not as bad as all that. The lass is young and strong. She'll be all right." Surprised, Hayley turned.

The tavern-keeper's wife smiled at her, concern in her features. "Let me see to that bath. Of course your sister can't stand one, but you can sponge her off. I'll bring fresh rags to bandage her ankle, too."

With another pat, she was off, closing the door behind her.

Hayley looked after her, her fears somewhat eased. The woman's disapproval of their appearance seemed to have gone when she saw how ill Darryl was.

But still, if anyone came around asking about two blue-eyed flaxen-haired lasses, she'd remember them.

Coldness went through her. For all she knew, people might already have been here, asking about them.

She and Darryl could trust no one. Ever again. Not even Conn Merritt, who appeared so decent, so kind and honorable.

Any new person they encountered would add to the danger. She'd stay here in this room with Darryl until they left in the morning. Her stomach growled loudly. She was so hungry!

Conn had given her bread and meat at midday, and Darryl had eaten a little. But midday was long gone.

A knock sounded on the door. Hayley hastened to it and swung it open. A pretty, fresh-faced young woman, vaguely resembling Mrs. Warner, stood outside, holding a tin tub.

Hayley reached for it. "Here, let me take that."

The girl shook her head and came in. "Oh, no, I couldn't let you do that!"

She deposited the tub in the middle of the floor. "I'll bring up the pails of water." She smiled and left.

It was passing strange to be treated like this, almost like a member of the gentry, Hayley thought. Merely because she and Darryl were with Conn Merritt, who obviously was held in high esteem by these tavern-keepers.

She felt Darryl's forehead again, and thought it seemed a tiny bit cooler.

Half an hour later, she stepped out of the tub, washed and clean, feeling much better.

She'd already sponge-bathed Darryl and put poultices on both her hand and ankle. Wearing a fresh nightdress the inn-keeper's wife had provided, Darryl slept peacefully, her fever-flush less bright.

Hayley put on her own borrowed nightdress and combed her hair. Her stomach once more growled loudly.

Again, there was a knock on the door. She opened it to the same girl, bearing a tray this time. "Mr. Merritt bade me bring this to you and your sister."

Hayley appreciatively inhaled the wonderful smells wafting off the tray. Meat smells . . . fresh-baked bread. Oh, heaven!

"Thank you." Hayley smiled, and this time the girl let her take the tray.

Darryl roused enough to drink a good bit of broth, and even ate some bread and cheese. Much cheered, Hayley made her own meal and left not a crumb on the tray, then slipped into the clean bed beside her sister.

Across the room, the other bed stood empty. Conn Merritt's bed. A strange sensation went through her at the thought of him sharing their room.

When would he come up? He'd been a gentleman and let them have privacy all evening, but soon he'd have to sleep if he were to drive the wagon and team the next day. . . .

Hayley's eyes closed on that thought and instantly she was asleep, exhaustion from the ordeal she'd endured claiming her at last.

Conn opened and closed the bedchamber door as quietly as possible. There was no candle lit to guide him, but a small amount of illumination came from the moon outside the many-paned window.

The near bed held two unmoving mounds. He made it to the bed against the far side of the room, and removed his boots and outer wear. With a weary sigh, he slipped under the covers.

Thank God, none of his acquaintances were staying the night here. He'd not had to explain why he had these two females in his care.

Even to George Warner and Freda. If George was inquisitive, he never showed it. Which made him an admirable tavern-keeper. Freda was dying to know everything, but she had sense enough to keep her curiosity in check.

The excellently kept tavern, along with their well-run farm, made the Warners a comfortable living. Freda wouldn't risk the Merritt family's future custom by prying into Conn's private affairs.

Damn good thing, too, because he was still questioning his recent actions himself.

And not looking forward to explaining them to Lavena when he got back home to Holly View tomorrow evening.

One of the mounds moved and uttered a small moan of pain. Anna. That protective urge he'd felt when he first saw her welled up inside him again. He hoped a hot meal, a good bed and some herbal doses had helped her.

The other mound remained utterly still. Jane. The devoted sister. Another feeling took its place beside the first.

One he didn't want to examine, although he couldn't deny it.

Jane stirred his blood. And he didn't want that, either. So he'd stay away from the lasses once he had them safely established at Holly View.

The girls had been badly used, he instinctively knew. They were wary and fearful, and he hated that. But soon, they'd feel secure and safe. Holly View was a wonderful place to live.

Lavena would raise a ruckus, but there wasn't anything she could do. The farm was his, by deed from his father and by virtue of his long, hard years of work on it. Lavena expected her son to inherit, and he probably would.

God knows, Conn had no wish to ever marry again. Or to produce an heir for the property. No, his nephew Ellis would serve very well in that capacity.

CHAPTER FOUR

Conn came out of a deep sleep, hearing voices ... female voices ... how could that be? Females in his bedchamber ...?

"It's all right. Don't fret yourself. It's all right."

"No! No, he' s ... pushing me ... ohh ..."

Abruptly, the sleep fog left Conn, and he remembered the events of the previous day and evening. The bed creaked as he sat bolt upright. What was the lass mumbling about?

In the dim light coming through the window, he saw the other girl's sharp turn of head toward him. Then she quickly turned back to her sister.

"Hush ... A-Anna dear. You're just fevered and having a bad dream. Here, drink more of this tea."

"No ... tastes bad ... don't want it." The girl thrashed wildly around.

Conn could see Jane was having a hard time constraining her sister. He reached for his breeches, pulled them on, then padded barefoot across the room to stand beside Jane.

In the dim light, he saw Jane's startled glance.

"Let me help," he said in a low voice.

Her eyes widened. She quickly shook her head. "No. Go back to bed. You'll only make things worse."

Anna pulled herself out of Jane's grasp and almost slid out of the bed.

Despite Jane's refusal, Conn instinctively reached for her, grasping her shoulders in a gentle grip, holding her steady. She strained against him, sobbing, making incoherent sounds. Obviously, she was still in the grip of her nightmare, only half conscious. He held her resolutely, his firm grasp unwavering.

Jane made no more protests, and finally Anna went limp, falling back against the pillow.

Conn straightened, letting out his breath.

"Can you lift her head a bit and I'll try to get more tea down her," Jane asked.

Her voice was strained, but it had lost the almost hysterical quality of a few moments ago. Apparently, she was willing to accept his help now.

"Yes." Conn slid an arm behind Anna's neck and raised her slightly from the pillow. Jane put the cup to her sister's mouth.

"You must drink this," Jane said.

This time the other lass took the liquid into her mouth and swallowed. Obediently, she did the same again, and again until most of the cup was empty. Then she turned her head away.

"Thass all. I can't stand any more," she said, fretfully.

"Good girl," Jane soothed, patting her shoulder. "Now you can rest. And soon you'll be well."

"Yesss ..." Anna's voice drew out, drowsily. "Sleep. I need to sleep. . . ." Her eyes closed. Then she jerked her head up again.

Her blue eyes gleamed in the dim light. "But he's after me! I can't get away!"

Jane was there before Conn could react. "No one is here. You must sleep now." Her voice was low and comforting, with a lilt that rang pleasantly on the ear.

Once again Anna went limp against the white pillow. Her eyes closed. In a few moments, her breath became slow and regular in the rhythms of sleep.

Close beside him, Conn could smell Jane's clean scent, the fragrance of her fresh-washed hair. Again, he felt a stirring in his blood. In his loins.

No. He refused to acknowledge his feelings.

He moved a little away from her. "Why is she so afraid? What's happened to the both of you?"

Jane stood so still he thought she hadn't heard him, or wouldn't answer.

Finally, with a weary gesture, she brushed at her hair, which hung loose down her back, pushing it away from her face.

That soft flaxen hair, like silk . . . his hands itched to smooth down it, tangle it in his hands. . . .

"It's nothing. A man . . . on the ship caught Darryl in a corner . . . and was trying . . ."

She didn't finish. She didn't have to. Anger surged through Conn. He clenched his fists at his side.

"Did he hurt her?"

After a moment, Hayley said, "She's just . . . scared. And the fever has her confused."

Her voice sounded oddly wooden, as if she were holding in strong emotions.

As was he.

But a wholly different kind. He ached to turn to this girl beside him, pull her into his arms. Comfort her . . . and more than comfort her. Carry her to his bed across the room and make her his own.

His insane thoughts fair made his mind reel. He hadn't felt this way, wanted a woman this way since . . . Marie had spun her web around him . . . drawn him into marriage . . .

And then . . . and then . . .

His fists clenched tighter. He drew a deep breath and let it out.

"If she wakes again and you need aid, call for me," he said, stiffly.

"I think she'll sleep now. And by morning be much improved. But if she isn't . . ."

Her voice trailed off.

"If she isn't, we'll stay here another day and night," he assured her. "Or two, if need be."

He heard her relieved sigh. "Thank you," she said, her voice trembling, as if she'd feared he'd say he'd go off and abandon them here.

But then she gave him a quick glance, and he saw something else in her eyes. Another kind of fear, as if she equally dreaded staying here.

It hit him anew that these girls had suffered much more hardship than Jane admitted. Compunction for his lustful thoughts filled him. Once he got back to Holly View, he'd keep his distance from these two waifs, he vowed.

You'd better, his mind warned him. *Or you'll find yourself in a predicament of your own making that you don't want.*

"We'll see how your sister is in the morn," he said, his voice still stiff, and turned and walked across the room to his own bed.

He sat down and, his hand on his breeches' buttons, glanced across the room again.

Jane stood where he'd left her, her head turned his way.

His hands stilled. He swung his legs under the quilt, and sank into the depths of the feather bed. Once settled, he finished unbuttoning and tugged off his breeches.

He glanced across the room. In the dim light he saw two mounds under the quilt, and his tension lessened. He turned over on his left side and closed his eyes.

He devoutly hoped Anna slept peacefully the remainder of the night. Both for her sake . . . and his own.

In the morning, he'd wake early and be up and decently dressed and downstairs before either of the lasses stirred.

* * *

"Hayley . . . where are we?"

Darryl's voice, shaky and weak, accompanied by her shakes of Hayley's shoulder, woke Hayley.

Early morning light streamed through the one window. Hayley darted a glance across the room, relieved to see the other bed empty.

Especially since Darryl had called her Hayley instead of Jane.

Jane, Jane, Jane, she repeated to herself. She must tell Darryl their new names, impress upon her the importance of remembering them.

She winced. She'd told Conn Merritt many things that weren't true. Or at least glossed over the truth. One of which was that Darryl hadn't been abused. She hadn't dared reveal that. Many men would have blamed the woman. But Conn didn't seem that type of man.

You barely know him, she reminded herself.

But he'd been so kind. Taking them in. Last night helping with Darryl.

And so disturbing, his closeness making her breathless.

She quickly pushed that thought aside and turned to Darryl, a relieved smile curving her mouth.

Darryl's face had lost the fever-flushed rosy red of the day and night before. The wildness had gone from her eyes too.

But fear still lingered in the tenseness of her jaw, in the wary expression in her eyes.

Hayley drew her sister close and hugged her. Darryl was still a bit over-warm, but the fever was on the wane. It would be safe to travel today. "I'm so glad you're better."

Darryl hugged her back, then pulled away. "So am I, but where are we?" she asked again, more urgently than before.

"At a tavern," Hayley answered, carefully, so as not to alarm Darryl further. "Do you remember the man who carried you to his wagon yesterday?"

Darryl frowned, then nodded. "Yes . . . he was very strong. . . ."

Her jaw tightened, her eyes widened. "Who is he? Why did

he bring us here? Oh, Hayley, have they found out that I killed Oscar?''

"Hush, hush," Hayley soothed. "No, of course no one has found out."

Let that be true, she prayed, silently. "The man's name is Conn Merritt and he owns a farm and he's taking us there to work for him," she finished in a rush.

Darryl's face relaxed a bit, but she still looked wary. "What if he wants us for the same reasons Oscar Pritt did?"

Yes, what if he does? Hayley had asked herself that same question.

"We have no choice. I had to grasp this chance for help. But he's a decent man," she said, firmly. "He's behaved in all ways as a perfect gentleman."

Darryl's mouth twisted. "Gentlemen can have the best of manners and still be rogues."

Hayley nodded to accept the truth of that remark. "Yes, I know. But I'm certain this Conn Merritt's decency goes deeper than the surface. Somehow, I feel that."

Darryl gave her a fearful, searching look. "You defend the man very stoutly, sister."

Hayley felt her face warming, and hoped Darryl didn't notice. "He probably saved our lives," she reminded Darryl. "Of course I'm grateful."

Darryl's tongue came out and ran across her still-swollen lips, encountering the almost-healed cut. She drew in a sharp breath. "Naturally. But don't let it go farther than that! Men are such beasts!"

Compassion for Darryl's ordeal filled Hayley. She gave Darryl another hug. "Not all men," she told her. "Our father was a kind, gentle man."

Darryl drew away, her face set in hard lines. "He was the exception. All they care about is relieving their own lusts."

Her sister's hurt went deeper than the physical pain she'd suffered, Hayley realized. Much deeper. And only time would get her over this anguish.

Or would anything ever heal her?

Again, she pushed away her disquieting thoughts. She had other things she must worry about.

Their very survival.

"Hush, hush," Hayley said, soothingly. "Don't get yourself worked up. We must be ready to travel today. To get us to Conn Merritt's farm. Where we'll be safe. Everyone will be looking for us toward Philadelphia."

She emphasized the last words, hoping that would make her believe they were true, that their pursuers were searching in the opposite direction.

But they didn't. How could she and Darryl ever feel safe again?

Darryl drew back, her expression calmer. "Yes, you're right, Hayley. Let's get ourselves together."

The new names. She must tell Darryl.

After she did, Darryl's eyes widened. "How clever of you to think of that. Anna. Our grandmother's name. And Jane, the squire's wife."

She gave Hayley a worried look. "But how will we ever remember? And if we slip . . ."

"We won't. We mustn't," Hayley said, firmly. "Just keep repeating them over to yourself until they seem natural."

Darryl nodded. "Yes, of course that's what we must do."

But her voice sounded dubious, Hayley thought.

"We're going to be all right," she told Darryl, forcing a sureness she was far from feeling into her voice.

When Conn Merritt came back to the room, both Hayley and Darryl were dressed in the plain but clean gowns Mrs. Warner had provided, had breakfasted and were ready for travel.

Hayley assured him that Darryl's ankle and hand were much improved, and they went downstairs, Darryl insisting on walking with their combined aid.

George Warner was on hand to see them off, as affable as yesterday. "We always appreciate your custom, Mr. Merritt," he said.

"Your accommodations are excellent," Conn replied, nodding to the tavern-keeper's wife, who was smiling in the background.

The woman was cordial, but her glance was sharp, Hayley noticed, uneasily. She wouldn't forget their stay anytime soon.

Conn Merritt had procured another blanket for Darryl's comfort. Hayley spread it out on the wagon floor, settled Darryl and carefully stored the herbs Mrs. Warner had provided in her bag. Darryl went back to sleep at once, relieving Hayley greatly.

The night's sleep had taken care of her own exhaustion. She didn't feel like stretching out beside her sister. She glanced at the back of Conn Merritt's dark head, and a little shiver went over her.

Mr. Merritt, she reminded herself. She'd better get used to thinking of him as that or she'd slip and call him by his given name. And that would never do.

She didn't want to sleep on the wagon bed, but neither did she want to sit on the plank seat beside her new employer for the rest of this journey.

Those were the only two choices.

Hayley moved up to the front seat, sliding to the far edge. She wanted no more of those disturbing feelings this man created inside her.

He glanced over at her, his expression pleasant but reserved. "We'll stop for a midday meal and for you to tend to your sister. We should be home by late afternoon."

Home. No, not for her and Darryl. But maybe a place of refuge.

Hayley arranged her own features into the same expression as Conn Merritt's.

"Good," she said, not able to keep the deep relief she felt out of that one short word.

Oh, please God, she prayed, *let the place be far removed from the roads. Let us be able to hide away there and be safe!*

Fool, her mind mocked. *Can you really make yourself believe*

that can ever be possible? You're both runaway bound servants.
Darryl is a murderess.

No! She recoiled at that awful term. Her sister wouldn't hurt
a fly. She'd only been defending herself.

And I suppose you think the authorities will accept that?

Again, she forced away the thoughts. She was getting very
good at doing that, she told herself, wryly.

The day was fair and warm, the country wild and strange to
Hayley's eyes. Pine trees grew alongside sturdy oaks and
maples, as well as other hardwoods and glossy holly trees. The
sandy soil reminded her that the sea was not far distant.

The midday stop found Darryl eager for food and feeling
better. But she was noticeably tense when Mr. Merritt tried to
make conversation with her, and fell back into healing sleep
when they resumed their trip.

Their employer stopped once more in a tiny village for supplies, leaving both girls in the wagon. Hayley kept a tense
lookout. A few passing strangers gave them mildly curious
glances, but went on about their business.

When they resumed their trip, Mr. Merritt said very little,
for which Hayley was grateful. She found herself nodding off,
the bumpy rhythm of the wagon lulling her.

Like yesterday, when the movement ceased, Hayley awoke.

They'd pulled up at the rear of a large, two-story frame
house. Its weathered gray shingles, its leaded, diamond-paned
windows and steep gables looked so much like the squire's
house on the estate where her family had worked that she
gasped.

Behind the house, Hayley could glimpse outbuildings and
fields, with workers here and there. The house and its lawns
and grounds were neatly kept. All looked prosperous.

Surprise and consternation filled her. Since Conn Merritt had
used a wagon instead of a carriage, she'd expected him to have
a modest holding. Especially since he'd insisted on calling it
a farm instead of a plantation.

Now she realized he must have taken the wagon because he
was bringing supplies home.

How would she and Darryl fit into this household? Mr. Merritt had said he'd find them work. As housemaids? Neither she nor Darryl had done that kind of work. She forced down her worries.

Of course they could do the work, or learn to do it. They'd do anything they must in order to stay here where they'd have at least a measure of safety.

"Well, what do you think of Holly View?" he asked.

Hayley turned to him. Fond pride had been in his voice, was apparent in the rugged lines of his face. She saw he loved his home deeply. *Holly View.* She liked that name. And it was fitting. Glossy-leaved holly trees dotted the lawn.

She looked at the building again, and this time she saw the hominess of it, felt a touch of what Conn must be feeling.

"Lavender! Thyme and yarrow. Oh, how beautiful it is."

Darryl's voice from behind made Hayley jump. She turned to see her sister gazing raptly at what Hayley now recognized as an herb garden. If anything could help to heal Darryl, it would be this. Ever since she was a child, Darryl had loved working in gardens—especially herb gardens. That had been her job at the squire's estate.

"Yes, it is," Conn Merritt answered, his voice almost reverent. "Shall we go inside?"

He got down from the wagon, leaned over to help Darryl up and lifted her easily over the side.

"Lean on me," he directed. Darryl gave Hayley a fearful look. Hayley nodded encouragingly and, her reluctance obvious, Darryl let him support her. With Hayley behind, they walked up the flagstone walk, past the herb garden and a kitchen garden, to the sturdy wooden door.

He opened the door, revealing a big, pleasant room. White-washed walls brightened it, with sturdy dark beams overhead. A dresser, of polished dark wood, which could have stood in many a Suffolk kitchen, sat along one wall, gleaming pewter pieces and blue and white plates on its top and shelf.

Over his shoulder, Hayley saw a middle-aged woman, dark hair going gray, leaning over a scrubbed worktable, slicing a golden loaf of bread. A pretty gray and white cat curled around her ankles.

The woman glanced up sharply, her eyes widening.

Little wonder, Hayley thought. Darryl's bandaged ankle showed beneath the hem of her skirt. Her bandaged hand was also plain to see.

"I've found you help for the house, sister!" Mr. Merritt announced, stepping aside to let Hayley enter.

His voice was hearty, but it also sounded a little wary. Not as if he expected his statement to be warmly received, she thought uneasily.

"This is Jane Johnston and her sister, Anna," he went on. "My sister, Lavena Drake," he finished.

"Good day, Mistress Drake," Hayley said politely, bobbing a curtsy.

The woman's eyes widened even more. Ignoring Hayley's greeting, she put down her slicing knife and stood erect. She was a tall woman, with a marked resemblance to her brother.

"You were to return with one girl, Conn. And I expect my helpers to be able-bodied," she said, severely.

He ignored her first words and gestured to Hayley. "This lass is that, Lavena. The other will be over her injuries in a little while."

His sister sniffed her disbelief. "They both look as if a strong wind could blow them away. Where on earth did you find these waifs?"

Anger trembled through Hayley at the woman's disdainful words. All that she and Darryl had endured washed over her, making her lose her caution.

She raised her firm chin and before she could curb her tongue said, "We're not waifs, Mistress. We know how to work and have done aplenty of it since we were but young children. We'll earn our keep."

The moment the words were out, Hayley was appalled. What had she done? Had she ruined their chances to stay here?

Lavena Drake's mouth dropped open. Finally, she closed it with a snap. She turned to her brother.

"I'll have no kitchen wenches who give me back talk. These two will never do. You'll have to return them whence they came and bring a strong, sturdy woman."

Darryl gasped and a sob escaped her. "Oh, please don't send us away from here!" she begged.

Her heart sinking, Hayley slipped her arm around Darryl to console her, again berating herself for speaking out and ruining their chances to stay here in this lovely place.

"I'm sorry," she said. "I should have held my tongue."

The other woman acknowledged neither her nor Darryl's words. She just kept on glaring at them.

"No, Lavena, I will do no such thing," Conn Merritt said, his deep voice very firm. "They are here to stay and you will have to accept that."

Hope rose in Hayley. She turned to him with a smile of thanks. She saw only his profile, his strong features stubbornly set.

Silence fell in the clean, pleasant kitchen. Brother and sister eyed each other, two strong wills clashing, each trying to beat down the other.

Hayley held her breath. Who would win? Would he let his sister have her way in this household matter in the end, in spite of what he'd just said?

Finally, Lavena Drake lowered her glance to the loaf before her. She once more picked up her slicing knife.

"Very well, have it your way," she said, stiffly. She glanced up again, the knife gesturing as she talked. "But if these two cause trouble, or steal anything, they will be put from the house."

Hayley's cheeks burned, but this time she bit her tongue to keep it still, holding her arm firmly about Darryl's waist to keep the swaying girl from falling.

"I take full responsibility for their behavior," Conn Merritt said, his voice also stiff, but Hayley detected a touch of relief in it, too.

He didn't enjoy going against his sister's wishes, she

deduced, and must generally let her have her way in household matters, else she'd not have been so willing to argue with him.

Lavena Drake sniffed again, her knife making perfectly even slices through the loaf. "See that you do."

"Lavena."

Something in her brother's voice made his sister look up from her task.

"These lasses have had a wearying journey and need rest. Anna must have clean bandages for her injuries and more herbs for her fever."

"Fever! What ails the girl?" she asked, sharply. "The whole household will be down!"

His mouth tightened. "It's not contagious. Her hand is cut and inflamed, but improving."

Lavena Drake let out her breath. "They can have the attic room the bound girl had. The bed is small, but will have to do."

He nodded. "It'll do for tonight at least. Tomorrow we'll see about making the room more comfortable."

The kitchen door opened. Hayley turned. A tall young man stood in the opening. He somewhat resembled Conn Merritt with his dark eyes and hair. But his frame wasn't as muscular, nor his bearing as confident.

He closed the door behind him and glanced at the group curiously. "I see you're back, Uncle Conn," he said.

His glance slid over Hayley to Darryl, where it lingered.

Darryl glanced up and caught the look, and Hayley felt her tremble against Hayley's steadying arm. A surge of protectiveness went through Hayley.

Once again she forgot caution, and gave the young man a slit-eyed look that made him blink in surprise.

"Yes," Conn Merritt said, wearily. "Ellis, this is Jane and Anna Johnston. They have come here to help your mother."

So this was Lavena Drake's son. He seemed much more agreeable than his mother, Hayley thought, glancing again at that woman.

Her lips were pursed. She glared at her son in disapproval.

Hayley sent her a silent message. *Never fear, my sister has no wish to entice your precious son. He's naught but a gangly boy, anyway.* Then she felt shame.

She had nothing against the young man. She just couldn't stand Darryl being hurt any more.

Hayley bobbed a curtsy, noting that this time Lavena Drake looked taken aback. Farm girls they might be, but they came from respectable folk and they'd been raised with manners and some education.

"I'll show you to your quarters," Conn Merritt said. "Take my arm," he added to Darryl. "The stairs are steep."

"I'll do that," the young man put in hastily, positioning himself on Darryl's other side.

Darryl shrank away from him, closer to Hayley.

"We will do fine. I'll help my sister," Hayley said.

He looked bewildered at Darryl's rebuff, but at once said, "I can show you the way."

His uncle sighed. "Go ahead."

His mother dropped her slicing knife onto the table with a clatter. "Ellis, go on about your evening chores. *I'll* see to this matter."

"My chores are finished, Mother. I came in for supper."

"Supper will be a bit late today. Bring in the milk and butter."

Her stern tones left no room for argument. Her son departed the kitchen.

Lavena Drake turned her attention to Hayley and Darryl. "If this must be done, let's get it over with."

She gave her brother a challenging look.

He returned it, then left the kitchen by the back door, closing it a bit harder than was necessary.

"Come." Without looking at the girls, she led the way into a small hallway with dark, polished floors, off which steep back stairs rose.

Supporting Darryl, Hayley followed. She'd show this woman how wrong her estimation of them was, Hayley vowed. She wouldn't give her a chance to find fault with them. Her new employer's support couldn't be counted on if his sister complained about their work.

Their security here was very shaky. She must never forget that.

And anyway, they both had pride! They'd do good work in any case.

Halfway up the flight, Darryl's ankle turned and she stopped and moaned with pain. "We're almost there," Hayley soothed her.

Mistress Drake turned impatiently, waiting for them to catch up with her.

A stab of fear snaked through Hayley. How could she expect the woman to be willing to let Darryl stay if she couldn't work for perhaps a fortnight or more?

At the top of the stairs, she led them down another hall with gleaming, polished floors, this one wider and longer. At its end rose yet another flight of even steeper steps.

Somehow they managed, but the walk had done Darryl's injured ankle no good, Hayley realized, seeing her sister's face grow paler with every step.

The attic had several small rooms. Lavena Drake opened the door to one and stood aside to let Hayley and Darryl enter.

A narrow bed, a chest, and pegs along the wall completed its furnishings.

Hayley helped Darryl down onto the bed. Darryl let out a sigh of relief.

"I don't know what possessed my brother to bring you two here," Mistress Drake said, coldly. "Holly View belongs to him, so he has the final say. But let me assure you that the house is my province. And to earn your keep and wages, you girls will have to step lively. I'll tolerate no slackers."

"We're no slackers, Mistress," Hayley said, in a conciliatory tone. "We're used to hard work and will earn our way. But just now my sister is unwell. In a week or so, she'll be fine. But now she needs poultices for her ankle and her hand. I'll tend to these if you'll show me where your supplies are kept."

Again, as a few minutes ago, the other woman looked taken aback.

She said nothing for a moment, then nodded. "Very well." Without another word, she turned and left the room.

Hayley heaved a relieved sigh to be left alone with her sister for the first time since early morning. "How do you fare?" she asked.

Darryl shrugged. "I'm all right." She looked up at her sister, fear on her face. "Oh, Hayley, you shouldn't have talked to her like that in the kitchen! What if she persuades her brother to send us away? What will we do?"

"You're right, sister," Hayley said, her voice chastened. "But she angered me so, I forgot myself."

"You've changed," Darryl said, wonder in her voice. "You've become so brave, I scarcely know you."

"Perhaps I've become *too* brave," Hayley said. "I'll watch my tongue, and humble myself with Mistress Lavena. Although the woman is most unlikable."

Darryl sighed. "So she is. She's just like Mrs. Whitley. But we have to please her. If she complains too often to her brother, he's apt to send us away—and then ... oh, Hayley! I can't believe I killed a man! Even one so despicable as Oscar Pritt."

"You were only saving yourself," Hayley comforted her. "He shouldn't have used you so."

"But you know as well as I do that no one else will accept that, will believe us. We'll be hunted down! I will hang!"

"No, you won't," Hayley said, firmly. "We'll work hard and please Mistress Lavena, and we'll be safe."

Oh, how she wished she could truly believe that!

What they should do was stay for a week or two, only long enough for Darryl's physical injuries to heal. Hayley could work, earn some coin.

Then they should continue their flight.

Her heart quailed at this thought. Only yesterday they'd been hungry and thirsty, exhausted and dirty. At the end of their resources.

How could she persuade Darryl they must leave here?

How could she persuade *herself* of that?

Conn Merritt's strong-featured face came into her mind's eye. A shiver tingled down her back.

He'd promised them a refuge here. And he seemed a man to keep his promises.

You fool, her mind told her. *Do you really believe if he knew the truth about you and Darryl, he'd give you a room in his house?*

CHAPTER FIVE

Hayley paused to talk to Darryl, who was busy in the herb garden, on her way to the hen coop to collect some eggs for Lavena.

By now, a month after their arrival at Holly View, Hayley and Darryl had long ceased thinking of any of the family in formal terms.

The bright June day was lovely, birds singing, the sun on her back warming her all the way to her bones. Her morning stint in the small dairy was finished; now she was on call for whatever Lavena needed done during the remainder of the day.

Darryl was absorbed in her weeding. Her woven basket swinging from her arm, Hayley watched for a few seconds. Darryl carefully plucked a weed away from a flourishing lavender plant, then stroked the herb with gentle fingers.

Darryl had always loved gardening, but something new and deeper had been added since they'd come to live at Holly View. The gardens were her refuge. She retreated to them at every opportunity.

Lavena saw Darryl's knack at caring for growing things, and left her alone. Lavena was house-proud. Her domain was inside.

She seemed relieved at having the gardening chores taken from her shoulders.

Hayley was her somewhat unwilling helper with the housekeeping, but she quickly learned the necessary skills. Unlike the large estate in Suffolk, the dairy work here took only a small part of her day.

During these weeks, Darryl's injuries had healed. At least her bodily ones. The inside wounds she'd suffered were still there.

And might be for a long time to come.

Thank God, Darryl's courses had come at their regular time. She wasn't with child by Oscar Pritt. Hayley repressed a shudder. That would have been too terrible to endure!

Darryl glanced up and saw her and smiled. "The thyme I transplanted is coming along well."

Her voice was as pleased as if she'd announced her lover had just proposed marriage. Probably more so, Hayley thought, wryly.

"That's good." Hayley smiled back, relief at her sister's improvement mixed with ever-present anxiety about their still precarious situation. Each time a stranger came onto the farm, her heart stopped. Part of her uneasily told her she and Darryl should have left here before now—as soon as Darryl's injuries had healed.

Left here. If only that were all that was required! To take their proper leave, travel on south in a wagon or carriage.

Instead of fleeing in the dark of night, taking to the woods again. Getting lost. Running out of food.

Maybe dying this time.

Neither of them had been able to face that yet.

They kept putting it off. For one thing, they had very little coin saved. Not enough to buy food for their journey. And where would they find food to buy even if they did?

No place. They wouldn't dare stop anywhere. They'd have to take food from the household here. And even if they left their few coins in payment, Lavena would be sure to go to the nearest authorities.

Hayley swallowed. Lavena would be only too happy if they were exposed as frauds . . . and worse. Much worse.

Once Lavena had their descriptions posted, and the searchers knew they'd gone south instead of north, they'd have little chance of escaping this time.

Familiar sick tension went through her. They weren't safe here, but they'd be in even more danger if they fled.

Or was she only fooling herself into believing that because she didn't want to leave?

Hayley glanced up at a sound. Ellis strode up the walk toward them.

"Good day, Jane . . . Anna." He gave them both a wide smile, then paused, glancing at Darryl. "The herb garden has never looked so well."

His voice had softened on the last words, his lingering gaze at Darryl revealing even more of his feelings.

"Thank you." Darryl's voice was stiff and she kept her head down. The strained line of her neck bespoke her tension and her reluctance to show more than mere politeness to Lavena's son.

But Ellis wasn't easily put off. He leaned over and plucked a sprig of lavender, so close to Darryl's hands, his fingers almost grazed hers. He tickled her nose with it.

At the touch, Darryl's body grew rigid, and she jerked her head up, her mouth opening in surprise at his wide, teasing grin.

Hayley saw the rosy flush staining her sister's cheeks. Hayley held her breath, thinking Darryl would smile back. But she didn't. She put her head down again and moved backward a bit, out of Ellis's reach.

His face fell. He stood there awkwardly, twirling the lavender sprig in his fingers. Finally, he flipped it over into the herb patch and walked on to the kitchen door, standing open to the warm sunshine.

"Ellis is a good young man," Hayley said as the silence drew out. "I'm sure he'd do nothing to harm you or anyone."

Darryl jerked her head up again. Her cheeks were still pink, her features tight. "How can you expect me to look on any man with interest after . . ."

Her voice trailed off. She glanced away.

Hayley's heart softened. It was too soon. She should have said nothing yet.

Yet? What did she mean? How could she fool herself into believing anything could come of Ellis's interest in Darryl?

But there was no point in talking about their ever-present fears here in the lovely garden this morning.

"I don't. I . . . just think it might help you if you could be friends with Ellis."

"Leave me be, Hayley," Darryl said, turning again to her tasks.

Hayley heard more steps and glanced up again. This time Conn strode up the walk. His black hair gleamed in the sunlight and his brown eyes were deep and soft. His muscular body moving along the walk called to something deep inside her.

As always in his presence, Hayley felt that peculiar awareness flowing into her, intensifying her senses. It was disturbing . . . yet she enjoyed it, too. She couldn't deny that.

He paused as he reached Hayley. "Have you seen Ellis? He was supposed to bring a pail of water to the fields."

Conn seemed to be trying hard to keep an impatient note in his voice and manner, Hayley thought. As if he had to make an excuse for being here. For being in her presence.

That thought made her pulse quicken.

She smiled at him, and all her bodily responses deepened even further. "He just went into the kitchen."

Conn smiled back, his gaze lingering on her just as Ellis's had on Darryl a few minutes ago. " 'Tis a good day for growing the crops. We've had few enough this year with all the rain."

"Yes," Hayley agreed, unable to move her eyes away from his.

"So you are off to find some eggs?" He nodded at her basket, abruptly bringing Hayley out of her daze and reminding her of her undone task.

She drew in her breath. "Yes, and I must be about it." She

passed by him, the narrowness of the walk bringing them very close to each other. His skin smelled of the warm sun and the earth he toiled in, pleasant scents to her farm-bred nose.

"Jane! Where are my eggs?"

Lavena's annoyed voice came from behind. Hayley stopped and turned. Lavena stood in the kitchen doorway, frowning, hands on hips.

"I'll be only a minute," Hayley promised, quickening her steps.

"Those girls are nothing but loplollies!"

Hayley heard the Suffolk term for a careless and lazy worker and almost smiled. Almost. But apprehension overruled her amusement. Lavena only used the country words when she was truly exasperated. Then they flowed from her mouth unthinkingly.

And in spite of Conn's defense of them, they might still be sent away.

For Lavena saw them as threats. After a month here, Hayley realized why. Conn couldn't hide his attraction to Hayley, although he tried hard.

And widowed Lavena's only son, Ellis, stood to inherit the prosperous farm if Conn didn't marry and produce heirs.

Of course, a man as handsome and virile as Conn surely would marry in time. It was passing strange he hadn't already. Most of the marriageable young women of the area must have been after him long before.

"That isn't true, Lavena. I've never known you to be so hard on any of our household help as you are with Jane and Anna."

Conn's voice was loud and carrying. His defense eased Hayley's fears a bit. But only a bit.

She was realistic enough to know that at least some of Conn's defense of them was because he felt . . . something for Hayley.

But men's feelings for women were fickle, could change overnight. Both she and Darryl knew this from experience with the local lads back home.

And Lavena was blood kin. Conn's closest blood kin. That

meant a lot. Perhaps more than anything else, if it came right down to it.

Hayley stopped short, realizing the way her thoughts had turned. Was she intending, then, to use any feminine wiles she possessed on Conn? To lure him to her . . . for what purpose?

She didn't, couldn't, expect marriage. When Conn wanted to marry, he'd have his pick of the daughters from other prosperous farms in the area.

Then was she considering allowing him to bed her? Just to try to keep her and Darryl here? The thought wasn't as repugnant to her as it should have been.

Because deep in her heart, she knew if that happened, it wouldn't be only for that reason.

She was drawn to Conn so strongly, had been from the first moment she saw him, that more and more often thoughts of lying in his arms occupied her mind. Her dreams.

A hen cackled loudly from inside the henhouse, announcing the creature's successful completion of her task.

Hayley hurried inside the warm, dim building and began expertly plucking eggs out from under unwilling fowl.

Her thoughts went back to their Suffolk cottage, and a sharp stab of homesickness and loneliness for her dead parents went through her. Oh, why hadn't they all stayed safely in England? They'd had a good enough life, hard, but satisfying.

If they'd stayed, her mother and father would still be alive. Not lying somewhere **at** the bottom of the cold sea. Darryl would still be an innocent maid. Or wed to one of the local lads. Not a fearful husk of her former vibrant self.

And as for herself?

She had no answer for that.

But one thing she knew. She wouldn't be here, on this alien soil, waiting, fearing each day someone would come onto the farm and take her and Darryl away.

Perhaps take Darryl's very life away.

And she wouldn't be foolishly pining for a man she'd never be able to have as a husband.

* * *

Conn watched Jane leave, her flaxen hair, pulled into a knot in back, shining like moonbeams in the sunlight. Her lissome body, although decently clad in a long, dark skirt and laced bodice, swaying as she walked.

He felt his own body hardening in response to that innocent movement. Or was it innocent? Perhaps the girl knew exactly what she was doing, was deliberately inflaming his senses.

His mood darkened at that thought. Just so had Marie walked, just so had he reacted to it . . . and to other things. And to what end had those awakened desires driven him?

Misery and heartache. Betrayal and loss.

"Are you going to stand on the walk all day?" Lavena asked tartly from behind him. "It's only mid-morn, and your breakfast eaten just an hour ago."

Her sharp words pricked his self-absorption, made him aware he was standing on the kitchen walk, lusting after a girl he had no business showing any interest in.

"The day's warm, sister," he retorted, striding past her. "As the master of Holly View, I believe I may be allowed to return to the house for water when I thirst."

From behind him, he heard Lavena's sniff. "You should take a pail with you to the fields."

"I labor hard and I prefer water fresh from the spring. Is that too much to ask? And where is Ellis? He was supposed to have fetched the water."

Conn heard the sharpness in his own voice and frowned.

Lavena had turned sharp-tongued since her loss of husband and home, but during this last month, the two of them had scarcely exchanged a dozen civil words.

Ever since he'd brought Anna and Jane here.

He knew why, too, and that knowledge made him even more irritated with Lavena.

She feared his interest in Jane. Hide it as he tried, he knew she was aware of it.

He'd never told her he wouldn't marry again, but he knew

she'd believed he wouldn't. And that suited her purposes very well.

Perhaps it didn't suit his own.

Instantly, he pushed down that errant thought. Of course he wouldn't let those choking bonds enclose him again!

He wasn't that much of a fool.

But he couldn't deny he burned for the comely girl who'd now disappeared from sight.

And the thought of trying to coax her into his bed without marriage was also abhorrent.

You're truly on the horns of a dilemma, aren't you? his mind mocked him. *So what are you going to do about it?*

Nothing. Since neither choice was to his liking, he'd simply avoid the female as he'd planned to do from the beginning. Stay away from the temptations she represented.

And that will be so easy, won't it? Since you see her about the farm a dozen times a day.

No, it wouldn't be easy. But it was what he'd do.

'Tis better to marry than to burn, his mind teased him.

CHAPTER SIX

"Sweet Jesu! Not again!"

Conn surveyed his ruined field—trampled cornstalks, with bean runners up the sides, the squash plants underneath reduced to pulp.

The culprits—half-a-dozen cattle belonging to his neighbor on the west, Vaughn Walbridge—were still at their depredations.

"Haw! Get out of here!" Conn and Gustav Anderson, a former bond servant who'd stayed on after his term of servitude and was now Conn's right-hand man, picked up sticks and began herding the animals toward the knocked-down section of fence they'd come through.

"This can't go on," Conn told Gustav between tight lips. "Walbridge is the poorest excuse for a farmer I've ever seen."

The rail fence was sloppily constructed, new and also erected by the Walbridges. And a good distance over the Merritt property line.

"He is that," Gustav agreed.

As Gustav and Conn got the last animal back across the

fence, Conn saw figures approaching from the Walbridges' land. His mouth tightened more.

Vaughn and his son, Radley.

He was fed up, Conn decided. And today they were going to have it out. The Walbridges had bought the farm from the widow of an old friend. Conn heartily wished they hadn't.

Vaughn fancied himself a member of the gentry, although he wasn't. And as such, menial work was beneath his dignity. But he couldn't afford enough workers to tend to everything, so he and Radley did a good deal of the work, or tried to.

"Hallo, Merritt!" Vaughn called. "Wait up."

Conn waited, fuming, until the two men reached the fence and stepped over the fallen rails. And kept walking instead of replacing them, as any decent farmer would have done. They were truly loplollies, as Lavena would say.

Vaughn reached out his hand, and Conn had little choice but to shake it. The man's grip was weak, his hands soft like a gentlewomen's. Conn turned to the son, and repeated the performance. Radley was a decent enough boy, but somewhat thickheaded. His shock of brown hair fell over his forehead and his pale blue eyes had a slightly vacant expression.

"Sorry about this," Vaughn said, his voice bluff, gesturing to the fence. "Those scalawag cattle the Widow Steen sold me just won't stay in their pasture."

Conn gave him a level look. "The Steen cattle are good stock. The fault lies in the fence. Or lack of it."

Radley's eyes widened, as if he couldn't believe anyone would dare to criticize his father.

Vaughn also looked taken aback. "Now, here, here, man," he blustered. "I don't quite like what you're implying."

Conn bit back the hot retort on the tip of his tongue. This needed to be discussed in a civilized manner if he expected to get anywhere with this man.

"This fence needs to be propped up for now," he said instead.

"Of course," Walbridge said. "Come along, Radley."

Conn, followed by Gustav and the two other men, lifted up

the knocked-over rails and braced them as well as they could. The Walbridges weren't of much aid.

Keeping his temper with difficulty, Conn said, "Shall we go to the house and have a mug of beer and talk about the problem?"

Vaughn looked surprised, but gratified, which irritated Conn even more. Now the man thought Conn was backing down.

"Sounds like a splendid idea. Splendid!"

"Go on back to the fields," Conn told Gustav. "I'll manage this."

Gustav nodded and left. Conn wished Ellis were as steady and dependable as this man. Of course Ellis was young yet, he reminded himself. In time he'd surely improve.

Aren't you a bit hard on the lad? his mind asked him. *Why do you persist in seeing him as he was five years ago? Can't you stand the thought of him becoming an equal partner as you've led him to believe all these years?*

Conn frowned at his wayward thoughts. Of course it wasn't that. He was a fair man and he always kept his word.

"Come along, Radley," Vaughn again told his son.

Radley followed his father like a lapdog, although he had to be at least twenty-one or two.

"You have a wonderfully productive acreage, Merritt," Vaughn said as they headed toward the house.

His voice was so condescending Conn gritted his teeth. "Yes, it's a good farm. My grandfather and father worked hard to make it so. It was wilderness when they purchased it. And I'm trying hard to improve it."

"You mean this wasn't one of the land grants?" Vaughn asked, surprised.

"No," Conn answered shortly. "We paid for what we have with our coin—and our sweat and blood."

Reaching the back of the house, Conn saw Anna was, as usual, at work in the gardens. The kitchen garden this morn. She didn't glance up at the sound of their approach. In fact, she seemed to shrink down inside herself in that peculiar way of hers, as if trying to make herself smaller so no one would notice her.

Vaughn shot a glance her way, Conn noticed. A look composed both of appreciation for her beauty and a gleam of lust in his piggy eyes.

"New addition to your household?" he asked.

"Yes," Conn said, briefly, not liking that look.

They'd reached the door and Conn swung it open.

Jane was alone in the big, cheerful room. She turned and glanced their way.

Like her sister, Jane kept to herself. But why did the sight of the neighbor men make her blue eyes widen in surprise and what looked for all the world like fear?

As always, the sight of her sent unwanted emotions coursing through him. She hardened his body. She sent lustful desires rampaging inside him.

She gladdened his heart.

He quickly pushed down all those unwelcome thoughts. Especially the last one. He wanted no woman to make him feel good just to be alive. Just to be a man.

"Jane, fetch beer for all of us," he said, brusquely, and motioned his two companions to sit at the big, polished table at the other end of the room.

Jane looked a bit startled at his tone, as well she might, but nodded and quickly set about her task.

Never mind that he should have shown the two men into the library or at least the study. The kitchen would do well enough for this conversation.

Vaughn seated himself, his tight profile showing that he recognized the social slur. Radley sat, too, but his face showed no displeasure.

His gaze was fixed on Jane, following her deft, quick movements with his eyes, as if he'd never seen anything like her in his life.

Swift anger sped through Conn. He half-rose in his chair. Who did the stripling think he was, looking at Jane in that manner? A handsome stripling, he had to admit, his anger increasing.

"Sir, is something amiss?" Vaughn inquired, his voice a bit frosty.

Conn lowered himself again. "Yes, *sir*," he said. "There's much amiss. And we need to reach some kind of an understanding."

"I assume you're speaking of the cattle."

Jane carried a mug-laden tray to the table and handed the beer around.

Her hand brushed Conn's sleeve as she gave him his mug. He felt the tiny touch all the way up his arm. He gritted his teeth again at his inability to ignore her charms.

"Yes. I'm indeed speaking of the cattle. And your poorly erected fence—which is not on your property line, but a distance over on Merritt land."

He huffed out a sigh. He'd brought the two men here so this could be talked over in a civilized way, and an excellent start he'd made! And mostly because of Jane's disturbing presence.

Vaughn drew himself up in offended pride, but not before he'd taken a big swallow of the excellent beer, Conn noted.

"Sir, I take offense at your words and tone!"

"And I take offense at finding your cattle devouring my crops!" Conn shot back, not able to help himself.

Out of the corner of his eye, he saw Jane watching with openmouthed surprise from the fireplace, where she'd retreated, a big stirring spoon in her hand.

"Why are you standing there like a ninny? If you have no work, I can find—"

Lavena's sharp voice ceased. She stopped, halfway through the doorway from the hall. Conn glanced at her. Her face had turned red. She swallowed.

"Excuse me, gentlemen, I knew not you were here," she apologized, the sharpness in her voice changed to embarrassment.

Vaughn rose and bowed. "Good day, madam," he said. "You're looking well this morn," he added, gallantly.

"Good day," Lavena answered, trying to draw her dignity back around her. "Do you have all that you require?"

"Yes, indeed."

"Good." Lavena hurried across to the fireplace and jerked the spoon away from Jane. With a flurry of skirts, she turned to the big pot simmering over the flames.

Conn turned back to the two men at the table, forcing his anger down, determined to get this matter settled. "There is no need for any of us to get up—"

Lavena screamed. A high, fearful sound. A loud splash followed. Conn jumped from his seat.

Jane stood, holding the leather fire bucket. Lavena's long skirt was drenched, water dripping down onto the floor.

"Are you all right?" Conn asked.

"Of course I'm all right!" Lavena snapped. "The foolish girl has near drowned me. And all because of a stray spark!"

Jane drew a deep breath and put the bucket back in its place. "I'm sorry," she told Lavena. "But it looked as if your skirt would go up in flames."

"I've had many a spark hit me, with no untoward effects," Lavena said, frigidly.

Conn let out his breath. This "meeting" was turning into a farce. "Gentlemen, let us finish our beer and our talk," he said, his voice loud enough to send his sister the message to leave the room.

At least Lavena wasn't dense, he thought, thankfully, or was it just that she had to change her soaked clothes? In either case, she left, signaling for Jane to follow.

Jane did, and Conn forced his eyes away from the innocently provocative sway of her hips.

Or was it innocent? He heaved a sigh of relief as the hallway door closed behind the two women.

Vaughn and Radley had taken his suggestion. Both held their mugs to their mouths and took large draughts. But Radley's head was turned as he, too, watched Jane leave the room.

Conn decided he also badly needed a drink of beer. When he replaced his mug, it was more than half empty.

"Now, shall we try to settle this problem?" he asked.

Vaughn, his mug emptied, had apparently decided bluster wasn't the way to go. "I had no idea the fence was over on your property," he said.

Of course you didn't, Conn told him, silently. But continuing this argument wouldn't remedy the problem.

He nodded. "Mistakes can happen," he answered. "I'll help you rebuild the fence with stronger posts and in the right location."

Radley was still looking at the closed door through which Jane had gone. *And that's no concern of yours,* Conn reminded himself. *Unless the lad does something more than stare.*

Vaughn cleared his throat. "That's a most generous offer, Merritt. I must admit these rough jobs are a mystery to me." He gave a hollow laugh. "I should just leave it to my workers, eh?"

Conn smiled tightly. "That might be a good idea. This afternoon, shall we say, to make a start? An hour after dinner?"

Vaughn nodded. "An hour after dinner, then."

Conn finished his beer and set the mug down. "It's been a productive talk, gentlemen," he said.

Vaughn took the hint. He rose, puffing a bit as his portly frame almost didn't clear the tabletop. Radley rose, too, and Conn followed the two men out and walked with them back to the fence line.

Fortunately, the cattle hadn't tried the fence again in their absence.

Once more, the men shook hands and the father and son headed back to their home.

Conn stood for a few moments, watching their figures dwindle in the distance. Then he walked around the field, assessing the damage the cattle had done.

It wasn't as bad as he'd thought at first. He must have caught them before they'd had time to destroy much. Still, he'd have to replant. And it was nearly too late for that.

His mouth tightened. And Walbridge hadn't offered to pay for the damage. He didn't look forward to having them for neighbors. Maybe Walbridge would realize soon he wasn't cut out for this kind of life and sell his holdings.

Wishful thinking, Conn told himself, wryly. That was too much to hope for.

Frowning, he glanced at the sky, where rain clouds were beginning to form.

Damn and blast! They were in for more rain. They wouldn't be able to rebuild the fence this afternoon, and the crops certainly didn't need the rain. The corn was stunted already from another overly wet season such as this summer was turning out to be.

A noise behind him made him turn. Jane stood there, carrying a bucket of slops for the hogs, looking miserable and worried.

And delicious and beautiful.

How would her lips taste under his? Her soft breasts feel against his chest?

Conn tried to push these unwanted thoughts far back in his mind as he always did.

But this time they wouldn't go.

He tightened his face so she couldn't see how she affected him.

"Yes, what is it? Is something wrong?" he asked, deliberately making his voice brusque.

You don't want to talk to her like that, his mind told him. *You'd like to whisper love words in her ear, tell her how much you want her in your bed.*

Jane set the bucket on the ground. She looked down at her feet, then up at him again. Her expression had changed. She now looked resolute, her shoulders straight, her chin raised a bit.

Her bodice covered her decently, but Conn could fancy he saw the cleft between her breasts, imagined how it would feel to press his mouth there . . . and other places . . .

"Are you going to send Anna and me away?" she asked,

her voice trembling a bit on the last word despite her effort to
look strong and brave.

Conn stared, her unexpected question effectively stopping
the erotic images in his mind. "What on earth would make
you think that?"

"Because Mistress Lavena hates us. Everything I do is
wrong, according to her. Today, when I poured the water on
her, she told me I was doing something daft and that she was
going to give us the sack."

Jane's words tumbled out of her mouth, her lapse into the
Suffolk country accent a sign of how disturbed she felt.

Conn's face tightened in true anger. He well knew Lavena's
feelings toward Jane and Anna had only hardened during the
past weeks. His sister was careless around the fire, and more
than once a stray spark had landed on her skirt. Jane was only
trying to help, as Lavena must have known.

"My sister isn't the owner of Holly View. She doesn't make
these kinds of decisions."

Jane had pulled herself together again. She lifted her chin a
bit more, but one hand worrying the edge of her bodice gave
away her tension.

"Are *you* pleased with Darryl and me?"

I'm more than pleased with you, he told her, silently. *If you
knew how I felt about you, you'd never have come out here
alone.*

Her eyes widened and she backed up a step. For a moment
he thought he'd spoken his lustful thoughts aloud. Then he
realized his expression must have given him away.

"Yes, I'm quite . . . satisfied with you and your sister," he
finally said. "You need have no fears I'll send you away."

Silently, he cursed himself. His voice had given him away
even more.

But Jane backed up no further. She stood her ground, and
something in her own expression made his heart lurch in his
chest.

"Jane . . ." he said, moving forward cautiously. He heard
her quick intake of breath.

And then she moved forward herself just as he was doing.

It suddenly seemed hard to breathe. They were standing so close he could see the pulse in her throat. He knew her physical reactions must be similar to his own.

Not exactly, his mind said. *Pray she doesn't glance down at your breeches, or you'll scare her far away.*

A tendril of her corn-silk hair had come loose from its knot at one side, forming a beguiling ringlet which trailed along her cheek.

Conn extended his work-hardened fingers and let the ringlet curl around one of them.

She drew in her breath sharply. Her small hand came up, and just as lightly her fingers traced around the square line of his jaw.

That gossamer touch undid him.

He reached for her and she reached for him. Her soft body seemed to melt against his hard one, creating heat wherever she touched him. His hands trembled on her back as he urged her closer; his mouth trembled as he pressed it against her full, soft lips.

Honey from the sweetest nectar couldn't taste the way her mouth did accepting his touch, returning it, inviting more.

She opened her mouth to him and he drank from it, deeper and deeper . . . until he felt dizzy with the waves of sensation flooding him.

No other woman had ever made him feel like this. He was drowning in her, caring about nothing but this moment. He scooped her up in his arms, feeling her lightness, wondering how her lush curves could be contained in such a small body.

He looked down at her. Her eyes were closed, her golden lashes forming a curved arc on her cheeks. A faint rose flush stained her fair skin.

She was the most utterly desirable woman he'd ever seen.

And he must have her . . . now.

A spreading oak stood at the edge of the field, its branches forming a pool of shade under it. Conn carried Jane toward it, his whole being intent on the feelings surging through him.

Overhead, a crow let out a raucous cry as it swooped toward the oak. The sound startled Conn. He stumbled over a fallen limb near the tree, almost dropping Jane, roughly jostling her before he regained his balance.

Jane's eyes shot open. Their glances met. He didn't know what his eyes said, but her own gaze swiftly changed from startlement to shame.

She squirmed in his arms, struggling to be free. "Let me down," she begged, her voice shaking.

He did as she asked, setting her gently on her feet again.

She smoothed her clothes, then after one last wide-eyed look, like a frightened woods creature, she fled without a backward glance.

Conn stared after her, his pounding heart slowly returning to normal. Long before his inflamed body did.

"You cursed idiot!" he berated himself. "The first time you're alone with the girl and you almost took her here on the grass under a tree."

Hayley, running as if the hounds of hell chased her, heard his angry voice. Although she couldn't make out his words, she could imagine them.

Conn was no more happy about the events of the last few minutes than she was. She well knew he constantly fought his attraction to her. Just as she did the feelings he aroused in her.

What had happened back there? Some unseen force had drawn them together, despite their unwillingness.

You didn't fight it very hard, her mind said.

No, she thought, bleakly. She hadn't fought it at all. She'd been mesmerized, her mind blanked out, only her body alive and responding.

Responding shamelessly! If that crow hadn't cawed just then, what would have happened?

She knew. She'd have let Conn take her, because her body was telling her that was what she also wanted.

Her breasts throbbed where they'd pressed against his hard chest. Her lips felt hot and tender. A hollow place farther down ached to be filled. . . .

Conn wasn't coming after her, she realized in a few moments, and slowed her pace.

A stitch jabbed her side; her breathing came fast and loud. Her hair, half undone, straggled over her shoulders. Altogether, she was a sight, and she had to make herself presentable before she reached the house.

If Lavena saw her like this . . . Hayley shuddered and didn't finish the thought. She found another tree and scooted under it, tidying her hair and clothes before resuming her walk back to the house.

Conn had told her she need not fear being sent away from Holly View. But how long would he hold to that resolve if Lavena kept on complaining about her and Anna? Soon, he might tire of the unpleasantness and decide to find other servants who suited his sister, to close Lavena's carping mouth.

Perhaps he'd only reassured her today because he wanted her.

And he'd have had her, too, if the crow hadn't intervened.

She'd toyed with the idea of allowing Conn to possess her to try to assure their continued safety here. She'd been horrified at thinking those thoughts. That she could, in effect, sell herself to him in return for staying here.

And now she'd almost given herself to Conn simply because of the desires of her body. There had been no forethought, no calculation of advantages to be gained.

Only feeling and touch had been real. Nothing else had mattered.

Oh, she was a fool indeed!

She should never have come out here.

But the two strangers to her, the neighbor men entering the kitchen, had scared her witless for a few moments until she realized their presence had nothing to do with her or Darryl.

But that had made her realize anew her vulnerability. Darryl's even more so. Any day they could be found here. They should leave now. Before that happened.

Flee as they had before. Skulk through the woods. Run out of food and water.

And maybe next time no kind stranger would find them, take them in.

Maybe the next time they'd die in those woods.

Despite the risk of staying, there was worse risk in running again. And no one in this household had mentioned a search for two girls of their description. Cilla must have done her work well. The search must be going on toward Philadelphia.

As always, her thoughts circled and returned to the beginning.

No, they must stay here. It was far safer than the alternative.

That thought had sent her flying out with the pig slops as an excuse to find Conn, to gain reassurance from him. . . .

The pig slops. Where was the bucket? She'd left it back there with Conn. She *couldn't* go back for it, and Lavena would be sure to notice its absence. And if Conn brought it back, that would be even worse. Lavena would scold her for carelessness, for leaving the bucket outside.

What could she do?

She was nearing the barn. Maybe she could find another bucket there and take it to the house. To her relief she did, and hurried on.

She took a deep breath of the fresh air, filled with summer fragrances, and tried to forget her troubles.

A few drops of rain fell, and she looked at the cloud-filled sky. More drops fell. She hurried her steps even more.

Ahead of her, she saw Darryl still working in the kitchen garden. Darryl seemed to be growing a little stronger every day, for which she was deeply thankful. And Conn had just assured her they could stay here.

But could she depend on that promise?

She tried to ignore those thoughts of Conn. But that was no easier than trying to forget she'd been in his arms only minutes ago.

No easier than trying to deny that, despite her feelings that

it was safer to stay here than to run, someday the fear she and
Darryl would be found could easily become reality.

And the strangers in the kitchen would be there for her and
Darryl.

CHAPTER SEVEN

Darryl carefully balanced the bucket of vegetable peels and scraps she carried to the pigsty. She hated to leave Hayley in the kitchen with Lavena's scolding even worse than usual today, but what else could she do when Lavena thrust the bucket at her? Nothing, of course, except obey her.

"Thass just how it has to be," she said, her voice overloud in the mid-morning summer air, the sibilant hiss of the "thass" sounding odd to her ears now that she'd been here in the Colonies for almost three months.

Odd and ill-educated, considering she and Hayley could read and write well. Their squire had been unusually generous, allowing her and Hayley to attend tutoring sessions arranged for his own children.

A wave of homesickness swept through her. Oh, to be back in their small cottage, with her parents alive and well! Not in this place, far away from anything they knew.

"What has to be?"

Ellis's unexpected voice from close behind startled her, made her tilt the bucket so that some peels spilled onto the ground. She quickly knelt to retrieve them, the unwanted mix of fear and attraction she always felt in his presence overwhelming the homesickness.

"Here, let me help," Ellis said, his voice rueful. He knelt close beside her.

"No! I can do it." She edged away from him.

"It was my fault you spilled them. I shouldn't have come up on you so suddenly."

Ellis scooped the last peel off the ground, then stood, the bucket dangling from his big hand.

"Why are you so scared of me, Anna? I'm not going to hurt you."

His puzzled frown, the hurt look in his dark eyes, the way his black hair gleamed in the sun, began to soften something cold and hard deep inside Darryl's body. Ellis was friendly and considerate. He'd shown her and Hayley only kindness since they'd arrived here . . . .

That means nothing! her mind told her. *Men only want one thing from a woman. And they don't care how they get it. You must never forget that!*

The cold knot tightened again. She tilted her chin up and looked at him. "I'm not fearful of you," she said, her tone as even as her expression.

Ellis's frown deepened a bit. "Then why do you try to run away every time you see me?"

Darryl swallowed, the words she wanted to say clogging her throat. *I fear you because a man brutally used me and I'll never trust another one!*

No, she couldn't tell him that. Not ever. But what could she say that would make him leave her alone?

Leave her alone, yet not be angry with her or Hayley.

That would give his mother an added advantage in her never-ending battle with Conn to send them both away from Holly View.

And what would happen to them, then? Where could they go to be safe . . . from what she'd done.

She'd killed a man!

Tears sprang to her eyes. One spilled over, down her cheek. She quickly brushed it away, hoping Ellis hadn't noticed.

One quick glance showed her he had.

His frown deepened. His mouth tightened. He took a step forward, toward her, then stopped.

Darryl's heart gave a thump. She stepped back, away from him. She felt her eyes widening in added fear.

A chagrined expression replaced what she'd thought was anger on Ellis's face.

"I'm sorry," he said. "I shouldn't have tried to rush you. I know you're not yet ready. But I just . . ."

His voice trailed off.

Darryl drew in her breath at the new look on his face. Not that unabashedly admiring expression she'd grown accustomed to. Well, yes, there was that, but something had been added. Something deeper . . . softer.

It reminded her of the look her father had often given her mother over the years . . . a look of caring . . . of love.

Her heart thumped again. She pushed the thought away.

"I won't press you now," he told her. "I'll wait until you're ready. Until you're over whatever it is that's scared you so much."

He paused. His features became resolute. "Unless you tell me I have no hope. That you find me repulsive."

She stared at him, instantly rejecting his words. That would surely make him angry with her! She couldn't risk it.

Something behind her last thought crowded forward, demanding to be recognized.

She couldn't do it, anyway, even if it represented no danger.

Because it wasn't true. He wasn't repulsive to her. He could never be.

Her tongue came out and wet her lips. They stood for long moments, their gazes locked.

At last Ellis smiled. "I'll wait for you," he said, softly.

He turned and headed for the sty, pitching the bucket of scraps over the fence. The pigs squealed and jostled each other in their eagerness to get at the unexpected food.

Darryl stood with her feet rooted to the spot, watching the strong movements of Ellis's arms, seeing how the muscles flexed in his back, in his thighs. . . .

A shudder went through her. She forced herself to move, to go back to the house.

"Wait!" Ellis called from behind her. "You'd better take this back with you."

In a moment he was at her side, holding out the empty bucket. For a second she saw again that burning look; then he quickly blotted it out.

"Mother will expect you to bring it back."

"Yes." Darryl took the bucket. In the exchange her fingers brushed his. Another shudder she couldn't repress went through her.

And Ellis saw it. He seemed to be seeing everything today. A satisfied look came over his face.

"Head on back. You don't want to anger Mother."

"No," she agreed. She turned and walked away.

Ellis watched her go before returning to his own duties in the fields. Frustrated desire mingled with concern for Anna. As well as another, deeper emotion.

He'd just told Anna he'd wait for her. Those words had to mean more than just wanting her in his bed.

Love?

He tasted the word in his mind, nodded and accepted it. Yes, that was what it had to be. The feeling a man should have for a woman he wanted for his wife.

And which was so often absent in the marriages he'd known. His father hadn't had that feeling for his mother, he didn't think. Or if he had, he'd lost it before Ellis was old enough to notice. His parents had tolerated each other. Then his father had died when he was twelve, leaving debts that required his mother to sell their own nearby farm.

His mother had become hard and bitter over the loss of their home. She'd had no choice but to move them in with his Uncle

Conn, whose wife had recently died. Conn hadn't seemed to mind his mother's newly sharp tongue. He'd seemed lost in grief, only half-noticing what went on around him then.

Eight years later, he'd changed. Hardened, like his sister. And, also like her, he'd never remarried.

Now that might also change. It was obvious Conn was mightily attracted to Anna's sister.

And was having about the same luck as *he* was, Ellis thought, wryly.

But today something had changed just a bit. Not only for him, but also for Anna. His spirits rose as he remembered the look she'd given him a few minutes ago.

He smiled at the memory. She didn't find him repugnant.

No, something else fueled her distancing herself from him. Something that had nothing to do with him.

He wished he knew what it was so he could help her fight it. But he didn't. And her fear was so great he had to bide his time, keep his patience, until she was able to tell him.

It wouldn't be easy to try to win her. Especially with his mother's strong disapproval, which she made obvious at every opportunity.

But he could do it. He would *have* to do it.

Because he intended to have Anna for his wife.

CHAPTER EIGHT

Conn came in and shook the rain from his outer jacket, then hung it on its peg by the door. He glanced at Lavena, sitting at the worktable, peeling potatoes.

He was relieved she was alone in the kitchen, neither Anna nor Jane in evidence.

Are you trying to pretend you don't miss seeing Jane's flaxen head bent over the fire? his mind mocked him. He ignored it.

The less he saw of Jane, the better.

"Take off those muddy shoes and leave them by the door to dry," Lavena commanded without lifting her head from her work.

Conn grinned wryly at his sister's bent head, but complied with her command.

Lavena didn't seem to be in a good mood. When was she ever? He didn't relish the argument he was sure would follow when he told her what he wanted to do.

He firmed his mouth. He had to figure out some way to make her come around. After his visit with Aunt Agnes today, he knew there was no other choice.

Conn went to the beer keg in the corner and served himself

a mug, then pulled out a chair across the table from Lavena. He took a long swallow.

"I stopped in at Cedarwood to see Aunt Agnes today," he said.

Lavena lifted her head, her glance cool. "Oh? And was your visit pleasant?"

Conn placed his mug on the table. "Of course. You know Aunt Agnes and I've always gotten along splendidly."

Lavena sniffed. "As she and I never have."

Conn took a deep breath and released it. *Patience,* he told himself. "That isn't entirely Aunt Agnes's fault."

Lavena sniffed again. "It's not entirely *my* fault, either. And I don't know why you insist on calling her Aunt. She's no kin of ours."

"She's the closest thing to an aunt that we have now."

Lavena shrugged. "I manage to get along with the family we have left. I don't feel the need to call that cantankerous old woman aunt."

Conn closed his eyes. *Give me strength,* he prayed.

"Have you forgotten how she helped out when you and I were down with a fever as children and nearly died?"

Lavena finished the last potato and stood. "How could I forget when every time we see her she tells that story? Why, by now she truly believes she saved our lives."

"Maybe she did," Conn countered. "Our mother certainly thought highly of her."

"Well, I don't," Lavena snapped. She picked up the bowl, walked to the hearth and slid the potatoes into the pot of simmering fish stew.

Conn narrowed his eyes at her rigid back. All right, appealing to Lavena's softer side wasn't working. Perhaps her softer side had shriveled away and died. It was time to use whatever guile he possessed.

He released a loud sigh. "What a pity. I was going to suggest that we ask her to come here to Holly View to live."

Lavena turned so fast she almost lost her grip on the empty bowl. She grasped it just before it fell, then straightened.

"You were going to do what?"

Conn shrugged. "Forget it. I don't know how I ever could have had such an insane idea, considering how you can't get along with her."

He sighed again. "But she looked so pitiful today. In bed with one of her heart spells. And I don't think that housekeeper of hers is attentive enough."

"Then let her hire a new one. She has plenty of money."

Conn nodded. "Yes, that's true. And her plantation is still very prosperous. When she dies, which can't be too far in the future, she'll leave a big estate. Shame she has no family to leave it to."

He glanced at Lavena. She stood in the middle of the floor, stiff as a ramrod.

"Of course, she's told me many a time that she wants to leave everything to us." Conn shook his head. "But, naturally, I said we wouldn't consider it."

He got up from his seat and stretched widely.

Lavena's expression had changed. Her mouth was hanging open in shock.

Conn suppressed a smile.

"You're right. Aunt Agnes can hire a new housekeeper, one who'll do the job properly, and be a companion to her. And then Aunt Agnes can leave everything to *her*."

He glanced at Lavena. "Would you happen to know of someone suitable? You women keep up with such things in the community."

"Maybe you were too hasty, brother," Lavena said, her tone markedly milder. She walked across to him and sat back down. She gestured to his chair. "Sit down again and let's discuss this matter."

Conn forced a surprised expression onto his face. "Why, there's nothing to discuss. Since you and Aunt Agnes don't get along, we must find a suitable woman to stay with her."

Lavena looked uncomfortable. "I never said I *couldn't* get along with her. I only said she was difficult. But of course, if she's ill and truly in need, we must offer her a home here. After all, as you just said, we *are* her oldest and dearest friends.''

Conn scooped up his mug and went to the beer keg. He didn't want any more, but he wasn't able to hide his amusement. His back turned, his mouth twitching, he let out a third mighty sigh.

''I don't know, Lavena. I'm afraid it just wouldn't work out. It would put a lot of extra work on you.''

''Nonsense. I'm strong and hearty. And there are Jane and Anna to help.''

Conn gave himself only a third of a mug and came back to the table. ''You know how she likes to goad you,'' he said. ''Especially these last two years since Warren died.''

''I can handle that,'' Lavena said, briskly. ''The poor old woman is just entering her dotage. I'll pay no attention to her prattle.''

Conn frowned. Lavena's words might not be far off the mark. Aunt Agnes's mind did seem to be slipping a bit. The last few times he'd visited her, she'd talked to him a lot of the time as if he were still a boy.

''That I would like to see,'' he told Lavena. ''You've very little patience with anyone.''

Lavena firmed her mouth. ''I've plenty of patience when it's needed.''

Conn lifted his mug and saluted her. ''All right, I'll argue no further. Then you're in agreement we should offer Aunt Agnes a home here for the rest of her life?''

''Yes.'' Lavena's voice was firm. ''It's clearly the Christian thing to do. And I've never been one to shirk my duty in those respects.''

Conn gave his sister a warm smile. ''We'll ride over tomorrow and try to persuade her. It might not be an easy thing to do. She may insist on hiring someone to stay with her.''

Lavena looked a little alarmed. ''I'm sure between the two of us we'll be successful,'' she said.

I'm sure of that, too, Conn told her, silently. *If all the hints she gave me today were any indication. How lonely she is, now all her friends are dead and gone. How she's always considered us her family.*

"I hope we can," he said, letting doubt remain in his tone.

And he did have doubts, but not the ones Lavena thought.

Maybe he shouldn't have done this.

Now he'd have *two* tart-tongued women to deal with, instead of only one.

But Aunt Agnes was a good soul, kind and generous in her own way.

Conn shrugged and dismissed his doubts.

He couldn't have done anything else.

"Let's get you settled in, Aunt Agnes, so you can rest after your journey," Lavena said, her voice solicitous. "I've seen to it that your room is as comfortable as possible."

Lavena shot a cool glance at Hayley, who was refilling the flowered porcelain pitcher on the stand beside the four-postered bed. She nodded curtly and motioned for Hayley to leave.

Hayley suppressed a smile. Lavena acted as if she'd single-handedly readied the big, airy room for Mrs. Townsend.

Which wasn't true, of course. Hayley had done it, working in the evenings after her other chores were finished.

The old woman's gaze was vague as she glanced around the room. "It looks very pleasant," she said.

Lavena smiled, and led Agnes toward the bed. "Now, you just lie down here and rest until dinner."

Agnes stopped halfway across the room, shaking off Lavena's hand. "I don't believe I want to," she said, a stubborn note in her voice now.

Lavena looked surprised, then a little irritated, Hayley thought. No wonder. She was used to issuing orders and having them instantly obeyed.

"Of course you do, Aunt Agnes." Lavena walked to the bed and patted the mattress. "See how lovely and soft the bed is. It will feel so good."

Agnes frowned and stood her ground. "Lavena, I am not a

child to be cajoled,'' she said, the stubbornness in her voice stronger.

Lavena also frowned, then quickly erased it. ''Of course you aren't,'' she said. ''I only thought—''

Agnes lifted her hand imperiously. ''Never mind what you thought. You've always been a headstrong little girl. Sometimes I despair of you ever growing out of it enough to find yourself a suitable husband. Now, I want to go downstairs and see Conn. He's such an impish child, but a dear one, all the same.''

Now surprise hit Hayley, who was still standing by the washstand. Why, the old woman was in her dotage!

Hayley well remembered her own grandmother sinking into that sad state. One moment she'd be talking as sensibly as anyone, the next she'd ramble on about things long past and people long dead as if the happenings had taken place yesterday and the people were still alive.

No wonder Conn felt he had to offer the old woman a home now that she had no family and wasn't in good health.

Lavena finally said, ''Of course, Aunt Agnes, whatever you like.''

Lavena turned and glared at Hayley. ''Jane, I told you to go downstairs!''

Hayley's heart thumped. ''Yes, ma'am.'' She hastened to the door.

Closing it, she heard the old woman say, ''Why, Lavena Drake! What a way to talk to that pretty girl. She has such a sweet smile and lovely manners.''

Hayley didn't know whether to feel relieved or even more anxious. Agnes's approval would probably only make Lavena dislike Hayley and Darryl even more than she already did.

Hayley took the back stairs. At the bottom she encountered Dolly, Lavena's gray and white cat, and stooped to pet her. ''You don't have much longer to wait for your kittens, do you?'' she asked.

The cat meowed and rubbed her head against Hayley's hand, her very rounded body moving clumsily.

Lavena loved this cat, Hayley thought. And the cat loved her. That must prove there was some softness left in Lavena.

Hayley sighed. But it was well hidden, and only Dolly seemed to bring it forth, she thought, opening the door to the kitchen.

She stopped just inside the room, her heart racing.

Conn sat at the kitchen table, his fingers curled around a mug of ale. She'd expected him to be back in the fields long before now. His strong profile, his black hair tied back on his neck, affected her as the sight of him always did.

She wanted to run to him, put her arms around him, feel his warmth surrounding her.

Since that day in the cornfield, two weeks ago, she'd not been alone with him.

She'd taken great pains not to be alone with him.

Her memories of those few moments she'd been in his arms were with her all the time, try to banish them as she would.

He glanced toward the door, his face tensing as he saw her. Their gazes locked and held.

Hayley trembled. Was Conn also remembering those moments they'd held each other, kissed each other?

"How is Aunt Agnes settling in?" he finally asked.

Voices from the front hallway came floating in. Hayley shrugged, hoping the gesture looked offhand. "She doesn't want to rest. She wants to see you."

Hayley paused, then said, "She says you're a dear boy even if you are full of impishness."

Conn gave her a startled look, then shook his head. "It's hard to see Aunt Agnes like this. She's always been so sound-headed, her mind so sharp."

As she'd hoped, that intense moment between them had been redirected. "I'm sure she still is sometimes," Hayley said. "I could see that just in the few minutes I was with her. As my grandmother got old, she knew none of us. She lived completely in the past when she was a young girl."

"Do you have no family left at all—either in the Colonies or England?" Conn asked.

Sadness enveloped Hayley. "Only a few distant cousins."

"Do you never wish to return to England?"

"Of course I do! I wish my parents were still alive and we were back in our cottage. A dozen, a hundred times a day I wish we'd never gotten on that ship!"

That was true, as far as it went. But it wasn't the entire truth. A hundred times a day she was glad she'd come.

Because Conn was here.

"It must be terrible to be without any family at all," Conn said, sympathy in his brown eyes. "Sometimes it's hard for families to get along, but being alone would be much worse."

"Yes."

Their glances met again. And held. Something grew between them as it had in the field. Conn half rose from his seat, pushing back his chair. Hayley took a step forward to meet him.

The door from the front hallway suddenly opened. Lavena entered, her lips pursed, then turned and held the door for Agnes.

The old woman came in, her carriage erect, her expression alert. Her glance fell on Conn, still half out of his chair.

Agnes smiled and held out her arms. "Conn, dear boy! Come and give your old Auntie a hug! It's been so long since I've seen you."

Hayley swallowed. He'd brought the woman here less than an hour ago.

Conn pushed the chair back farther, and walked over to her. His expression was a mixture of fondness and sadness as he put his arms around the old lady and kissed her wrinkled cheek.

"I'm happy you've come to stay with us," he told her.

Agnes's smile dimmed. Tears came into her faded blue eyes. "I'd be glad to visit you, but I wish dear Warren were still alive and we were still at Cedarwood. We were so happy!"

For the moment, her mind was lucid again. And her poignant words reminded Hayley of her own parents, her own loss. She held back tears and hurried to the fireplace, stirring the stew that bubbled in the big iron pot.

"I wish that, too. Warren was a good man," Conn said

gravely from behind her. "But since it can't be, I hope you'll be content with us."

The old woman sighed. "Oh, I shall be. Especially if that sweet girl across the room can attend to my needs."

Lavena huffed. She walked over to Hayley and took the spoon from her fingers. "Go out and bring me some eggs," she ordered, her voice cold. "I must make a custard for dinner."

"Yes, ma'am," Hayley said, quietly. She found the egg basket and walked toward the outside door.

"You'll enjoy my custard, Aunt Agnes," Lavena said, her voice now cloyingly sweet. "It's very good, even if I do say so myself."

"It isn't polite to prattle on about your talents, Lavena," Agnes said, reprovingly. "But then, you always did have that fault. And instead of growing out of it, I do believe it's gotten worse as the years pass."

Hayley quickly let herself out the door and closed it behind her, struggling to contain her amusement as she walked down the stone walk.

Darryl glanced up from the herb garden, her hands full of rosemary she'd been transplanting. "What is so funny, sister?"

Hayley walked over to Darryl, her eyes dancing. "If I don't miss my guess, Lavena's met her match."

Darryl looked puzzled. "What do you mean?"

"Mrs. Agnes Townsend. She's gotten Lavena livid twice within the last few minutes."

Darryl's mouth dropped open. "Do you mean that old lady has bested Lavena?"

"Yes. And what's more, Mrs. Townsend likes me! She asked if I could attend to her needs."

Darryl's face closed. She dropped her handful of herbs on the ground. "That will only make Lavena treat you worse."

Hayley sighed, her merry mood dissipating. "I know, but it's so nice to have someone in this house who actually *likes* me."

Darryl's expression didn't lighten. "You already have someone who *likes* you. Perhaps too much."

Hayley felt her cheeks redden. Had Darryl seen that look she and Conn had exchanged in the kitchen a little while ago?

Don't be a ninny, she told herself. Of course she hadn't. The windows were too small, Darryl was too far away.

"I don't know what you mean," Hayley said, forcing herself to look straight into her sister's eyes.

Darryl's expression changed, became fearful. "Yes, you do! I can see it in your eyes. Oh, Hayley, you can't let yourself succumb to Conn's charms. You *can't* trust him! Or any man!"

Her face crumpled. Sobs erupted from her. She bent over, holding her stomach.

Stricken, Hayley rushed to her, knelt beside her, cradled Darryl in her arms. "Hush, sister," she said, softly. "I've succumbed to nothing. Nor will I."

Darryl lifted her tear-streaked face. "What if he demands that you do? Must we run away yet again? Where could we go?"

The desperation in Darryl's voice chilled Hayley to the marrow. Over the last few weeks she'd thought she saw signs of Darryl's healing. Now, it was brought home to her how fragile her sister still was.

Darryl couldn't survive another headlong flight through the wilderness. She'd barely survived the one. Perhaps wouldn't have, if Conn hadn't rescued them.

Hayley had to take care of her until she was once more her happy, confident self. No matter how long it took.

Or what she had to do to insure they stayed here. Where they had good food, comfortable beds. Where an illusion of safety and peace surrounded them.

Where they could sometimes forget that at any moment men might be searching for them. Might find them and take them back to the horrors they'd escaped.

Even if it meant letting Conn take her to his bed. The very thing she'd just promised Darryl she'd never do.

Oh, yes, that would be such a sacrifice for you! Her mind mocked her hypocrisy.

No, it wouldn't be a sacrifice. Now, this minute, she burned for Conn. Wished she were in his arms, pressed against his hard body, his lips hot on hers, melting her . . .

"Sister? Must we flee again?"

Darryl's trembling voice brought her back to the reality of the moment.

"No. We won't have to leave here." Hayley made her voice sound positive. She didn't feel that way inside. But Darryl mustn't know that.

"But I've seen the way Conn looks at you," Darryl continued, her voice trembling. "And how you return his looks."

Hayley forced a smile. Her sister was very observant. It would be difficult for anything to go on she didn't know about.

"You're imagining things because you're afraid. And from now on, with the old woman to tend to, I'll be far too busy for any of the kind of looks you think you've seen."

Darryl gave her a searching look, then finally smiled back and wiped her eyes. "I'm such a weakling. What's gotten into me?"

Hayley stroked her sister's hair. "You'll be all right. You must give yourself time."

Behind her, she heard the kitchen door open and close. Oh, Lord, if that was Lavena . . .

Quickly, she rose, brushing off her skirt and picking up her egg basket. Half-turning, she saw Conn approaching. Relief mixed with tension filled her.

"Dry your tears," she whispered to Darryl, and hurried down the walk toward the henhouse.

Behind her, she heard Conn's rapid footsteps. She rounded the turn, and the garden was out of sight. She tried to walk faster, but he soon caught up.

Thank goodness Darryl couldn't see them.

"What is your hurry?" he asked, as he drew abreast of her.

He was much too close. They were almost touching. She felt his heat, caught that mingled scent of earth and man that was distinctly his own.

Her breath came faster. She tried to edge away. His hand

caught at her arm. Even through her sleeve, his fingers heated her skin.

"Let me go," she pleaded.

"I can't," Conn said, his voice strangled. "I've tried. I lie on my bed and listen to the night birds and I burn for you."

Her heart lurched. He was saying the words she longed to hear.

That she *shouldn't* long to hear!

"I lie awake thinking of you, too," she heard herself say.

They'd reached the relative seclusion of the henhouse. Hayley hurried inside. Conn followed, his hand still on her arm.

It was dim and cool inside, with the soft sounds of the hens clucking on their nests.

"Look at me," Conn said, his voice still with that odd, tight sound.

Hayley turned as if she had no choice.

Conn's dark eyes blazed into hers with an intensity that made her gasp.

"Come to me," he said, his voice low and husky. He dropped his hand and held out his arms.

Hayley walked into his embrace and at once his warm, hard arms enclosed her, brought her against his chest, just as she'd dreamed of. . . .

She lifted her face to his and his head swooped down, his mouth claiming hers in a deep kiss that she wanted to never end.

At last, gasping for breath, they broke apart. Hayley gave him a frightened look and moved backward. "We mustn't do this!"

Conn's mouth tightened. "Don't you think I tell myself that a hundred times a day? I can't help myself. I want you in my bed! I can think of little else since you came to Holly View."

Desire mingled with fear in Hayley's breast. Here it was. What she'd told herself she'd do if it came to this. To ensure their continued safety here. Or what she and Darryl had managed to convince themselves was safety.

And to give in to the need that throbbed through her body.

"I . . . feel the same," she whispered. "I want to be in your bed."

The words had been said. They couldn't be taken back. Hayley made her gaze firm, unwavering.

Conn's look was made up of desire and something else, just as hers must be.

"Jesu! What is the matter with me?" He smacked his fist against the wooden wall of the henhouse.

Without another word, he turned and left the building.

Hayley realized what that other expression in his eyes had been.

Fear.

As strong as her own. Maybe even stronger.

CHAPTER NINE

"Here you are, Mrs. Townsend." Hayley placed the breakfast tray carefully across the older woman's lap. A few drops of tea sloshed out of the delicate cup, onto its saucer.

"Oh, I'm sorry!" Hayley quickly wiped up the drops with the napkin she'd brought.

Agnes laughed and arranged herself more comfortably in bed.

"Don't take on so, child. I'm not used to being waited on and this is a treat for me. So is not having to sit across the breakfast table from Lavena and watch her pretend she likes me. She never has liked me and the feeling is mutual. I know she's just doing it because she wants to ensure I leave my money and property to her and Ellis."

Hayley tried to keep her lips from curving upward, remembering how offended Lavena had been when, two days after Agnes arrived, the older woman told her she couldn't stand Lavena's prattle so early in the morning and planned to take her breakfast in bed from now on.

Hayley didn't mind bringing the tray up every morning. She was growing fonder of Agnes each day.

"I don't believe Lavena will ever become a woman who doesn't drive a body crazy to be around," Agnes went on. "She's much worse the last few years."

A piece of bread in her hand, she glanced up at Hayley, then quickly down again.

"Of course, maybe she'll change. After all, she's young yet. Just as Conn is. But Conn has the makings to become a fine young man someday."

Hayley could keep her lips still no longer. They twitched upward into a smile.

Agnes looked up again, their glances meeting.

Hayley's smile broadened into a grin. "You're no more in your dotage than I am, are you?"

Agnes's eyes widened. "Why, whatever are you talking about, Jane? Who are you, anyway? Lavena has set a stranger to care for me!"

Hayley's grin faded. She clamped her mouth shut. Oh, what had she done? Why had she blurted that out? Agnes's last words were high-pitched, verging on hysteria.

Or make-believe hysteria?

She'd gone too far to stop now. She had to take a chance and find out. "You know perfectly well who I am, Mrs. Townsend. And you also know Lavena and Conn are full-grown now."

She kept her gaze level on the other woman's, holding her breath, hoping she hadn't gone too far.

After a few moments, Agnes's lips began to twitch. The movement turned into a smile. "I knew you were a clever girl the moment I saw you. How did you figure this out?"

Hayley let out her held breath in relief. "My old grandmother was long in her dotage before she died. She lived with us. She didn't act as you do."

Agnes nodded, as if pleased. "Yes, you are very observant. Does anyone else know?"

Hayley considered. "My sister—and maybe Co—Mr. Merritt suspects."

At her near-slip, Hayley felt her face warming. She'd not seen him alone since that second time he'd kissed her.

A week and two days ago.

That was the way she wanted it. *No, you don't,* her mind told her. *Stop lying to yourself.*

And she was certain Agnes's shrewd old eyes didn't miss a thing. "But not dear Lavena," Agnes said. "No, that one is too full of bitterness these last years to care about anyone else."

Hayley's innate honesty made her protest this. "She loves her son very much."

Agnes nodded. "Yes, that's true. And she wants him to make a good match when he marries. She's not at all happy that Ellis has eyes for no one but your pretty sister."

Hayley's heart skipped a beat. What else had Mrs. Townsend noticed? How should she reply to this remark?

"Your sister is attracted to Ellis, too, I think," Agnes said. "But she's been wounded in her body and spirit and is not yet healed."

Hayley stared. This woman had discerned more in the few times she'd seen Darryl than Lavena had in all the weeks they'd been here.

"Yes," Hayley finally said. "We lost our parents only a few months ago." She hoped Agnes would be satisfied with this and not probe deeper.

"What happened, child?" the old woman's concerned voice asked. "Tell me."

Hayley told her about how her parents had died aboard the ship, what she'd told Conn about searching for family in Philadelphia, then heading south and Conn finding them. She suddenly found herself wishing she could tell her all of it.

But of course she couldn't. Fear hit her at the unwanted reminder of what would happen to them if they were found.

Mrs. Townsend looked at Hayley for a moment after she'd finished. "I'm sorry for the both of you. You and Anna have lost much. And your family is the worst of it. But you haven't told me all. You're still hiding something."

Hayley drew in her breath. She opened her mouth to deny that.

Agnes held up her hand. "It's all right. It's none of my business. I know you and Anna are good girls."

She tilted her head and gave Hayley a measuring look. "This, too, can just be between the two of us."

Their glances locked again. Hayley knew what she meant. Finally, she nodded. "All right. I'd better go now."

At the door she turned and gave Agnes an inquiring glance. There was one thing she had to find out.

"Why are you pretending your wits are addled?"

Agnes's hand, holding a spoonful of porridge, paused halfway to her mouth. "Because it's enjoyable to me, child. Not many things are now, except eating and having some laughs. And Lavena needs someone to bring her down a peg or two. She gets away with far too much."

Hayley looked at her a moment.

Agnes shrugged. "All right. That's not really the reason. I've never been able to keep from letting Lavena get under my skin. I've discovered this is the easiest way to keep her from gaining control over me. I keep her off guard, don't you know. And as you say, I think Conn sees through my playacting."

She sighed. "I miss Cedarwood more than I expected. I know my housekeeper is taking good care of the house, and Conn is keeping an eye on the overseer to see that the farm is properly run. But I miss my own house!"

Hayley nodded, touched. "I'm sure you do. Why don't you ask Conn to take you to visit oftener?"

Agnes shook her head. "No, that will only make me long even more to have things back as they were. And I know that can never be."

"Yes. I'm sorry there's nothing I can do." Hayley put her hand on the door latch.

"Don't worry about it, child. I'll be all right. Now I have a question for you," Agnes said. "Why are you trying to pretend you have no interest in Conn?"

Hayley's hand, still on the door latch, froze. The silence drew out.

Finally, Agnes waved her hand. "Go on downstairs. You don't have to answer that one, either."

Hayley quickly turned the latch and opened the door enough to leave.

"And I've seen the sheep's eyes Conn sends your way when he thinks no one is looking. But he's as big a ninny as you are, and he also has losses."

Agnes's voice floated out as Hayley closed the door and hurried downstairs, her face burning.

Was she so transparent, then? Was Conn? She knew Lavena suspected the attraction between her and Conn. But she'd never directly mentioned it to Hayley.

So Mrs. Townsend thought both she and Conn ninnies? Because they didn't act on their feelings? Would she actually approve if they . . . her mind veered away from that unfinished thought, because it evoked disturbing mind pictures for her.

She and Conn lying together, lips and bodies pressed tightly together . . .

Her face flushed. Her body heated.

She shook her head to clear it. She'd reached the bottom of the back stairs by now.

Dolly meowed at her from her nest under the stairs. Several tiny kittens lay against her, nursing.

Smiling, Hayley paused to pat the cat. "Your babies are so sweet," she told her, rising.

She swung open the door into the kitchen.

Lavena, busily stacking candles into the box on the wall, turned. "Well, it certainly took you long enough to get back down here! Go punch down the bread dough. It's almost risen too much."

Hayley hastened to the worktable and began kneading the fragrant, elastic dough, her thoughts still on Agnes Townsend's last remarks.

Losses? What did Mrs. Townsend mean by that? Was she

referring to bad crop years . . . or other things . . . emotional losses?

Probably both, Hayley decided. Conn's parents were dead, and Lavena had mentioned that several younger brothers and sisters were buried in the family burying ground. Just as her own parents had lost three children.

At last she had to face the one thought she'd been holding at bay.

Surely, Mrs. Townsend hadn't meant that she would approve of a *marriage* between Hayley and Conn.

Not if she knew the truth about you and Darryl, her mind said. *How can you ever hope to make a decent marriage?*

She thumped the bread dough vigorously, trying to shut out the bleak thoughts.

"What are you doing?" Lavena asked, her voice shrill. "The dough needs no more pummeling! Go ahead and shape it into loaves so it'll be cooked before midnight. And when that task is done, I've many more for you. You and your sister are not being paid to loll around bedchambers talking to old women who aren't in their right minds."

Hayley pressed her lips together. Why couldn't Lavena ever give her or Darryl a kind word?

Yes, she and Agnes Townsend did have a secret between them. She could see how fooling Lavena into believing her wits were addled was amusing to the old woman.

But they had more than one secret between them. Agnes Townsend knew Hayley was hiding something. Even if she didn't know what it was.

The always present fear clamped down, painfully tightening her stomach.

She liked the old woman, but could she trust Agnes Townsend not to speak of this to anyone else? Not to get other people in the household wondering about them?

She might as well, because there was nothing she could do about it, Hayley decided in a moment.

The last thought she'd had before Lavena's tirade teased at her mind, wouldn't leave it.

Marriage. Marriage to Conn. Was that a possibility? In England such a union would be rare. But this new country was different. Here there wasn't such a huge gap between master and servant.

Conn's own forebears were from common folk, who'd gained their holdings by hard work. And hadn't Conn admitted he badly wanted her in his bed? As *she* wanted to be there? Wasn't mutual desire often the prelude to marriage?

You're forgetting something, her mind whispered. *You have other problems to worry about. How could you ever tell Conn you and Darryl are runaway bond servants?*

That your sister killed a man? Do you think you could convince him that the deed was justified? That what you've done since then is?

Her stomach clenched even tighter.

And even if she did convince him, what good would that do?

Conn couldn't protect her and Darryl from what they'd done even if she were his wife.

Conn opened the kitchen door and closed it quickly to shut out the wind and rain.

Jane was busy at the fireplace. Anna polished pewter at the worktable. Lavena and Aunt Agnes sat at the kitchen table drinking a mid-afternoon cup of tea.

Lavena's face was serious. Obviously, he'd caught them in the middle of an ongoing discussion.

"Margaret is such a dear, sweet girl," Lavena said. "I've long thought she and Ellis would make a good match."

Wiping off his wet hair with the towel that hung by the door, Conn smiled. His sister had pushed Ellis at their neighbor's daughter for the last couple of years. Lavena was even more anxious now that Anna had come into the household and Ellis was showing such an obvious interest in her.

He glanced quickly toward Jane. She was turned away from him. As always, just the sight of her—her profile, with her small straight nose, her high brow and cheekbones, her curvy slight-boned body—made his own body tighten, made all that swirl of unsettling feelings start up inside him.

He turned just as quickly away and hung up the towel on its peg.

What was he going to do about this situation? Nothing, as he'd done these last weeks, growing ever more lustful by the day. Ever more sleepless at night.

And more than that. Not only lust drove him. He wanted more than that from Jane. He wanted her in all ways.

But he also feared to give in to his desires. He'd done that before, let physical cravings draw him into marriage. . . .

No! He wouldn't think of that. It was over and done with, years before.

"Yes, I believe going to the Findley party would be enjoyable," Agnes agreed. "I haven't been out of the house since I arrived, more than two weeks ago."

He heard Lavena's indrawn breath. "Oh, but Aunt Agnes. I thought you'd be happy to stay here with Jane to look after you. You haven't been well lately. You're still grieving over Uncle Warren's untimely death, and—"

"Fiddlesticks! Warren's been dead two years. I'd love to see some lively company for a change. And besides, Lavena, you're getting old enough now you need to get out and mingle with some young people yourself."

Conn glanced over at his sister. Her lips were tight, and a frown drew her brows together.

He frowned himself, wondering if he'd done the right thing when he'd more or less tricked Lavena into agreeing to bring Agnes here to live. How long could Lavena keep on being solicitous and kind to the older woman? And all because she wanted a portion of her property for herself and Ellis.

And therefore, was always careful to say nothing to offend the old lady. No matter how provoking she became.

And he had to admit Aunt Agnes went out of her way to provoke Lavena.

These days no one knew what would come out of Aunt

Agnes's mouth. Sometimes, as now, she was as lucid as anyone, and yet a minute later, she was back in the days of his and his sister's childhoods.

Sometimes he wondered if Agnes was truly as confused as she appeared. Could it be possible that this was only an act she put on? Just to amuse herself at Lavena's expense? He could hardly blame her. Sometimes Lavena embarrassed him with her fawning over the old lady.

Despite himself, he glanced over at Jane again. She'd half-turned toward the two women at the table, a wistful expression on her face.

Why, she'd also enjoy the festivity at the Findleys' the other two were discussing, he realized. Naturally, she would. She was young and lovely.

"But I'd planned a special supper for you that evening, Aunt," Lavena said, her voice placating. "The blackberries are ripe and I'll make my blackberry fool, and—"

Conn saw his honorary aunt glance at Jane. Something flickered in her old eyes. She waved her hand imperiously.

"I can have your blackberry fool any night, Lavena. Besides, I'm not at all sure you're sufficiently trained to prepare that delicacy. You're still very young, you know."

She gave Lavena an equally imperious look. "I intend to go to the party. And since you're so concerned that I'm properly taken care of, Jane can go with me. And her sister, too."

This time Lavena's gasp would be audible through the outside door, Conn thought, his gut tightening at the thought of Jane at the party, surrounded by admiring men.

Of course that was impossible. Jane was a servant here. She couldn't be included in the invitation.

He stole a glance at Jane. She stood like a statue, staring at the two women sitting at the table. Anna, too, stared. Both of the girls looked dumbstruck at the suggestion. As well they might.

"Aunt Agnes! What are you thinking of? Why, why . . ."

"Stop sputtering like a half-cooked chicken," the older woman said. "Jane and her sister are cousins of the family, come for a visit. I'm sure we can find something suitable for them to wear."

Jane moved forward, her movements jerky. "Anna and I couldn't do that, Mrs. Townsend," she said.

Aunt Agnes glanced up at her. "Of course you can, girl. Your manners and speech are as good or better than anyone else's. You and Anna will have a grand time."

Jane shook her head. "No, no, we can't go."

Conn stared at her. Her voice held a note of desperation, almost fear. She and Anna kept to themselves, were not forward in any way, but why would she fear this suggestion, as odd as it was?

Aunt Agnes raised her chin and gave Jane a piercing look from her old eyes. "Yes, you can, my girl," she said, a strange note in her voice. She held Jane's gaze for several moments.

Jane's face paled. Finally, she turned away, with no more protests. Across the room, Anna stared at her.

"There! Everything is all settled," Aunt Agnes said, her voice satisfied.

He saw Lavena swallow. There was a silence. Then finally, his sister nodded. "All right," she said, tightly. "If that's what you wish, we'll try to arrange it. But it's most irregular."

Agnes waved her hand again. "Old age has privileges, you know. And this *is* what I want."

Lavena got up from the table. She turned to Jane, her mouth still tight. "Girl, come and get these dishes. And then help my aunt back to her bedchamber."

Jane hastened to obey, her face averted, as if she didn't know Conn was in the room.

She did, though. He was sure of that. There seemed to be some kind of connection between them, some kind of awareness. . . .

And he ached to walk to her, pull her into his arms and kiss her until she was breathless.

And then take her to his bed.

He was insane.

Conn went to the door, opened it to the force of the driving rain and left.

Lavena stared after him. "What in the world is Conn doing? Going back into this storm? He can do no more outside work today."

"Leave the lad alone, Lavena," Agnes advised. "He's just trying to learn to be an adult, and sometimes it's hard to do."

Lavena jerked herself up from the table. "Oh, Aunt Agnes! Conn is thirty years old! I am forty-five!"

She strode across the room to the door to the back stairs, flung it open and left.

Agnes shrugged, her eyes twinkling.

"I believe I'll stay downstairs for a while today, Jane dear. I'm feeling much stronger than yesterday."

CHAPTER TEN

"We'll have to go on without Conn," Agnes, seated with the others in the parlor, said impatiently.

Frowning, Lavena shook her elaborately coiffed head. "No, we should wait a little longer."

"Whatever is the matter with you, Lavena? We can't arrive late at the gathering!"

Lavena's frown smoothed out as she turned to Agnes.

"Of course you're right, Auntie," she said. "But it just isn't the thing to do, to appear at a soiree without the head of the family."

Agnes let out a deep sigh. "We've been preparing for this event for two weeks. And we've spent most of today getting dressed. Surely, you aren't going to let these lovely girls lose their chance to shine!"

Agnes, dressed in widow's black, turned to Hayley and Darryl and gave them her widest smile. And a wink that she took care Lavena didn't see.

Hayley smiled back, but felt her face warm. She glanced down at her blue velvet gown, borrowed from Lavena, and far more elaborate than anything she'd ever owned or worn. Its lace and tucks, its fine linen scarf, made her feel uncomfortable, not herself. And the stays she was unaccustomed to wearing made her feel as if she couldn't take a deep breath.

Darryl's green satin gown was somewhat plainer, but still the finest gown she, too, had worn.

In vain Hayley had tried to beg off from coming. Agnes had reminded her that they had some small secrets between them, and that had ended Hayley's protests.

Of course, Agnes didn't know what those secrets were, but that didn't matter. If Agnes decided to start probing and asking questions, no telling where it would end. Maybe with their true identities revealed.

Maybe with them found and punished.

Maybe with Darryl hanged.

When Hayley told Darryl Mrs. Townsend suspected they were hiding something, and was gently blackmailing her, Darryl had paled. She, too, had reluctantly agreed they must go. They were caught in the middle, between Lavena and Agnes, and although they didn't want to incur Lavena's wrath, neither did they want to anger Agnes.

In any case, how could they refuse? Especially once Lavena had, however reluctantly, agreed and the plans had been made. Despite the elaborate ruse, they were still servants here. They still had to do the bidding of their employers.

Or, as in this case, their employers' guest.

They must go, although it was too dangerous for them to go anywhere, let anyone see them.

The butterflies that had been in Hayley's stomach all day started beating their wings again.

Lifting her head, she encountered Lavena's renewed scowl. Which puzzled her.

Conn's sister's outrage at the idea of Hayley and Darryl attending the party had abated since the day Agnes had proposed the plan and Lavena had agreed.

She hadn't objected to two of her gowns being altered. She'd even helped Hayley with the blue one she was wearing, saying Hayley was too clumsy for the delicate work.

Now, because Conn wasn't yet back from his stock-buying trip to Derryville, all her ill humor had returned.

"Come!" Agnes said, rising with the aid of her cane. "We must go or we'll be late indeed."

With ill grace, Lavena led the way across the polished wood floor to the wide front door. The carriage sat in the drive, waiting.

The weather had turned chilly for an early September evening, and the women adjusted their cloaks, then walked down the broad steps, Ellis alongside to see they had no difficulty.

At the carriage, Ellis carefully seated Agnes, then reached for Lavena's hand.

He cast a sideways glance at Darryl, and Hayley realized he must be anticipating taking her hand to help her inside.

A clattering of hooves came from behind. Lavena turned sharply, as did Hayley.

Conn drew his bay gelding, Tristan, to a stop behind the carriage. Even with his breeches and coat travel-stained, his hat askew, and lines of weariness etched into his face, the very sight of him made Hayley's heart leap in her chest, her breathing quicken.

Lavena's frown disappeared, replaced by a smile. "Brother! We'd given up on you. We'll return to the parlor and wait while you change clothes."

"Nonsense! Go ahead. I'll change and follow on Tristan." Conn fastened the horse's reins to a post.

Hayley watched the swift, sure movements of his hands, a shiver twisting down her spine. She remembered how his hands had felt holding her that day in the field . . . the other time . . .

Lavena's frown returned. "But we should wait," she protested. "It isn't seemly for us to go ahead."

"Lavena, will you get yourself in here and let us be going?" Agnes's impatient voice said from the depths of the carriage.

"But I don't think—"

"We're wasting time with this futile argument," Conn said. "Go ahead."

His glance fell on Hayley, standing beside Darryl in the

drive, moving from the top of her head, covered by a small lace cap, down her cloak-covered body, the blue gown peeking out at the bottom.

Hayley shivered again, feeling the glance as if he'd touched her, leaving heat in his wake.

Abruptly, he turned and headed for the house.

Lavena's chest rose and fell. Her lips tightened as she looked after him. She whirled toward Hayley and Darryl.

"Don't stand there like ninnies. Let us be going!"

She entered the carriage, disdaining Ellis's proffered hand. Hayley and Darryl hastened behind, Darryl managing to get inside before Ellis could touch her.

Someday, I'll not be able to keep my temper, Hayley thought as she carefully arranged her borrowed skirts around her. *I'll tell her how angry she makes me, what a sour and sharp woman she is, and then we will be forced to leave here.*

The memory of her and Darryl's flight through the woods came into her mind. The horror of it. How Darryl had nearly died . . . how she was still far from recovered from what she'd endured. How she might never recover.

Hayley's anger deflated. No, she'd keep her anger at Lavena's hard ways from showing. She had to.

She and Darryl weren't used to harsh words. They'd be better off if the squire and his family hadn't treated them so well, she thought. Many, if not most, servants weren't treated so well. Either in England or the Colonies.

We have a roof over our heads, she reminded herself, as she often did. *We have good food to eat, a comfortable bed and room of our own. That is more than many people ever have.*

And all this could end in an instant. Maybe it would tonight. One of the guests at the Findleys' party could point a finger at them. Denounce them as frauds . . . and worse.

Don't be absurd, she told herself. How could anyone connect them in their disguise as cousins of the family to two runaway bond servants, missing for months now?

Maybe the search for them had been abandoned. Or was still

going on in the north. In Philadelphia. If not, why had no one discovered them here before now?

"Jane, dear, do stop fidgeting and try to enjoy the evening," Agnes Townsend said, wine glass in hand. She sipped at the wine, then continued. "My goodness, you'd think you and Anna had never been to a small affair at a neighbor's house."

Agnes gave Hayley a merry half-smile.

Hayley forced herself to return it, although she was irritated at the old lady. Of course, Agnes knew that Hayley and Darryl never had been to such an affair as this. And how could they possibly enjoy it since they were here under false pretenses?

And terrified of being discovered for who they truly were. Of course, Agnes didn't know that. To her credit, Hayley believed the old woman thought she was doing a good deed and genuinely wanted them to have a good time.

Everyone had accepted her and Darryl as the people they pretended to be. This was due in large part to Agnes Townsend's gleeful coaching for the last two weeks on their supposed background, which Agnes had made up out of whole cloth. If anyone thought it odd that the old woman needed two companions, no one had said anything or even raised a brow.

But Agnes had created an impossible situation, Hayley realized. Eventually, some of these people would come to Holly View, would see her and Darryl working, would realize they were actually servants.

But there was no use worrying about that now, she advised herself. You and Darryl must get through this evening without raising anyone's suspicions.

The dining room where they sat was painted a brilliant yellow, with elaborately carved furniture which Mrs. Findley had taken pains to inform everyone was made by Chippendale.

As Agnes, drawing heavily on the privileges of old age, had requested, Hayley sat on one side of her, Darryl on the other. Margaret Findley, the pretty daughter, flanked Darryl, with Ellis beside her.

Wishing he were next to Darryl, Hayley knew. He kept leaning forward so he could see Darryl. Across from their group, Lavena sat with Walter Findley, the son of the household, and the two Walbridge men.

Lavena's expression had been smugly pleased that Ellis was seated beside Margaret. But her expression changed to a frown every time her son looked Darryl's way.

And, just like Hayley, she kept shooting quick, anxious glances at the dining room doorway.

For the same reason? Was Lavena watching for Conn, too?

The group was almost finished with the meal, which had begun with a fruit cup, then roasted quail, with several more courses after that.

And Conn still hadn't arrived. Had he decided not to come, after all?

Disappointment shot through Hayley at this thought, making her admit to herself how much she'd looked forward to seeing him and, as much as she'd dreaded this party, being in his company for several hours.

A situation which never happened at Holly View. Conn ate his meals almost indecently fast, then hurried back to his work. In the evenings he seemed always to have something he needed to attend to in the barns or elsewhere outside.

The rest of the meal passed in a blur to Hayley. Once in a while, someone addressed a comment or a question to her, which she managed to answer.

Finally, they left the table and retired to the Findleys' wide front hall, painted a bright blue and furnished with chairs and settees.

"We've started using it as a summer parlor," Louisa Findley chirped. "That's all the rage now."

"The color is exquisite," Lavena said.

Her voice had lost its usual crispness, Hayley noted. She sounded as if she were only making the polite response expected of her.

And now she darted glances toward the front door. Was she

still watching for Conn? And if so, why was she so nervous about his arrival?

Which Hayley had given up on. Surely, he'd decided not to come.

Louisa preened. "Yes, I believe I made a wise choice. It's quite the fashion in London, now."

Agnes made herself comfortable on the settee she shared with Hayley and Darryl.

She poked Hayley in the ribs. "That blue's bright enough to put your eyes out, if you ask me," she said behind her opened fan. "The woman always was a fool for fashion."

Hayley managed a smile for Agnes, then felt other eyes on her. Vaughn Walbridge was giving her and Darryl a curious look.

With a jolt, she remembered that day in the kitchen when he and his son were there and Lavena's skirt had almost caught on fire. No doubt he'd also seen Darryl in the garden.

Renewed fear replaced her other emotions. What was he thinking about them? Had he realized they were servants that other day? She'd come in with Lavena, and both had served the men, so he couldn't have been sure . . . and Lavena also often worked in the gardens. But he could have found out. . . .

"Mistress Jane, are you quite comfortable?" Radley asked from behind her chair.

Hayley swallowed, trying to dismiss her fears. Vaughn was probably only upset at his son's attentions to her, which she certainly wasn't encouraging. She wished Radley would stop hovering over her.

Ellis was beside Darryl, much to Darryl's discomfiture. Out of the corner of her eye, she caught another displeased glance from Margaret Findley. That Margaret had an eye for Ellis was obvious.

Margaret got up in a flurry of silken skirts, to lead the guests in dancing, choosing Ellis as her partner.

His reluctance to leave Darryl was so painfully clear Hayley winced.

"Will you honor me with this dance?" Radley asked.

Hayley tensed. She didn't want to dance with him. That was one thing Agnes had neglected to coach them in.

But she couldn't refuse. She didn't dare do anything that would draw attention to her and Darryl, make anyone suspect they weren't who they pretended to be. And Agnes's cousins would certainly know how to dance.

However, she and Darryl were supposed to be here to tend Agnes's needs. She turned to the older woman with a hopeful, questioning look.

Agnes waved her hand dismissively. "You and Anna go ahead and enjoy yourselves," she said. "I'll be fine. If Warren were here and I still could, I'd be out there showing you young people a thing or two."

Swallowing nervously, Hayley rose and took Radley's arm as she saw the other women doing with their partners.

Hayley stiffened as Margaret's brother Walter gallantly asked Darryl to dance. For a long, frozen moment, Darryl looked as if she would jump out of her chair and flee the house.

Don't do it, Hayley silently willed. *You have to go along with this.*

Finally, Darryl smiled and rose, letting Walter lead her out into the middle of the wide hall.

Relief flowed through Hayley, but they still didn't know how to do this dance.

Oh, would this evening never end?

Jacob Findley bowed before Lavena. Lavena rose, looking as if she'd rather be anywhere but here.

Hayley managed to follow the moves of the dance, finding it similar to village dances she'd learned as a child. She saw Darryl was managing all right, too.

In the midst of a turn, she heard the front door open and close. Her stomach tightening, she glanced toward it.

Oh, he had come after all!

A maidservant behind him, Conn stood in the doorway, resplendent in fawn-colored, fitted knee-breeches and a braided coat of dark brown. Shining silver buckles adorned his shoes.

As it had earlier this evening in the drive, Hayley's heart leapt in her chest.

Conn's glance swept over the merrymakers. Finally, it settled on Hayley, moving from her capped head down the elaborate gown to her toes.

His face blanched, his body tensed and his gaze stayed fixed on Hayley.

Hayley felt her own face pale. What was wrong? Surely the sight of her in the borrowed finery couldn't be so unsettling to him. After all, he'd known from the beginning she and Darryl would wear two of Lavena's gowns.

Did he fully realize for the first time that his two servant girls were dancing in a well-to-do neighbor's hall, pretending to be of that class?

Or was the reason a simpler one, a more welcome one? Could he be upset because she was dancing with Radley? After all, Conn had admitted he wanted her in his bed.

But he fought against those desires. He didn't want to have them. And besides, that wasn't a jealous kind of look.

Conn finally tore his gaze from Hayley and walked to the nearest chair. Once seated, he accepted a glass of wine from a servant's tray and drained it.

Somehow, Hayley got through the dance and then another one. Finally, Radley seated her beside Agnes again, brought her a glass of punch and took an empty chair beside her.

Conn sat across from her, still looking straight ahead of him as if he'd received some kind of terrible shock.

Winded, others also dropped into seats.

Lavena took a chair as far from Conn as she could. After one quick glance at him, she turned away, biting her lower lip.

"Glad you could make it, Merritt," Jacob Findley boomed. "But buying new stock takes precedence over these get-togethers. Especially since our harvest is turning out to be another poor one. Blast all the rain we've had!"

"Don't say that," Vaughn Walbridge said, jovially. "Lest next year we have a drought."

"We've already had that, two years ago," Jacob returned, sourly.

"Were you successful in your stock buying?" Jacob went on after Conn made no reply to either man's comments.

"Moderately so," Conn finally said, his voice clipped and strained.

Hayley lifted her head a little and gave Conn a sideways glance.

He was tilting his refilled wine glass again. When he put it back on the small table beside him, it was once more empty.

He looked as if it was all he could do not to bolt from the chair and the room.

Hayley wished with all her heart she could do just that.

For the past weeks, since that last encounter, when both had admitted their mutual desire, Conn had made sure they weren't alone together. As had she. But he'd never before been rude, never openly showed he couldn't stand to glance her way.

Her confusion grew. Something was very wrong and she had no idea what it was.

"What do you think of the pirate raid on the Bay last week?" Jacob Findley asked.

"Glad we live this far inland," Vaughn Walbridge answered.

Jacob laughed. "Nowhere in Delaware is very far inland."

"Maybe we should stop fighting Pennsylvania's claim on our colony," someone else put in. "They'd certainly give us more protection from the pirates than the Maryland side."

"All this mess needs to be settled," Conn suddenly said. "It's been going on too long, with none of us sure where we stand."

"There's talk of having some men skilled in surveying sent from England to complete the boundary lines," Vaughn said. "Mason and Dixon, I believe they're called."

"Bah!" Jacob rebutted. "There's always talk. We need some action."

"Well at least we don't have the trouble with our Negroes that they have down south," Louisa Findley put in.

"No, we have it with our bound servants," her husband

answered. "One of my cousins is a housekeeper on a big plantation on the Brandywine, and she says they've had a lot of trouble with runaways."

Hayley froze in her seat. Could they possibly be talking about Oscar Pritt's plantation? Mrs. Whitley? Or maybe Burle Porter's?

"Yes, that's true. Always a lot of that going on. I heard around there's a runaway bond servant girl being looked for," Vaughn said into a silence.

Hayley's heart thumped, then thundered in her chest. She didn't dare glance at Darryl. Were the searchers now in this area?

Could this explain Conn's strange behavior? Had he, too, heard this story and put the pieces together?

CHAPTER ELEVEN

All her muscles tensed, she waited for Con to rise to his feet, point his finger at her and Darryl and denounce them in front of all these people.

But why were they looking for only one girl? That didn't make sense. When Oscar's body had been found, and Darryl was missing . . .

Another thought hit her, a new one. As far as they knew, only Cilla and Oscar had known Hayley was at Oscar's plantation.

And Oscar was dead.

What if no one knew she and Darryl had escaped together? What if Burle Porter's men were only after *her?*

Or Oscar's men were only after Darryl?

Cilla might have told, but she'd helped them escape. She was tough and wily and she liked Hayley and Darryl.

If Burle Porter had come to Oscar's plantation to look for Hayley, he might have suggested the two sisters were together.

But unless someone had seen her there, or Cilla had confessed, no one could know for sure.

There could very well be two search parties after them. One for Hayley . . . another for Darryl . . .

Why hadn't she and Darryl ever considered this possibility?

"Nothing unusual in bond servants trying to escape," Conn said. "Too many people treat their indentured people abominably."

Conn's voice sounded almost back to normal, only a small edge to it.

He hadn't discovered their secret, or he wouldn't be saying these things.

Hayley's relief left her limp. Whatever was wrong with him, it had nothing to do with their fugitive status.

"True, true," Jacob Findley agreed.

Louisa sniffed. "Most of them are from the lower classes. They don't respond to kind treatment."

"Oh, you're so right!" Lavena chimed in. "Our last girl had no gratitude whatsoever. She left the very day her bond was fulfilled, with not a backward look or thanks for all we'd done for her."

"Clara was a good worker," Conn said, his voice cold. "She left because she married and wanted a home of her own."

Lavena drew herself up, giving her brother a haughty glance, obviously furious her brother would contradict her in public.

Hayley caught her breath at the look on Conn's face as his gaze met Lavena's. His jaw was clenched again, his mouth tight, his eyes narrowed.

The anger left Lavena's face, replaced by what looked like a mixture of fear and regret. She cleared her throat.

"You're right, brother," she finally said. "I—I guess I'd forgotten that."

Amazement went through Hayley. Never, since she and Darryl and come to Holly View, had she heard Lavena apologize for anything she'd said or done.

And never had she seen such a look on Lavena's face.

All this must have something to do with Conn's reaction when he entered the house a few minutes ago.

Something to do with the way he'd stared at Hayley as if he were seeing a ghost.

"Bonnie lass, I heard, with flaxen hair," Vaughn said.

Fear stabbed at her midsection. The searchers were after them. Or one of them.

Still not daring to look toward her sister, Hayley fought down the urge to reach up and tuck every wisp of her hair under the linen cap she wore, hoping Darryl hadn't done that.

Something in Vaughn's voice made Hayley risk a sideways glance at him. He was looking her way. She jerked her gaze away, certain every eye in the room was turned in her and Darryl's direction.

"She's got dark eyes, though, so that combination shouldn't be hard to spot."

Dark eyes?

Relief flooded Hayley, making her weak. These searchers weren't after her or Darryl, but some other poor unfortunate female.

The ones after them, and surely there were people looking for them, must still be searching in the other direction, toward Philadelphia as they'd hoped.

"She won't get far by herself," Walter said, his voice casual, as if he were discussing a stray dog.

"No," Vaughn agreed, his tone just as offhand as the younger man's. "Likely to die in the woods somewhere."

Hayley risked a glance at Darryl. Her sister was looking her way, her eyes wide, her lips curved into a relieved smile.

Hayley's answering smile accidentally included Radley, who was also glancing her way. He returned it with a gratified smile of his own, his face lighting up.

"Do they have dogs out?" Conn asked, his voice hard and tight.

"Can't say," Vaughn said. "You know how these things are. Stories get passed around and changed."

"Yes," Conn answered. "Unfortunately, I do."

"Oh, enough of this gloomy talk!" Margaret Findley said, rising. "Let us dance again."

She turned to Ellis, smiled widely at him and held out her hand.

Ellis politely rose and escorted her to the dance area, but not without a longing backward glance at Darryl.

Radley rose and bowed to Hayley. "Will you do me the honor?"

Hearing his confident voice, Hayley realized he'd misinterpreted the smile she'd given him a moment ago.

She couldn't refuse. Even if they'd had a reprieve, danger still surrounded them and would continue to for a long time.

Maybe forever.

"Of course." She rose and placed her hand on his arm.

Conn deliberately kept his eyes on Vaughn, on Jacob. On his sister.

On everyone but Jane, now dancing with that Walbridge stripling.

Not that it made any difference. He was aware of her with every breath he drew, every heartbeat. But he couldn't stand to look at her. Not tonight.

He was over the shock the first glimpse of her in that damned gown, dancing with Radley Walbridge, smiling up at him, as she no doubt was doing now, had caused when he walked into the house.

But a mixture of feelings still surged through him. Bitter anger had been predominant at first.

That had faded. Now he was back to the powerful desire he felt for Jane no matter how he fought it.

And she was again dancing with that gangly boy. His jaw tightened. Maybe he wasn't such a boy after all. Radley was openly defying his father with all these attentions to Hayley. Conn's jaw tightened more. He hadn't thought Radley had the guts for that.

It was clear the elder Walbridge was trying to push his son in the direction of Margaret Findley.

No wonder. The Findleys had the largest, most prosperous plantation in the area. Walbridge could certainly use some of the dowry money Margaret would bring to her marriage.

But it was also clear Margaret preferred Ellis. Who wasn't interested in her but in Anna.

Conn moved impatiently in his seat as most of the other guests drifted toward the dance area.

Oh, to hell with all the intrigue! He liked things open and direct.

He could stand it no longer. He turned and glanced at Jane. Her back was turned, but she wouldn't be glancing in his direction, anyway. Could he blame her? After the look he'd given her when he entered?

Damn it all, he couldn't help it. He'd been so startled, so disbelieving. Lavena would hear from him later on tonight.

His arrogant sister had gone too far this time. To let Jane wear *that* gown.

A new thought hit him. Maybe Jane had known . . . maybe Lavena had told her and she'd gone along with it . . . no, he instantly dismissed that idea. Jane wouldn't have.

Would she?

Didn't he still believe he could never trust a woman after what Marie had done? Yes . . . maybe . . . maybe not.

But there would be no reason for Jane to do this. How could she have thought it would advance her cause?

What cause? The girl was not making advances. These last few weeks she'd avoided him as assiduously as he'd avoided her.

And she'd smiled very warmly at Radley several times tonight. Danced with him earlier.

Was dancing with Radley right now.

His mood darkened. Didn't that prove she was fickle? That she cared nothing for him?

He wished *he* was dancing with Jane.

Damn it all to hell! Why couldn't he hold to his vow to have nothing to do with her, so this unwanted attraction would die a natural death?

Unwanted? his mind mocked him. *Surely, you're still not trying to convince yourself of that.*

No. He wasn't.

He wanted Jane so fiercely it was all he could do to keep from getting up from his chair, striding to her, picking her up and carrying her to the nearest bed.

He held himself rigidly against the miserably uncomfortable chair in this pretentious house.

Until he could stand it no longer.

He got up from his seat and headed toward the dance floor, just as the dance ended.

"May I have this next dance?" he asked, forcing a smile he didn't feel onto his face.

Radley opened his mouth to protest, then apparently thinking better of it, closed it again and moved back.

Jane looked at him for a moment. Then, her smile no more genuine than his own, she nodded and stood silently beside Conn, waiting for the music to begin once more.

When it did, they linked hands and joined the group of dancers. That small touch undid Conn. As they moved through the steps of the dance, his hands tingled to caress Jane. His lower regions ached fiercely to possess her.

Then don't be a fool. Give in and take what was offered to you. The girl is willing. She told you she wanted to be in your bed. What are you waiting for?

What, indeed.

The dance momentarily had them facing each other. He looked at her. Their gazes met and held.

He drew in his breath. Everything else fell away. The other people moving around them, the babble of voices and laughter . . . everything.

The desire he saw in Jane's eyes must surely be mirrored in his own.

Her clear blue eyes, her slightly parted lips, told him she still wanted him as much as he wanted her.

"Why have you been avoiding me?" he asked her.

Her eyes widened. "Avoiding you? Why, whatever are you talking about?"

"I haven't forgotten what you told me in the hen coop," he

whispered in her ear as they came close together with the dance movements. "And soon I will hold you to that promise."

They swooped away from each other, then neared again. "I promised you nothing," Jane said.

He smiled at her. "Ah, but your eyes did. Your body did."

She jerked her gaze away, rosiness flooding her cheeks.

Satisfaction filled him. Jane may have smiled at Radley, but she hadn't given him such looks. Nor would she.

Because Conn's hesitation was over.

Conn looked over at Lavena to catch her gaze on him. Deliberately, he gave her a narrowed-eyed, cool glance.

His sister flushed a deeper pink than Jane. She jerked her head away.

Lavena's wicked little prank hadn't worked out the way she'd planned.

No, it had only served to cause him to stop his vacillation.

Soon Jane would be in his arms and he would be partaking of the delights of her lovely body.

CHAPTER TWELVE

"Good morning, Anna."

Darryl, on her knees weeding the kitchen garden, jerked her head at the sound of Ellis's voice. He stood a few feet away on the stone walkway leading from the kitchen door.

Smiling. That warm smile that sent fear and panic racing through her, and at the same time brought strange, unwelcome feelings to life.

She didn't smile back. After a few moments she nodded, then lowered her head again and pulled a weed beside a cabbage plant, adding it to the neat pile beside her.

"Did you enjoy the party at the Findleys' last night?" Ellis asked after another moment.

The other fear, fear for her very life, shot through her.

Why was he asking her that? Was there an insinuating tone to his voice? Was he remembering what that horrible Vaughn Walbridge had said about the runaway bond girl? Had he seen her and Hayley's terror at first? Had Ellis managed to put two and two together?

She swallowed, her mouth and throat dry as dust.

"Well, did you?" Ellis persisted.

He wouldn't leave until she answered him. The warm September sun beat down on her face, starting a trickle of perspiration at her temples. She lifted her head again, forcing a smile so he wouldn't see how agitated she was.

"It was very pleasant." Her voice sounded raspy dry, too. And parts of the party had been pleasant, she had to admit.

Ellis's smile faded, a frown replacing it. "Then I take it Walter Findley was a 'pleasant' dancing partner?"

The fear wrapping its tentacles around her insides eased. No, he didn't suspect anything. Of course he didn't. How could he? But why was he asking her this?

"Yes," she said, primly. "Mr. Findley is a good dancer and a genial companion."

Ellis's frown deepened. "Then that's why you chose to dance with him all evening?"

"You must have found Margaret's dancing to your liking, also, since you were her constant companion," Darryl said, coolly, then drew her breath in.

Why had she said that?

Ellis's eyes widened in surprise, the frown smoothing out. The corners of his mouth turned up. "Mistress Margaret Findley holds no interest for me."

Darryl felt her face warming. She lowered her head again and jerked another weed out of the ground with more force than necessary.

"Anna," Ellis said, softly, from a closer distance. "Why do you care how many dances I shared with Margaret?"

She looked up again to see he was now only a few feet away. Again, that disturbing mixture of emotions trembled through her body. "I don't care. What gave you that notion?"

Ellis's half-smile became a grin. "Nothing. Not a thing in the world. Your sister received much attention from Radley Walbridge. But she seemed none too happy."

"Jane and I would prefer to be left alone."

Ellis's grin remained in place. "Oh? Is that so? Somehow I had a different idea. She didn't seem to object when Conn danced with her. Both of them seemed to enjoy it very much."

He moved a little closer.

Darryl fought down a wave of panic, and forced herself to hold still, not move back, away from him. "You're wrong. Mr. Merritt may have, but Jane was merely being polite."

"You're fooling yourself. Sooner or later you'll have to face that."

She shook her head so violently, the handful of weeds she held fell to the ground and scattered. "No, I'm not. Jane and I . . . aren't interested in men. We never will be."

He gave her an incredulous smile. "How can you possibly say these things? You're both beautiful, sweet, wonderful girls. Surely, you want homes, husbands, families of your own someday?"

Somehow he'd come very close now. He stooped so that their faces were level with each other. "Why are you so afraid, Anna? You have nothing to fear from me."

He reached out and touched her shoulder, squeezed it gently.

Panic overcame her. She scrambled backward, overbalanced and fell between the vegetable rows. Ellis quickly knelt, reached for her shoulders and gently raised her. "I'm sorry. Are you all right?"

She nodded, rasping out, "Yes." Her heart fluttered with fear at his touch. *More than fear,* her mind told her. She ignored it.

They looked at each other.

"Anna?" Ellis whispered. "Oh, Anna!"

His head lowered to hers. His lips brushed hers lightly.

Darryl drew in her breath. Despite herself, her lips parted.

Ellis groaned deep in his throat. His mouth touched hers again, softly.

For an instant, Darryl closed her eyes, her heart pounding in her chest, returning his kiss.

What was she doing?

She opened her eyes, jerked herself away from him and scrambled to her feet.

Ellis got to his feet, too. Chagrin filled his face. "I'm sorry.

I told you I wouldn't do that. That I'd wait until you were ready. And you're not."

Darryl was too shaken to speak while the moments ticked by and their gazes were still locked.

Her fear was ebbing.

But not the other feelings Ellis's kiss had aroused in her.

Slowly the tenseness in Ellis's face relaxed. A small smile teased his lips upward again.

He got to his feet. "I must be going back to the fields."

He touched a hand to his forehead and sauntered off, whistling a familiar tune. After a moment, Darryl realized it was one of those tunes the musicians had played for the gathering at the Findley house.

Her face burned in earnest now. Her lips tightened. She returned her attention to the garden patch, pulling weeds with such vigor that Lavena, coming out half an hour later, blinked in surprise.

"For once you've done a good morning's work," she said.

Darryl kept her eyes lowered. Could Lavena never give a word of praise without canceling it out with disapproval? "Thank you, Mistress."

"Now, pull me some green onions for the dinner stew, and keep on with your weeding until the meal is ready," Lavena said, crisply.

Darryl obeyed, pulling the pungent vegetables out of the ground and handing them to the other woman, the sandy loam soil still clinging to them.

Still thinking about her recent encounter with Ellis, Darryl watched Lavena go back to the house.

She tried to push away the memory of Ellis's tender kiss, but it wouldn't leave.

Darryl admitted to herself she'd lied when she'd told him she cared nothing about how much time he'd spent with Margaret Findley.

She did care.

Fear twisted her insides again at this admission. No! She didn't. She couldn't. She wanted nothing to do with any man, ever again. How could she have forgotten that vow? How could she have forgotten the danger she and Hayley were in?

They'd talked in their attic bedroom last night after the Findleys' elegant party. Shared their fear when they'd thought the search party was after one of them.

Hayley had told her about realizing that no one might have discovered that Hayley had been at Oscar's plantation, that no one might have known they were together. Therefore, no one might be searching for two girls together. She'd been amazed they hadn't considered this before.

But this new knowledge didn't really help their situation, Darryl told herself, spirits plunging again.

What should they do? Run away again? They'd received only a small amount of wages so far. Where could they go with so little money?

Where could they go anyway that would be any safer than here at Holly View? Unless they could somehow manage to get far away. Which was impossible.

They had to stay here. They had to hope that no one would find them.

They had to pretend to themselves and to each other that they were safe even if in their hearts they knew better.

CHAPTER THIRTEEN

"We should have twice as many apples as this. Damn the everlasting rain!"

Conn transferred the contents of the small picking basket to a bushel-sized one, then handed it back to a worker standing on a ladder propped against an apple tree.

He frowned at the lowering sky, which had been threatening rain all day. Every man he could spare was in the orchard, because today was the first one this week it hadn't rained all day long. Apples were rotting on the trees and falling to the ground.

Gustav looked at his employer reprovingly. "You should be thankful for the bounty that you have. Many this year have much worse harvests."

Conn huffed out a sigh. " 'Tis hard to be thankful when crops have been bad for the third year in a row."

"We're fortunate the moon is on the wane. Otherwise, we wouldn't have been able to pick today."

Despite his ill-humor, caused by more than the sparse harvests, Conn found himself grinning at his eternally optimistic foreman—who insisted on planting and harvesting by the moon's phases.

Most of the time Gustav seemed to be right, so Conn went along with his decisions.

"What would happen if we did pick during a full moon?" Conn asked, in a bantering tone.

"The fruit would rot during the winter storage," Gustav said, severely, then grinned himself. "Let us hope that Perdita does not foal until the new moon. The foal will not prosper if she does."

"Then let us certainly hope and pray she waits a few days," Conn agreed, wholeheartedly. Perdita was his prize mare. Her foals were beautiful and sound. This one due would sell for a good price come spring.

And by spring they would be needing coin for seeds and supplies, more so than any previous year.

That thought made his gloom return. Along with the other matter that gnawed at him, it gave him no peace.

Nearly two weeks had passed since the night of the Findleys' party.

The night his sister had played that abominable trick on him.

The night he'd decided he was finished with his ambivalence. Decided he would soon have Jane in his bed.

He'd had his say with Lavena. To his amazement, she'd apologized for what she'd done. She'd never intended for things to happen as they had, she'd insisted. If he hadn't been late—

Conn had cut her off, expressed his outrage, then left. They'd been very cool with each other since, but he knew a thaw was imminent. It was too damnably hard on the nerves to be at odds with someone you saw several times a day. And who was your closest blood relation, besides.

And he hated grudge-holding. He'd seen too many families broken up because of senseless feuding over long-ago happenings.

But just the same, he'd watch Lavena with a closer eye from now on. He knew what she was after, and he'd not allow her to dictate his life.

And his plan to soon have Jane in his bed wasn't coming along as he wanted. He'd been too busy with the crops to try to make an opportunity to talk to Jane alone.

Talk to her? his mind jeered. *That's not what you want to do.*

No, he admitted. She was an intelligent and interesting girl, but his thoughts were on matters of the flesh. And his bluntness throughout their conversation during that dance at the Findleys' party hadn't helped. Now, she avoided him even more than before.

Had she indeed changed her mind, as she'd insisted during that brief talk? Was it only his own arrogance that had made him think different?

"Here's another full one!"

Conn came to himself with a start. He grasped the basket, emptied it, then handed it back to the worker.

A figure appeared at the far end of the orchard. For an instant, hope rose; then he saw it was Ellis, carrying a pail of drinking water in each hand.

Conn watched as he approached. The boy was filling out these last months. Becoming a man. Why had he never noticed that before?

His mouth tight, Ellis sat the pails down with a thump. The pewter dipper in one of them clanged against the edge.

Conn gave his nephew a surprised glance. What ailed the boy? "Something wrong?" he asked.

"No," Ellis said, shortly. "I'd better get back to the house to see if Mama has any more 'chores' for me to do."

He turned and strode away from the orchard.

Conn stared after him, not knowing what to make of Ellis's behavior. "What ails the boy?" he asked Gustav.

Gustav walked over to stand beside Conn. He shook his head. "He's no boy, Conn. He's a man now. Maybe it's time you and his mother recognized that."

Conn raised his brows. "I was just telling myself that. But I don't treat him as a boy. He does a full day's work like any of the workers."

Gustav gave Conn a wry smile. "Maybe that's the problem. He's *not* one of the workers. He's going to own this farm one day unless you remarry and have sons."

His words took Conn aback. He stared at Gustav. "I vowed never to remarry when my wife died," he said, stiffly.

"I know. I remember," Gustav said. "But things change. You're still a young man. You might want sons of your own one day."

Sons of my own. Why did that notion make a glow of warmth go through him now? It never had before. A son that would have his dark coloring. One that would have flaxen hair and blue eyes . . . maybe some daughters, too . . .

Again, he came out of his woolgathering and dismissed the errant thoughts.

Or tried to.

"I doubt that," he said, curtly. "So you think I don't treat Ellis fairly?"

Gustav clamped a big hand on Conn's shoulder. "No, I don't. He's old enough now you should be considering making him a full partner."

Conn gave him a level look. "I don't need a partner. I have you to run the things I can't take care of."

"We're not talking about what *you* want," Gustav pointed out. "We're talking about Ellis."

"You're right," Conn said, after a moment's silence. "When I was Ellis's age, my father accepted me as a partner. He probably thought I was too young, too."

"No doubt," Gustav said, dryly. He dropped his hand from Conn's shoulder and hurried over at a worker's call to empty a full basket of apples into the big container.

Leaving Conn staring after him. Uneasiness coiled inside Conn. He didn't like change, he knew that much about himself. He resisted it, as most people did.

But change was upon Holly View. He had to face it, decide what to do about it. As Gustav had just said, he couldn't go on treating Ellis as a stripling. Since Marie's death, the boy had been brought up to believe he'd inherit Holly View. He'd been trained to someday take over as its master.

But, Conn realized, somewhere inside himself he hadn't accepted that. Somewhere inside, he'd secretly harbored the belief that his own sons would take over from him.

So where did that leave Ellis, his hardworking, dependable, trustworthy nephew?

Out in the cold, that's where.

No! Conn repudiated that.

Just because he burned to have Jane in his bed, just because he was determined that would come about, didn't mean anything else had changed.

His views on marriage certainly hadn't. Or the trustworthiness of women. Marie had led him a merry chase, luring him, promising him the delights of heaven if he would only wed her.

Which he'd done.

And which he had bitterly regretted from his wedding day on.

No, the promise of sons could not lure him again into that institution.

Hayley's arms were tiring. Why was the butter so long in coming today? She'd pushed the wooden dasher up and down in the big wooden churn for more than half an hour. Maybe it was the weather. It was rainy and close today. She felt as if she could hardly breathe.

"Close weather, hard to bring the butter."

Her mother's remembered words rang in her head; her mother's features came into her mind's eye, bringing quick tears to her eyes.

Oh, *how* she wished that her family were still all alive and safe in their Suffolk home. She remembered how all of them had prayed over the proposed move, seeking some sign it was the right thing to do.

Hayley's mouth tightened. God had given them no sign,

either way. So they'd done what they thought was best, the
only thing that could give them hope for a better life.

And now, to what end had it come? Her parents at the bottom
of the sea. Darryl a runaway bond servant and a . . .

No, she couldn't say the word. Her sister was no murderer,
only a desperate girl trying to save herself from a brutal man.

As for herself . . .

Hayley's mouth tightened more. Her own situation was little
better. She was also a runaway bond servant. Subject to harsh
penalties if she were caught.

Worst of all, she was in love with a man who didn't love
her.

She drew in a breath as that last thought resonated in her
mind.

She was in love with Conn?

Yes, she admitted. When had that happened? There'd been
no one moment, she realized. Her feelings had grown over the
days, the weeks, the months she'd been here.

Had crept upon her unawares until this moment, when she
fully realized how much she cared for him . . .

A sound made her glance up. Her heart thumped, her hands
stilled on the churn dasher. As if her thoughts had conjured
him, Conn stood in the low doorway.

As usual, he wore an old shirt and worn breeches, his black
hair pulled back with a leather thong. As usual, the mere sight
of him played havoc with all her senses.

He seemed to be taking in all of her, too. Hayley was suddenly
conscious of her soiled apron, her hair coming loose at the
sides.

"I see you're busy," he said, after a moment. He paused.
The incipient frown pulling his dark brows together smoothed
out, replaced by a smile that looked a little forced.

"Yes," Hayley said. She tried to think of something else to
say, but failed. She couldn't even return his smile. Her face
felt frozen.

Her mind was filled with her thoughts of a few moments
ago. *She loved him.* She drew in her breath, feeling a hot blush

stain her cheeks, remembering the last time he'd given her such a searching look.

At the Findleys' party. She'd never forget the look he'd given her when he came into the hall. As if the mere sight of her had shocked him speechless.

She still didn't know what had caused it.

Then, later that evening, when they were dancing, their eyes had met again . . . Conn had told her she would be his. Her face grew warmer as she remembered. . . .

"When will you be finished here?" Conn asked, after another interminable few moments had passed.

"Not more than a half hour," she answered.

Conn nodded, as if her answer pleased him. "Good. I would like to talk with you."

Her heart leapt again. "All right."

"I'll be out along the fence line separating my property from the Walbridges'."

He turned and left, leaving Hayley staring after him.

What could he want to talk about?

It had to be something concerning the two of them.

The last time they'd been alone together, both of them had admitted their desire for each other.

And Conn had plainly shown he intended to fight his feelings. After that he'd avoided her until the night of the party. . . .

He could also want to talk to you about that runaway bond servant Vaughn Walbridge mentioned, her mind said. *Maybe that talk made him realize how very little he knows about you and Darryl.*

Fear replaced the other feelings, and she fought it down. No! That couldn't be it. If he suspected anything like that, he wouldn't have waited all this time.

With renewed vigor she resumed the churning. The butter soon formed. Hayley pressed the golden mounds into two glass bowls, then stamped them with the mold carved into the bottom of the churn dasher, an H and V for Holly View. The letters were prettily entwined, symbolizing this place, its peace and stability.

Would she and Darryl ever attain peace and stability again? How was that possible?

She looked at the finished butter for a moment, until tears blurred her vision. She blinked them away, and swiftly finished cleaning the dairy, then took the butter to the springhouse. It was cool and dim inside, mossy-smelling. She carefully placed the covered bowls on one of the shelves.

Outside again in the still, overly warm day, she pushed her errant curls back under the mob cap, removed her soiled apron and hung it on a peg on the dairy wall as she passed.

Conn was nowhere in sight. She glanced around. How long was the stretch of fence separating the two properties?

She walked along the zigzag fence, trying to catch a glimpse of him in the distance.

Ahead of her, she saw one of the Walbridges' cows. On the wrong side of the fence. Behind it and to the side lay scattered rails which the animal must have just knocked down.

Oh, Conn would be angry! She hoped no other cows had preceded it and were now trampling the corn Conn planned to harvest in a few days. Glancing around, she saw no others.

Relieved, Hayley found a long tree limb on the ground and hurried her steps. She'd herded many an errant cow home in Suffolk. She should be able to get this one back on its side of the fence before it wandered further.

"Go on! Get over there!" she yelled as she approached.

Hayley stopped short, fear sweeping over her. Slowly, she retreated, her hand clutching the tree limb.

The animal snorted, then slowly turned to face her, its eyes glaring from its huge red head.

The beast in front of her, its nostrils flaring in rage, was no docile cow.

But an angry bull.

While she continued to slowly back up, the bull lowered its head and pawed the ground.

Then lunged at her.

CHAPTER FOURTEEN

Farther down the fence line, Conn heard the sounds. And knew what they were.

The Walbridges' blasted cattle had torn down the fence again. For the third time since he'd helped the man do the repairs.

"Dammit!" he swore, jerking around to head back, then froze, terror rushing through him.

An enormous bull, pawing and snorting, advanced on Jane.

His new bull, not the Walbridges' How had the beast gotten out of its pen?

Conn scooped up the pole with a hook on its end he'd brought with him because he planned to move the bull later. Thank God he had it! He took off at a run.

"Come on, you coward, pick on someone nearer your size!" Conn yelled, hoping to divert the animal's attention from Jane.

The bull ignored him and lunged at Jane. Conn's heart stopped, but not his feet.

Jane turned toward the fence, neatly sidestepping the beast. Its blind forward movement sent it crashing headfirst into the fence. Another rail toppled under the animal's onslaught, smashing into its head. The bull bellowed in pain and rage, then turned his enormous body toward the human who was thwarting him.

Jane stood at bay, backed against the fence. "Climb over it!" Conn yelled.

Then, his heart stopped again. Jane raised the tree limb she carried, and moved toward the bull.

"Holy Mother of God!" Conn swore. The crazy female was going to try to put the end of the limb through the ring in the beast's nose! She'd never be able to manage it. The limb was too flimsy, her strength too slight.

And all his workers were still over in the orchards, picking apples. No one was close enough to hear him call for help.

"Hey! You spawn of Satan!" Conn bellowed, running faster. "Come after me!"

The bull paused for an instant, swinging its big head in Conn's direction, then snorting its defiance at this other human who dared to challenge it.

Conn went limp with relief as Jane scrambled over the fence during the momentary reprieve. Thank God there were still enough rails left to keep the bull from following her.

Again, the big animal bellowed its fury because Jane had escaped, then turned his attention back to Conn, advancing on him.

He had only one chance, to successfully manage what Jane had planned a few moments ago.

"Run for the fence!" Jane's voice was full of fear for him.

"I'm too far away!" Conn kept his gaze steady on the bull. At what he judged the right moment, he thrust the pole forward, aiming the hook toward the ring in the bull's nose.

He missed, grazing the bull's flared nostrils.

The creature gave another rage-filled bellow and, head lowered, lunged again.

Feeling its hot breath as it lumbered by, Conn shivered. Its sharp horns missed him by only inches.

A piece of tree limb struck the beast. "Come and get me!" Jane yelled. Another piece of limb smacked against the bull's head.

Pain mixed with fury in the bull's bellow. It stopped, turning toward the source of its aggravation.

Just long enough for Conn to again thrust the pole forward. This time he managed to slip the hook through the ring, and jerked it sharply.

"All right, you misbegotten creature! Come along."

Jane watched Conn lead the now-docile animal to its shed, then disappear inside with it.

Her knees suddenly gave way and she sat down with a thump just inside the Walbridges' side of the fence. She was shaking all over. She drew her knees up in front of her, putting her arms around them, lowering her head to her arms.

Oh, how close that had been! How easily the bull could have killed either her or Conn. Or both of them. Her trembling increased. She felt cold all over.

Conn was suddenly crouching beside her, his arms around her, pulling her close.

"Are you all right?" his urgent, rough voice rasped in her ear.

Her throat was so dry she couldn't speak. Instead she nodded.

He rocked her back and forth in the circle of his arms, uttering broken words, half-finished sentences.

His words and actions flowed over her like soothing balm, relaxing her, stopping her trembling.

Finally, she lifted her head to see him staring at her, concern and fear plain in his frown, his tense features.

And something else was there, too.

Hayley drew in her breath at what she thought she saw in his eyes.

"Do you know how frightened I was?" Conn muttered.

Hayley moistened her dry lips. "Probably about as frightened as I was when the bull almost got you."

His face softened. He reached out a hand to stroke her hair back from her forehead. Her cap had come loose and hung around her neck, freeing her hair.

"You brave little idiot. I can't believe you were willing to tangle with Edgar."

Hayley grimaced. "I wasn't brave. I thought he was one of the Walbridges' cows until too late. And he certainly doesn't act like an Edgar."

His face softened even more, and a hint of a smile turned up the corners of his mobile mouth. "No," he agreed. "I believe we'll have to rename him Brutus."

"That would be more fitting."

"I was so afraid the bull would get you. It was so close!" Her voice trembled on the last words.

"So you'd miss me if the bull had killed me?"

Something different was in his voice, too. "I couldn't stand for anyone to die such a horrible death," she answered, evading his question, lowering her eyes.

"Ah. So you don't like the sight of blood, is that it?"

She felt his gaze on her eyelids, heating her . . . she looked up again. "I wouldn't enjoy the sight of your blood flowing from a mortal wound."

The upward movement of his lips had turned into a real smile. "Neither would I relish the sight of your own blood spilled," he said, softly.

His hand, which had been caressing her hair, moved down. One of his long fingers traced the outline of her lips.

Hayley's trembling started again. "You're cold," Conn said. "Shall I warm you?"

His fingers were rough against the soft skin of her lips. But it was a wonderful kind of roughness. Her lips burned where he touched her. Burned for more of his touch.

Her tongue came out and moved along the length of his finger. She felt him stiffen, heard his quick intake of breath.

His hand slid down to her chin and tilted it upward.

For a long moment their gazes met and melded.

Just so had they looked at each other that day in the field . . . and that evening in the Findleys' hall . . .

"Let us proceed with the warming," Conn's husky voice said. Slowly he lowered his head toward hers.

Hayley's lips parted, and she lifted her head to meet his advance. When finally their lips met, a long trembling sigh escaped her. She closed her eyes, letting the intense pleasure of Conn's touch flow over her.

The kiss deepened, became more than a kiss. Gently, Conn pushed her backward onto the grass, and lowered himself beside her.

"Are you becoming warm?" he murmured into her ear, while his hands still stroked her, evoking wondrous sensations.

"Yes, oh, yes!"

She felt his fingers fumbling with the laces of her bodice, felt them give way, gasped when his warm mouth settled itself on one breast, his tongue making hot, lazy circles around the nipple through her shift.

Oh, she'd never imagined a man's touch could feel so good. Could make her forget everything but wanting more of it . . . wanting the ultimate giving there could be between a man and a woman.

Conn's mouth left her breast to find her eager lips again. His tongue delved within her mouth, found her own tongue.

Instinctively, Hayley met his thrusts and parries, as if she'd done this a hundred times before.

"You feel so good," he said, lifting his head to take a deep, ragged breath. "You belong in my arms. I want you, Jane. I've wanted you since that first night at the tavern."

His admission heated her further, prompted her to make one of her own. "I've also wanted you from that first night."

She smiled at him. Her smile held such sweetness, Conn sucked in his breath.

"I love you, Conn. I—I think I've loved you all this time, too."

With that sweet, loving smile still on her mouth, Jane held out her arms to him, welcoming him to her embrace.

Trusting him enough to give herself to him without any promises, any words of love.

A wave of strong feeling swept over Conn. Feelings that he'd never before had. Never even known existed.

Astonishment followed.

Was this love he felt?

Crouching over Jane, his knees pressing against her sides, his lower body throbbing with urgent need, he stared into her wide blue eyes.

Finally, he leaned back, then moved away so that he was sitting beside her.

Jane's eyes were full of surprise. She drew herself away, then sat up and turned toward him.

The surprise had left her eyes and the bright blue seemed to have dulled. "I shouldn't have said that. You've never given me any indication that you . . . cared for me."

Her voice was dulled, too. She inched away a bit more.

Conn reached for her hands and covered them with both of his own. The lure of her lips was drawing him in again, beguiling him toward that whirlpool of desire. . . .

He had to say this while he still could, before his body took completely over again.

"You're right. I've never given you any indication that I wanted anything more than to possess your body."

She pulled at her hands, trying to free them. Her face had reddened with embarrassment.

"Wait," he commanded, softly. "I'm not finished."

He tugged at their entwined hands, pulled her closer. "I never knew I wanted anything more until . . . you looked at me that way just now, told me you loved me."

Her hands stilled in his grasp. He found her gaze and again held it.

"I love you, too. I want you to marry me."

The words sounded right and good.

Not like the first time he'd asked a woman to marry him.

He pushed away that dark thought. This was different. *Jane* was different.

Her pupils widened until there was only a line of vivid blue left. Her lips, swollen from his kisses, parted. "What did you say?"

He smiled at her tenderly. "I think you heard me. I'd be

very honored if you would give me your hand and heart in marriage.''

Where had all his hesitation, his mistrust gone? Conn wondered. How could his feelings have done such a complete turnaround in these few minutes?

He didn't know. Nor did he want to try to find out. This felt right. So very right. A tumble in the grass such as he'd thought he wanted—with no strings attached, nothing but a physical coming together—had suddenly not been enough.

''I want to spend the rest of my life with you, Jane.''

Those words sounded and felt right, too.

''So what do you say? Have I become totally repulsive to you in these last few moments? Have you decided you'd rather entertain Radley's suit?'' he asked, teasingly.

Bewilderment came over her face. ''Radley? What are you talking about?''

Maybe he wasn't teasing, he realized, the dark thoughts that hovered at the edge of his mind trying to return.

Maybe he just had to make absolutely sure.

''You gave him several fetching smiles at the Findleys' party. And danced with him more than once.''

''Those things meant nothing,'' she protested. ''You know there's no one but you.''

He saw her swallow. ''It's just that I never expected this. Never hoped—''

A clanging of cowbells came from close by. A loud moo followed, then another.

Conn scrambled to his feet, his half-teasing banter forgotten. ''What the hell?''

Two of the Walbridge cows headed purposefully toward them.

Conn grabbed for Jane and helped her to her feet. Her blush was darker, and she fumbled with the lacings of her bodice.

Damn it all to hell! At this moment he'd love to make winter beef out of these miserable animals!

He grasped Jane's shoulders, determined not to let this end in farce.

"Say yes, Jane," he urged. "Now!"

Jane's lips trembled. "Yes, Conn, oh, yes!"

She left her bodice laces half undone, flung her arms around him, moved against him so their bodies touched their full length and sought his lips.

Conn pulled her even closer, sighing as his hard, heated body began to lose its tension.

"I don't want us to have a long betrothal," he said, lowering his mouth to hers, kissing her until they both gasped for breath.

"We must tell Lavena and your sister," he added.

He felt her body stiffen against his own. She drew away a little, looking up at him, her eyes troubled.

"Lavena?" she whispered. "And . . . Anna?"

"Yes, of course," Conn answered. He claimed her mouth in another kiss that ended only when a cow nudged his leg and he almost lost his balance. He let her go regretfully and stepped back.

"But that will have to wait until tonight. Now, I must hurry with dinner and spend the afternoon building a more secure pen for that bull. I'll see you at the house in a few minutes, after I check on the bull again."

Hayley laced up her bodice decently again and watched Conn's confident strides take him away from her. The dazed, incredulous joy she'd felt only a few moments ago was now mixed with foreboding.

Darryl wouldn't take this most surprising news well.

No, of course she wouldn't. Hadn't she begged Hayley, with tears in her eyes, not to let herself feel anything for Conn? Hadn't Hayley all but promised Darryl that she wouldn't?

Even while she knew that was impossible because it had already happened?

As for Lavena . . . Hayley's heart quailed at the prospect of facing her. How would Lavena react when Conn told her he wanted to marry Hayley?

Wanted to marry her!

Joy swept over her again. She still could hardly believe that. And she didn't truly think Lavena could change Conn's mind.

Did she?

No. Of course not. Conn didn't let his sister rule his life.

But she *was* his sister. His closest living relative.

Hayley smoothed her rumpled skirt and tucked her hair under her cap again.

Other thoughts tugged at her mind. She tried futilely to push them away.

Are you planning to marry Conn without telling him the truth about yourself and Darryl?

Yes. She was. She had to. There was no other choice. She couldn't risk Darryl's life. Conn might understand and forgive her for not telling him she and Darryl were runaway bound servants. He could buy their bonds.

But he couldn't protect Darryl from a murder charge.

No one could.

If she wanted to marry Conn, she had to keep silent.

And she wanted to marry him with everything inside her. She couldn't give him up.

Fear battled with her love.

The love won.

She'd somehow live with these secrets locked inside her. Hope and pray no searchers would ever find them.

And now she'd put all this aside and glory in the reality of Conn's love for her. And hers for him.

At least until she had to face Lavena.

She glanced at the September sky, blue and cloudless again for the third day in a row, for which the apple harvesters were rejoicing.

It was dinnertime. After the butter-making she was supposed to have returned to the house to help Lavena with the meal. It was a wonder Lavena hadn't come looking for her.

She pictured Lavena coming upon her and Conn wrapped in each other's arms, and despite her gasp of horror at that scene, all those delicious feelings swept over her again.

Conn loved her! Only minutes ago he'd told her he wanted to live with her all his life.

Hayley drew herself up and walked toward the house, holding the feelings close, refusing to dwell on her fears or the trouble to come with Lavena.

Nearing the house, she saw Darryl wasn't in the garden. She walked across the cobblestones and entered the kitchen through the open doorway.

Darryl was taking fragrant loaves of bread out of the oven built into the side of the fireplace.

Agnes sat at the kitchen table, peering at some embroidery work she held in her hands. She glanced up and gave Hayley a warm smile.

Standing before the dining room door, a steaming bowl in her hands, Lavena jerked her head around, frowning at Hayley.

"Where on earth have you been?" Lavena scolded. "I had to take Anna away from her weeding to help me with dinner."

You don't truly want to know where I've been and what I've been doing, Hayley told her silently.

"The butter was a long time in coming," Hayley said, hurrying to take the bowl from Lavena.

Lavena didn't relinquish her hold. "Never mind," she snapped. "You go help your sister. It's past time to have the meal on the table."

She jerked the door latch down impatiently and swept on into the dining room.

Feeling very self-conscious, Hayley walked to the hearth. Darryl handed her a loaf, curiosity in her eyes, then something else as she glanced at Hayley's face. And then her gaze traveled down to her toes.

Hayley felt her face warm. Oh, Lord, had she not laced her bodice all the way? Were her kiss-swollen lips a telltale giveaway? Grass stains on her skirt?

Darryl's face closed. She picked up another loaf and took it to the worktable.

Still holding her loaf, Hayley bit her lip. Conscious of other eyes on her, she glanced up.

Agnes was giving her a bright-eyed look, full of mischief. "The butter must have given you quite a tussle," she said. "You have a distinctly rumpled look."

Embarrassment swept over Hayley. Following her sister to the worktable, she decided she had to say something to explain her appearance. "Conn's new bull got loose. It chased me."

Darryl's eyes widened. "Are you hurt?"

"No. I—I jumped the fence."

"Is the beast still loose?" Lavena demanded, coming in from the dining room, obviously having heard Hayley's last words.

Hayley glanced up at the older woman. "No. Conn got it back into its shed."

Lavena's gaze sharpened. "What were you doing out in that field?"

Hayley stared at her, speechless. She could think of no explanation that would satisfy Lavena, and now Lavena's gaze was traveling down Hayley, too.

"For heaven's sake, leave the girl alone, Lavena!" Agnes said. "You should be thankful no one was hurt."

Hayley heard a noise, and glanced toward the door. Conn entered, followed by Ellis.

Conn looked at Hayley and smiled. A smile that quieted her fears, made her smile back.

"If you're talking about the bull, then yes, you should, Lavena," he said. "If Hayley hadn't been so quick and clever, she might have been killed."

Lavena cut a last slice of meat before she looked up. "She shouldn't have been out there in the first place," she snapped.

Hayley felt her face reddening again. She lifted the meat platter, to take it to the dining room. A hand grasped her sleeve and she stopped.

"Wait a minute," Conn said. His voice was annoyed. "I wasn't planning to talk about this until tonight, but I can see I must do it now."

Hayley gasped. Was he going to tell everyone about . . . them . . . now?

A quick look at his determined face confirmed this.

Heart hammering, she put the platter back on the worktable, and straightened. Conn stood beside her, his hand still on her arm.

"Talk about what?" Lavena demanded.

Out of the corner of her eye, Hayley saw how absolutely still Darryl stood.

Conn released his hold on Hayley's arm, and slid his arm around her waist. She thrilled to his possessive touch even while her whole being dreaded the next few minutes.

"I've asked Jane to become my wife and she has accepted," Conn said, his voice firm and sure.

Behind her, Hayley heard Ellis's delighted "Ha!"

Agnes clapped her hands. "What wonderful news!"

Lavena froze. Then the carving knife she held dropped to the floor with a clatter. "You can't be serious!"

"Of course I'm serious. Do you think this is a joking matter?"

Very slowly, Lavena stooped, picked up the knife and laid it on the worktable.

"How could you even think of taking this . . . servant girl for your wife?" she asked, shrilly.

"Lavena, that will be enough," Conn said, coldly. "This is none of your affair."

"It is! Wasn't I the one who stayed by your Marie's bedside until the very end? Until both she and the babe had died? Heard you vow you'd never marry again?"

CHAPTER FIFTEEN

Hayley felt as if she'd been turned to stone. Conn's arm about her waist tightened until it hurt.

"Lavena, I don't want to hear any—"

"But you will hear me," Lavena's angry voice cut him off. "How can you even think of marrying a girl like this after the wife you had? Marie came from one of the best families in Delaware. She was beautiful, accomplished."

Hayley could stand no more. She twisted herself out of Conn's grasp, turned and headed for the open kitchen door, and ran headlong down the walk, blinded by tears.

Angrily, she brushed them away. How could she have been such a fool? Hadn't she found it very strange that such a handsome man as Conn had never married? Why hadn't she suspected that he had? That his wife had died?

She heard footsteps behind, rapidly overtaking her, and tried to run faster. At the end of the walk, she turned right, toward the orchards, then remembered all the workers would be there, picking apples.

Hayley swerved, turned, and ran full into Conn's hard chest, knocking the breath out of her.

He grasped her arms, steadying her. She tried to jerk away again, but his grip tightened.

"Let me go!" she said, her voice shaking.

"No," Conn said, flatly. "Not until we go somewhere private to talk. I have some things to tell you."

"What can you add to what Lavena said? Didn't you think I should know you've already had a wife?"

His face was strained. "I thought you knew. After all, it's not a secret. I was sure Lavena would have told you I was married before."

After all, it's not a secret.

Hayley swallowed. No, something like that wouldn't, couldn't be. And it was certainly a wonder Lavena hadn't mentioned Conn's first wife. If only to make Hayley see she had no place in their family.

Marie was beautiful, accomplished. From a grand family. Everything she *wasn't.*

Marie hadn't been a runaway bond servant. Her sister a murderer.

And Marie had died in childbirth. How Conn must have suffered. Maybe was still suffering.

"Lavena told me nothing." Hayley said. "But someone should have! Little wonder your sister thinks I'm not a fit wife for you! How can I ever be anything but a poor substitute for a woman such as that?"

Conn drew his breath in sharply, then let it out. His face tightened more. "Come," he said, trying to pull her along with him as he headed toward a back field. "We must talk."

Hayley dug in her heels, staring at him. "Why? Do you deny what Lavena said is true?"

A muscle tightened in his strong jaw. He said nothing for a moment, then finally said, "No, I don't deny it. Lavena said what she believes is true. But it's not all of the truth."

Confusion filled Hayley. "What do you mean?"

"Damn it! Will you come with me? So we can talk in private?"

Hayley swallowed. "All right. Now, please let go of me."

"If you promise not to run away again."

"All right," she again said.

They walked silently to the big hay field beyond the corn-fields, finally reaching a newly stacked hayrick where Conn stopped and turned toward her.

Conn raked long fingers through his black hair, his brow furrowed. "I didn't want to talk about Marie. I don't even want to think about her."

Hayley sucked in her breath. His voice sounded so peculiar. Flat and yet full of anger . . . and something else . . . something almost like hate.

"Why not?" she asked, her voice low and hesitant.

He was silent so long this time, she didn't think he was going to answer at all. Then he lifted his head and looked Hayley full in the face.

"Because she was a liar and a whore. When she married me she was already pregnant with another man's child. On our wedding night she taunted me with that fact, told me what a fool she'd made of me."

Hayley's knees felt as if they'd hold her up no longer. She sat down beside the hayrick and leaned against it. She opened her mouth, then closed it again. What could she say to him?

"I see you're shocked. So was I," Conn said, bitterly. "Marie was beautiful . . . as my sister said. And accomplished. And from a wealthy family. She was wildly sensual. She said she loved me and she drove me insane with desire. Which, she told me, could only be satisfied if I married her. So I did."

He gazed down at Hayley, his face drawn up in tight lines. He looked ten years older than he had an hour ago.

When they'd lain in each other's arms and told each other they wanted each other . . . and she'd told Conn she loved him.

Just as his faithless wife had done.

She'd kept her own secrets from him . . . just as his faithless wife had done.

Her heart jerked in her chest. No! It wasn't the same. She'd done nothing out of malice. Only to save her sister.

But isn't the result just the same? her mind asked her. *He thinks you keep no secrets from him.*

"I married her, and entered into Hell," Conn continued, his voice still that horrible mixture of flatness and deep anger. "No one else ever knew what kind of person she truly was. She delighted in telling me how many men she'd enticed into her bed before me."

Hayley finally found her voice. "Is that why you fought so hard against your feelings for me?" she whispered.

"Yes. I've never been able to love or trust another woman since Marie died. I've never *wanted* to until I met you."

He sank onto the newly shorn meadow grass beside her, reaching for her hand. His warmth curled through her body as his long fingers curled around hers, comforting her.

"Jane, I do truly love you. And I believe that you love me. You're not like Marie. You're decent and kind and trustworthy, not a deceitful liar. You told me that you wanted me, yet you asked nothing from me. Even today, you offered your sweet love like a flower offering its nectar to the bees. No teasing, no flirting, no trying to entice me into marriage."

Cold swept over Hayley, like a winter wind sweeping through the Suffolk countryside. The loving words he'd just spoken to her fell away from her consciousness as if they were nothing but chaff from the haying scythe.

You're not a deceitful liar. I trust you.

What would he say to her if she told him the truth about herself and Darryl? That they were runaway bond servants.

That Darryl had killed a man.

She could imagine what he'd say. What he would do.

His fingers tightened around hers. "What's wrong? Are you unable to forgive me for not telling you what kind of a marriage I had?"

Mutely, she shook her head. Her throat felt so dry she couldn't have spoken right then.

"I'm sorry," Conn went on. "I know that I should have. When I saw you in Marie's wedding dress at the Findleys' party, I knew what Lavena was trying to do. I should have told you that night.''

Hayley's throat became dryer still. She licked her lips for some moisture. ''The dress I wore was your . . . wife's wedding dress?''

Sick horror filled her. Her voice was a croak. She wondered if he could understand her words.

He nodded, his lips tightening. ''Yes. That's why I acted like such a fool when I saw you. I was so furious with Lavena for pulling that trick. I knew why she'd done it, too. It was her way of reminding me you weren't Marie—that you'd never be like Marie. Thank God!''

Oh, but she was more like Marie than he knew. She, too, was planning to enter into marriage with him while hiding a terrible secret. A secret she couldn't reveal no matter how much she wanted to.

Darryl's life depended on her keeping her silence. She couldn't do anything to endanger her.

''Something is wrong,'' Conn said, caressing her cheek with his work-roughened palm.

She shivered at his touch, wishing with all her heart she could tell him the truth.

But she couldn't. Not now. Maybe not ever.

You have to be strong, she told herself. *And not give in to what you so yearn to do. To drop your burdens upon Conn. To give them to him to resolve.*

He couldn't resolve them. No one could.

She desperately fought to keep tears from forming again. She managed a weak smile.

''Nothing's wrong. I—I only wish my parents were here. I've missed them so much.''

Conn's face grew tender. He smiled back. ''Of course you do, Jane. It was a great loss for you and Anna.''

Anna. Jane. The two false names rang in her head like harbingers of doom. The man she loved and would marry didn't even know her real name. Might never know it.

She lifted her hand and curved it around Conn's hard jawline. "Yes. But now I have you. And maybe Anna will. . . ."

Her voice trailed off. She couldn't very well tell him she hoped her sister and Ellis would someday make a match of it, despite Lavena's opposition. Despite their desperate plight.

Conn smiled. "My nephew will win your sister," he said.

A tremor went through her. He seemed almost able to read her thoughts. She hoped he never perfected that ability completely. She forced another smile. A wider one.

"I've no doubt you are right," she agreed.

Conn pulled her to him and kissed her, a long, lingering kiss that she was helpless to resist. She kissed him back, pouring all her love into it.

Praying that somehow this would all turn out right, no matter how hopeless the snarl seemed now.

To Hayley's intense relief, Lavena was nowhere in sight when Hayley and Conn got back to the house.

Darryl washed the dinner dishes at a worktable. She glanced quickly at Hayley, then as quickly away.

But not before Hayley saw her sister was not angry. Her relief spread.

"Your dinner is on the hearth," Darryl said, her voice even.

Agnes, back in her rocker with her embroidery, gave them a wide, delighted smile, then fixed her gaze on Conn. "So you finally got up enough gumption to ask this sweet girl to marry you. High time, too, if you ask me."

Thank God the older woman apparently wasn't going to mention Conn's wife. Was going to act as if all that didn't matter.

Conn tilted his head. "Why, Aunt Agnes, do you really think I'm old enough?"

Amazement went through Hayley. His voice held no hint of the emotional scene they'd just gone through. And he was also finally letting Agnes know he hadn't been taken in by her playacting. That he knew her brain was as sharp as his own.

Agnes blinked in surprise. "Watch your mouth, young man," she finally said. But Hayley saw a twinkle in her eyes.

"I always do around you, Aunt Agnes," Conn said, solemnly.

Hayley's tension eased a bit more. Maybe it would be all right after all. Maybe no one would ever come looking for her and Darryl. Maybe they could stay here forever in this wonderful place.

And you'll never tell Conn how you deceived him? her mind asked. *How do you think you can ever be truly happy keeping these secrets?*

"And when is the wedding to take place?" Agnes asked.

"Soon," Conn said, glancing at Hayley, smiling.

But something in his eyes told her this light mood was only a pretense. Telling her the horrible truths about his first marriage had opened up the wounds his wife had inflicted on him.

They hadn't healed. They still burned rawly.

He'd never be able to forgive another deception such as that.

And he wouldn't have to, Hayley told herself. She'd never betray him with another man. The secrets she kept were to protect her sister's life.

Hayley forced a smile. "Whatever Conn wants," she said.

"Lavena's nose is out of joint, but she'll recover," Agnes said. "Once she's over the shock that now Ellis won't inherit Holly View. That you two will soon be started on your own sons."

Hayley felt her face redden at Agnes's frankness.

Beside her, she saw Conn stiffen.

"God willing, that will happen," he said in a moment, his voice uneven. "But Ellis won't be pushed aside."

Understanding washed over Hayley. Agnes's words must have brought back the horrible memories of his wife's death.

The death of the child everyone believed to be his son.

She longed to reach out a hand to comfort him, but couldn't bring herself to do it, here in front of Darryl and Agnes.

"I'll get the food on the table," she said instead, hurrying to the hearth, where Darryl now poked up the fire.

"Your places are still set in the dining room," Agnes said.

"All right," Conn said, then walked through the open door into the other room.

"I think I'll have another cup of tea with you two," Agnes said, reaching for her cane, then getting up and going after him.

Leaving Hayley and Darryl alone in the kitchen.

Hayley picked up a bowl and stood. She looked full at Darryl.

Her sister's mouth curved in a faint smile. Darryl reached out a hand and placed it on Hayley's arm.

"Now we'll be safe, sister!" she whispered. "How did you manage to entice him into marriage?"

Hayley stared at Darryl, feeling all the blood leaving her face, as she remembered how, weeks ago, she'd told herself if need be she'd lie with Conn to ensure their staying here.

Remembered how she'd admitted that would be no sacrifice.

Today, Conn had taken her into his arms and kissed her, more than kissed her. Indeed, they'd almost made love. Would have if Conn hadn't stopped.

She'd thought of none of that. She hadn't thought at all. She'd only felt. Only wanted to stay in Conn's embrace forever.

"I never dreamed this would happen," Darryl continued in that soft whisper. She frowned at Hayley. "Oh, sister, I hope he'll be gentle with you. That you won't have to endure what I . . ."

Her voice trailed off. She bit her lip.

Hayley squeezed her sister's shoulder. "You don't understand. I agreed to marry Conn because I truly love him. He's a good man."

"It's all right. You don't have to pretend with me," Darryl said. "Thank you for doing this for me."

Hayley's consternation grew. "I'm not pretending," she protested.

Darryl put her finger to her lips, shaking her head warningly. "We must bring in the food." She turned away to pick up another bowl, handed it to Hayley.

Moments later, Hayley headed for the dining room with a tray of food and a pot of tea.

Agnes sat next to Conn, her hand on his arm. She glanced up, smiling, as Hayley placed the food on the table.

"Come, sit down here and eat," she said.

Hayley saw two places set at the table. She stared at the older woman; then realization flooded over her.

Now that she was to be Conn's wife she would sit at the table with the family.

And what about Darryl? How could she sit in here, leaving her sister in the kitchen to eat by herself?

Agnes's smile widened. "Of course, from now on you and Anna will both eat with the family," she said. "Now, come, sit."

Hayley lowered herself to a chair across the table from Conn. He, too, gave her a smile, the dark, bleak look gone from his eyes.

"You must be hungry," he said.

"Yes," she answered. But she wasn't.

Guilt throbbed through her. She should never have let Conn kiss her. She should never have accepted his proposal. She should have. . . .

What? Fled with Darryl into the woods again? Tried to find another place of refuge?

Turned herself and Darryl in to the authorities? Let Darryl be hanged for killing a brutal man who had badly used her?

No, she couldn't have done any of these things. The only safety she and Darryl had was in remaining here. And hoping they wouldn't be found.

Marrying Conn would assure that she and Darryl stayed here. *But she hadn't accepted his proposal for those reasons!*

Darryl didn't believe that.

A cold lump formed in Hayley's stomach.

And Conn wouldn't believe it either, if he ever found out the secrets she kept from him.

CHAPTER SIXTEEN

Hayley paused at the springhouse door, watching the bustling activity at the barns. She glimpsed Conn's black hair among the group of farm workers and her pulse increased.

Another gust of wind hit, rocking her on her feet. A flash of lightning zigzagged through the roiling, dark storm clouds.

Hayley squeezed her eyes shut, her whole body tensed, waiting for the loud thunderclap. When it came, following close on the lightning, she shuddered.

She'd never get used to these dreadful storms here in this new land. And this one wasn't just an ordinary storm.

Conn had said last night they must prepare for what might turn out to be a hurricane, since the storm was lasting so long. He'd gone on to explain what a terrible kind of storm that was, sometimes destroying many lives and property.

Again, she glimpsed Conn and drew in her breath. He was leading his favorite mare, Perdita, out of the barn. She was a beautiful bay. Hayley had fallen in love with her the day she'd found Conn grooming her in the barn and the mare had nickered at Hayley as if she were a long-lost friend.

Hayley had always loved horses, from the time she was a

child and her father had set her up on the back of old Nellie, their cart horse, laughing when she showed no fear and crowed with delight.

Hayley forgot her task of bringing more milk and butter to the house, and ran toward Conn.

"Conn!" she called when she neared. He turned his head and smiled when he saw her.

"Where are you taking Perdita?" The mare whinnied at the sound of Hayley's voice, and Hayley reached out a hand to smooth her head.

"The horses will be safer in the open. They know how to find the most secure place during these storms."

Conn kept walking toward the far field, and Hayley hurried to keep up with him. "But aren't you worried she might foal?"

He let out a sigh. "Of course I am. But this is still the safest thing to do. They'll be fine unless the storm hits us dead on."

Even two weeks after the turbulent day when Conn had asked her to be his wife and she'd agreed, Hayley thrilled at the thought. She had to pinch herself every morning when she awakened, to convince herself it hadn't just been a dream.

That it was actually true. They would soon be married.

His black hair was coming loose from its restraining thong in back. It curled in the damp air surrounding them. His profile, facing her, with its strong, even features, made her heart thump in her chest.

She lifted a hand and gently squeezed his arm, wanting, needing the physical contact with him.

A muscle flexed beneath her fingers, making her realize just how tense he was.

"Don't do that," he said, throwing her a rueful glance. "It makes me want to take you in my arms and kiss you until you've no more breath left."

She took her hand away, her skin still feeling the warmth of his skin under his shirt. "That would be wonderful, but I'm not trying to tempt you now. I just need to touch you."

He shot another glance at her, this one warmer, and also

surprised, as if her simple words were ones he'd never heard before.

Maybe he hadn't, she thought, taking little running steps to keep up with him. Maybe his wife Marie had never said such things to him before they were married.

And she must not have after they were wed, since Conn had said she'd taunted him with her unfaithfulness on their wedding night.

Hayley turned the thoughts off. That was all over and done with. She would make Conn a good, loving wife. They would be happy and content.

How can you believe that when you're keeping dark secrets from him, when at any moment you and Darryl may be found out? her mind asked her.

"I'd better go back," she said, regret in her voice. "Lavena sent me to the springhouse to bring extra supplies to the house."

"I'm sure you're finding her bark not so severe as previously," Conn said, a twinkle in his dark eyes.

"No, Lavena doesn't scold so much as she did," Hayley agreed, trying to respond in kind, to make her voice light. "But if I don't get back now, that won't be true, I fear."

Another gust of wind, stronger than any before, came tearing across the open field they were now in, throwing Hayley off balance, making the mare give a frightened whinny and try to rear.

Conn controlled her with difficulty, swearing under his breath. "Go on back," he told Hayley, his voice tense. "Get in out of this before it gets any worse."

"All right. Be careful," she told him, hearing the fear in her voice.

"I will. Go on now."

Hayley turned and ran, another gust hitting her as she neared the barn, this one knocking her to her knees.

Real fear hit her as she got to her feet and wrenched open the springhouse door. She grabbed the food from the shelves and put it into the wooden buckets she'd brought, then hurried back to the house.

Leaves, twigs and small tree branches littered the ground already. Some of the more delicate herbs had broken stalks, she saw, hurrying up the walk. Darryl would be brokenhearted if the herb garden was destroyed.

A noise made her glance up as she approached the house. Lavena was at her bedchamber window, pulling a heavy storm shutter closed. Her jaw tensed when she saw Hayley, but she said no words of reprimand. She pulled the other shutter closed, leaving Hayley staring at an expanse of solid wood, where a moment before there had been diamond-paned glass.

All the other upstairs windows were similarly shuttered, Hayley saw, and most of the downstairs ones, giving the house a dark, bleak look, as if they were preparing for a siege.

She opened the kitchen door and went inside. A big pile of wood was stacked by the fireplace, where Ellis had put it this morning.

Darryl turned from the fire, where she stirred a kettle of stew. Her face was set in tense lines, too.

Avoiding Darryl's gaze, Hayley gave her what she hoped was a reassuring smile. After a moment, Darryl returned it, but Hayley saw the tremble of her lips. Darryl feared these New World storms even more than Hayley did.

Darryl, who used to fear nothing. Hayley pushed away her sadness at this thought.

Agnes was refilling the candle holders on the wall.

"There you are," Agnes said. "Thank goodness. You were gone so long we were worried you'd fallen or had a tree limb strike you."

"No, I'm fine," Hayley said. "I—I just saw Conn taking Perdita to the fields and talked to him a moment."

Agnes gave her an impish smile. "Of course you did. Even with a storm coming, it's only right you'd want to be with your future husband for a moment or two."

Hayley still avoided Darryl's gaze. She'd been dodging being alone with her sister since the day Conn had asked her to be his wife, even to going to bed only after Darryl had already gone to sleep.

For the first time in her life, she felt uncomfortable with Darryl. She hated it.

But didn't know what to do about it. Darryl still believed that Hayley had managed to somehow trick Conn into marriage so that they'd no longer have to worry about Lavena sending them away.

Darryl wanted to hear nothing about the love that Hayley felt for Conn, or that he felt for her. She shied away from any discussion of it, making Hayley realize anew, with dismay, that Darryl was still far from recovered from her ordeal with Oscar Pritt.

The feelings between men and women had led to what she'd endured from that brutal man, and she still couldn't accept the thought of any pleasure coming from such contact.

Or if she did, she still feared it.

"I'll put these in the pantry," Hayley said, carrying the buckets across to the storage closet. She opened the door, and the fragrance of fresh-baked bread filled her nostrils. The shelves held several extra loaves Lavena had baked this morning as well as the normal supplies.

Hayley placed the bowls of milk and butter in the heavy wooden chest made for that purpose, and laid cloths over the bowls to preserve the coolness they still held from the spring-house.

Lavena came into the kitchen just as Hayley reached the worktable. She gave Hayley a hard glance, her mouth pursed, then quickly smoothed out her features.

"We need to close the shutters on these kitchen windows soon," she said.

The thought of being completely shut up in the darkened house gave Hayley a sense of foreboding. She hoped Lavena would wait as long as possible before this final step.

Maybe the storm would slack off, veer away from them.

And maybe Lavena would come to accept and like her and Darryl.

Both possibilities seemed equally remote. Lavena's voice

sounded half-strangled, as if her struggle to be polite to Hayley was almost more than she could stand.

Out of the corner of her eye, Hayley saw Agnes's grin. Despite her tension from anticipating the worsening storm, Hayley fought to control a smile herself. She had to admit that observing Lavena's efforts amused her, too.

But she could understand the older woman's difficulty. Two weeks ago, in the space of an hour, Hayley had gone from a servant to soon-to-be mistress of Holly View.

Lavena had an even harder time with Darryl. As Hayley's sister, Darryl was also now in a different position. Both girls still did the work they'd done before, of course—everyone worked at Holly View—but Darryl and Hayley now sat at the dining room table with the family, entered into the conversations.

Which, thankfully, had dealt no more with the search for the runaway bond servant girl. It was all too easy to imagine another search party was nearing them right this moment. Hayley tucked that thought in the back of her mind, too.

They had other things to worry about now.

"What else needs to be done?" Hayley asked Lavena, making her voice neutral.

"We need more water," Lavena answered in the same colorless tone. "Take two buckets to the springhouse."

Outside, a hard gust of wind slammed against the house, and a crash followed.

Agnes started, dropping one of the candles she held onto the floor. "The storm is getting worse, Lavena. You can't send the girl out into it again!"

Lavena pursed her lips. "We need the water, but I'll go myself."

Hayley quailed at the thought of going back into the storm, but she lifted her head. "No, you know what further preparations need to be made and I don't. I'll go."

Agnes opened her mouth, then closed it again. Hayley saw her hands were shaking. Why, the older woman was as fearful of this storm as Hayley.

"I'll go," Darryl spoke up. "The stew is done, and needs only stirring once in a while."

"All right," Lavena said.

Hayley gave her sister a quick look, then blinked in surprise. Darryl's face had taken on a resolute expression, her lips tight. Hayley remembered that look from the days before Darryl had turned into the fearful person she now was.

Her eyes told Hayley not to interfere, that she intended to do this.

Darryl got two empty buckets from the pantry and opened the door against a rush of wind that slammed it back against the wall.

Hayley moved forward. She couldn't let Darryl go out into this alone. "I'll go with you."

Darryl frowned at her and shook her head. "No, you stay here and help," she said, her voice strong and commanding. "I'll do fine."

Before Hayley could protest again, Darryl had slipped out the door, closing it firmly against the storm.

Hayley stood frowning, indecisive, then behind her she heard an indrawn breath, and a sharp little cry.

She whirled. Agnes held her hand to her chest, her face white.

Catching Hayley's alarmed glance, she tried to smile. "It's just one of my little spells," she said. "I'll be all right."

Without warning, she sagged in her chair.

Hayley, Lavena behind her, sprinted across the room in time to keep the older woman from falling to the floor. Carefully, Hayley supported her, and eased her back into her chair.

Agnes's breath was coming in shallow little gasps. "My chest hurts," she said, in a shaky voice completely unlike her usual firm tones.

Even empty, the wooden pails were heavy. But she was strong from years of farm work. She could do this, Darryl told herself. A wind gust slapped against her, making her stagger and drop one of the buckets.

She picked it up and continued on, closing her mind against the terror that pushed against her like a black blanket.

What had gotten into her at the house a few minutes ago? She'd listened to Hayley agree to go back out into the storm, and suddenly had become ashamed of her own cowardice. She'd spoken up before she'd thought.

The springhouse seemed so far away, with the wind bowing the tree limbs down until they looked as if they must snap. Some of them did. Just ahead of her, at the end of the walk, a big branch thudded against the stones, then bounced up, making her dodge back to keep it from striking her.

Darryl's heart thundered. She felt her breath coming in fast little gasps, making her dizzy. She stood for a moment, forcing herself to take deeper, slower breaths. Finally, her head lost that light, floating feeling; her panic subsided a little.

At last she reached the springhouse. Beyond, workers were still in the barnyard, securing everything loose they could, or taking items inside the barns. She caught sight of Ellis's dark head as he held a halter fastened to one of the horses. He paused to give an order to a worker, who nodded and hurried off.

She didn't see Conn. Ellis seemed to be in charge, and handling those duties well. A strange feeling welled up inside her. For a moment she didn't know what it was. Then she realized it was pride.

She felt a glow of pride that Ellis was strong and capable.

Dismayed, she tried to push the feeling away, far back in her mind. But it stubbornly refused to go.

Hayley and Conn's betrothal seemed to have increased those manly qualities in Ellis. He didn't share his mother's anger at it. No, like Agnes, he was frankly delighted with the new state of affairs.

He'd been giving her newly confident glances since that day two weeks ago. As if the betrothal had given him new hope for his own suit.

Seeming to sense her intent look, Ellis turned his head toward

her. Darryl jerked her head around and tugged at the springhouse door latch.

It wouldn't budge. Frustrated, she tugged harder. It opened
so suddenly she staggered, grabbing onto the side of the door.

She hurried inside with her heavy buckets and knelt beside
the gurgling, constantly running stream. She took a dipper
hanging from a peg and dipped water into her first pail.

Another gust of wind shook the sturdy building, alarming
her. The gusts were coming more frequently now, and were
stronger. She had to hurry.

"Why in hell are you out in this? Has Mother no sense?"

Ellis's voice, rough with concern, came from behind, making
her jump.

She turned her head. He stood behind her, a frown furrowing
his brow. His clothes were wet from the intermittent rain,
flattening his shirt to his chest.

Why had she never before noticed just how broad his chest
was?

She caught her breath at that errant thought and quickly
turned back to her task. "We need the water," she said over
her shoulder. "Everyone else was busy."

She set the first bucket aside and started dipping into the
second, her movements jerky.

Ellis swore again and then was beside her, taking the dipper
from her hand. Moments later, the bucket was full, and he
stood, holding out his hand to her.

"Come on. Let's get back to the house before all hell breaks
loose."

Darryl looked at his extended hand. It, too, was big and
capable. But it also could be gentle . . . very gentle.

She scrambled to her feet, reaching for one of the buckets.

"I'll take them." Carrying one in each hand as if they
weighed nothing at all, Ellis walked to the door. Darryl hastened
to open it.

They hurried through, gasping as wind-driven rain hit them
full force.

"Walk behind me," Ellis said. "That will protect you some."

She did as he bade, and they struggled toward the house. The rain drove down so hard now she could see nothing in front of her, could barely keep her footing. It stung like sleet, drenching them both to the skin in moments, making her shiver with cold.

A flash of lightning seemed to light up the whole sky in front of them, followed closely by thunder so loud it seemed directly overhead. A huge oak tree made a sound like a human groan, then fell with a tremendous crash right across the path.

Terror swept over her, increasing her trembling.

"Hang on to me," Ellis said above the tumult.

She grabbed at the loose tail of his shirt, and hung on for dear life as he led her around the spreading branches of the big oak. Its huge exposed roots dripped soil like tears.

Darryl fought for breath as the wind and rain relentlessly pounded them. Would they never reach the safety of the house? Had Ellis strayed from the path?

Finally, the house's blessed bulk loomed ahead. The shutters were closed now, the entire house dark. Lavena flung the kitchen door open as they approached. Behind her, a few flickering candles lit the gloom.

"Quick, get in before you flood the place," she said.

They did, Lavena slamming the door so close behind them, Darryl's skirt would have caught if it hadn't been so wet and clinging to her. She removed her soaking cloak and hung it on a peg.

Ellis lowered the buckets to the floor and gave his mother a frown. "Why did you send Anna out in this?"

Lavena tried to return his look, but her glance faltered. "It wasn't this bad when she left," she finally said. "Come to the fire. You're soaked."

"I have to get back to help Conn finish up outside. This is going to be a bad one."

He turned to Darryl, his dark gaze finding hers, probing, lingering.

She couldn't take her eyes away, although she knew her face revealed far more of her feelings than she wanted it to.

Ellis turned and hurried to the door.

Darryl watched as it closed behind him. Fear for his safety filled her, blending with other, unnamed feelings.

What if another tree fell? And he couldn't get out of the way in time?

Anything could happen out there now. The look they'd exchanged a moment ago could be the last one they'd ever give each other.

"Get out of those wet clothes, girl, before you catch your death."

That was Agnes's voice, but strangely weak and faltering.

Darryl looked around dazedly, realizing she was shaking as if she had a chill.

Close to the hearth, Agnes sat in an armchair, pillows piled behind her. Her face was pale, and she looked older, somehow shrunken.

Hayley stood by Agnes's chair, holding a steaming mug, her face worried. "Drink some more of this tea," Hayley urged, extending the mug.

Agnes waved it away, making a face. "Not now. It tastes and smells so bad, I won't be able to keep it down."

Hayley sighed, putting the mug on the mantel. She raised her head and frowned at Darryl. "You're shaking like a leaf. Go up and put on dry clothes," she said. "Or you'll get sick."

Darryl nodded numbly, then took a candle and headed for the door to the back stairs. Finally reaching the attic bedchamber she and Hayley shared, she set down her candle on the small chest. Hurriedly, she stripped off her wet clothes and donned dry ones.

She fumbled with the tiny buttons, her back to the shuttered window. Mixed with the driving rain another screaming gust of wind battered the house.

Before she could move, a loud crack came from the window, then the sound of breaking glass.

The howling storm tore into the room, bringing shards of flying glass with it.

Terrified, Darryl hurled herself onto the floor, crawling toward the bed, her only thought to get under it.

CHAPTER SEVENTEEN

"What was that?" Lavena asked, her voice alarmed. "It sounded like a window breaking upstairs and something falling."

New fear shot through Hayley's veins.

Darryl was in the attic.

"Yes. Stay here with Agnes. I'll go." Hayley ran for the back stairs.

The door to the attic stairs was open, and Hayley heard the howling of the storm from the bottom step. It was too loud to still be outside the house.

Wild urgency driving her, she ran up the stairs and flung open the door to the bedchamber she and Darryl slept in.

Wind-driven rain blew through the broken panes of the window. A shutter hung by one hinge; the other was completely gone. Water ran in rivulets over the floor.

Darryl lay sprawled face-down, amid shards of broken glass. Part of a big tree limb lay beside her.

"Darryl!" Hayley screamed, running to her sister, broken glass crunching under her feet. Hayley dropped to her knees beside Darryl, feeling a jabbing pain as a glass shard pierced her knee through her skirts. Her sister lay still as death.

Hayley turned her over. Darryl's eyes were closed. Blood streaked her face from two cuts on her forehead.

"Darryl, can you hear me?"

There was no answer. No movement. Hayley's fear increased.

Then she saw the rise and fall of Darryl's chest. Weak with relief, she gently patted Darryl's cheeks. "Wake up, Darryl."

Darryl still lay motionless, and Hayley's fear returned. Her sister might be mortally injured. She had to get her downstairs, but she couldn't carry her. She must get help.

Hayley scrambled to her feet and ran down the two sets of steps, bursting into the kitchen just as Conn and Ellis closed the outer kitchen door behind them, the wind and rain trying to follow them inside.

Wild-eyed, Hayley ran for Conn.

"Dar—Anna's in our room hurt. I can't wake her up," she gasped out.

A tiny part of her mind wondered if anyone had noticed her near-slip. Then that worry was swallowed up and forgotten in her greater concern for Darryl's life.

Neither man stopping to remove his outer clothing, Ellis tore up the back stairs before her last words were out, Conn behind him, Hayley following in their wake.

By the time she reached the bedchamber, Ellis had picked Darryl up and was holding her carefully in his arms. His face was pale beneath its normal brownness, his mouth tight.

Conn moved aside, and Hayley grabbed the quilt off the bed and followed the two men downstairs.

Back in the kitchen she spread the quilt on the floor and Ellis, his face still tense with fear, gently laid Darryl on it.

"What on earth happened?" Lavena shrilled.

Conn waved her to silence. Agnes, who'd been dozing, opened her eyes and struggled to sit up, subsiding with a gasp.

Darryl's eyes were still closed. The cuts on her forehead still oozed blood, but didn't look too deep, Hayley decided, carefully probing for broken bones.

Everything felt all right.

So why was Darryl insensible? Hayley continued her gentle touches, finally discovering a rising lump on the back of Darryl's head.

"Something must have hit her when the window blew in," she said. "Probably that tree limb on the floor."

Ellis, crouching beside Darryl, nodded, looking even more worried. He touched her cheek, his hand lingering.

"Lavena, why are you standing there like a lump?" Agnes asked. But her voice was only a shadow of its former robustness. "Go get the smelling salts!"

Hayley heard Lavena's sharp intake of breath. Then the woman hurried across the room to the shelf where the household remedies were kept.

"Here," she said a few moments later, handing the vial to Hayley.

Hayley held the vial under Darryl's nose. For a few moments nothing happened. Then Darryl began to stir and moan. Finally, her eyelids fluttered open and she gave Hayley a dazed look.

"Wh—what happened? Why does my head hurt so?"

"The storm blew out a window. Something hit you," Hayley explained.

"Oh." Darryl nodded, then closed her eyes again.

"A window is out upstairs? Ellis, go tend to it before the house is flooded," Lavena said.

Ellis didn't seem to hear her. He crouched by Darryl, his eyes fixed on her again still face.

He looked up at Hayley. "Will she be all right?"

Hayley nodded. "I think so. She just needs rest now. But we must rouse her if she sleeps too long. One time my father was hurt like this, and that's what we were told to do."

"Ellis, did you hear what I said?" Lavena said, her voice louder. "This . . . girl will be perfectly all right. There are enough of us to tend to her."

Ellis whirled, glaring at his mother. "I don't care if the

entire house floods. I won't leave Anna until I'm sure she's recovering."

He turned back to his vigil by Darryl's side.

Lavena gasped, her eyes widening. "Well, I never," she said in a moment.

"I'll tend to the window," Conn said. "Are there boards in the house?"

Lavena gestured to a few old boards by the fireplace. "There. I was foresighted enough to see to that." She sniffed, obviously still upset by what Ellis had said to her.

Conn turned to Hayley. "Will you help me?" he asked.

Hayley nodded, rising. "Of course, as soon as I tend to Anna's cuts."

"Lavena, you can do that," Conn said. "You're right, we must board the window before the house floods."

For a moment there was silence. Then Lavena said, "Naturally, I will tend to Anna's cuts. Jane, you go ahead with Conn."

"Aunt Agnes, are you ill?" Conn asked, seeming to notice for the first time all the pillows piled around the older woman in the chair.

Agnes waved her hand, dismissively. "Just a weak spell. You know I have them now and then. This storm is bad. It's very upsetting."

As if to prove her words, the storm suddenly increased in intensity, wind and rain pounding against the house. The old structure shuddered.

Hayley held her breath, waiting for one of the shuttered kitchen windows to break, the door to crash open.

But the house held firm against the now-incessant pounding.

"Come on," Conn said, heading upstairs with the boards and a handful of nails, Hayley hurrying behind.

Water dripped from Conn's clothes as they hurried up the stairs to the attic.

Water now covered the bedchamber floor, and more poured in from outside.

"Here, hold the nails." Conn gave Hayley a handful. Fighting the wind and rain, he forced a board against the broken pane and taking a nail from Hayley's extended hand, hammered it to the sill.

In a few minutes, the window was patched tightly enough that the fury of the storm could no longer breach it.

"Thank God, that's done," Conn sighed.

Hayley's tension eased a bit. The window was repaired. Darryl would be all right. Aunt Agnes was recovering from her spell. The storm seemed to be getting no worse.

And she and Conn were alone together.

She pushed that stray thought aside. Her feet were soaked from the wet floor. Her left knee throbbed from the cut she'd gotten earlier.

"We must get this water off the floor before it goes through the ceiling," Hayley said. "I'll go down and get buckets and rags."

Conn reached out and grasped her arm. "Wait a moment."

His warm hand on her arm sent a thrill through her. "Why?" she asked, innocently.

"I think you know." He pulled her closer to his soaked body, so that she felt every work-hardened muscle.

She raised her face and he lowered his and their lips met. Hayley sighed in joy, circling her arms about his neck, molding herself to him.

The kiss deepened. Hayley felt Conn's lower regions awakening, and a shudder went down her spine. How she longed for their wedding night to arrive. How she wished it were tomorrow instead of several weeks away.

Conn's hand curved around her bottom, bringing her tightly against his arousal. She let out a whimper and her tongue snaked into his mouth, finding his and curving around it.

"You little minx," Conn muttered. "If you keep this up, I don't think I can wait for our wedding."

Loud footsteps pounded up the steps. "What is taking so long?" Lavena demanded from the door. "The lower rooms will be ruined!"

Hayley jumped back, but Conn was slow to release her. His

dark eyes held the promise of delights to come, making her pulse race.

Lavena came inside, holding buckets and rags. "What a terrible mess. We must clean it up at once."

"Go back down with Anna," Conn told Hayley. "I'll help Lavena with this."

"Anna is doing fine," Lavena said, tartly, already sweeping the broken glass into a pile. "My son's making sure of that."

And Lavena doesn't like that one bit. Hayley hesitated for a moment, then grabbed a rag herself and began to mop up the water behind Lavena's brisk broom.

There was no harm in leaving Ellis with Darryl for a little longer.

No harm at all.

By the time they all three went back down to the kitchen, the storm's fury seemed to have abated just a bit, Hayley thought.

The wind and rain still pounded against the house, but as she'd thought upstairs, it wasn't getting any worse.

Ellis still crouched beside Darryl, one of her hands enclosed within his. Darryl's eyes remained shut, but her color was back to normal. A neat white bandage covered the cuts on her forehead.

Hayley knelt beside her sister. "Anna, wake up," she said. "Open your eyes and talk to me."

After a moment, Darryl's eyelids fluttered up and her blue eyes focused on her sister. "My head still hurts," she complained.

"And it will for a while. You got a hard blow. We found the branch that blew in and hit you. It was a stout one."

Darryl moved her head a little, grimacing, looking at Ellis.

Her eyes widened when she saw his hand holding hers. Her mouth made a surprised O, and she tried to tug her hand out from within his grasp.

Reluctantly, he let go. "Thank God you're all right, Anna," he said, his voice unsteady. "I couldn't have borne it if anything had happened to you."

For a moment, Darryl's gaze stayed on his; then she turned away and closed her eyes again. "I'm very tired," she said. "I must sleep."

Sister, You're doing a bit of playacting, Hayley told her, silently. *You're not as immune to Ellis as you'd have him and all of us believe.*

Hayley pulled the quilt up over Darryl to her chin, then settled down beside her.

Conn and Ellis went upstairs to change into dry clothes, then came back down to wait out the storm.

Ellis settled down again beside Darryl. Conn restlessly prowled the room, pausing to smile at Hayley now and again. Lavena went ahead with supper preparations, Hayley helping her. Agnes dozed, muttered in her sleep, woke now and then.

The room grew even darker as the evening drew toward night. And almost unbearably close.

Finally, Hayley lifted her head. "Is it just my fancy, or is the storm abating?"

Conn paused in his circuit between the windows and the fire and nodded. "It's not your fancy. The worst is over. And the house is still standing. With little damage, I believe."

"If all the plaster doesn't fall onto our heads from that attic, it will be only God's mercy preventing it," Lavena said.

"Quit predicting doom and rejoice that we still have a roof over our heads," Agnes said from her chair, her voice almost back to its usual strength.

"Aunt Agnes, stop giving me orders," Lavena snapped.

Hayley glanced at Agnes in time to catch the older woman's grin.

"Why, Lavena, don't you know that furnishes me with one of the chief pleasures still left to me in this life? I'm determined that I will manage to get you grown up to be a sensible, competent woman, if I just keep at you long enough."

Lavena whirled, her face tight with anger. "Be quiet, you silly old woman. I'm tired of you picking on me day and night. I am not a girl. I'm a middle-aged woman, with a grown son."

Agnes smiled again, even more wickedly. "Why, of course,

I know that, Lavena dear. I'm no more in my dotage than you are.''

Lavena's mouth dropped open. "What do you mean?"

Agnes drew herself up in her chair, so that she sat straight.

"This storm we've just endured frightened me half to death, so that I had a heart spell. It made me face the fact that sometime I won't recover from one of them."

"You've got a lot of good years left," Conn protested.

Agnes shrugged. "That may be so. And then it may not be." She looked at Lavena again and sighed. "Too bad that I must stop teasing you, Lavena. It's been so entertaining. But I must if I want my lawyer to believe that I'm in my right mind."

"Aunt Agnes, what are you talking about?" Conn asked.

Agnes sighed again. "I've been studying this over, Conn, dear, and my mind is made up. As soon as things are back to normal from this storm, I must act on my decision."

"What decision?" Lavena asked, sharply.

Agnes smiled at Darryl, then turned to Hayley.

Finally, her glance returned to Conn.

"I've decided to change my will. I'm going to leave my property to these two sweet girls."

CHAPTER EIGHTEEN

No one said anything for a long moment. The storm sounds were suddenly loud in the room.

Hayley stared at the old woman she'd come to love like a member of her family over these past weeks. She couldn't believe what Agnes Townsend had just said.

Lavena's face had turned ashen. "You are out of your mind! You can't do that."

Agnes gave her a straight, firm look.

Lavena moved back a step.

"But I can," Agnes said. "I have no family members left alive. I may do with my property as I will."

"You are not of sound mind," Lavena said, her voice shaking with anger. "Everyone knows that. Why, you ramble on as if you don't know if it's today or thirty years in the past."

Agnes's mouth quirked. "Only to you, Lavena."

"Not just to me," Lavena protested. "Half the time you think Conn is a child, as you think I am."

Agnes shook her head of white hair. "Conn has long known I was only pretending."

"That's not true! It can't be true." Lavena jerked her head around to stare at her brother.

Conn looked uncomfortable, then finally nodded. "I'm afraid it is, sister. If you'd paid more attention instead of buttering Aunt Agnes up for your own gain, you'd have soon realized what was going on."

Lavena stared at him. "I've been doing no such thing! I've merely been taking care of a sick old woman, who isn't even a member of our family."

Conn frowned. "As far as I'm concerned, she's as much my aunt as any of my blood relations ever were. More so than most of them. And Agnes didn't ask to come here. We had to persuade her, if you recall."

"And that was all your doing! You told me Agnes was going to leave her property to a housekeeper if we didn't."

Conn sighed. "So I did. I wanted you to agree to let Agnes come here. And I knew you didn't want that. I couldn't think of anything else that would work."

Lavena's face turned brick red. "That doesn't alter the fact we've cared for her night and day for months."

Conn frowned. "I don't believe you've done much of that. Any time I was around, Jane or Anna was in attendance. Besides, most of the time, Aunt Agnes is as spry as you or I."

"Will you two stop acting and talking as if I'm not in the room?" Agnes asked.

She gave Conn a severe look. "So you tricked your sister into agreeing for me to come here?"

Conn looked even more uncomfortable. "I didn't want you staying at Cedarwood with only a housekeeper."

Agnes turned to Lavena, her face serious. "Yes, I'd planned to leave my property to you and Conn and Ellis. You didn't have to butter me up. I would have preferred that you and I have an honest relationship. Admit to each other that we don't get along and probably never will."

Lavena opened her mouth, then closed it. She looked from Agnes to Conn. Then her glance landed on Hayley.

Her face hardened. "You're the sly one, aren't you? Coming

in here, pretending to be so sweet and good. And all the time you were plotting to take away what was rightfully ours.''

Conn stepped across to his sister, took her arm. ''That will be enough, Lavena. Come on, you need to sit down.''

Lavena shook his arm off. ''Leave me alone,'' she hissed. ''I speak only the truth.''

''No, you speak out of spite and thwarted greed,'' Agnes said, sadly. ''Your son will have an equal share in this prosperous farm. Neither of you have any need of my property. You have a secure home here.''

''There's been no security since these two girls came here,'' Lavena cried. ''They've disrupted this household. Schemed and plotted for their own benefit.''

''You're wrong. They've brought life and love here,'' Agnes said. ''Both of which have been sadly lacking for a long time.''

''Enough of this!'' Conn said, loudly. ''Lavena, you will stop talking in such manner about my future wife and her sister. *Now.*''

Ellis joined the group clustered around Agnes Townsend. He gave his mother a cool look. ''Yes, Mother. I don't want to hear any more such remarks about Anna.''

Conn sighed, heavily. ''I'm to blame for part of this. I knew you and Aunt Agnes have never gotten on. I thought it would work out somehow, but I was wrong.''

Lavena slowly looked from one person to the other. When she finished, she repeated the procedure. Finally, she walked blindly across the room, fumbled for a chair and lowered herself heavily into it. She sat there, staring at the shuttered windows.

Despite the woman's cruel words about her and Darryl, Hayley felt a twinge of pity. In the last few minutes, Lavena's world had been shaken up and changed completely.

Or at least she believed so.

Hayley moved to stand before Agnes. She arranged the older woman's pillows in a more comfortable position. ''It was kind of you to think of us, but of course, Anna and I can't accept the gift of your property.''

Agnes tilted her head. ''Why not?''

Hayley gave her a perplexed look. "Because as Lavena says, it wouldn't be right. They've been like family to you all these years, and now you're living in their house."

Agnes nodded. "That's true, and I'm grateful. Warren and I did well for many years. He left much more than enough money for me even if I live until I am truly in my dotage. Conn and Lavena and Ellis will of course inherit that."

Hayley's frown deepened. "Even if that's so, why should you want to give anything to Anna and me?"

"Because I *like* both of you, you silly girl," Agnes said. "I want to be sure both of you are taken care of."

She smiled at Hayley again. "Not that I don't expect Conn to be a generous husband, but it's always nice for a wife to have something of her own. And I'm sure Conn won't object."

Her last words silenced Hayley. She stared at the older woman, unable to think of anything else to say.

"And as for your sister, a girl as pretty as Anna will not remain a maid for long. I expect all this will even out in time."

Agnes glanced at Ellis.

His eyes widened. Then he abruptly turned and went back to Darryl's side.

"So, have we had enough excitement for one day?" Agnes asked. "The storm seems to be abating. Soon you'll all have to go out and assess the damage. In the meantime, let's have some stew. I am famished."

"Be careful," Hayley told Conn as he and Ellis left the house after they'd eaten.

It was nearly dusk, and the storm had died down into mild wind-driven rain. Leaves and tree limbs covered the ground like a carpet. Here and there, a tree had fallen.

"Don't worry," Conn told her, a warm feeling going over him at her concern. How long had it been since anyone had cautioned him like that? Shown real care for his welfare?

Not since childhood. Not since his mother had told him these things.

Certainly Marie never had.

His mouth twisted. No, his wife had never cared for him. All her professions of love had been lies to entangle him into marriage. He grimaced impatiently.

Why was he thinking about Marie so much these days?

Ever since he'd asked Jane to be his wife.

He tried to dismiss the thoughts, but the best he could do was push them into the back of his mind.

God, what a day this had been!

First the storm, and Anna's injury, which, although he'd not let Jane know, he'd feared was far more serious than it turned out to be.

Then, Aunt Agnes's astounding announcement.

He frowned, regretting he'd manipulated Lavena into accepting that Aunt Agnes share their home. But he hadn't seen any other way of managing that feat, and he hadn't dreamed anything like this would happen.

He shook his head. When Aunt Agnes made up her mind about something, nothing on earth could sway her.

But he wished she hadn't done it. He would always take care of Jane.

Aunt Agnes's prosperous farm would have been perfect for Ellis. As he remembered the old woman's remark about a girl as pretty as Anna not remaining single, his frown deepened.

The old girl was wily as a serpent. She knew Ellis loved Anna. She expected them to marry. In which case, her half of Aunt Agnes's farm would become Ellis's anyway.

As by law, Hayley's half would be his. But he'd draw up papers giving her control of her property.

Lavena, of course, wouldn't accept any of that. Especially the thought of Ellis marrying Anna. His sister was moving around like a sleepwalker, still in shock. But at least she was no longer insulting Jane and Anna.

She'd get over it in time, because she knew she'd always have a home here at Holly View.

Or did she?

The thought struck him forcibly that possibly some of Lavena's outrageous behavior today came from fear.

Maybe she thought that when he and Jane married, Jane would find some way of getting her out of the house. He shook his head.

He saw Ellis give him a quizzical look.

Conn turned to him. "Do you think your mother feels she won't be welcome at Holly View after Jane and I marry?"

Ellis blinked in surprise. "I don't know. I'd never thought about it."

"Neither had I until just now, when I was trying to figure out why Lavena was so overwrought today."

"She didn't expect Aunt Agnes to do what she did." Ellis answered.

"Of course not. None of us did. But your mother will always have a home at Holly View. I thought she knew that."

"Maybe you should tell her," Ellis said. He gave Conn a direct look. "Do you intend to make me a full partner?"

It was Conn's turn to be surprised and a little annoyed. He didn't like being put on the spot. After a few moments he said, "Hasn't that always been the plan?"

Ellis nodded. "Yes, but that was before you decided to re-marry. And to have sons of your own."

"That will be God's will," Conn said, realizing he was being evasive.

A flicker of anger came into Ellis's dark eyes. "If you've changed your mind, I want to know. If so, I'll start looking for land of my own."

Conn stared at his nephew as if he'd never before seen him. "You'd leave Holly View?"

Ellis's jaw clenched. "I won't stay on here as just a paid worker."

"What has brought all this on?"

"I, too, want to marry and have my own family. Is that so hard to understand?"

Conn suddenly remembered Ellis's hovering over Anna today. Defying his mother. "No. Of course it isn't."

He looked at Ellis. Truly looked at him from head to foot. He wasn't a boy any longer. This last year he'd filled out. He was tall as Conn now, almost as muscular.

Ellis was a man. And as Gustav had reminded Conn recently, it was time he recognized that and set things straight.

Conn clapped Ellis on the shoulder. "I hope Anna accepts you soon. She'll make you a fine wife."

Ellis nodded again. "I know that."

"As soon as we clear up from the storm, you and I will also go to our lawyer and have papers drawn up. I want you as my full partner, Ellis. You're a good man. And you've been pulling your weight around here for quite a while. I'm sorry I've been so slow to recognize it."

Ellis stared at him as if he couldn't believe his ears. "Do you mean that?"

"Of course I mean it."

Ellis grinned. "Thank you, Uncle Conn." He held out his hand.

Conn took it, grinning back a bit wryly. "No thanks needed. You've earned this. And you can leave off the 'Uncle.' Makes me feel like an old man."

"All right, Conn."

"We'd better get a move on. It will soon be full dark."

"Yes," Ellis agreed. "I hope the storm damage isn't too bad."

Conn sighed. "We certainly don't need that on top of a bad harvest again this year. You may not be getting such a prize with this farm."

"I think I am," Ellis said. "Next year will be good, I'm sure."

Conn laughed. "Always the eternal optimist, aren't you?" He remembered just in time to leave off the "boy" he'd almost added.

Ellis laughed, too. "Why not be?"

Why not, indeed? Conn asked himself. It would certainly make a person feel better. He might try it himself. Ever since Marie's death, he'd felt little but gloom.

Now he was ready to make a new start with Jane.

"You may have something there," he told Ellis.

As they approached the outbuildings, his thoughts turned to Lavena again.

He felt sorry for his sister—or rather for the pleasant girl and woman she used to be during their childhood and her marriage.

Losing her husband and her farm soon after that had soured her on life. He'd tried to help her for a long time, been patient with her sharp tongue. But years of listening to it had wearied him. And no amount of kindness shown her seemed to help. So finally, he'd stopped. Begun being as sharp-tongued as she was.

Maybe the shock of tonight's events would change her. Soften her a little. Make her more like the sister he still missed.

He gave a wry smile at his fancies. And maybe the moon would turn to green cheese while he watched.

He assessed the damage to the outbuildings. The smokehouse door hung by one hinge swinging in the wind, but the dairy and henhouse seemed to have come through with little damage.

"It could have been worse," he told Ellis. "I remember one hurricane that hit us full force when I was a child. We had to rebuild most of the outbuildings."

"Yes," Ellis agreed. "And the house fared well. Only one broken window."

Conn's face sobered as the barn came into view. "Dammit," he swore.

A huge tree limb had blown across one end of the stable, and still lay there, crushing the roof. "Thank God the horses weren't in there."

"Yes, thank God," Ellis agreed again. Like Conn, his face was somber. "But we don't have enough sawed lumber for the repair."

Conn gave an absentminded nod as he hurried on to the barn, to assess the extent of the damage.

Gustav was already there, pulling at his chin as he walked around the structure.

He glanced up at their approach. "It is bad." He shook his grizzled gray head. "A lot more structural damage than it appears at first."

Conn let out a discouraged sigh. "And we don't have time to saw the lumber now. We must get the rest of the harvest in, such as it is."

Gustav nodded, his face thoughtful. "Yes, but there is another way."

"What?" Ellis asked.

"We could tear off this whole section and rebuild with logs. Logs are stronger and a lot faster to put up than sawed lumber. Look at the log structures the early Swedes built that are still standing."

Ellis nodded. "That's true. I've seen many of them when we've gone north."

"As have I," added Conn.

"I think we should do that," Ellis said, his voice decisive.

Conn gave him a surprised look, mixed with a bit of irritation. When had Ellis thought he could make big decisions like this?

Conn opened his mouth to tell his nephew so, and then closed it.

Hadn't he just told Ellis he'd make him a full partner as soon as possible? And with that position came the right to make decisions about what was done on the farm.

He nodded at Ellis. "I agree with you. It would be the best thing to do."

Ellis blinked, then smiled. "We need to get started right away."

Gustav nodded, gravely. "But I believe we can wait until tomorrow. It's nearly dark now."

"Have you checked the livestock?" Conn asked Gustav.

"Not all. The cows and sheep are fine. So is Edgar."

"Then let's go see about the horses."

A knot of worry formed in Conn's stomach as they headed for the field they'd turned the horses into. Soon they were all accounted for—except Perdita.

Conn and Ellis exchanged a frowning look. Gustav was

peering into a far corner of the field. "I see her," he said. "She's not moving. I believe she is foaling."

"Let's go bring her in," Ellis said, and before Conn could move, he was loping across the field.

Hayley threw another anxious glance at the kitchen door, which remained closed. Conn and Ellis had been gone for hours. It was full dark now. The wind and rain had subsided to occasional gusts and squalls.

Why weren't they back?

They must have encountered some kind of emergency. Or what if they'd been caught by falling limbs and were lying injured and trapped?

She tried to wrench her mind away from such thoughts. Of course they were all right. It was unlikely both would be hurt at the same time, and if one was, the other would have come to the house for aid.

Hayley turned away from the window.

Lavena, without eating a bite of supper, or speaking another word to anyone, had retreated to her room.

Darryl, to Hayley's intense relief, had gotten up soon after Agnes's unbelievable announcement and eaten a generous bowl of stew. At least Hayley didn't have to worry about her sister's injury.

But where was Conn?

"Jane, you may as well stop fretting and go see what's keeping Conn and Ellis," Agnes said from her armchair near the hearth.

By the light of the fire and a candle, she was again busily knitting, her color back to normal. "None of us will have any peace until you do."

She'd like nothing better. But she shouldn't leave Agnes and Darryl downstairs alone.

"Go on," Darryl urged from the hearth, where she'd put on another log. "We'll be fine."

Something in her voice made Hayley glance her way. Hayley

caught a glimpse of the same kind of worry and fear she felt, before Darryl smoothed out her face.

Darryl was worried about Ellis's safety. A ray of hope went through Hayley. As she'd thought earlier, Ellis's concern for Darryl's injury had brought Darryl and Ellis closer together. Had weakened the shell Darryl had enclosed herself in since . . .

Since Oscar Pritt had violated her and she'd killed him.

Hayley pushed away the cold fear that always hit her at that thought.

No use dwelling on it. That wouldn't help. Deal with what has to be done here and now, she commanded herself.

"All right, I will," she said. She hurried to the wall and took her cloak off its peg, drawing the hood securely around her neck.

Behind her the kitchen door opened. Hayley whirled, to see Ellis closing the door behind him. He was exhausted-looking.

"We need a bucket of hot water," he said, urgency in his voice.

"What's wrong? Is Conn hurt?" Hayley burst out.

Ellis wearily shook his head. "No, no. It's Perdita. She's foaling and the foal's turned wrong. Conn must turn it."

Before the words were out of his mouth, Hayley was across the room, filling a bucket from the big pot of water hanging over the fire.

Ellis's glance found Darryl. Some of the tired lines left his face as he smiled at her. "Are you all right?" he asked.

Darryl's cheeks pinkened. "Of course," she said.

"Thank God. I was so worried."

"There was no need to be," Darryl said, primly, her cheeks warming a bit more.

Ellis crossed the room, took the bucket from Hayley's hands. "Thank you."

"I'm going with you," Hayley said.

"There's no need," Ellis protested. "We can handle this."

"I'm sure you can, but nevertheless I'm going." Her firm voice left no room for argument.

"You may as well save your voice," Agnes said. "If you don't agree, she'll follow along behind you."

Ellis frowned, then nodded. "All right, come along, then, but Conn won't like it."

You may be wrong. Conn might like to see me, she told Ellis, silently.

Aloud, she said, "I'll take along some hot broth from the stew." She found an empty jug and walked to the hearth.

"Yes, that would be good, we're both tired and hungry," Ellis agreed.

"I'll do that," Darryl said, taking the jug from Hayley. She quickly filled the jug with broth and capped it.

"Here, have some now." Darryl handed him the jug.

Surprise filled Ellis's face as he took the proffered jug. He smiled at her. "Thank you."

Darryl gave him a return smile. "You're welcome. I hope all goes well."

"It will. Conn is experienced in these matters."

Hayley tried to keep her own smile from looking so gratified. Out of the corner of her eye she saw that Agnes smiled too.

Darryl suddenly seemed to realize everyone was looking at her. Her face reddened, and she turned and went back to the hearth.

Ellis drank a portion of the contents, then handed the jug to Hayley. He gave Darryl one last glance, but she was turned to the fire, stirring it with the poker, although it didn't need it.

The walk to the barn, in the windy, rainy dark, following in Ellis's surefooted wake, made Hayley glad she hadn't started out alone. The night was dark and moonless, and she'd have strayed from the path many times before reaching her destination.

At the barn, she gasped at the damage to the stables. A flickering light came from a stall in the sound part, and Hayley heard soft murmurs as they approached.

Conn soothed Perdita, who was straining and heaving, her sides slick with sweat. The strong features of his face were set in lines of worry and exhaustion.

"Here. Let's get at it." Ellis set the bucket of water down beside Conn, handing him a sliver of soap.

Conn turned, surprise going over his features when he saw Hayley. "What are you doing here?"

But he didn't look or sound displeased.

"I wanted to come," she said, simply.

Conn nodded, then quickly scrubbed his hands, shaking the moisture from them when he'd finished.

Staying out of the way, Hayley watched as Conn inserted his hand into the mare and slowly and carefully performed the delicate maneuver.

Minutes later, a long-legged chestnut foal stood on trembling legs beside its mother, nuzzling at her sides while Perdita nudged it gently in the right direction.

Conn washed his hands in the bucket again, while Ellis rubbed Perdita dry.

"She's so beautiful," Hayley breathed, awed and enchanted with the miracle of birth.

Conn came to stand beside her, sliding his hand around her waist beneath her heavy cloak. "Perdita always throws good foals," he said, satisfaction in his voice that all had ended well. "And as you say, this little filly is a beauty."

She shivered at his touch, the feel of his big hand working its usual magic on her senses. She wanted to melt into his arms, here, now, let his mouth and touch possess her.

She remembered the broth she'd brought. "Here," she said, handing him the jug. "Drink this. You look as if you need it."

Reluctantly, he withdrew his arm and did as she asked. After he'd finished, Hayley slipped the jug back into her cloak's capacious pocket.

Ellis finished rubbing Perdita dry. He glanced at Hayley and Conn, still standing very close together, then picked up the bucket. "I'm going back to the house if you don't need me any longer."

"Go ahead," Conn said, absentmindedly, his head turned toward Hayley.

Ellis left.

She drew in her breath. Passion smoldered in Conn's dark eyes. He wanted her as much as she wanted him.

She turned toward him and lifted her head for his kiss. He groaned deep in his throat and covered her mouth with his own. She pressed herself closer to his hard body, feeling his arousal, his need for her as great as hers for him.

And she felt something else. His wet clothes, the incipient shiver that had nothing to do with the fire leaping between them.

She forced herself to break the contact of their mouths, to move away from him. "You're chilled to the bone. You must go back to the house and get out of these wet clothes or you'll take a bad chill."

He frowned at her, frustration drawing his mouth into a tight line. At last he reluctantly nodded. "You're right."

"Let us go, then." Hayley started to turn away, still feeling desire throbbing through her with every heartbeat.

He grasped her arm, holding her back. "Wait," he commanded.

She turned to look at him.

"Will you come to my bedchamber tonight?"

She drew in her breath at his words, knowing what they meant. Knowing she wanted that, too. With everything inside her.

"Yes, I will come."

CHAPTER NINETEEN

The house was finally quiet, a late-night calm pervading it. All were abed and asleep, Hayley hoped.

Except for Conn, of course. Her heartbeat quickened.

No, he must be awake. Lying on his bed. Waiting for her. Her heart seemed to be crowding her chest until she could scarcely breathe.

She quietly slid out of the bed she shared with Darryl, casting a quick glance toward her sister.

Darryl's breath was even and regular. The sleep of the exhausted. But she was out of danger now.

Hayley could slip away without fear of leaving her sister alone.

But she was fearful of what this night would bring.

No . . . not fearful. She joyfully anticipated what would happen between her and Conn.

But still . . . something nipped at her nerves, made her quiver with a kind of anxiety.

Before this night was out, she would be a maiden no longer.

The quiver nipped at her again. She pushed it aside, concentrating on the joy she felt.

She tiptoed to the door, turning as she opened it to glance again at Darryl. Her sister hadn't moved. She still slept, peacefully.

Hayley closed the door behind her, blessing its silent hinges. She walked down the attic stairs to the second floor. The long hall stretched before her. Agnes's bedchamber was the first on the left, Lavena's next to it. Then Ellis's. On the right was a small chamber used as a storeroom.

Next to it was Conn's bedchamber.

Hayley shivered as she looked at Conn's door. All she need do was walk over, push the latch down . . . and Conn would welcome her inside. . . .

Wouldn't he? What if he'd changed his mind since they'd returned from the barn with the welcome news of Perdita's successful foaling?

She glanced down at herself. Clad only in her shift, she felt woefully underdressed. Maybe she should go back upstairs and put on her day gown.

Maybe she should go back upstairs and stay.

She hesitated, then half-turned to flee. A noise stopped her, made her whirl.

Conn stood in his doorway, wearing only his breeches.

Hayley drew in her breath. She'd known his chest was broad, but . . . not how magnificent he would look standing before her like this, with his black hair tousled, his dark eyes gazing into her own, the smile on his firm, sensual lips beckoning to her.

He moved back a step, his outstretched hand beckoning to her, too. "Come," he said, his voice low and soft.

Her heartbeat quickened. She hadn't made a fool of herself by coming to his chamber. He still wanted her . . . just as she wanted him.

She walked inside. His bedchamber was familiar to her. She'd been in it many times before, cleaning. She'd often smoothed up his bed, with its coverlet of dark blue, dusted the small chest alongside it, swept the bare, polished wood floor with its small wine-colored rug by the bed.

But tonight, dimly lit with two small candles on the chest,

it looked different. The bedcoverings were turned down, invitingly.

Her mind gave Hayley pictures of her lying on the bed, Conn bending over her. . . .

He drew her farther inside and closed the door. He stood there looking at her for a long moment, his dark face serious, his hand still warm on her arm.

"I've had second thoughts since I left you earlier," he said. "I didn't intend to press you. If you want, we'll wait until our wedding night."

Wait? How could she wait until that time still weeks in the future? She shook her head. "No. I don't want to wait," she assured him.

A slow smile curved his lips upward. "I hoped you'd say that. Neither do I."

His hand slid around her shoulders, pulled her closer. Like her, he'd bathed. He smelled cleanly of soap, with an undertone of some scent that was all his own. She'd know it anywhere.

His hard, bare chest pressed against the softness of her breasts. She felt the warmth of his skin through the thin cloth of her shift.

Nothing had ever felt so good . . . except the touch of his lips on hers . . . the feel of his hands sliding down her back . . .

She pressed herself closer against him, molding her body to the hard contours of his own. She lifted her head. Amazed at her boldness, she whispered, "Kiss me."

Jane's soft body against his own inflamed Conn, made him tremble with desire. He gazed down at her upturned face, his heart melting with love. Her wonderful blue eyes, fringed with long, honey-colored lashes, gazed into his. Her fair skin, her long, flaxen hair, now loose and flowing down her back, shone in the flickering candlelight.

She was altogether desirable.

"I will do that," he answered, lowering his head, claiming her lips with his own. She tasted so delicious. Her mouth was so sweet, so sweet.

Part of him wanted to linger like this forever . . . and another, more urgent part, demanded he go faster, reach that ultimate joining they both craved. He fought that part, knowing he must go slowly.

He closed his eyes, savoring the feel of her softness against his hardness . . . his fast increasing hardness.

He drew away a little, wanting to prolong this, not wanting to rush Jane. But her nearness, her touch sent arrows of flame through him. He could stand little more of this without exploding.

Her flushed face, her slightly open mouth, made him groan, made him renew the kiss, deepen it. His tongue sought hers and found it. For a moment she hesitated, then circled her tongue around his, and they began the age-old mating game.

At last they drew apart, both gasping for breath. Her round breasts rose and fell beneath the thin cloth of her shift, the rosy nipples clearly outlined.

Conn's hot mouth found one, suckled it. Jane's soft gasp, her tighter grip on his shoulder, inflamed him more. His lower body tightened, heated. He drew in a shaky breath and lifted his head, smiled down at her.

"Why are we standing in the middle of the room when a comfortable bed sits just over there . . . waiting?"

She stared at him, her eyes widening. Her tongue came out and licked at her delectable lips. "I don't know," she finally whispered. "Why are we?"

"No reason!" Conn scooped her up in his arms and strode across the room. He threw the bedcovers all the way back with one hand, and laid her gently onto the sheet.

Her shift outlined her body . . . the body he longed to touch, to caress.

To enter and claim as his own.

"We have too many clothes on." He tugged at the shift's hem, Jane lifting herself to aid his efforts. In a moment, it was off.

He drew in his breath. Her pale, lovely body glowed in the candlelight. Her full breasts, with their rosy nipples, were still hardened from his kisses. Her waist nipped in, then rounded below into lush curves.

His gaze lowered. The sight of the pale curls between her slim thighs tightened his body even more.

"Beautiful," he breathed. "You are surpassingly beautiful."

Without warning, a sharp pain hit his chest. He had a sense of déjà vu . . . as if he'd spoken these very words before . . . in just this manner . . . in just this place.

Marie. Oh, God, Marie.

For a moment, the vision of Marie's lush body, her black hair tumbling over her white shoulders, her mocking smile, superimposed itself over Jane's.

Violently, he pushed the image aside, banishing it to the darkest part of his mind. No! Jane was in no way like Marie. She was good and sweet and truthful. Deceitfulness was foreign to her nature.

He would not let memories of his hellish marriage spoil this night.

Swiftly, he rid himself of his own clothes, slid into the bed, drew Jane to him, gasping as the full length of their naked bodies touched, then clung together. "You feel so good," Conn whispered, his tongue curling around her earlobe.

Hayley shivered at that touch, so small, yet somehow so intimate. She pressed herself closer to Conn's body, tingles of delight quivering through her nerve endings at every place bare flesh met bare flesh.

She'd never dreamed anything could feel so wonderful. So right and perfect.

She pressed herself closer, gasping again as Conn's manhood, hard and long, pushed against the softness at the juncture of her thighs.

A small thrill of fear shot through her. Soon he would be inside her . . . and how would that feel? Would it hurt? How could it not?

Conn's lips found her breast again, with no barrier of cloth between them now. His tongue circled a nipple, leaving a trail of heat. Then his teeth nipped at the tip, tugging gently. He moved to the other breast.

Deep inside her, something tightened, and an ache began. A feeling of incompleteness . . . that only Conn could resolve . . .

She slid a hand up to curve around the muscled hardness of his shoulder, let it slide downward to find the nipples on his own chest, tease them with her fingertips. She felt his instant tension, and moved her hand farther downward . . . let her fingers circle in the dark curls there. Then lower still.

Conn jerked himself away from her, his breath coming in short gasps. "Do you know what you're about, Jane?" he asked. "I wanted to go slowly, but if you do that for another moment, I can't be responsible for my actions."

She stared at him in the dim light, her fear vanishing, glorying in his feelings for her, her power over him. Her lips curved upward.

"Maybe we've waited long enough," she suggested, then drew in her breath at her boldness of speech, her own sudden wish to complete what they'd begun.

He blinked in surprise, then smiled himself. "Perhaps you're right." He moved over her, his bent knees straddling her.

Fear hit her again for a brief moment, then as quickly left. This was Conn. He had never hurt her. He never would.

She wanted this as much as he did.

He found her lips again, and lowered himself until their bodies again touched from mouth to toe. They fit together perfectly as if they were made for each other. Conn left her mouth, kissed a trail from her throat down to her stomach. He curled his tongue into the small indentation of her navel, then moved lower. . . .

Hayley's body involuntarily arched against his seeking mouth. "Enough," she cried. "Enough."

He lifted his head. "Oh, no, it's not nearly enough, sweet. Before this night is through, we will have tasted all the delights that men and women can pleasure themselves with."

Hayley moved her legs restlessly. "That's not what I mean. I—"

"I know what you mean." He smiled down at her. "I know just what you mean."

Gently, he nudged her thighs apart and pressed himself against her. Hayley tensed against the pain she expected, but all she felt was a slight discomfort, and then he was inside her, filling her.

She gasped with relief and delight.

He stopped, looking down at her. "Are you all right? Am I hurting you?"

"No," she reassured him. "You're not hurting me at all."

His smile returned. "Good." His voice contained both satisfaction and relief. He sought her lips again, his tongue thrusting into her mouth while his body sought its own completion inside hers.

Hayley's untutored body seemed to know what to do, she found, her delight increasing. She wrapped her arms around Conn's neck and closed her eyes, abandoning herself to pure feeling and touch, glorying in the heat and the movement, the instinctive rhythm their bodies fell into.

The candle sputtered and went out, leaving them in a heated darkness that only intensified the feelings. Conn's mouth sought hers again and again as he made her his own, until she wasn't sure where his body left off and hers began.

She felt herself drawn up and up into a vortex of pure pleasure. The darkness was splintered with light, with a feeling she'd never known existed. Conn gasped into her mouth, holding her tightly, ever more tightly. . . .

Finally, they lay beside each other, bodies still clinging. Conn's heart thundered against her breasts. Against his chest, her own heart echoed its beat, her body trembling in satisfied exhaustion.

"You are sweet, so sweet," Conn murmured in her ear. "I never dreamed it would be like this, since you are . . . were a maid."

"Neither did I," Hayley said, drowsily. She moved a little nearer to him, curved her hand around his waist. Her eyelids fluttered closed and she slept.

Conn held her while his body slowly returned to normal. Remembering, savoring what had happened between them. He'd expected awkwardness, some fear and pain for Jane. Having to go slowly to ease the newness for her.

None of that had happened. Jane had fitted into his arms, welcomed him into her body as if they'd been with each other a dozen, a hundred times before.

There had been no awkwardness at all. She'd moved with him like a dream.

Their moments of joy had come almost together.

That place of darkness in his brain stirred. *So did Marie please you until you were lost,* it whispered, silkily, like an evil serpent. *You never dreamed Marie had given herself to other men before you, until she told you . . . afterward. Laughed at you for being such a gullible fool.*

His body grew rigid. He listened to the voice for a moment . . . considered its words . . .

No! Violently, he rejected those thoughts, forced the darkness into the back of his mind.

He must forget Marie. He must not let her spoil his forthcoming marriage to Jane.

Jane was good and beautiful and true, he repeated to himself like a litany. Just because she'd responded to him with abandon and passion didn't mean she'd had other men before him.

It only meant she loved him as he loved her, he told himself, firmly.

Regretfully, he woke her, sending her off to her own chamber with lingering kisses.

"Soon, my darling, we'll sleep the night together," he whispered as he quietly opened the door for her.

"Yes." She gave him a smile of such sweetness his heart turned over.

He watched her go and went back to his lonely bed, wishing Jane were still enfolded warmly in his arms.

And sleep was a long time in coming.

CHAPTER TWENTY

"You be the fairest maid who ever wed."

Darryl's voice cracked on the last word. She'd lapsed into Suffolk country talk this morning as she helped Hayley prepare for her wedding.

Her sister was making a valiant effort to pretend that she felt lighthearted and gay. That this was an entirely joyful occasion.

Hayley swallowed, her throat tight with conflicting emotions. How she wished this day could be wholly merry, full of the joy of the occasion, with no undertones of fear and grief to mar it.

But of course it couldn't. Not with things as they were.

She gave her sister a smile. "I hope that I am at least present-able," she answered, trying to keep her voice light.

Darryl managed a wan return smile. "Your gown is lovely."

Hayley looked down at the gown in which she would be married in less than an hour. Its embroidered overskirt, ivory petticoat and pleated underbodice made it by far the nicest gown she'd ever worn.

No, not worn, *owned,* she corrected herself.

Far more elaborate than this was the blue velvet one she'd
worn to the Findleys' party.

Which had been Conn's first wife's wedding gown.

A knot formed in her stomach at this thought, and she quickly
brushed it aside.

"Yes," she said, "How I wish our parents were here today."

Darryl nodded, her face growing sober. "I miss them so
much."

"As do I. Your gown is also beautiful," Hayley quickly
added to get the sad look off her sister's face.

Darryl wore a plainer blue gown, but its taffeta bow and
gauzy scarf were very becoming to her. She shrugged, but she
glanced down at her gown and smoothed one of the bows.

The small gesture heartened Hayley. Her sister was gradually
coming out of her shock and fear. She could take pleasure in
a pretty gown once more.

Darryl gave her a sudden direct look. "Are you going to tell
Conn about . . . us?"

Hayley's already tight nerves drew even more strained.
Hadn't she asked herself this question on many a sleepless
midnight?

And come to the same conclusion each time.

"Of course not," she said, calmly. "You know I wouldn't
do that."

Darryl's direct gaze didn't waver. "That is fine now, before
you are wed. But what about after . . . when you and he . . ."

Sister, sister, Hayley wanted to tell her. *Our wedding night
will hold no surprises for me. Will not tempt me to loosen my
tongue after passion has lowered my defenses. Conn and I've
already come to know each other in the deepest sense a woman
and man can, and more than once.*

But of course she couldn't say that.

Darryl still refused to believe that Hayley was marrying Conn
because she loved him.

Darryl still feared the physical ties that bound a woman to
a man. Feared what the marriage would do to Hayley.

And what it might do to Darryl, too.

"I will never tell anyone," Hayley again reassured her sister, putting the ring of conviction into her voice.

Darryl visibly relaxed. A faint smile even turned up her lips a tiny bit. She moved to Hayley, embraced her and kissed her. "I do wish you happiness, sister, dear," she said. "It's just that I don't see how—"

"Either of us can find any peace or security with the secrets we must hide?" Hayley finished.

Darryl nodded. "Yes," she said, the somberness back in her eyes.

Hayley expelled a sigh. "We must keep our spirits up, and hope no one finds us. That they'll finally give up the search."

"Do you think 'tis likely? For a murderess?"

"We've heard nothing more of a search being conducted in this area lately," she reminded Darryl. "Except for a middle-aged man that Conn mentioned a few days ago. And no one has ever spoken of a search for a murderess."

Darryl nodded again, then lifted her head. "I'm sorry to be so glum on your wedding day. I promise that I'll say and do no more to spoil it for you."

"Thank you. Now, I suppose we'd better go on downstairs."

"Yes. I wish no one else were coming. I do so fear to meet strangers who might look at us and remember someth—"

Darryl broke off, put her hand over her mouth. "I am sorry again."

"It's all right," Hayley reassured her. She, too, wished no strangers had been invited to the wedding. It was bad enough that the Findleys and the Walbridges would be there. She didn't look forward to listening to Louisa Findley's complaining, to trying to avoid Vaughn Walbridge's sly glances for the evening.

But there would be several other families, too. Strangers, as Darryl had said.

She tried to dismiss the disturbing thoughts, straightened her shoulders and walked down the attic stairs with Darryl. Last night had been the last time they'd share this bedchamber.

Tonight and every night thereafter, she'd share Conn's bedchamber on the second floor.

Openly. That would be such a relief.

They walked down the second flight, then entered the kitchen. It was bustling. Lavena had hired two local girls to help with cooking and serving. Now they hurried to and fro, with Lavena, dressed in a new gown, giving crisp orders.

Agnes sat in her usual chair by the fire. Today she was dressed in her best dark green gown, garnet ear bobs in her lobes. She glanced up and gave Darryl and Hayley a delighted smile.

"Girls! You both look so lovely."

Lavena paused for a second. She nodded at them, her expression neutral.

Since the day of the hurricane when Agnes had announced her plans to leave her property to Darryl and Hayley, Lavena had been a changed woman. She kept to herself now, quieter than Hayley would ever have thought possible.

She was no longer overtly critical of Hayley and Darryl. In fact, she seemed to have lost interest in life, going about her chores by rote, and retiring to her chamber as soon as the day's work was finished.

Hayley felt sorry for the older woman now that her sharp tongue wasn't lashing her twenty times a day. Agnes's decision had shocked Lavena so profoundly, sometimes Hayley thought she'd never get over it.

And she wished Agnes had never made that decision, although she knew it eased Darryl's mind, gave her a feeling of security she'd never dreamed she could have.

"It's almost time for the ceremony. The minister is here, and all the guests," Agnes continued, her old face alight with anticipation. "I declare, we do have a houseful. We invited more than enough people as it was, but the Findleys brought along a cousin and her fiancé."

"Two more people won't make any difference," Lavena spoke up, still in that colorless voice.

"But a sourer-faced woman I've never seen than that Mrs. Whitley," Agnes continued. "No wonder she's a widow. Her husband was probably glad to die to get away from her."

Hayley stiffened. *Mrs. Whitley?* She gave Darryl a sideways glance. Her sister's eyes were wide. She clenched her hands at her sides. Hayley tried to dismiss her fears.

This couldn't be the same woman who'd been Oscar Pritt's housekeeper. What would she be doing here?

"And she looks as if she hadn't had a good meal in ten years," Agnes went on, shaking her head. "Can't understand why any man in his right mind would want to marry her. She won't be able to warm his bed on cold nights."

Hayley's alarm increased. A very thin, sour woman? Although Hayley had never seen the woman, that perfectly fit Darryl's and Cilla's description of Mrs. Whitley.

"She's a good, churchgoing woman," Lavena said, still in that colorless voice. "Louisa Findley told me all about her. She had a respected position as a housekeeper on a big plantation in the north of Delaware. She is very knowledgeable about running a household."

With a rush, Hayley's memories of the Findleys' party returned. Someone had mentioned a cousin who worked as a housekeeper on a northern plantation. She and Darryl had been worried for a few moments, then had forgotten it in the shock of the announcement of a search for a runaway bond servant. . . .

Darryl moved closer to Hayley, then reached for her arm. Darryl's fingers were like ice gripping Hayley's flesh.

Fear drummed in Hayley's veins. Her leg muscles were jumping. It was all she could do to keep from grabbing Darryl's hand and running headlong from the room, from Holly View.

She forced herself to remain still. She hoped her expression didn't show her feelings.

"My goodness, but you look pale, dear girl," Agnes said sharply. "Come, do sit down. I know how you feel. I well remember how I felt on my wedding day. Why, I fainted dead away, if you can believe that."

Gratefully, Hayley sat on a cushioned bench beside Agnes, moving over to make room for Darryl.

"I'll go get the milk from the springhouse," Darryl said, her voice tight and breathy.

"No, it's too soon," Lavena said. "Wait until after the ceremony."

The marriage ceremony. Dear God, how could she stand in front of Mrs. Whitley and repeat her marriage vows?

Would the woman stand up during the ceremony and denounce her as a runaway bond servant . . . Darryl as a murderess?

Hayley's knees felt weak and shaky. She managed to stiffen them.

The door to the back stairs opened. "It is time," Conn's deep, dearly loved voice said.

Hayley slowly lifted her head and glanced across the room.

Conn's dark eyes were full of love as he gazed at her. Love for her.

He trusted in her, believed in her.

"You look beautiful," he said. "Come, let us go in and say our vows to each other."

She took his arm. Let him lead her into the other room.

The parlor had been transformed into a bower with sweet-smelling flowers. The door to the dining room was open, flowers in it, too.

She tried not to meet anyone's eye, or look directly at the smiling faces, gazing at her and Conn.

Hayley never knew how she got through the ceremony, never remembered later what she'd said, but they must have been the right things, because no looks of horror appeared on any of the faces in the room.

Afterward, as she and Conn faced the gathering as a newly wed couple, her glance found Darryl.

Her face white and drawn, Darryl was staring toward a thin woman in the back of the room.

The woman stared back, her eyes hard, her lips pursed.

Their nightmare had come true.

CHAPTER TWENTY-ONE

Hayley, still standing with Conn's warm hand encircling her waist, watched her sister.

Darryl stared back at Mrs. Whitley, as bemused as if the other woman were a poisonous snake and had bewitched her with fangs and hisses.

Hayley quailed inside. *Don't show how you fear her,* she silently told Darryl. *That's what she wants.*

Ellis stood beside his mother, giving Darryl a frowning, puzzled look.

"Let us toast the newly wed couple!" Agnes cried. She beckoned to one of the serving women, who hastened over with a tray of filled wine glasses.

Hayley forced herself to turn her attention and her glance away from Darryl and the other woman.

Conn took two glasses and gave one to Hayley, his smile warmer than his hand. His glance was warmer still, full of promises.

Couldn't he feel the sudden tension in her body? Couldn't he see her answering smile was forced? That she was scared to death?

Agnes took a glass of wine and lifted it. "To Conn and Jane Merritt. May their union be joyful and fruitful."

Beside her, Lavena dutifully raised her own glass, her face impassive.

Glass clicked against glass amid approving murmurs from around the crowded room.

Hayley could feel Mrs. Whitley's glare. Although the woman had never seen Hayley, she must realize who she was, from her resemblance to Darryl. And surely the entire story of Hayley's escape from Burle Porter's plantation had been revealed after she and Darryl fled.

Leaving behind a dead man.

Hayley's skin felt icy cold. Her knees were shaking again. Maybe everyone would attribute it to bridal nerves.

What difference did it make, anyway? Soon, any minute now, Mrs. Whitley would raise her long, thin finger and point it at Darryl and then at her and denounce both of them as runaway bond servants, frauds and murderers.

The roomful of people had started talking to one another. Rigid with tension, looking straight ahead, Hayley smiled until her face hurt, while she and Conn accepted congratulations as Mr. and Mrs. Connard Merritt.

Jane Merritt. A stranger's name. Why had she never given any thought to the fact her married name was false?

And what did it matter? She would have no marriage now.

Despair hit her, rolling over her in sickening waves.

Why hadn't Mrs. Whitley said anything? What was she waiting for?

Hayley made herself look around the room again. Darryl was nowhere to be seen. Neither was Mrs. Whitley. What did that mean? Surely, the woman hadn't forced Darryl out of the room?

No, that was impossible. Someone would have noticed.

Somehow, she and Conn were sitting side by side, in the places of honor. Accepting more congratulations and being served food and drink. Hayley kept a constant surreptitious lookout for Darryl or Mrs. Whitley, her fears mounting with every passing moment.

Ellis, holding a wineglass, stood off by himself, a frown still on his face. Like Hayley, he kept glancing toward the door.

Where on earth could Darryl and Mrs. Whitley be? Did Mrs. Whitley have someone drag Darryl off? Was her sister even now arrested?

Of course not, the sensible side of her mind told her. *Don't you think that would have caused enough commotion you'd have noticed?*

Then where are they? she screamed, inwardly.

Conn sought her cold hand and warmed it under his own.

"Why are you nervous, sweetheart?" he murmured in her ear. "I hope we can soon get away from this prattling crowd and . . . be by ourselves."

"It's not every day a woman becomes a wife," she managed to say.

Not many marriages begin and end the same afternoon, either, her mind added.

She glanced around the room again. Her breath caught in her throat.

Darryl and Mrs. Whitley stood side by side in the doorway from the dining room. While she watched, Darryl nodded cordially to the other woman.

Mrs. Whitley stiffly returned the nod, then walked toward a middle-aged man who was talking with Vaughn Walbridge. He greeted her with a fond smile, then found her a seat. Her fiancé, someone had told Hayley.

What on earth was going on?

Smiling, Darryl made her way toward Hayley. Ellis started to walk toward her, then changed his mind and stepped back, still frowning. She didn't seem to notice him at all.

Darryl's cheeks were flushed, Hayley saw, her eyes bright. She looked for all the world as if she had nothing more serious on her mind than greeting her newly wed sister with wishes for a happy future.

Darryl stopped before Hayley. She hugged Hayley, then kissed her cheek. "Sister, I'm so happy for you."

She turned to Conn, hugged him, too, kissed his cheek. "I'd like to borrow Jane for a few moments," she said, prettily.

Conn gave her a curious glance. No wonder. He'd never seen or heard Darryl like this. So at ease. So much the way she used to be before those terrible things had happened to them and their family.

"Of course," he said, then gave Hayley a loving, smiling glance. "But don't keep her too long."

"I won't," Darryl promised. Her gaze met Hayley's. She gave Hayley a tiny nod, as if to tell her everything was all right.

Hayley rose and followed her sister through the crowd, into the kitchen, where the serving girls still bustled about. Lavena was there, too, her back turned as she directed a girl.

Darryl put her finger to her lips and led Hayley out the door to the back stairs, closing it behind her, shutting themselves into sudden silence.

One of the kittens came out from its nest under the stairs and meowed at Darryl, plainly wanting her usual attention.

Darryl scooped it up and hugged it, then gently set it down again. "Later, Mischief," she promised. She turned to Hayley. "Come on, quickly."

Hayley followed her up the stairs to their bedchamber, where Darryl closed the door behind them, and whirled to face Hayley.

"What has happened?" Hayley asked, her voice urgent.

Darryl took in a breath and released it. "A great deal, sister dear. Mrs. Whitley's no longer a threat to us."

"What?" Hayley cried. "How can that be? I saw the look she gave you when she first saw you."

Darryl nodded. "But did you see how politely we parted company later?"

"Yes," Hayley admitted. "By what miracle did this happen?"

"No miracle. We went outside to talk . . . and discovered

both of us have more to lose by revealing certain things than if we keep quiet."

Hayley stared at her. "Do you mean she agreed not to say anything about us to the authorities?"

"Yes. And in exchange I agreed not to let anyone, especially her well-to-do fiancé, know that not too long ago, she warmed the bed of her employer."

Hayley's mouth dropped open. She gazed at her sister with admiration. "How could you think of doing that?"

Darryl shrugged, the animated look leaving her face.

"When one is desperate, the mind works very cleverly. Mrs. Whitley is desperate, also. This is her chance to marry well, be taken care of in her old age. She's not going to let anything ruin that for her."

Hayley swallowed. "Even if it means . . ."

"Yes, even if it means letting a murderess go free," Darryl finished, a bitter edge to her voice. "Or what the world would consider a murderess."

Hayley went to Darryl, hugged her close. "Do you think she'll keep her word?"

"Oh, yes. She has too much to lose, and nothing to gain but spiteful satisfaction if she turns us in. We're safe . . . for the moment, anyway."

For the moment. The words rang hollowly in Hayley's ears. Was the rest of their lives going to be like this? With never a feeling of real security?

"You were very brave and clever," Hayley told her. "I wouldn't have. . . ." Her voice trailed off.

"You wouldn't have believed that this pitiful shell I've become could rally like that?" Darryl finished, still with that bitter note in her voice.

She straightened her shoulders, firmed her mouth. "As I said, sister, desperation oils the mind's hinges. I'll do anything to keep from being hanged for killing Oscar Pritt."

"And so will I to keep that from happening," Hayley answered.

She would, too. She had to. Even if it meant that Conn would never know the truth about his wife.

Not even her true name.

She summoned a smile for Darryl. Brave, clever Darryl, who'd used her courage and her brains wisely today.

Who was almost back to her old self again.

Hayley linked her arm in Darryl's. "Let's go back downstairs."

"Yes." Darryl smiled at her. "You must return to your new husband." Her smile faltered for a moment, then recovered.

She gave Hayley a look full of caring. "I know that you and Conn deeply love each other," she said. "I'm sorry for what I said that first day. You could never enter into marriage without love."

"Thank you, sister," Hayley said, her voice husky.

For the first time since the day Conn had asked her to marry him, she felt the old, cherished closeness to Darryl.

Darryl touched her sister's cheek, tears bright on her lashes. Then she blinked them away and smiled.

"Mrs. Whitley promised she'd soon develop a terrible headache and would have to leave the festivities."

Hayley let out a relieved sigh. "Thank God for that."

She'd go back downstairs, she'd smile and be polite to the guests.

And she would try to make Conn a good, loving wife.

The kitchen was empty, to Hayley's surprise. She lingered a moment, dreading going back into the crowd of people. Darryl scooped up a platter of sliced meats. "I'll take this in. Are you coming?"

"In a few moments."

"Don't be long." Darryl smiled at her and turned to leave. As she opened the door, she almost ran into Ellis. The platter wavered in her hands, and he caught it before it fell.

"I'll carry that in for you," he said.

Darryl hesitated, then relinquished it. "All right."

The door closed behind them.

If anyone could win over her sister, could make her forget

the terrible events that had befallen her, it would be Ellis, Hayley thought. He had patience and to spare.

And he'd need all of it.

She walked to the fire, held out her hands to the blaze. She was still trembling with reaction from the terrible fright she'd had with Mrs. Whitley. She must get herself under control before she went back in to Conn.

To her husband.

A different kind of shiver went over her at that thought. Conn loved her enough to make her his wife. She loved him just as much.

The door to the dining room opened, then closed. Hayley sighed. Her solitude was already invaded. She turned, expecting one of the serving girls.

Radley Walbridge stood just inside the door, looking at her. He was dressed well today—his blue waistcoat quilted and embroidered, silver buckles gleaming on his shoes.

Hayley sighed again, then managed a smile. Radley was tedious, but at least he'd always liked her.

He walked across to where she stood, looked down at her, a sad look now on his handsome face. "How could you wed him?"

At a loss for words, Hayley stared at him in amazement.

He reached down and captured one of her hands. "When you know how I care for you."

She recoiled. The smell of liquor on his breath was overpowering. "Don't be ridiculous. Why, you hardly know me!" She jerked at her hand, but he was much stronger than she.

"I knew from the first moment I met you I wanted you for my wife."

"Jane. What are you doing in here?"

Conn's voice erupted into the room.

Radley started and dropped her hand, then moved away and turned toward Conn.

"Merritt, I was just congratulating your new wife," he said in a falsely hearty tone.

Hayley cringed. How much had Conn heard? Only those last

words with Radley holding her hand? Oh, how she'd like to pick up the fire pail from the hearth and hit Radley over the head with it.

Conn walked across to where they stood. Hayley smiled at him, reached out her hand.

Without smiling or taking her hand, he turned away, toward Radley. "I accept your felicitations on our marriage," he said, coldly.

Radley nodded. "Yes, well, I must go." He bowed, then hurriedly left the room, his gait a bit weaving.

Conn stared after him, his profile showing her the muscle clenching in his jaw.

Was he jealous of Radley? Oh, that was absurd. Then she remembered the remark he'd made about her dancing with Radley at the Findleys' party.

Remembered what his first wife had been like.

Should she try to explain? No, she decided. That would only draw attention to the incident. She'd give Conn an opening, let him question her if he wanted—and she hoped he'd realized Radley was in his cups.

She reached out her hand again and laid it upon the hard muscles of his forearm. "Conn," she said, softly. "What is wrong?"

For several more moments, he kept his rigid stance. Then she heard him exhale. He turned back to her, still not smiling, but at least not scowling now.

"Anna told me you'd stayed in here. I was looking for you."

His voice was even, not showing the anger she was certain he'd felt, might still feel. She forced another smile.

"Yes. I dreaded to face all those people again. I'm glad you're here. Do we have to go back in there?" The pleading in her voice was genuine. She truly didn't want to go back to the crowd.

But she also wanted to allay any dark thoughts he might have had about finding Radley here with her. She couldn't bear it if he had any suspicions, however foolish, of her being like his first wife.

You're more like her than you want to admit, her mind said. *You've deceived Conn, just as she did.*

But it's not the same! she silently protested. *I have to, unless I'm willing to see Darryl hang for murder.*

Conn kept his serious expression for moments longer. Then he smiled at her. "I believe it's forgivable for the bride and groom to slip away to their chamber. But we must say our good nights first."

That prospect made her shudder. She slid her hand up his arm, fitting it inside the curve of his elbow. "I suppose, then, we'd better go back."

"It will soon be over," he promised her, his smile widening, warming. He bent and kissed her lightly, then more deeply.

"You're mine now, Jane," he said. "I don't want anyone to forget that."

His possessive kiss and words sent a thrill through her. "And you're mine, too," she reminded him, tilting her head up toward him, meeting his dark gaze with hers.

His face lightened at her words. "Yes. And I most certainly won't forget that."

A cozy blaze crackled in the fireplace in Conn's bedchamber. Two small armchairs were drawn up before it. Conn sat in one, holding a glass of wine. Firelight flickered through it, changing its garnet color to ruby.

He'd removed his waistcoat, wore only his fine white shirt, partly unbuttoned, revealing the dark curls on his chest. His black hair was rumpled. Hayley ached to open his shirt all the way, to rumple his hair even more.

But she wouldn't. She would let him make the first move.

Still in her own bridal finery, Hayley sat in the other chair, her hands outstretched toward the welcome heat of the fire, her glass of wine sitting on a low chest between them.

She stole a glance at her new husband and drew in her breath. In profile, his strong, regular features looked hard and set. A muscle in his jaw flickered.

Was he thinking about finding her with Radley in the kitchen? Was he still upset about it?

Surely not. Surely he'd realized long before now that meant nothing. If Conn had seen Radley holding her hand, he'd realized Radley had taken her unawares, that his words were prompted by the liquor he'd consumed, not by anything she'd said or done to encourage him.

Hadn't he?

Why hadn't she explained fully to him?

It was too late now. She didn't want to bring it up to give it undue importance. Perhaps he wasn't even thinking about that. Maybe he was just tired.

She felt her body tensing with worry, and reached for her wine. She took a generous swallow, savoring its heat as it slid down her throat. She reached across the space separating them and touched her glass to his. The crystal gave off a tiny, bell-like ring.

"Everyone toasted our health and our new life. But we didn't," she said.

He turned his dark head toward her.

Hayley smiled at him, slowly and sweetly. She lifted her glass. "May our life together be long, happy and . . . fruitful."

When his own smile came, it dazzled her.

"We will make it so." He touched her glass with his again and they both drank.

When Conn put his glass down on the chest, it was empty. He reached for the decanter and poured himself another glass and drank it. After he set the empty glass down this time, he left it there.

He lifted his head and looked at her, his dark eyes gleaming. He took her wine glass out of her hand and set it beside his own. "Are you ready for bed, Mrs. Merritt?"

Hayley nodded, relief filling her. Whatever had been wrong with Conn, if, indeed, anything had, he seemed to be over it. He was once again the man who'd almost made love to her on the sweet meadow grass.

Who *had* made love to her in this very chamber several times before.

Conn rose, took her hands and lifted her to stand before him. She went into his arms and they kissed, long and deeply.

Hand in hand, they walked toward the bed. Conn sat down on it, kicked off his shoes and quickly shed the rest of his clothes. Gloriously naked, he beckoned to her, pulling her down on his lap.

She gasped as she felt how very ready he was. He kissed her, making quick work of her gown fastenings while doing so. He slid the gown off her shoulders, kissing his way down the exposed flesh as he went. Her shift was next, sliding to her waist.

"You are so beautiful."

Conn successfully fought down the last remnants of his dark thoughts. He looked at Jane's delectable breasts, and felt himself hardening even more.

His wife. His beautiful young wife.

He'd keep repeating those words to himself until no vestige of Marie's memory colored them. Until only Jane's face and body, her essential sweetness and goodness filled his mind's eye.

He would forget he'd seen Radley Walbridge holding her hand in the kitchen, heard him murmuring to her. Seen her flush.

Why hadn't he asked Jane about that? Was he afraid of hearing what she'd say?

More importantly, why hadn't Jane explained without him asking?

He'd forget all that. It hadn't meant anything. It couldn't mean anything. It was plain Radley had been drinking. His uncertain gait proved that. The man was obviously attracted to Jane, and just got a little carried away.

So he would put it out of his mind and spend the night making love to his lovely wife.

In moments the remainder of her clothes lay on the floor with his own. He lay down on his back on the bed, pulling her with him. The feel of her soft breasts pressed against his chest, her lower body against his hardness, inflamed him with desire.

"You are mine, all mine," he exulted, raining kisses down her face, her throat. "I love you more than I can say."

She gave a little gasping sigh and smiled. "I love you, too. And I will love you forever." She sought his lips, pressed her own against them.

A wave of happiness went through Conn. This was a new start. They would have a good marriage.

He gave himself up to the kiss, to her lips and body, as desire swept them both into a world of sensual delight.

CHAPTER TWENTY-TWO

Darryl opened the back stairs door into the kitchen and stopped short in the doorway.

The room was empty except for Ellis. He sat at the kitchen table, a tankard of ale lifted to his lips. Seeing her, he set it down with a thump and quickly rose.

Darryl whirled, started to retreat, then stopped. She was acting like a simpleton. She couldn't run like a silly goose every time she saw Ellis.

Mischief, the calico kitten who now followed her everywhere and slept on her bed at night, tumbled down the last stair and ran over to her, rubbing against her ankles and purring. Mischief was a comfort now that Hayley no longer shared her bed since her marriage to Conn a month ago.

"Anna," Ellis said from behind her. "Don't run away just because I'm here."

He was so close she felt his warm breath on her neck. She gave an involuntary shiver, hoping he didn't notice. "I'm not running away," she said without turning.

"That's what it looks like to me."

"I—just remembered something I left upstairs." *Where was*

everyone? Why didn't someone come in and rescue her from this encounter?

"Fine," Ellis said, his voice firm. "Go on and get it and I'll wait."

She tensed even more. This wasn't going to be easy. "I'm sure you have work to do," she got out.

Where was Hayley? Agnes? She'd even welcome Lavena right now.

"Since the harvest is in, and the barn's nearly rebuilt, work has slacked off. I have free time now and again."

She was beginning to feel like a true lack-wit standing with her back to him. She felt a light, warm touch on her neck and jerked sideways.

"Must you always act as if I'm planning to attack you every time I touch you?" he asked.

"You startled me," she said, defensively.

"Will you face me?" Ellis demanded. "Your back is nice, but I'd prefer talking to your face."

Reluctantly, Darryl turned.

Even in his working clothes, Ellis was a very good-looking man, she had to admit.

He smiled at her, making a peculiar little ripple move down her spine. "That's much better."

No, it wasn't better. She was too close to him. He was affecting her in a way she never wanted to be affected again. He was making her feel like a woman.

A woman with desires and needs.

Needs that only a man could fill.

Panic overtook her.

She could never trust a man again.

She backed up, knowing the panic showed on her face.

Ellis's smile faded, a concerned look replacing it. "What's happened to you, Anna? What man has so abused you that you fear them all?"

His mouth tightened. "Tell me who the bastard is and I'll kill him."

No, you couldn't. That would be impossible. He's already dead.

A wild impulse to tell him everything rose up in her. What a wonderful relief that would be. She could tell him and he'd take care of it. Take care of her . . .

She opened her mouth to do just that, and then sanity returned. What was wrong with her? He couldn't mend this horrible mess. Couldn't protect her and Hayley. No one could. Their only protection was continued silence.

She shook her head at Ellis. "You're wrong. I'm not afraid of all men. I'm not afraid of you. I just never plan to get involved with any man . . . to ever marry."

His angry expression faded. He gave her a straight look. "And you'd have me believe that you aren't drawn to me as I'm drawn to you?"

She nodded. "That is right," she said, trying to make it sound convincing.

He took a step nearer, put his hand on her arm. She tried to retreat, but his touch felt so good. Maybe she could enjoy it for a few moments. . . .

"I don't believe that. You aren't telling the truth."

His voice was soft, yet compelling. Again, shivers trembled up her arm, down her spine. His dark eyes bored into hers, demanding.

She swallowed. "Yes, I am," she said, faintly.

"No. You're not." He took a step nearer. Gently, he drew her closer.

She didn't resist this time, but let him pull her against his hard body. She rested her head on his chest. His strong, steady heartbeat comforted her, made her feel secure. Some of the constant fear she'd carried all these months eased.

"See, there, that isn't so bad, is it?"

Ellis's soft voice tickled the hair at her temples, made her shiver again. "No, it's nice," she whispered, leaning a little farther into his embrace.

"Nice . . . yes . . . it's very nice."

She felt his warm hand tugging at her chin, tipping her face upward. Again, she made no resistance, only staring at him bemusedly as his head lowered to hers, a lock of his dark hair falling forward.

She lifted her hand, smoothed the hair back, marveling at the feel of it, not rough, as it looked, but a burnished black, smooth with a man's smoothness. . . .

She heard his indrawn breath, the involuntary tug of his hands to draw her closer still.

"Anna," he whispered. "I want to kiss you. Will you let me?"

No, of course she wouldn't. That would be insane.

She tried to shake her head, but her beguiled body refused to make the gesture.

Instead, her lips parted and her head tilted farther upward toward his lowering one.

The first brush of his mouth upon hers made her gasp.

But not retreat.

Ellis pressed his lips more firmly against hers, moving gently across them. She returned the kiss. It seemed impossible not to.

A small satisfied sound came from Ellis. His hands roamed on her back, caressing, pulling her closer to his firm body. She melted against him, her head swimming at the smell of him, the feel of him.

Through the fog surrounding her, she became aware of his lower body pressing against hers. His hard lower body.

Panic flooded her, made her gasp for breath.

She jerked back, pushing against his chest. "Let me go!"

Ellis released her, stepping backward himself. "What's wrong?"

Darryl wildly shook her head. "Everything. Leave me be. Just leave me be."

He regarded her steadily for a few moments, then nodded. "As you wish. But you care for me, no matter how much you try to deny it. And we'll overcome this fear of yours. However long it takes."

He turned and left her standing there in the hallway. Left

her feeling bereft even while the panic still coursed through her body.

Slowly, her short, shallow breaths evened out, regained a normal rhythm. Her heart stopped thundering against her chest wall.

She tried to retreat to that inner place where she felt nothing for Ellis. Where her thoughts were concentrated on her love for Hayley and her fears for their safety.

This time it didn't work.

Ellis's face, his warm lips moving over hers, his strong arms encircling her, remained in her memory, made her own body involuntarily tighten in response to the memories.

We'll overcome these fears of yours, no matter how long it takes.

Could that be possible? Could a time come when the thought, the feel of a man's body against her own didn't frighten her witless?

The thought and feel of *Ellis's* body pressing against her, loving her?

She swallowed, the rest of the panic subsiding. Cautiously, she let this last thought linger, become a part of her.

Maybe it was possible. Maybe someday she could fully welcome Ellis into her heart. Her body. Maybe she could love him back the way he yearned for her to do.

That will be fine, her mind said. *But that won't help with the rest of your problems. Even now, someone may be coming to find you, take you back.*

Hang you.

Conn glanced around his—no, *their* bedchamber with approval. It looked dim and cozy with only one candle lit. Their own little love nest.

One candle was all they needed. He knew Jane's body like his own by now, even if it was scarcely more than a month since they married.

Every curve and hollow . . . and she knew him. Knew how to send desire flaming through him with just a touch . . .

He smiled as Jane removed her undergarments, then quickly reached for her nightrail. Her innate modesty, even after a month of marriage, both amused and touched him.

Not like Marie. His first wife flaunted her naked body, finding a cruel satisfaction in the fact he still desired her, even after she'd revealed her faithlessness.

His mouth tightened. What a fool he'd been. He'd vowed never to be such a besotted idiot ever again.

Yet here he was, exactly as before. Desiring this woman who was his wife so deeply, his thoughts were never far from her no matter what he was doing.

He pushed the dark thoughts far into the back of his mind. No, this wasn't the same as his first marriage. Of course not. Jane was good and sweet and faithful. There wasn't a hurtful bone in her delectable body. She loved him and tried very hard to be a good wife to him in every way possible.

A task at which she was supremely successful. His body began hardening at the thought of their nights together. "Wife, you may as well leave off your nightrail. 'Twill not stay on long in any case."

She glanced at him, a smile curving her lips.

"Are you sure? Might you not want an entire night's rest? There have been few lately."

Her pink lips curved upward even more. An urgent wish to press his lips against hers rose in him. A delightful mixture was his wife—modesty blended with a forthrightness that often surprised him.

He got up from his chair and swiftly shed his own garments. She gave a mischievous glance at the evidence of his readiness and tossed her nightrail to the foot of the bed, then walked to meet him, her arms outstretched.

He loved her body. Her long, slender legs, her nipped-in waist, her rounded, full breasts.

Which, now that he noticed, seemed even fuller than before, yet she'd not gained weight elsewhere.

Jane came into his arms, wrapping her arms around his waist. Conn pulled her closer, lowering his head to meet her upturned one, kissing her.

Her breasts pressed against his chest, inflaming his need. He took his mouth away from hers, lowered his head to her breasts, gently tugged at a soft, pink nipple, which to his gratification, at once hardened in response.

"You seem to have added a bit of weight, wife," he murmured. He lifted his head, giving her a smile.

Her face flooded with color, the half smile fading. Her wonderful blue eyes gazed into his, something odd in their depths. "Yes," she said. "That's true."

"Not that I'm complaining. It's in delightful places."

She visibly swallowed. "There's a reason for that. I—I've been waiting for the right moment to tell you. Perhaps it's now."

Conn gave her a puzzled look. "Right moment? What are you talking about?" Anxiety suddenly filled him. "You're not ill?"

Jane quickly shook her head. "No, no. I'm perfectly well."

She took a deep breath and then smiled, her eyes searching his. "I'm with child."

Conn stared at her, feeling as if all the breath were knocked from his body. His burgeoning desire fled, replaced with a complex mixture of emotions.

A dark memory rose within him. Marie, on their wedding night, telling him of her pregnancy, taunting him that it wasn't his child.

He fought against it, banished it. Forced the good feelings to the surface.

"Wife, that's wonderful news. I'm so happy." And so he was. Of course he was. The wife he loved deeply was carrying his child.

And so soon after the marriage . . .

Why had she been so hesitant to tell him?

Another dark thought raised itself. Jane and Radley in the

kitchen, on their wedding day. Radley holding Jane's hand, murmuring something to her . . .

Swearing inwardly at himself, he banished that thought, too, and enfolded Jane into his arms.

"How long have you known?" he asked her.

"Only a week or so."

Of course it couldn't have been long. They hadn't been married long. . . .

Damn it, he *wouldn't* let his mind do this. Let it spoil this moment of joy.

He reached down and found Jane's chin, tilted her head upward. He gazed into her eyes, smiling tenderly at her, made his voice firm and sure. "You've made me very happy. Now we must pray that all will go well with you . . . and the babe."

A smile curved her lips. She stroked his cheek with her hand. "I'm sure it will. I am from sound stock. My mother was slightly built, like Anna and me, yet she birthed five children with no difficulty."

A nip of anxiety tugged at his insides. He'd never thought about Jane's smallness in that regard before. But of course what she said was true. He remembered women talking about wide-hipped females with approval, saying they were fashioned for easy childbirth.

But he mustn't let Jane see his apprehension or the dark thoughts. All he would let her see was his excitement and joy.

"That's good. I'm sure you're right. Now, let us get to bed. It's late."

He scooped her into his arms, feeling the lightness of her body, another stab of fear going through him.

Marie had been several inches taller than Jane, a good bit heavier. Yet she'd not been able to successfully birth a living child.

The child that, even now, everyone thought had been his own son.

Savagely, he banished that unwelcome thought. Jane would be all right. The babe would be all right.

He carried her to the turned-back bed and gently laid her

down on the sheet. Smiled at her. "You must get plenty of rest now."

Jane smiled back, reached for him. "I will, but it's not that late."

His desire had completely departed. Conn lay down beside her, turned on his side and pulled her close against his chest. "As you said, we've had few full nights of sleep since we wed. I think this should be one of them."

He felt her stiffen. Even in the one candle's dim, flickering light, he saw the tension in her eyes. "Of course you're right. Good night, dear husband."

"Good night, lovely wife," he said in return.

Jane pressed her mouth against his. She seemed to be seeking something more than their usual good night kisses. Some kind of reassurance . . .

Chagrin hit him. What a fool he was. Of course she needed reassurance. Jane knew about Marie. Knew the dark thoughts that still lingered in his mind.

No wonder she'd seemed a bit hesitant to tell him about being with child.

Conn smoothed her flaxen hair back from her forehead, and returned her kiss with a gentle thoroughness that made her relax against him.

He pinched the candle out and settled down to sleep, Jane still nestled sweetly against him.

He couldn't relax. He wasn't at all sleepy.

The vision of Jane and Radley together in the kitchen swam into his mind once more.

Don't be a bigger fool, he advised himself. When would she have had time for dalliance, even if she were so inclined? How could she possibly have secretly met Radley with no one the wiser?

But despite himself, one thought kept running around in his mind.

What if there was another reason for Jane to be hesitant about telling him she was with child?

CHAPTER
TWENTY-THREE

"We have something to tell all of you," Conn said, his voice firm.

His arm around Hayley's waist also felt firm and reassuring. Yet at the same time, his grip seemed a bit too tight.

Almost as if he were trying to reassure himself as well as her. Tension grew in her stomach.

It was the morning following the night she'd told Conn about the babe-to-be. Breakfast was over, although everyone was still in the dining room.

All during the meal she'd dreaded this moment, her stomach so tight she had to force herself to eat, knowing she must think of the babe's well-being above all else.

How would Lavena react to this news? With the anger and resentment she'd undoubtedly feel? Would she show those feelings openly? No, probably not. Lavena had shown no strong feelings since the night of the storm.

Darryl, too, would be surprised.

"Jane is with child," Conn said baldly.

Pride and happiness rang in his voice. Was there anything else? Some dark emotion she didn't want to put a name to?

Agnes gave a delighted gasp and clapped her hands. "Splendid!" she cried, beaming at them.

Agnes seemed to have completely recovered from her attack on the night of the great storm. Although much of her acerbity had gone, since Lavena was no longer amusing to tease.

Hayley's glance moved to Lavena. Conn's sister's face showed little emotion, but something flickered in the depths of her eyes.

"Congratulations," she finally said, her voice as neutral as her expression.

Darryl sat very still. When Hayley's glance met hers, there was no wondering what Darryl's feelings were.

Hurt and surprise. But she quickly smiled, got up and walked over to Conn and Hayley.

"That's wonderful, sister," she said, hugging Hayley and smiling at Conn.

"Yes, it is," Hayley agreed, a relieved smile easing the tension in her face.

"You must take better care of yourself, Jane," Agnes said, her glance moving over Hayley's small frame, lingering on her narrow hips.

A stab of worry hit Hayley, despite her brave words the night before. The truth was, her mother was larger-built than either Hayley or Darryl. And she'd come close to dying after the birth of Hayley's younger brother, who'd been stillborn.

"Of course," Hayley agreed, summoning a wide smile.

Ellis rose from his seat. He, too, hugged Hayley and beamed at her. "I couldn't be happier if the babe-to-be were my own," he said.

He gave Darryl a sideways glance.

Hayley was sure Darryl caught the look, but she didn't blush with embarrassment. Instead, she steadily returned the glance.

"I must be off to see how the barn repair progresses," Ellis said.

Conn squeezed Hayley's waist again, then released her. "I, too, must be off." He grinned at Ellis. "Although I don't know why I bother. Ellis seems quite capable of running the farm all by himself.''

Ellis grinned back, instead of looking uncomfortable as he would have a few weeks ago. ''Oh, Gustav and I still need you from time to time,'' he returned Conn's good-natured banter.

''I'm glad to hear that. Well, shall we go?''

Ellis nodded and the two men left the room.

''Let's have another cup of tea,'' Agnes said. ''It isn't every day we get such news.''

''All right,'' Lavena said, to Hayley's surprise.

Darryl poured the tea for both women, then she and Hayley started clearing the table.

''You girls, too. Come, sit,'' Agnes urged.

Hayley caught Darryl's sideways look. *I want to talk to you,* it said.

Glad enough to postpone her talk with Darryl, Hayley poured the two additional cups and seated herself. Reluctantly, Darryl also sat back down in her chair.

Finally, after a few more minutes of talk about the coming baby, Darryl rose, followed by Hayley. She carried a stack of dishes to the kitchen, Darryl close behind her.

Darryl firmly closed the dining room door and put her load on the worktable. She straightened, looking at Hayley. ''Why didn't you tell me about the babe?''

Hayley blinked. Darryl's voice sounded exactly as it used to when they still lived in Suffolk, before all the terrible things had happened. Firm, a little bossy, as older sisters' voices usually did. Cheer rose in Hayley.

''Well, sister, dear, I only told Conn last night. Don't you think my husband should be the first to know?''

Darryl's expression changed. Became a little chagrined. Finally, she nodded. ''Yes, of course, you're right, but . . .''

Hayley shot a glance at the dining room door. Still securely closed. She backed toward the hearth, beckoning for her sister to follow.

When both stood close together before the cheerful blaze, Hayley finished Darryl's question, in a low tone.

"But will this change my vow not to tell Conn the truth about us?"

She grimaced at the words, hating the way they sounded, as if she and Darryl were common criminals, hiding from authority.

Which of course everyone else would consider them to be.

Including Conn? Would her husband believe and understand?

Her stomach tightened again. How would she ever know the answer to that question? And it didn't matter anyway. He couldn't protect Darryl from being hanged for killing Oscar Pritt. No one could.

Darryl nodded, her lips tightening.

Hayley squeezed her arm and managed a smile. "Of course it won't change my vow," she said, forcing firmness into her voice. "Nothing ever will."

Darryl visibly relaxed. Then her mouth quirked in a wry smile. "So we'll go on as we have. Living every day in fear of being found out."

Hayley sighed. "Yes. But as time passes, we'll be safer. There's been no word about any searches that fit our descriptions. Either they've given up, or as we hoped are still hunting the other way, toward Philadelphia."

Darryl gave her a straight look. "They'll never give up the search for a murderer."

She couldn't reassure Darryl on this point because it was true.

Hayley returned the look, holding Darryl's gaze. "No, but the more time that passes, the less attention will be paid to it. That's only logical."

Finally, Darryl nodded. "You're right. Now, shall we finish clearing the table?"

"Yes."

Hayley followed her back to the dining room, wishing with all her heart it was possible to feel nothing but joy and happiness that in a few months she would have a baby to love and care for. Her and Conn's baby.

But it wasn't. Not only must she continue to lie about her

very identity to her dearly loved husband, but she sensed that darkness inside him still remained.

How long would his first terrible marriage continue to haunt him?

"Oh, Gipsy is the most beautiful filly I've ever seen." Hayley stroked the fast-growing animal's head and it butted against her hand, wanting more.

Perdita nickered, as if in agreement, and Hayley laughed, her eyes meeting Conn's.

He leaned against the stall door, his own smile almost as foolishly fond as her own.

The last four months had been a time of peace and joy. Their love had grown as fast as the babe inside her. And it must be a lusty boy, because for four months gone, she was large indeed.

"Yes, I'll have to admit I agree," he said, "I've decided to keep her instead of selling her in the spring. That is, if we can get through the rest of the winter with enough coin left to get us started again in the spring."

His voice changed on the last words, became laced with worry. The January day was mild, but Hayley shivered, pulling her cloak more tightly around her.

A spasm of dizziness passed over her. She fought against staggering, but didn't entirely succeed.

Conn's firm hand gripped her waist. "Are you all right?" The worry in his voice had intensified, becoming concern for her.

She couldn't add to his worries. Although these dizzy spells came on her often lately, surely nothing serious was wrong. They'd pass.

Hayley nodded, forcing a smile. "I only stumbled over something."

Conn glanced down. "I don't see anything. But you must be more careful."

He reached under her cloak and patted her softly rounded

belly. ''Maybe we should send for the midwife to stay with you until the babe's birth.''

She quickly shook her head. ''No, that would be foolish.''

And the midwife's fee would further deplete Holly View's lean coffers.

''I'm fine,'' she reassured him, widening her smile, seeking his eyes.

He finally smiled back, the worry lines between his brows disappearing, his dark gaze filled with love for her.

And nothing else? Did she dare hope the dark memories had been erased from his mind during these past weeks? That the thought of the coming babe now brought him nothing but joyful anticipation?

She moved closer, put her hands on his shoulders and lifted her head for his kiss. He pulled her close, his hand warm on her waist beneath the cloak, his lips warm on hers, his heart beating steadily against her own.

''I love you,'' he whispered, his warm breath further warming her.

''And I love you,'' she whispered back, feeling happiness bloom inside her, fill her, until there was no room left for fears or worries or doubts.

Conn's lips met hers, covered hers, moved over them with a seeking pressure that weakened her knees.

Dimly, she heard the barn door open, then close. Heard footsteps in the distance.

Conn sighed, then reluctantly released her and stepped back, his eyes still soft with love and tenderness.

He turned and let them both out of the stall, then secured the latch.

''Conn,'' Ellis's voice said from behind, filled with a strange urgency. ''There's someone here who insists on seeing you.''

''You're damned right I do,'' a harsh male voice said. ''And now, too.''

She'd heard the voice before, but for a moment Hayley couldn't place it. When she did, she sucked in her breath, and whirled.

A swarthy, beefy man stood there, legs spread far apart, covered with an expensive cloak. A jagged scar marred his forehead.

His glance settled on Hayley and his full lips curved up in an unpleasant, satisfied smile.

"So here you are at last. Your master will be glad to see you. And where's your sister? I can't wait to get my hands on her. Left me for dead, she did."

Hayley's dizziness returned with a rush, along with encroaching darkness. Desperately, she fought against it, but knew she was losing the battle.

The last thing she heard was Conn's swearing, and then his strong arms caught her as she fell.

CHAPTER
TWENTY-FOUR

Conn stooped and gathered Hayley into his arms. Anger coursing through him, he scowled at the man.

"Who are you? What do you mean, coming to my farm, saying such outrageous things to my wife?"

The man looked startled, then smiled.

"Your wife, eh? Well, well. Isn't that interesting. And from the looks of things, she's also in the family way. I'm Oscar Pritt and I have every right to be here."

Grim-faced, Conn stepped forward. "The hell you do. You scared my wife half to death. Now, get out of my way so I can take her back to the house."

The man moved backward, but the satisfaction was still on his face. "Go ahead and tend to your wife—but then we need to have a little talk."

"Get out of here," Conn warned. "When I get back, I don't want to see you. You obviously have the wrong person." He walked past the other man.

"I've made no mistake," he said. "And you'll see me, all right. Unless you want Burle Porter here, taking your wife away. She's one of his runaway bond servants. And marriage isn't allowed during the indenture time, as I'm sure you know.''

Conn stopped in his tracks, holding Jane closer to him. "What in hell are you talking about?"

"This woman's sister is *my* bond servant. Your wife ran away from Mr. Porter's plantation to mine. Her sister hid your wife, then tried to kill me when I discovered their plan to escape."

He touched the scar on his forehead. "After knocking me over the head with a poker, they ran away."

A chill trickled down Conn's spine at the man's words, his confident tone.

It hit him forcibly that he knew very little about either Jane or Anna. From the beginning, he'd sensed they were holding something back, but he hadn't pried. Finally, he'd dismissed those feelings. Dismissed, too, the fear they both seemed to feel most of the time.

Maybe he shouldn't have. Could this man possibly be telling the truth?

He instantly rejected that. No, the thought was absurd. Timid Anna trying to kill this man? Jane helping her? Both of them running away from their masters?

No, impossible. Jane couldn't have deceived him like that.

Then why had Jane fainted at the sight of this man?

A memory of the first time he'd seen Jane and Anna slipped into his mind.

Anna's hand and ankle injured, both she and Jane disheveled and hungry. Lost and penniless.

The chill down his spine intensified. Again, he tried to dismiss the thoughts. He took a deep breath and another step forward.

Jane stirred in his arms and sighed. He glanced down to see her eyelids fluttering open. Her blue eyes looked dazed.

"Why are you holding me?" she asked. "Where are we?"

"Awake again, are you, little lady?" Oscar Pritt said from behind Conn. "You had better stay awake this time."

Jane stiffened and gasped, fear filling her eyes. "I'm sorry. I'm so sorry," she whispered to Conn.

She struggled to get out of Conn's arms. He lowered her to the earthen floor of the barn, still grasping her waist to steady her.

The chill was spreading all through his body, deepening into pain. What was she sorry about?

Jane's back was rigid beneath his hands. He turned her to face him. "Do you know this man? Does he have some claim on you and Anna?"

The fearful, guilty look in her eyes was all the answer he needed.

His stomach ached, as if someone had given him a killing punch.

"Yes. I couldn't tell you, Conn," she said, her voice full of fear and guilt, too. "I couldn't betray Darryl. We thought she'd killed him."

"Darryl?"

"That's Anna's true name. Mine is Hayley."

He stared at her in disbelief. "So you lied about everything? Even your names?"

She shook her head. "No! Not everything. Just . . . what we had to. We were afraid to tell anyone the truth."

The pain inside him grew. "You couldn't trust any of my family? Couldn't ask us to help you?"

She swallowed, then shook her head. "No."

"Not even me, your husband?"

She bowed her head, didn't answer.

Anger, swift and violent, hit him. His mouth tightened, his hand tightened on Jane's—no, *Hayley's*—waist until she drew in her breath.

He released his hold. She swayed for a moment, then steadied herself.

Oscar Pritt walked up to stand beside Conn. He gave a cold, unpleasant smile.

"I don't know what the magistrate will make of all this," he said to Hayley. "Of course, both your indentures will have at least a year added to them. And your lovely sister will get a long prison term for what she tried to do to me."

Hayley whirled on him, her eyes flashing with fury. "What about what you did to her? Forcing her into your bed, raping her!"

The other man's smile vanished. His eyes narrowed. "What kind of lying nonsense have you dreamed up? Do you think that hogwash will stand in a court of law? That the judge will believe your sister and you over me? A man of property?"

He shook his head. "I'll have to hand it to you both. We'd searched all over the north, far away as Philadelphia. Couldn't conceive of you two heading into the wilderness. You might have gotten away with it if one of your husband's neighbors hadn't told the local magistrate about two girls matching your descriptions living on this farm."

Walbridge, Conn thought, his jaw tightening. It had to have been him. He'd been furious about his son's interest in Jane. No, not Jane, he corrected himself. *Hayley.*

Why had the man waited so long? *Hayley* was no longer a threat to Radley.

It must be because Conn had penned up three of his cattle two weeks ago, when they'd again knocked down the fence and raided Conn's field. Penned them and refused to return them until Walbridge properly rebuilt the fence.

Conn's mouth tightened. Why was he wasting thought on that? To keep from facing this situation?

Pritt gave an insolent glance around. "Looks as if you did well for yourselves, too. Prosperous place."

Hayley gasped. "You're twisting everything. Darryl and I had no choice. You brutally used her. She hit you in order to escape."

Oscar gave her a pitying look. "You may as well stop lying. Do you know how many bound females try to use the excuse of being wrongly used? What is your proof?"

His voice rang with self-righteous unction.

"The magistrate will see the truth," he went on. "That you and your sister tried to kill me to prevent the two of you from running away from lawful indentures. And nearly succeeded."

Hayley stared at him. Then she moved backward, her face

paling even more. "You're twisting things again. We had no choice. We had to do what we did."

Oscar gave her an insolent smile. "No choice? You and your sister signed the indenture papers without being forced."

"We had no money. We would have starved."

He shrugged. "So Burle and I saved your and your sister's lives."

Conn had had enough. Blind with confusion, rage and betrayal, he grasped the other man by the throat and shook him, wanting to squeeze the life out of him.

"Conn, stop! You'll kill him," a voice pleaded.

His wife's voice.

The second woman in that position who'd lied to him. Tricked him. Deceived him.

He let go of Pritt. The man dropped to his knees on the ground, wheezing for breath.

Ellis appeared, his face grim. "Do you need help?"

"No. Leave, Ellis," Conn commanded. "This is none of your affair."

"I believe it is, but I'll leave. For the moment at least." He disappeared from sight.

Out of the corner of his eye, Conn saw Jane—no, *Hayley*—standing to the side, her face white.

His deceitful wife. Who hadn't trusted him enough to tell him the truth about anything.

Anything?

Even who was the father of the babe she carried?

He drew in his breath as this dark thought entered his mind, followed by a memory of Radley Walbridge in the kitchen with Hayley on their wedding day.

Conn tried to dismiss the thoughts. He wasn't able to.

What was the truth? What his wife had said, or this man's accusations? Or something in between?

How would he ever know? How could he ever trust Hayley again?

But he couldn't let this man take the two of them away, no

matter what they'd done. That thought was appalling. He well knew many masters misused their female bond servants.

Then why are you doubting your wife's story? his mind asked. *Do you believe this man you detest on sight?*

No. Yes. Hell, he didn't know!

If Jane—no, damn it, *Hayley*—could live with these secrets all these months, how many more secrets might she have been comfortable with?

Finally, Oscar glanced up, coughing. "You'll pay for manhandling me like that. I'll see you do."

Conn gave him a cold look. "Tell me what both bonds cost. I'll pay for them, and something extra for your trouble with An—Darryl. You might decide it's not the most advisable thing to go to court over this."

He made his last words enough of a threat they were unmistakable.

Pritt blinked at him, then unsteadily got to his feet and brushed off his trousers. He looked at Conn as long moments ticked off.

Finally, he said, "All right. I'll accept those terms. Burle Porter gave me authorization to settle his claim on your wife."

Conn's anger grew. So these men had planned this all along, knowing full well he'd agree.

"Tell me what the price is," he said, tightly. "And show me the bond papers."

The man brought a pouch out from the pocket of his cloak and held it out.

Conn took it, glanced through the indenture papers inside. All was in order.

The amount Oscar named made Conn's stomach knot. It would take almost all their buffer of protection to tide them over the rest of the winter. If any crisis occurred, they would have little left for seeds in the spring and all the other usual seasonal expenses.

But it must be done. He couldn't let this man take his wife's sister away, back to servitude.

Neither could he let Porter take Ja—Hayley away. That was unthinkable. His wife. His *pregnant* wife.

"Let's not waste time. Wait here and I'll bring you the money."

Pritt, his confidence returning by the second, shook his head. "I believe I'll just go along with you."

Conn nodded, stiffly, although everything inside him protested. To take this odious man inside his home, have this sordid story revealed to his family, was almost more than he could stand. But he had to.

He turned to Hayley, who'd stood mutely while he negotiated for her freedom. "Come," he said.

Eyes cast down—in guilt? shame?—she walked beside him to the barn doorway, Pritt having the sense to walk behind them.

Ellis and Gustav stood outside, both grim-faced.

"It's all right," Conn told them, between jaws so tight they ached.

They nodded, but Ellis fell in behind as they walked toward the house.

How could anything ever be all right again? Conn bleakly asked himself. The happy, contented life he'd thought stretched ahead of him had been torn down around his head.

His wife, whom he'd trusted with his life, had lied to him. Deceived him. And he'd never know to what extent. He'd never be able to untangle the web.

Or ever again trust her.

Lavena was alone in the kitchen, kneading bread. She glanced up, her eyes widening in surprise as the four people entered.

"Where's Anna?" Conn asked, curtly. "This man has business with her."

"With Anna?" Lavena asked, surprise in her voice.

"So that's what she's calling herself now, is it?" Pritt said, his voice all righteous indignation.

Hayley shuddered. He sounded for all the world like a man

who'd been badly wronged. How could she expect anyone to believe her or Darryl?

The door from the back hall opened. Darryl stood framed in the opening, the kitten who followed her everywhere twining around her ankles.

At the sight of Pritt, her face tightened in shock. Her hand came out to hold the door frame, the knuckles whitening from her grip.

"You—you're not dead," she finally gasped.

Pritt moved forward a few feet. "No thanks to you and your sister," he sneered. "If Mrs. Whitley hadn't soon found me, that might well have happened."

Mrs. Whitley had lied to Darryl, Hayley thought. She'd let them go on believing Oscar was dead. All this time they'd lived under a cloud of unnecessary fear.

Darryl's blue eyes were huge in her white face. "You've come to take me back."

"Yes, that's indeed why I came," Oscar said, ominously.

Darryl crumpled toward the floor.

Ellis leaped forward, Hayley behind him. Ellis reached her in time to keep her head from hitting the hard wood surface.

He knelt beside her, supporting her. Hayley hovered nearby. The kitten mewed, piteously.

"He won't take you away," Ellis said, his voice rough with emotion. "I won't let him."

Darryl moaned, then struggled to sit up. "I'm to stay here then? Both of us are?"

"Yes," Conn said, tightly. "I'll pay your and your sister's bonds. Mr. Pritt's agreed to that, and so has Mr. Porter."

"I'll pay your and your sister's bonds," Conn had said, not "my wife's."

His voice had been cold as ice.

He believed what Oscar Pritt, who'd been so plausible, so horrified at her "lies," had said.

Hayley glanced across at Conn. He was turned away, as if he couldn't stand the sight of her.

She fought back despairing tears. Conn thought she'd connived with Darryl, tried to kill Oscar Pritt, just to be free of their bonds.

Maybe Conn even thought she'd enticed him into marriage.

As his first wife had done.

Her despair grew.

The door to the back hall opened again. Agnes stood framed in its opening. Her glance fastened on Darryl.

"Anna! Whatever is the matter?"

Darryl glanced up and tried to smile. "It's nothing. I'll be all right." She struggled to rise, and with Ellis's aid, did.

Agnes, reassured as to Darryl's condition, turned her gaze upon Oscar Pritt. "And who might you be?" she asked in her abrupt way.

Oscar, obviously mistaking her for the household's mistress, bowed. "Oscar Pritt, ma'am," he said.

Agnes frowned. "Oscar Pritt," she repeated, "Now where have I heard that name?" Her face cleared. "Oh, yes, now I remember. A former housekeeper of yours, a Mrs. Whitley, was a guest at Conn's and Jane's wedding."

Oscar's mouth turned up in a grimace. "You must mean Mr. Merritt's and *Hayley Armstrong's* wedding," he said.

Agnes's frown deepened. "What are you talking about?" she demanded.

"This woman"—he gestured to Darryl—"is a runaway bond servant whose real name is Darryl Armstrong. She tried to kill me," he said, quite openly enjoying saying these things. "And the other one"—he gestured toward Hayley—"aided and abetted her."

Ellis took a step forward, his dark eyes glaring, fists balled. "If you don't get out of here this instant, I'll flatten you."

Oscar gave him a raised-eyebrow glance. "We haven't transacted our business yet. I wouldn't be so hasty. I might change my mind about my agreement with Mr. Merritt."

"Lavena, will you go get our money bag?" Conn asked his sister.

Without protest, she slipped through the open doorway and upstairs.

''Not taking any chances, eh?'' Oscar asked.

''No,'' Conn said, coldly. ''None at all.''

His glance lingering on Darryl, Oscar smiled. ''On second thought, I've decided I want to keep this female's bond.''

Hayley jumped to her feet, fear coursing through her body. ''You can't keep her!''

Ellis also got up, his face a mask of fury as he faced Oscar. ''You can't and you won't.''

''That's right,'' Conn said, tightly. ''We made an agreement.''

Oscar's smile widened. ''But no money's changed hands. Nothing's in writing yet.''

Agnes opened her mouth, then closed it again. Her mouth tightened, her eyes narrowed into slits.

Lavena came hurrying back into the room, handing Conn a worn leather pouch.

''Thank you, Lavena. Now if you'll find me paper and pen.''

His mouth a hard line as he stared at Oscar, Conn held up the pouch. He moved a step closer. ''You'll take the money for Darryl or leave empty-handed.''

Hayley drew in her breath. His voice was so icy it made her shudder.

Ellis also moved closer to Oscar, his hands clenched at his sides, his face as tight and angry as Conn's.

Oscar looked from one man to the other. He swallowed. ''Well, now, I believe I've changed my mind. Keep the wench. What use is she to me?''

A rush of relief filled Hayley. *Thank God, thank God!*

Beside her, Ellis relaxed his stance a bit, but still glared at Oscar.

Conn nodded. ''Good. I'm glad the matter is settled.'' He took the bag to the worktable and removed coins from it.

Lavena returned with paper and pen.

Conn wrote on the paper for a few minutes, made a copy, then handed the paper to Oscar. ''I believe this covers our agreement.''

Oscar warily took the paper and read it. "I guess that will do," he said, grudgingly. "Now, the money, if you please."

He was trying hard to regain the upper hand, but not quite succeeding, Hayley saw. He feared these two men. Good! She wished they'd knock him senseless.

And would that help your situation any? her mind asked. *Would that return Conn's love and trust to you?*

"We're not quite finished," Conn said, his voice still cold and remote. "Agnes, will you and Lavena and Ellis witness mine and Mr. Pritt's signatures?"

They finished the transaction, Oscar frowning in displeasure the while. Conn held out the coins. "The papers, please."

Oscar took the proffered money, then, his movements reluctant, handed Conn the bond papers.

"Thank you," Conn said, biting out each word. "Now, you'd best be on your way."

Oscar's head swiveled toward Darryl, his slow gaze traveling down her body.

Darryl shrank back, her eyes wide and fearful. Hayley's skin prickled. She felt as if he'd undressed her sister with his eyes.

Ellis moved forward again, but Agnes was quicker. She raised her cane and jabbed it hard against Oscar Pritt's chest.

Taken by surprise, he staggered, fell to one knee.

"Get out of this house, you unutterable slime," she said, her voice loud and authoritative. "If you ever so much as put your foot on this property again, I will set the bull on you."

His face beet red, Oscar rose to his feet and brushed off his trousers. "I'll leave with great pleasure."

He turned and left the kitchen, slamming the door behind him so hard the dishes on the dresser shelves rattled alarmingly.

Agnes turned to Hayley, gave her a satisfied smile, then turned to Darryl.

"I suppose we have to remember to call you girls by your rightful names. That shouldn't be so hard, now that I've regained my wits. Darryl and Hayley. I like those names. Got some character to them. I always did think Jane and Anna were too namby-pamby for spirited girls like you two."

Hayley stared at the other woman. Did Agnes truly think that all that needed to be addressed was the fact that Hayley and Darryl had been using names other than their own during their time here at Holly View?

Ellis moved back beside Darryl. Protectively close.

He'd heard all that went on in the barn. Heard Hayley say Darryl had been violated.

Many men would have considered her sullied.

But Ellis had been outraged on her behalf. He wanted only to protect her.

Oh, yes, Hayley thought, her sister belonged with Ellis!

"I like the name Darryl better, too," he said. He smiled at Hayley. "And Hayley."

A tide of warmth flowed over her. Agnes and Ellis were making it plain that whatever had happened in the past, none of it mattered now, that they would give their full love and support.

But Lavena was silent. Hayley glanced her way. The older woman's expression was impassive.

"I must get back to my bread dough or it will never rise." She walked to the worktable, and began kneading the dough again.

Some of the warmth fled. Lavena would give no support, but also it appeared, no additional enmity.

And Conn?

The warmth completely left. She forced herself to face him. His expression was stony. He stared at her as if at a stranger.

"Darryl and I must explain what happened," Hayley said. "And how sorry we are to have deceived you all these months. How grateful we are that you bought our bonds. We know it will cut deeply into the farm's reserve funds."

Her apology caused no softening of his features.

From behind her, Agnes said, "Whatever you girls did, I'm sure there were good reasons for it. And neither of you look up to anything else today."

"But we must tell you," Darryl said, her voice trembling.

"All that can wait until later. I think we've had enough turmoil for one day."

Somehow, Hayley managed to return the old woman's smile, but shook her head. "No, it can't wait."

With a sigh, Agnes sat down in her chair and waved her hand. "All right. But we need some tea to sustain us."

"I'll prepare it," Darryl quickly said.

"Let me." Lavena went to the dresser for the teapot.

"I must get back to the barns," Conn said, abruptly. He turned and left without a backward glance at anyone.

Agnes huffed. "Isn't that just like a man?" She smiled at Hayley again. "Don't worry, dear. He'll calm down and get over this. Just give him a little time."

Darryl was looking at her anxiously.

Hayley forced another smile. "I hope that all of you can forgive us for what we did."

"Of course we can and will," Agnes said, emphatically, thumping her cane on the floor for emphasis. "And that includes Conn."

But did it?

Conn wanted to hear no explanations. He still thought she and Darryl were conniving females who'd do anything to further their own causes.

Like his first wife.

Who had betrayed him in the worst way a woman could.

She longed to follow him, try to make him listen to her. But she'd do better to wait until tonight, when they were alone in their bedchamber. Maybe then he'd believe her. Realize she'd had no choice.

You had a choice, her mind told her. *You could have fled from Conn's kisses. Refused his offer of marriage. Now you're hopelessly entangled in his life. Carrying his child. There's no way out.*

She didn't want a way out. She deeply loved Conn and this babe of theirs inside her. Somehow she'd make him believe her, trust in her again.

And now she and Darryl had to tell their story to these three people who'd also trusted them.

Taking turns, they did, punctuated at intervals by Agnes's gasps and expressions of outrage, Ellis's growls of anger. Lavena said nothing, just sat and listened.

When they'd finished, Hayley felt a deep sense of relief. It was over at last.

The relief fled almost instantly.

No, it wasn't. She'd have to do this same thing again tonight. Alone with Conn in their bedchamber.

Agnes got up from her chair and came over to where Hayley and Darryl sat on the cushioned bench.

Tears stood in her eyes. She reached out and hugged Hayley, then Darryl.

"You girls have suffered and endured much. I wish you had told us all this when you first arrived. But I can understand why you didn't dare. You thought you'd killed a man!"

Agnes shuddered. "I wouldn't have dared, either."

She sighed and shook her head. "What a pity. You suffered all these months for nothing."

"It wouldn't have been nothing if Oscar Pritt hadn't been willing to take the money and leave," Hayley said.

"If he hadn't left, I would have knocked him senseless," Ellis said. He glanced at Darryl and gave her a warm smile.

Darryl gave him a small smile in return, then looked down at her lap.

Hayley realized her sister still couldn't believe that Ellis blamed her in no way for what had happened.

And Oscar appearing here today had brought back the horrible things he'd done to her. Had probably set back her recovery.

Today, what they'd feared all these months had finally happened. They'd been found. But nothing else after that had gone as they'd expected.

Oscar wasn't dead. Darryl wasn't a murderess. Their bonds were paid. They were free women.

They should both be half giddy with relief and happiness. But they weren't.

Darryl still had demons to fight. Maybe she'd never conquer them.

And maybe Conn would never believe Hayley or trust in her again.

CHAPTER
TWENTY-FIVE

Seated at the supper table, Ellis gave Anna a sideways glance. No, not Anna. *Darryl*. That name fit her better, as Aunt Agnes had said. It sounded strong and forthright, like her true nature.

She was eating with good appetite, and she seemed more relaxed than he could ever remember.

And why not? She no longer had a death sentence hanging over her. Or what she'd thought was a death sentence.

He grimaced. How hard it must have been for her to go through the days thinking every moment she might be discovered. Might be dragged off to jail.

Ellis was glad he'd stayed close outside the barn door and listened to the conversation when Pritt arrived. He'd known at first glance the man was bringing trouble, and had been determined to be ready for it if Conn needed him.

No wonder Darryl was so fearful of any man getting close to her. Now that he knew the full truth, he was amazed she'd let him kiss her. Touch her at all.

Another wave of anger went over him. He wished she *had* killed that bastard! He wished he could do it himself.

Agnes's instant declaration of Darryl's and Hayley's essential goodness, her belief in them, had made it much easier for the girls to tell their story. To humbly beg everyone's forgiveness for keeping these secrets.

How much they'd lost! And how brave they'd been. He could imagine Margaret Findley in such circumstances. She wouldn't have lasted a day.

He glanced at Conn, eating silently. That Conn was still very angry was apparent.

He hadn't wanted to hear any more explanations, and he hadn't come back to the house until a few minutes ago.

Since Pritt had been here this afternoon, he'd withdrawn from everyone.

Especially from his wife. During the course of the meal, Conn hadn't glanced Hayley's way once. Neither had he put comforting arms around her since they'd walked up from the barn with Pritt.

And Hayley desperately needed his comfort. That was obvious from her lowered head, her tense posture. Unlike Darryl, her anxiety didn't seem to be relieved at all.

Ellis frowned, trying to put the pieces together. Could it be possible Conn didn't believe his wife? That he'd accepted Pritt's version of what had happened?

No, Ellis instantly rejected that idea. Conn was no fool. Pritt couldn't have taken him in with his smooth explanations.

Anyone could see and hear Hayley told the truth. That she and Darryl had felt they had no other choice than what they'd done. Hell, anyone trapped in such circumstances could have, probably *would* have, done much the same.

Surely Conn could see that, too. How could he doubt the woman he so deeply loved?

"My, but everyone is very quiet tonight," Aunt Agnes said, her fork halfway to her mouth.

His mother said nothing, which was usual for her since the night of the big storm, just continued eating.

Neither did anyone else answer Aunt Agnes's comment.

Ellis decided he'd better. "I suppose we're all tired, after the day we've had."

Darryl glanced toward him. For a moment her blue eyes were clear and untroubled. Then a cloud came over her face, and he saw the fears he was used to seeing.

The difference was he finally knew the reason for them. And was sure it had nothing to do with him.

As he'd often told himself in the past, he could wait. Since at last he was certain waiting was what was needed. Now that Darryl no longer had her other fears, these remaining ones would disappear, too.

A vision of Pritt's heavy body, the innate cruelty he wasn't able to completely hide beneath his suave exterior, came into Ellis's mind.

He balled his fists, remembering the way Pritt had looked at Darryl before he left. As if he could see through her clothes.

And he hadn't wanted to sell her bond once he'd seen her again.

An uneasy frisson went over Ellis. But then he dismissed it. No, Pritt wouldn't dare try to come back, to take Darryl by force. He couldn't be that much of a fool.

That monster had violated Darryl's body . . . and her soul. And to what depths, Ellis couldn't know. Or how long it would take her to recover.

But she would recover. Fully.

Wouldn't she?

Was his love strong enough to help her through?

Of course it was, he told himself, firmly pushing down the doubts that tried to rise.

His jaw set. He'd make it so.

Hayley sat on the edge of the bed, undressing. Across the room, Conn sat by the banked fire, turned away from her.

He hadn't looked directly at her since she and he and Oscar Pritt had walked to the house this afternoon.

In profile, his face still looked set and hard, as it had when he'd left for the barns. And at the supper table.

She took a deep breath and let it out. She couldn't let things go on any longer.

Quickly, she finished undressing. Conn didn't glance toward her, give her a loving, desirous look as he had every night previous to this since their marriage.

She considered for a moment. Should she rise, go to him naked, press herself against him? Try to erase his somber mood with passion?

Try to make him forget that he doubted her? That he believed Oscar Pritt's smooth, lying words instead of hers?

How can you blame him after what his first wife did? her mind asked her. *You've feared from the beginning this would happen. Feared he couldn't forgive you.*

But I didn't really believe he wouldn't! she protested.

That was very foolish of you, wasn't it?

His first wife had lied to him. Betrayed him. Then lured him into marriage with passion. Conn wasn't yet able to see how different this situation was from that one.

Hayley's mouth set. She'd do nothing he could possibly suspect as a trick. She reached for her nightrail, put it on, then walked over, to stand between Conn and the fire.

He glanced up, his dark eyes cold and remote.

Her heart quailed. She longed to retreat, go crawl into the bed, roll herself into a ball and sleep.

She wouldn't, though. She had to be strong. Her very marriage depended on making Conn believe her.

Hayley held his gaze with her own. "Husband, we must talk."

His gaze flickered for a moment, but he remained silent.

Hayley forced her gaze to remain steady on his.

"Talking will not help matters," he finally said.

"Of course it will," she said quickly.

His face remained impassive. He stayed silent.

Hayley closed her eyes and prayed for strength. Oh, this was going to be harder than she'd thought. All she could do was tell the truth, repeat all she'd said earlier.

And hope he believed it.

"I'm sorry I couldn't tell you the truth about Darryl and me. I wanted to from the first day we met. But you must believe that Oscar Pritt lied. He violated my sister and she hit him with a poker to escape. She thought she'd killed him. We ran away to save our lives."

He kept on looking at her. "Why didn't you tell me all this when I found the two of you?"

His voice was as cold as his eyes.

The knot of tension in Hayley's stomach grew and tightened. "You know why. Because we were afraid to tell anyone."

"I could understand you'd feel that way at first. But not after you and I pledged ourselves to each other. I told you everything about Marie. Things I've never spoken of to another living soul."

The bleakness in his voice made an answering cold go through her body.

She knelt before him. Placed her hands on his knees, gave him a pleading look.

"I am so sorry for what we . . . I did. I will do anything to regain your trust. But you have to understand," she said, urgently. "If Oscar Pritt had died, you couldn't have protected us. No one could. Silence was our only defense."

"You'd have me believe you thought I'd turn you and your sister in to the authorities? If Pritt did all that you claim, he deserved to be killed. I'd have helped you all I could."

Hayley swallowed. His voice was still cold and hard. His legs were rigid beneath her touch.

"You're not being reasonable," she said. "How could you have protected Darryl from a murder charge? You heard Oscar Pritt today. Heard him deny everything I said, in such a plausible way. Do you really think a magistrate would have believed me over him?"

Conn savagely raked his hands through his hair. "Probably. At least possibly."

"And you think I should have risked that? Risked Darryl's life?"

Conn rose, so suddenly Hayley rocked back on her heels.

He stood, his gaze deliberately sweeping over her. Her soft, thin nightrail was stretched tight over her rounded belly. Conn's gaze lingered on it.

"You're exceedingly large to be only four months along with child," he said. "And all our nights together before our marriage were only a few weeks before we wed."

She gaped at him, for a moment not understanding his meaning. When she did, shock surged through her, along with the dizziness she often felt now.

She struggled to her feet, drew herself up. "What are you saying?"

"I can't forget that less than an hour after we had exchanged our vows, I found Radley Walbridge whispering to you, clasping your hand."

She felt a tide of red sweep up from her neck. Oh, God, he *had* seen that . . . and just as she'd feared, he'd misinterpreted it. In the worst possible way. Why hadn't she talked about it their wedding night?

"That . . . was not what it appeared to be," she said, hearing how weak her voice sounded. Her body felt weak, too. She must sit down.

She backed up, found her chair before the fire and collapsed into it.

"Radley walked in and said the most astonishing thing. He asked me why I hadn't waited for him, then grabbed my hand before I knew what he was about."

Conn's face was still impassive. "So you say now. Why didn't you say it then?"

"Because I was afraid to . . . stir anything up," she faltered. Oh, why had the dizziness hit now? Now, when she most needed to be strong, to convince Conn how wrong he was about all this?

"If what you say is true, what was there to stir up?" he asked, his voice relentless.

Hayley closed her eyes, fighting the weakness. The dizziness was worse than ever before. Blackness lurked just beyond her consciousness, waiting to claim her.

She couldn't defend herself. Everything she said sounded weak. Sounded like a lie. Even she could see that.

She could argue no further. She must make it to the bed before she fainted. Hayley rose, her head swimming, swaying on her feet.

"What's wrong?" Conn asked, sharply. "Are you ill?"

Mutely, she nodded, grasping the chair arms to keep from falling.

In a moment he was at her side, helping her to the bed. She sat on the edge for a moment, Conn's hands steadying her, then lay down on her back.

Conn bent over her, his face a mixture of concern and those other feelings she didn't want to see there. "Do you want me to call Lavena? Your sister?"

Darryl. Oh, yes, it would be most comforting to have her here . . . and she needed comforting so much . . . but she mustn't. She couldn't leave things as they were with Conn. Somehow, she had to convince him all his doubts were wrong.

She had to see his love for her in his eyes again.

"No. I want only you. Please stay with me."

She put all her love for him into her plea.

But she didn't see his love.

Concern was still there in his eyes . . . but so were the doubts, the suspicions.

"Of course I'll stay here. After all, you are my wife."

She hated the way he'd said those last words as if only duty motivated him. Not love.

He nipped the candle out, then turned from her and began undressing. Enough light came through the window to show the long lean lines of his back, his strongly muscled legs. A tide of longing went through her.

How badly she wanted to be gathered into his arms, held close. He donned the nightshirt she'd never seen him wear before, walked around the foot of the bed and slid under the covers.

Hayley battled her weakness and dizziness, the tears that now filled her eyes threatening to overflow.

Silence filled the room. Hayley sniffed, choked back a sob.

"Are you all right?" Conn asked, his voice cool.

She started to say yes, to reassure him as to the babe's welfare. Then she remembered his last remarks.

She had to convince him he was wrong. She sat up in bed. Too quickly. Her head swam, the sinking feeling returned. She stayed very still, and it finally subsided.

"No, of course I'm not all right," she said, forcing strength into her voice. "How could I be? When my husband has these terrible doubts about me?"

"I meant are you all right physically," he said.

She had to shock him. Nothing else could work. "Why do you care?" she asked. "When you think Radley Walbridge is the father of this babe I carry?"

She felt his body jerk, heard his sudden indrawn breath.

The silence drew out.

"I didn't say that," Conn at last said, his voice still cool.

"You may as well have said it." Hayley forced herself to continue, when everything inside her screamed to stop this, to turn to Conn, beg him to hold her, love her. . . .

But she couldn't. Not now. Not yet.

She heard him take in another deep breath, then let it out. "How could I not ponder on these things after what has happened?"

"You mean, after what's happened to *you*. I'm not Marie, Conn. I would never betray you in that fashion."

He suddenly turned to her, grasped her shoulders and loomed over her. In the dim light she saw his dark glance boring into hers.

"You lied to me. You didn't even tell me your real name. How can I trust that the rest of what you claim happened is true? That anything you tell me is true?"

She made her eyes hold steady, not waver under his intense stare.

"Because you must believe I love you. I'd never do anything to hurt you. What Darryl and I did was out of fear for our lives."

The tense lines of his face relaxed a bit, as did his grasp on her shoulders. Hope rose in her. She kept her gaze steady, not even daring a tiny smile.

Then, he dropped his hands and moved away from her. "How can I believe that you love me and not merely the security you've found here at Holly View? When you've told me you didn't trust me enough to think I'd help you."

He jerked his head around, the dark stare back in his gleaming brown eyes.

"I would have given my life for you," he said.

Fear hit the pit of her stomach. A deeper fear than before. *Would have,* he'd said.

Not that he still would.

She'd tried words and they hadn't worked. There was only one thing left to do.

Conn was lying on his side, facing her. Hayley moved across the few inches separating them, curved her arm around his neck, pressed herself against him. Or as close as she could get, with her rounded belly.

She felt him recoil at that touch. Desperately, she found his mouth with her own and moved her lips across his tightly drawn ones.

"Do not try that trick," he said, his voice cold as ice. "It won't work. Not this time."

"What do you mean? I've never tried to trick you."

"To my eternal shame I desired Marie even after she'd confessed everything. I won't be that kind of fool again."

A deeper cold than she'd ever felt went over Hayley. For the first time she saw that Conn's hurts and doubts went much deeper than she'd realized. Had even dreamed.

And might never be resolved.

Might destroy their marriage.

She summoned the last bit of her strength. "I'm not trying to make a fool of you. Or of myself. I'm only trying to show you that I love you. That I'll always love you."

Conn sighed. "Go to sleep. I won't desert you or the coming babe. You need have no fears of that."

Slow anger crept over her. Her hands fell away from his shoulders. "I don't want your pity. I want your love."

She drew away and turned her now-rigid back.

Conn said nothing, made no move to stop her withdrawal or answer her last words.

Tears came again. Angrily, Hayley brushed them aside.

She and Darryl were safe now. No longer must they fear being discovered, being dragged away, Darryl to face a hangman's noose.

She'd thought that longed-for state was all she needed to be happy.

But that was before she knew how fragile were the bonds of her marriage.

How shallow-rooted was Conn's love for her.

And maybe today's events had torn out those roots, left them dying on the hard earth.

Never to be revived again.

CHAPTER
TWENTY-SIX

"That embroidery around the neckline is lovely, Hayley," Portia Miller, the midwife, said.

Hayley managed a smile for the woman bustling about the bedchamber setting things to rights, then tossed the tiny nightgown she was stitching on the bed.

Her back had been aching on and off since last night. No doubt because she'd lain in bed all this time.

Four long months.

Ever since that horrible night with Conn after Oscar Pritt had come. She'd begun bleeding that night. The midwife had been fetched and had promptly dispatched her to bed for the duration of her pregnancy.

Hayley lifted her arms above her head and stretched widely.

"I am so tired of lying in this bed. Can't I get up and just walk about a bit?"

Portia shook her head, softening her refusal with a smile of her own. "No. We can't take any chances. Be patient. I predict only two or so more weeks and the babe will be here. Just in time for the summer breezes."

Hayley made a face. "How can you be that sure?"

"Because you're so big."

"Yes, I am," Hayley agreed with a sigh. "But that will be early. Are you sure the babe will be all right?"

"You've asked me that a hundred times. It will only be a week or two early. I feel confident it will do fine because of its size. And maybe you've miscalculated the time."

Startled, Hayley glanced at her. "No, that isn't possible. I . . ."

Her voice died away. Portia didn't know when Hayley and Conn were married. She wasn't trying to insinuate that Hayley had been pregnant when she and Conn said their vows.

Perhaps *before* they said their vows.

Hayley's mouth twisted.

Only Conn suspected that.

The door opened. Darryl entered, bearing a breakfast tray.

Hayley pushed down her disappointment. Not that she'd really expected it to be Conn. He never brought up her meals.

Conn no longer even shared her bedchamber. He'd told everyone he didn't want to take the chance of disturbing her.

But Hayley knew that wasn't the only reason. She'd seen the relief on his face when he'd suggested this arrangement and she'd agreed.

He didn't *want* to share her bed. He didn't even want to be around her.

Pain and sadness filled her. She tried to push it back. She couldn't let Conn's rejection of her destroy her life. Or her coming baby's.

Even if it had, she feared, destroyed her marriage.

Oh, Conn wouldn't cast her and the babe out, he'd already assured her of that. And he was such an essentially decent man, she had no doubts he'd keep his promise.

Sometimes she wished she could leave after the baby's birth. Take the child and . . . and what?

She had no place to go, no way to take care of herself and the child. Desolation swept over her. She tried to push it down, but bleakness remained.

Besides, no matter what Conn's doubts were, everyone else believed the child to be his.

And despite everything, Hayley still deeply loved him.

Darryl placed the tray across Hayley's knees. "Here. See that you eat every bite of this."

"I'll try." She forced down her dark thoughts and smiled at her sister.

Now that fear for her life no longer filled her waking thoughts, Darryl was almost back to her old self. And her manner around Ellis seemed easier as each day went by. That was one thing to be happy about.

Since Hayley had been ordered to bed, Darryl had taken over her duties in the household. Lavena seemed content with Darryl's work. Of course, no one really knew how Lavena felt these days. Her personality was so altered since the night of the great storm.

The door opened again and Agnes came in, huffing from the stairs, and leaning on her cane. She gave Hayley a disapproving frown. "Why haven't you eaten your breakfast?"

Hayley sighed. "Because Darryl brought it only two minutes ago."

"Humph. Well, see that you do." Agnes sat down heavily in the big armchair, letting out her breath in relief.

Hayley tried to hang onto Agnes's and Darryl's warmth and love, make it be enough.

But it wasn't. How could it be? She needed her coming babe's father.

She needed Conn.

Why couldn't he understand what she'd done was out of fear for Darryl's life? That she'd had no choice? If Darryl had killed Oscar Pritt as she'd thought, Conn couldn't have protected her. Her and Darryl's flight would have proved their guilt to the authorities. They wouldn't have believed Cilla, the only person who knew the truth.

No, confiding in Conn wouldn't have helped her and Darryl. It would only have brought Conn and his family down with them.

What she felt guilt for was staying on at Holly View. Letting herself fall in love with Conn. Agreeing to marry him. She and Darryl should have left as soon as they had a chance.

And long before now, you'd both be lying dead in the woods somewhere, her mind said.

Maybe. And maybe not. They should have turned themselves in. Since Oscar Pritt wasn't dead, Darryl wouldn't have hung.

But neither of you knew Oscar was still alive. And she could have been thrown into prison anyway. Or if not, her fate with Oscar would have been worse. You did what you had to. Conn should have realized that.

But he hadn't.

And why had those actions of hers led to his suspicions the child might not be his? It didn't make sense.

Even while she asked herself, she knew why. And it had nothing to do with sense.

It was because of Marie.

Her mood darkened further. Why couldn't Conn get over his first bad marriage? See how wonderful their own marriage could be if he'd come back to her, hold her in his arms, let the love she felt flow into him, heal him?

She tried to fight the bleakness and despair. Perhaps when his babe was born, Conn would change. How could he look at his own child's face and still keep his doubts?

You know he could, her mind said. *He's exceedingly stubborn. He hasn't softened an iota for these four months.*

And if that happened, the babe would know it, too. All three of their lives would become a living hell.

The dull pain in her back struck again, harder this time. Hayley grimaced, shifted her position. The pain persisted, became more intense . . . and now it seemed to be in front as well. . . .

She tensed, placing her hand on her stomach.

"What's wrong? Do you feel ill?" Darryl asked.

"Just a pain in my back . . . and now it seems to be in my front, too."

Portia Miller, her dust cloth forgotten, jerked her head up. "How long have you had these pains?"

Hayley shrugged. "Since last night. They're surely nothing."

Portia hastened to the bed, lifted the tray of food and handed it to Darryl. "How often do the pains come?"

Hayley frowned in thought. "Every few minutes. I don't know exactly."

"And has the baby been less active of late?"

Hayley's frown deepened. "Yes, I believe so." She glanced at the midwife. Portia's usual smile was gone. Her face was set in serious lines.

Hayley stared at the woman, fear sweeping through her. "Do you think something is wrong with the babe?"

"No," Portia assured her. "But it may be making its arrival sooner than we thought."

Hayley's fear increased. "But it's too soon."

Portia patted Hayley's hand. "Babes come when they've a mind to. You're so large. The child can't be too small."

"My heavens, no," Agnes put in. "It must be a strapping boy who can't wait to get into the world."

Hayley's sideways glance showed her Darryl's strained posture. She turned and tried to give her sister a reassuring smile.

Just then another pain started—wholly in her stomach this time. And stronger than the others. She closed her eyes, waiting until it passed.

"Darryl, go and tell Lavena to come up," she heard Portia say in low tones. "I must get the birthing supplies ready."

She heard the bedchamber door open, then close.

The pain grew in intensity, and Hayley felt sweat beading her forehead. Gradually, it subsided.

Hayley opened her eyes.

Agnes leaned forward in her chair, an anxious look in her old eyes. She sighed. "Giving birth is a hard, painful process."

Then a grin curved her lips upward. "Or so they tell me. But women say the reward at the end is so great, it's always worth the effort."

Hayley tried to pretend the older woman's words and manner cheered her. Agnes wasn't scared. She was certain everything would be all right.

Nothing would ever be all right again.

"Of course it will be," she said, forcing another smile for Agnes.

"That's my girl." Agnes thumped her cane on the floor for emphasis. "You'll do fine. I knew there was quality stuff in you girls the first time I saw you."

"I . . . feel as if you were truly my aunt," Hayley said, then bit her tongue. She shouldn't have said that.

"Well, I should hope so," Agnes said, indignantly. "I wouldn't want to think I was leaving my property to strangers."

"Thank you," she told the older woman.

Another pain struck Hayley just as the door opened again and Darryl slipped back in, Lavena behind her.

Hayley closed her eyes again. The pains were closer together, and growing in intensity. That had to mean the child would soon make its appearance, didn't it?

She tried to fight back the fears rising in her, concentrate on Agnes's cheerful words.

She was only partially successful.

What if the babe was too small to live?

And if it did, what kind of a future would it have, if its own father denied it?

Conn and Ellis entered the kitchen at dusk. The room was empty and strangely quiet. A pot simmered over the fire, giving off appetizing odors. A loaf of bread, covered with a cloth, sat on the worktable.

At dinner, Darryl had said it appeared Hayley's birthing time had come. But the midwife thought the birth was bound to go slowly since it was a first child.

Fear had shot through him. *It's too soon for the babe to be born.*

Unless it was conceived earlier than Hayley told him.

The mixture of feelings he'd struggled with these last few months had blended with the fear.

Anger, betrayal. Desire . . . and love.

He'd pushed them aside and he and Ellis had returned to the fields. The crops and the orchards were flourishing, due to the welcome correct mixture of rain and sunshine for the first time in four years.

They'd gotten through the winter with no further crises, and even after paying the midwife's fee, had enough coin to buy seeds. It looked as if the year would be profitable.

But once in the fields, he'd been unable to concentrate. He'd kept looking toward the house, expecting a summons.

"I suppose everyone is upstairs," Ellis said now, his voice sounding strained and anxious. He took off his work coat and hung it on the rack by the door. Although it was May, the weather had been blustery and rainy for several days.

"Yes, no doubt." Conn hung his own coat up, then walked across the room and poured himself a mug of ale from the cask in the corner. He lifted it to his mouth and took a hearty draft, hoping it would settle him down.

It didn't. Carrying his ale, Conn paced to the far end of the big room, then returned to the cask, where Ellis was filling his own mug, and refilled his own.

Back at the table, Conn held the mug to his mouth again. When he set it down, it was empty. He paced across the room and returned.

He glanced up to see Ellis regarding him with a cool expression. "So you are finally showing some concern about your wife and your coming babe?"

Conn frowned at him. Things had been strained between him and his nephew since the day of Pritt's visit.

Ellis obviously believed the story Darryl and Hayley had told that day. He'd been fiercely tender and protective toward Darryl from that moment on.

Just as clear was Ellis's disapproval of Conn since that day.

"Of course I'm concerned. What do you take me for?"

"That's a good question. I don't know what to take you for. Here you have a loving, beautiful wife who with her sister, went through hell before you brought them here. And since the day all that was revealed, you've treated her shamefully."

"You're going too far," Conn warned. He moved a step forward, his fists clenched.

Ellis put down his mug and faced him.

"Go ahead and hit me if it will make you feel better. God knows you need to do something besides brood and glower and ignore Hayley."

"This is none of your affair. You don't understand any of it, and I'd advise you to keep out of it."

"If there's a reason for your behavior, why don't you tell me what it's all about and maybe I *would* understand."

Conn stared at him. "I can't tell you. It's between Hayley and me."

Ellis gave an exasperated sigh. "How can you say that? Do you think I'm the only one who's noticed how you've neglected your wife? How you never talk to her, except the few words you must exchange? Never smile or laugh together? How you moved out of your bedchamber?"

Conn took a deep breath and let it out. "You know why I did that. So as not to disturb Hayley."

Ellis sighed again. Louder this time. "That was a supremely good excuse, wasn't it? To do what you wanted to do anyway."

"You'd better stop right now," Conn warned.

Ellis shook his head. "No. You need to talk about this. You've held something inside for months, maybe years."

A muscle in Conn's jaw twitched.

The other man's eyes narrowed. "You haven't been the same since Marie died. Some darkness has hold of you. I thought when you met Hayley, and married her, she'd healed you. But that didn't last. When Pritt spewed his pack of lies that day, you went back into that darkness. It's held you ever since."

"That's enough!" Conn stepped forward again, his fists once more balled. Then he stopped. He dropped into a chair at the kitchen table. Put his head in his hands.

When he lifted it again, Ellis was still looking at him, but his gaze had softened. "Talk to me, Conn," he urged. "Please talk to me."

Yes, talk to him, one part of his mind urged. *You must talk to someone about this before it destroys you . . . and Hayley.*

Don't be a fool, another part exhorted. *You can't bare your soul before this boy. Reveal those shameful secrets you've kept so long. Told no one.*

But he had told someone—Hayley. And in the telling he'd thought to find ease. But he'd only pushed the darkness in his soul back, not banished it.

He had to banish it. Or lose his heart, his soul. The part of him he'd given to Hayley.

And then taken away from her again.

"All right," he heard himself saying. "I'll tell you."

Ellis nodded. "Good."

When Conn finished talking, the big room was silent. A log shifted in the fireplace, sending up a shower of sparks.

Conn felt lighter, somehow, as if freed from a burden he'd carried far too long.

He lifted his head and gazed Ellis full in the eye. "Now, tell me how many kinds of a fool I am."

Ellis's dark eyes were full of compassion. There was no trace of the other emotions Conn had thought to see. Dreaded to see.

"You're a fool, all right. But not in the way you think. You behaved honorably with Marie when many men wouldn't have."

"Honorably?" Conn protested. "No, that wasn't honor, that was wounded pride. That was cowardice, fear to expose myself for a cuckold."

Ellis shrugged. "I don't see it that way. But in any case, that happened years ago. You were younger than I am now and you think me still a lad. Or at least, you did until recently."

He gave Conn a smile.

"The foolishness comes in with Hayley. Your wife who is upstairs at this moment giving birth to your babe."

Ellis waved Conn's protests away. "You know that's true. Somewhere inside, you don't doubt for a moment this is your child."

The door to the back hall opened, then closed. Conn glanced over. Lavena stood framed in the doorway, a worried look on her face.

"Conn. There you are. I'm so glad you're here. Hayley's laboring mightily to no avail—and is growing very weak. We fear for her life."

CHAPTER TWENTY-SEVEN

Conn shot out of his chair, a terrible fear filling him. "What do you mean? How could that be? She's young and healthy. Why are things going wrong?"

Lavena shook her head and walked farther into the room. Tears glistened on her cheeks. She wiped them away with a corner of her apron. "Women often die in childbirth. You know that."

Conn rapidly crossed the room and grabbed the doorknob.

Lavena's hand closed over his own. "Where are you going?"

He jerked her hand away, turned the knob. "To be with her."

She let out a relieved sigh. "Good. She's been calling for you. It might help her to see you, give her renewed strength." She took a breath. "She seems to fear you care not for her or the babe."

Conn was halfway up the stairs before his sister's last words were out of her mouth. When he reached the top of the stairs, he heard a moan coming from their bedchamber.

His heart constricted. He ran down the hall, turned the knob and let himself into the room.

Hayley lay upon the bed, her eyes closed, her face white as snow. As death. His fear deepened. His throat closed. He gasped for breath, and finally drew in a shallow lungful of air.

Darryl stood by Hayley's side, stroking her hand, murmuring soft words of encouragement. Agnes sat across the room. Her face was nearly as white as Hayley's and her body trembled.

The midwife, on Hayley's other side, glanced at him, frowning. Then she moved back a little, motioning for him to take her place.

Conn swallowed past the lump in his throat. His knees shook. He'd never been so afraid in his life. He reached for Hayley's other hand. Its coldness sent a new shock of fear through him.

A pain took her, doubling her up and making her moan again. When it was finally over, her eyelids fluttered open. Her blue eyes widened.

"Conn," she whispered hoarsely, as if she couldn't believe he was there.

He prayed to whatever gods might hear him.

Spare her and the babe and I'll never ask for anything else.

"I'm here, Hayley," he said. "I'll never leave you again."

She turned her head away. "Yes, you will. You don't believe in me or trust me. You don't love me."

"I love you with everything inside me," he told her, desperately willing her to hear. "If you die, I will die, too. I cannot live without you."

Another paroxysm took her, shook her until he could barely stand to watch. When it subsided, she looked at him, a new expression in her eyes. Hope.

"You no longer doubt me . . . or that the babe . . . is—"

He silenced her with a gentle, loving kiss. "No. I've been a fool. Now you must tend to your business of birthing our babe. You are not to worry about anything else."

She gave him a shaky smile and squeezed his hand. "I'll do that."

Another pain came. She closed her eyes, and Conn tensed. But this time she seemed to meet the pain, move with it, instead of fighting and fearing it. Conn's tension eased a bit.

Then she began to pant, her mouth open.

Conn gave Portia a glance of alarm. "What's wrong?" he whispered.

She moved him aside, smiling. "Nothing. Everything is finally right. Now you go outside and wait."

"No." Conn's voice was very firm, brooking no argument. "I promised I'd not leave her."

Portia opened her mouth, then closed it again. "All right, then stay you shall. But don't get in our way. The next while will be busy."

Conn moved back, but not far enough away that Hayley couldn't see him.

Time seemed to stand still while he watched, digging his nails into his palms. Hayley breathed in those shallow, panting gasps as the pains kept coming closer and closer together.

Finally, Portia leaned over the bed. "Hayley, you're doing very well. Now gather your strength and get ready to push your babe into the world. Can you do that?"

Hayley nodded, breathing in shallow panting gasps. She lifted her head and saw Conn and smiled at him.

Portia leaned toward Hayley again, lifted the covers to make a kind of tent around her. "I can see the babe's head," she told Hayley. "Come, push harder, just a few more pushes and it will be all over."

Hayley did as the midwife urged, while Conn dug his fingernails into his palms to keep from trying to help his wife with this impossibly hard task.

Why didn't men see this every time it happened? Why were they shooed away, until all was over? How could women go through this time after time? What courage they had. What unbelievable strength.

"Ah, here we are," Portia said, her voice satisfied. She lifted her head from the tent, held up a tiny baby, slapped it on the bottom, and it began crying lustily. She cut the cord with a pair of scissors.

Darryl hastened to her with a blanket, took the baby from

her and wrapped it securely. She beamed down at the babe and held it so Hayley could see.

"Oh, Hayley, you have a lovely little daughter. It's all over now. You can rest."

Hayley gazed at the babe, her face a mixture of exhaustion and joy.

Darryl moved to Conn, holding out the baby to him. Carefully, he took the precious burden. He gazed down at the babe.

"She's so small," he whispered. Awe and wonder filled his heart as he gazed down at the tiny red face in his arms.

This was his daughter, his and Hayley's. Together they had created this perfect little human being.

"Bring her to me. Let me see her," Agnes commanded.

Reluctantly, Conn returned his child to Darryl, who took it across the room to Agnes.

"One of the most beautiful babes I have ever seen," Agnes said, her voice gratified.

Portia was under the tent again. Conn heard her sharp intake of breath. She lifted her head, a look of astonishment on her face.

"You can't rest quite yet, Hayley dear. You have more work to do."

"Is something wrong?" Conn asked in alarm.

Portia shook her head. "No. Hayley, do you hear me? You must do yet more pushing."

Hayley turned her dazed face to the midwife. "Wh—what do you mean?"

"It's no wonder you were so big," Portia said. "There's yet another babe waiting to be born. Now, push, dear, push."

A few moments later, Conn heard another lusty cry. Portia swiftly and expertly performed the necessary chores, then wrapped the second baby in a blanket and handed it to Conn.

"Here, you may hold your newborn son, Mr. Merritt."

A son, too? He was bursting with pride and delight.

He glanced at Hayley.

Her eyes were open, she was smiling. And although her flaxen hair was wet with perspiration, her blue eyes were dark—

circled from exhaustion, she had never looked so beautiful to him.

He moved to her, holding the baby so she could see it.

"Our son," he said. "I'd like to name him Benjamin, after my father. If that's all right with you."

Hayley nodded. "That's a fine name."

Joy was in her face and voice as she looked at him, but also exhaustion.

And something else seemed to be there, too. Some kind of holding back . . . reserve.

Darryl moved to stand beside Conn, holding out the girl babe. "Here is your daughter, sister mine," she said, her face wreathed in smiles.

Hayley smiled back at her. "I'd like to name her Jillian, after our mother," she said.

Her smile for her sister was open, holding no undercurrents, as was her tired voice.

"If that's all right with you, Conn," she added, turning back to him.

That slight bit of holding back was evident again, he saw. He swallowed.

What could he expect after the way he'd treated her these last few months?

He was lucky she was even speaking to him at all.

"Of course. It's a beautiful name."

He sought her gaze and tried to put all the love he felt for her into his look, his smile.

She returned his smile, but after a moment her gaze fell away, her eyes closed. "I'm so tired."

"Of course you are," Portia said. "You've labored very hard and now you need to rest. All of you leave and let this new mother sleep."

The bedchamber door opened and Lavena entered, carrying warm bricks and blankets. She stopped just inside the door, her mouth dropping open.

"It is all over? And there are *two* babies?"

Darryl nodded, her voice full of pride and love. "Yes, indeed.

Look at them. How beautiful and lusty they are. You would scarcely know they were born early.''

Lavena's glance went to Hayley, who lay in an exhausted sleep. Frowning, she looked at the midwife. ''Is she all right?''

Portia nodded. ''She's very tired, but fine.''

Lavena's face cleared. ''Praise be for that. I was very worried.''

She placed her armload of supplies on a chair and held out her arms to Darryl. ''Here, let me hold my nephew . . . or is it niece?''

Darryl gave her the baby she held. ''One of each. This is Jillian.''

Lavena carefully took the baby into her arms. She gazed at the small face reverently. ''She is indeed wonderful.''

The baby's small face puckered up, and she began to cry.

Lavena gently rocked her back and forth until the cries turned into whimpers and then ceased. Lavena gave her a gratified smile.

''We may have to find a wet nurse,'' she said, authority in her voice. ''Hayley probably won't have enough milk for two.''

''That's true,'' Agnes said from her corner. ''Now, will you let me hold one of these infants? I can't wait any longer.''

Conn walked to her and gently placed his son in her arms. *Benjamin, his son. And Jillian, his daughter.*

The words sounded so good, so right to him. Of course these were his children. How could he ever have doubted that?

The dark memories no longer haunted him. Oh, they were still there. They'd always be there. But they'd receded to a far corner of his mind, stored with all the other hurtful things that had happened to him.

A heavy weight had been lifted. Cleansing relief flooded over him.

Everything seemed so clear now. As Hayley had tried to tell him, she'd had to do all she did, or risk her sister's life, and sell herself back into a servitude she didn't deserve.

Her only other choice would have been to leave Holly View. Leave *him*. His heart contracted.

Thank God she hadn't done that!

He'd been such a fool, but now it was all over. He was ready to be a good husband to Hayley. A good father to these babes.

Their life together stretched ahead of him, long and satisfying.

Hayley gave a small, tired sigh, then turned over in the bed.

Conn's happy thoughts came to an abrupt stop. He remembered the expression in Hayley's eyes before she went to sleep.

Love was there. But also doubt and anger.

The same emotions he'd felt these last months.

Could Hayley ever forgive him for his treatment of her? For his lack of support when she needed him the most?

Had his great awakening come too late?

CHAPTER
TWENTY-EIGHT

"You may as well tend to Jilly," Lavena said, looking up from the apple pie she'd just taken from the oven.

She put it down on the worktable and gave her niece a fond glance. "She has more appetite and a bigger mouth than Ben."

Hayley sniffed the fragrant pie appreciatively and nodded. She set a fresh-baked loaf of bread down beside the pie and went to the cradles in the corner.

As Lavena had said, it was Jilly whose small mouth was open, expressing her desire for food. Beside her, in his own cradle, her brother Ben slept peacefully.

Hayley sat down in the comfortable armchair and adjusted her clothing, then picked up the baby and put her to her breast. Contentment flowed through her as the baby greedily nursed. She'd never dreamed she could feel such a tide of love as she did for her babies.

Lavena glanced over at her, a fond smile on her mouth as she gazed at Jilly. "Sounds like a suckling pig, I do declare," she said.

Hayley still marveled at how much Lavena cared for the twins. She hadn't expected that. She'd thought Conn's sister would merely tolerate the babies from the distant plane she'd retreated to after the night of the great storm.

Now, that distance had receded. Lavena was back to her old self . . . well, almost. She was less bossy now. Less sharp-tongued. She and Agnes even got along tolerably well.

Mainly, Hayley suspected, because they both vied constantly for who would help tend the babies.

Not that Lavena extended her fondness to Hayley. No, she hadn't gone that far. That would be too much to expect, Hayley supposed.

A ray of warm July sunshine came through the diamond-paned window and lit the area.

The weather so far this year had been what farmers pray for and seldom get. Plenty of warm sunshine to make the crops grow and just enough rain—but not too much, like the previous two years. Conn and Ellis were jubilant. The orchards promised to bear bumper crops of apples and peaches.

And Vaughn Walbridge had sold his farm and he and Radley had moved away. The new owners were capable and careful about fences and good relations with their neighbors.

Life seemed almost too good to be true. Almost perfect.

The sunbeam retreated behind a cloud and a cloud fell over her thoughts.

What would make life at Holly View perfect would be having her and Conn's relationship truly the way it appeared on the surface.

The twins were now almost two months old. Conn still occupied the spare bedchamber he had before their birth. No one had said anything, but Hayley knew that soon he would have to come back to their shared chamber.

Or else everyone would know all was not right with them.

Hayley felt a lump in her throat. Would it ever be all right with them?

How could she ever again fully trust Conn not to abandon her emotionally? As he had during her pregnancy, when she'd so badly needed him.

The birth of his babies had seemed to work such a change

in him. She no longer saw the dark memories in his eyes that had kept him from believing her, from accepting that she'd made the only choice possible.

Besides leaving Holly View, never marrying him.

Oh, she couldn't have done that! She loved Conn too much. She knew he loved her, too.

And now she saw only love and joy in his eyes . . . mixed with a question when their gazes met.

When will you welcome me back? he silently asked her a dozen times a day. *How much longer will this last?*

Hayley closed her eyes, a tide of unhappy feelings going through her.

How could she ever be certain the darkness, the black suspicion, had left him forever? That it might not return at any time?

And if it did, this time it would certainly destroy them.

Jilly's greedy tugs at her breast ceased. She glanced down to see the baby asleep, her tiny rosebud mouth lax, her eyelids closed.

Gently, Hayley removed Jilly, laid her back in the cradle, then adjusted her own clothing.

A loud scream pierced the stillness of the room.

Hayley jumped up, horror in her eyes.

At the hearth, flames leaped up Lavena's skirts. She batted at them futilely, more screams erupting from her throat.

"Lie down and roll," Hayley yelled, running across the room.

Lavena, terrified beyond hearing, just kept screaming and hitting at the flames with her hands.

Hayley reached her, pushed Lavena down on the hearth, rolled her over until she no longer saw flames. She grabbed the fire bucket and, rolling Lavena back over, doused the remaining sparks with the water.

Lavena gasped for breath, terror still in her wide eyes.

Hayley set the fire bucket down on the hearth. She brushed Lavena's hair back from her face. "It's all right," Hayley soothed. "You're not hurt, except maybe for your hands. Let me see."

Obediently, Lavena held out her hands. "You have some small blisters on your palms, but that's all."

She smiled down at Lavena, who was now sobbing. "It's all right. Here, let me help you up. I'll find some salve for your hands, and then help you change your gown."

She supported Lavena as the older woman got to her feet. Lavena swayed, holding onto Hayley for support. Instinctively, Hayley hugged her, patting her on the back.

Lavena's arms came out, returned Hayley's hug. "I owe my life to you. I would have burned to death if you hadn't come to my aid," Lavena gasped out.

Warmth went through Hayley. It felt good to have Lavena's hug. But this closeness might not last. It was probably only Lavena's reaction to her fear and relief.

"I'm just glad you aren't badly burned," Hayley said. "You'd no doubt have done all right without me."

"No," Lavena said, drawing back to give Hayley a straight look. "I wouldn't. I was scared to death. I couldn't think straight. You truly saved my life and I'll never forget it."

"Anyone would have helped you," Hayley protested.

"Perhaps. But I've treated you and your sister abominably," Lavena said. "I've been ashamed of it for a long time, but couldn't bring myself to apologize to you. Will you forgive me?"

Hayley blinked, overwhelmed at Lavena's words and manner. "Of course I'll forgive you."

An impulse to equal generosity came over her. "It couldn't have been easy when Conn brought us here."

"No, but it was none of my business," Lavena said, sniffing, and wiping her eyes with her hand. "It's Conn's house and he's given Ellis and me a good home since my husband died. I should have been more grateful instead of trying to stop him from having a happy life, a good marriage. I've finally seen his marriage to Marie was a misery to him."

The kitchen door suddenly opened. Hayley looked up. Conn stood in the doorway, Ellis and Darryl behind him.

"What's that smell of burning?" Conn asked. Then his gaze

focused on Lavena. "Are you all right, sister?" he asked, sharply.

Lavena nodded. "Yes, I'm fine, thanks to your wife. The sparks got my skirt again, and this time I would have died if Hayley hadn't saved me."

Behind Conn, Hayley saw Darryl's eyes widen in surprise at Lavena's words, her humble tone.

Ellis hurried forward. "Are you sure you're all right, Mother? Your skirt is burned nearly off you."

Lavena smiled at him, holding out her hands. "Only some blisters. Now, I'd better get upstairs and change."

"I'll help you," Hayley said. "You're still shaky."

Lavena shook her head. "You don't need to bother. I'll be fine."

She gave Hayley another smile, one of real warmth, and patted her shoulder. "Thank you."

"You're very welcome," Hayley returned.

Lavena walked to the back stairs and closed the door behind her.

Hayley stared after her. Well. Would wonders never cease.

"Are you all right?" Conn asked from beside her, making her jump because she hadn't seen him move closer.

"Yes, I'm fine," she assured him. "I'm just glad I was here."

"So am I," Conn said fervently. "Lavena's always been so careless around the fire. I hope this cures her."

Hayley smiled at him, enjoying his closeness despite the doubts churning inside her. "I'm sure it will. She was terrified."

Her smile died as their glances met and held. A question was in Conn's brown eyes. The one she was used to seeing there. But now it seemed more urgent.

When are you going to welcome me into your bed again? Into your life?

She sucked in her breath. She wasn't ready for this. It was too soon . . . she needed more time. . . .

Conn's own particular smell assailed her nostrils. That mixture of fresh air, the outdoors, and pure male . . .

Hunger for him suddenly filled her. She'd missed that, she'd missed *him* so very much. How had she been able to do without him all these months?

She couldn't do without him a night longer.

She smiled at him . . . the smile going to her eyes, holding an invitation . . .

She saw him swallow, and his eyes lit up for a moment.

One of the babies moved restlessly in its cradle, then started making little snuffling noises.

Conn turned, smiling. "Either Ben or Jilly sounds hungry."

Hayley smiled back. "Ben. I just fed Jilly."

"I'll soothe him while you wash and change," Darryl said.

Surprised, Hayley glanced down at her soot-blackened hands and gown, then felt her hair straggling around her face.

Darryl hurried across the room, scooped up the baby and held him to her shoulder, patting his back and making soft sounds.

Across the room, Ellis watched her, his heart in his eyes.

Hayley swallowed a lump in her throat. What she would give to have Darryl married to Ellis. To have her sister holding a baby of her own.

And that would yet come, she told herself firmly. Darryl just needed a bit more time.

Conn walked across the room, and Darryl reluctantly gave him the baby. A look of infinite tenderness came over his face as he glanced down at his fussing son.

He looked up, his glance meeting Hayley's again. *I will come to you tonight,* it said.

She made herself hold his glance, not shy away. She gave him a tiny nod of agreement.

Perhaps when he held her in his arms once more and they again shared the delights of lovemaking, all her doubts would melt away like the welcome spring sun had melted the winter frosts on Holly View.

And what if that didn't happen?

What if they remained there? Dark and cold in her heart?

CHAPTER
TWENTY-NINE

Hayley set the wine decanter on the small table by the fireplace. The July night was warm and no flames blazed in it now.

She remembered the night of their wedding, when firelight had glowed through their wine glasses, turning the garnet liquid to ruby.

That night seemed a very long time ago. So much had happened since then.

Her pregnancy so soon after their marriage . . . Oscar's shocking arrival . . . Conn's withdrawal . . . the long dreary months she'd spent in bed before the twins' births.

She had nearly died during their birthing. And the twins with her. She shuddered at that memory.

If Conn hadn't come to her, hadn't sworn his love, that could easily have happened. Because she'd lost her will to live.

Conn had given that back to her, given back her life and that of their babies. He'd finally been able to understand and forgive her for what she'd done.

And she'd forgiven him. That had been easy.

It was the forgetting that was hard.

That might not even be possible.

But she had to try.

Everything inside her longed for a complete union with her husband. Not just the sharing of their bodies, which she had no doubt would be as wonderful tonight as it had been before.

She wanted something that had never been between them.

A sharing of the heart and soul.

Conn's dark memories had prevented that when they first wed. His torments had caused him to draw away from her when she most needed him.

Now his heart and soul seemed to be at rest.

And it was her own that could find no ease.

Behind her, she heard the bedchamber door open, then quietly close.

Her pulse raced. She glanced down at her filmy white nightrail, trimmed in lace. Darryl had made it for her, presented it to her just a few days ago.

Her hair was loose around her shoulders and neck. She had rubbed crushed rose petals on her skin.

She had done all she could to make herself appealing to her husband.

As always, the babies were with the wet nurse for the night, so Hayley might sleep and regain her strength.

They wouldn't be disturbed.

She felt Conn behind her. Then his hands were on her shoulders, caressing her. He pushed the fabric of her nightrail to one side, and she drew in her breath at the feel of his warm hand moving on her bare flesh. His hand slipped lower to cup the fullness of one breast.

It felt so marvelous . . . just as she remembered, only better. How had she been able to wait so long for his touch?

"Hayley," Conn whispered. "Come to me. I need you so."

She remembered those words from the first time they'd made love. When it was she who had come to this chamber, and he was waiting for her.

She slipped out of the chair and turned to him. He wore only his breeches. His wide shoulders, his deep chest made her gasp with the need to feel herself pressed against him.

His dark eyes held an intensity she had never seen in them before. His gaze roamed down her from head to foot. "You're so beautiful," he murmured. "I've wanted you for so long. I have died without you."

Shyness suddenly swept over her. She felt as she had that first night. It *had* been a long time since they'd shared their bodies.

And she had changed from that virginal girl. Her belly was slightly rounded now, her breasts bigger.

Would he still find her desirable when he'd seen all of her again?

She moved back a step. "I . . . have wine. Would you like some?" she asked breathlessly.

He held her gaze a moment longer, then nodded. "If you do."

Relief went over her at the reprieve. "Oh, yes, I do."

She moved to the table, poured wine into two glasses and handed him one.

He lifted his glass and held it toward hers. "Let us drink to a long and happy marriage."

His eyes told her he remembered those words, or ones similar to them, from their wedding night.

She lifted her own glass, listened to the faint chime as the crystal touched, then watched him over the rim of her glass as they both drank.

His dark eyes held no shadows tonight. Only a controlled passion . . . and love. Yes, she was certain she saw that also.

Hayley took another, deeper sip. The wine warmed her, eased some of her tension. She sipped again, until the glass was empty.

"Here, let me take that." Conn removed her glass from her hand and set it with his, also empty, on the table.

Conn turned to her again and held out his arms as he had that other night. "Come to me," he asked once more.

The wine had flowed all through her, warmed her, taken away her unease, her shyness.

Hayley moved into the circle of his arms and let them enfold her, give her the comfort and safety she'd felt those months ago.

She rested there for long moments, listening to their mingled heartbeats. Conn simply held her, caressed her shoulders and back, seeming as content as she was for each to just hold the other again.

Slowly, that feeling gave way to another one. She became conscious of the hardness of his body against her own.

Especially the lower regions.

Her heartbeat quickened as memories tumbled through her mind. She slid her arms around his waist and pressed herself closer to him.

Soon that wasn't enough, either. She lifted her head to him. He was waiting. "Kiss me," she whispered.

His face lightened. "I thought you'd never ask."

The first brush of his lips on hers was light as a butterfly's wing, yet it made her tremble, made her long for more.

Which Conn wasn't long in giving. The kiss deepened and deepened . . . all the remembered delights came flooding back over her.

At last, breathless, they drew apart. Conn gave her a slow smile. "We have on too many clothes."

She smiled back at those well-remembered words.

"Yes," she agreed. Then some of her tension returned. What would he think of her body now?

There was only one way to find out.

Soon, they stood naked before each other.

Conn's gaze feasted on her. She could actually feel its warmth. "I couldn't imagine you more beautiful than you were before, but I was wrong. Motherhood has ripened your body."

Her tension dissolved. "It's certainly changed it."

She allowed her gaze to sweep over him. "You haven't changed," she said. Her gaze went lower . . . lower still. She raised her head to give him a mischievous look. "Everything seems to be in fine condition."

"Come here, you little minx," he growled, reaching for her.

She came, willingly, gladly. When their naked bodies touched, she gasped and heard an answering gasp from Conn. Arms wrapped around each other, bodies pressed close, heat built between them until Hayley could stand no more.

She put her hands against his chest and pushed backward, until a few inches separated them. She gasped again. "I'm burning up. Enough."

He smiled at her. A slow and intimate smile that sent shivers dancing up and down her spine. "Oh, no, that wasn't nearly enough. Before the night's through, we'll both be consumed by fire."

"Yes," she answered in a breathless whisper, then turned and walked to the bed. When she reached it, she turned again and smiled at him over her shoulder. The same slow smile he'd just given her, teasing, hinting at delights to come.

"Beware," he warned, his dark eyes glinting. "Your teasing may get you into trouble."

"I certainly hope so."

"I think I must quiet your saucy tongue." In a moment he was beside her, holding her close, his mouth covering hers.

Eagerly, she returned the kiss and pressed herself even closer, willing her being to dissolve in his, her mind to stop its doubts.

Still holding her tightly, Conn lay on his side on the bed, tugging her down beside him. He lifted a hand and stroked her cheek. Then his hand strayed to her neck, down to her breasts, leaving fire in its wake.

"Touch me everywhere," she entreated him. "Just as you used to do."

He'd left the candle burning, and its dim light shadowed his face and made his brown eyes gleam, his white teeth flash as he smiled at her.

"I'll do that," he promised. He bent his head, and his lips followed the trail his hands had started. His teeth nipped gently at one breast, then the other.

She arched against him. "Oh, how I've missed your touch," she whispered.

"As I have yours," he answered. He picked up one of her hands and placed it on his throat. "Touch me, stroke me," he begged.

She felt the strong beat of his pulse beneath her fingers. His skin smelled of soap and that clean scent that was his own. It felt warm and smooth, enticing her to explore further. She eased her way down his chest, pausing to nip at his nipples with her teeth.

He moved restlessly beneath her and let out a small groan. She raised her head. "Have you had enough?" she teased.

"No," he growled. "Continue."

She slid her fingers through the curling dark hair on his chest, tugged at it, then moved her hand lower, then lower still.

Conn reached down and grasped her hand, holding it against him. She felt the swelling of flesh beneath her hand, felt her passion rise. . . .

Outside, a gust of wind sprang up, slamming a limb of the big oak against the house.

"It's going to storm," she murmured, delicately moving her hand and fingers.

"Let it," Conn answered, between his teeth. "Now get on with your work."

Hayley lifted her head and gave him a mock-surprised look. The guttering candle was almost out, but in its light she saw the gleam in his eyes.

"Work, is it?" she said. "I thought this was play."

"I'll show you play." He grasped her to him, rolled her over so that she was beneath him, his sinewy body pressing her to the bed. He looked down at her for a long, long moment.

"My beautiful wife," he said. "Have you forgiven me for my foolishness? Can you become one with me again?"

Her heart ached, longed for that. For a oneness they'd never experienced together. Surely, with both of them wanting it so much, tonight they could achieve it.

"I have long forgiven you," she said, with truth.

Now let the forgetfulness come, she prayed.

"I don't deserve you," Conn said. He kissed her long and deeply, then showered kisses on her face, her closed eyelids, down her throat, her breasts, her softly rounded belly, until he reached the curly nest of flaxen hair between her legs.

"Enough!" she cried again when his kisses lingered there, arching herself against him.

Outside, the storm gathered force. The tree limb banged against the house again, then the rain came, followed by a lightning flash and the crack of thunder.

Inside, snug in their warm bed, Conn and Hayley created their own gentle storm.

The joy and delight they'd always found together was still there, stronger than before. Their bodies seemed even more perfectly attuned to each other.

Conn's every movement drew forth an answering response from her, so that at the end, when they both came together in that final ecstasy, she truly felt as if they'd become one, body and soul.

At last, exhausted, panting, they lay enfolded in each other's arms. Against her breasts, Hayley felt Conn's heartbeat slow. Heard his breathing even out in sleep.

Outside, the storm still raged, but here, their own storm spent, they'd found peace.

Contentedly, sweetly, Hayley moved her fingers along Conn's cheekbones and cupped his square jaw in her hand.

He was her love and she was his. Just down the hallway, their two beautiful babies slept peacefully.

All was right in their world. All *would* be right, she told herself firmly.

Conn moved, restlessly, muttering something under his breath she couldn't understand.

She held her breath. It wasn't, it couldn't be Marie's name.

Of course it couldn't. All that was finished and over. She hadn't seen those shadows in Conn's eyes tonight. Or in the last few weeks.

But had she looked very hard? What if they were only pushed aside, not dissolved?

What if, maybe not tomorrow or next month, but someday, all the dark suspicions, the withdrawal came back?

With a rush, Hayley's doubts returned.

How could she trust that never to happen again? How could she make herself that vulnerable? That open to hurt?

Coldness invaded her, pushed out the warm contented feelings.

She couldn't stand that, not ever again.

It would kill her.

The coldness grew. Her only defense against that fate was to keep her wariness, her watchfulness.

She could share her body fully with Conn, just as they had done tonight. They had their lovely children to take satisfaction and joy in. All the rest of their lives here at Holly View they could share.

Hayley moved to Conn and snuggled against his warm body, letting his physical closeness bring back some of her contentment.

They had more together than most people. It would be enough. Tears filled her eyes, and she let them fall for a moment before wiping them away.

It *had* to be enough.

Because she couldn't fully open her heart to him.

She didn't dare.

CHAPTER THIRTY

Hayley came into the kitchen, carrying Jilly.

A beam of warm summer sunlight lay a path across the floor, brightening everything it touched.

Lavena glanced up from the worktable where she cut vegetables and smiled at both of them.

"You are late in rising, Hayley," Lavena said, but there was no censure in her voice and the smile went all the way to her eyes.

Since the day Hayley had doused Lavena's skirts, the older woman had treated Hayley as completely one of the family. Almost like a sister. She treated Darryl the same way.

Her thaw had been long in coming, but was all the sweeter for the waiting, Hayley decided. Life at Holly View was peaceful and happy these days.

"Yes, I'm a slugabed today," Hayley said, smiling back.

She felt her cheeks warm. She and Conn hadn't had a great deal of sleep last night. Other things had occupied their time. As always, their lovemaking had been wonderful.

Why couldn't everything be that way between them? Why

couldn't she get rid of the doubts and fears that plagued her still?

Conn knew, of course. They'd talked, ending with him telling her he understood. He could wait.

But for how long?

Eventually, her feelings would put a wedge between them. That was inevitable.

"You're no slugabed," Agnes said from her chair. "The twins aren't quite three months old and you had such a time with their birthing. You still need to rest and regain your strength."

Hayley gave her a smiling glance, to find Agnes's eyes twinkling at her. Hayley's flush deepened. Not much got past Agnes. It was obvious she hadn't forgotten her younger days with her husband.

"My strength is fully returned," Hayley said. Jilly squirmed in her arms and began the little snuffling noises, the rooting motions that signaled her awakening hunger.

"Let me hold her for a few moments before she gets all wound up," Agnes said, holding out her arms.

Hayley crossed the room and gave Jilly to her. Agnes rocked the baby back and forth, making soothing sounds as she beamed down at her.

"Go ahead and eat your breakfast," Lavena said. "We saved your portion."

"All right." Hayley retrieved her plate from where it was kept warm at the hearth and took it to the kitchen table. She quickly ate, mindful of Jilly's increasing fussiness.

"Here, let me feed her." She retrieved the baby and sat back down in her chair, adjusted her clothing, then put the baby to her breast.

"Where's Darryl?" she asked in a moment.

"Already out in the gardens," Lavena answered. "I've never seen such a girl for loving weeding and digging in the dirt."

Hayley smiled. "Yes, she's always been like that, since we were young children."

"Where she is, Ellis won't be far behind," Agnes said. "I

saw them talking in the gardens last night. And for once, Darryl wasn't backing off.''

"Good," Lavena said, finishing with her vegetables. She took them across the room to the big stew pot and placed them inside.

Another thing that had changed for the better, Hayley thought. Lavena no longer tried to fight her son's obvious interest in Darryl. In fact she now encouraged it. More than once lately, she'd mentioned a wish for grandchildren.

The kitchen door burst open with a bang. Startled, Hayley's head shot up.

Conn and Gustav, grim-faced, stood in the doorway, carrying Ellis, whose eyes were closed, his face very white.

Blood dripped onto the floor from his shoulder.

Hayley jumped to her feet, alarm going through her. "What has happened?"

Lavena jerked around. "Oh, my God, what's wrong with my boy?" She hurried across the room.

"He's been shot," Conn said over his shoulder as he and Gustav reached the parlor door, opened it and carried Ellis inside. They gently laid him on a settee.

Hayley and Lavena were close behind. Lavena ran to the kitchen, returning in a moment with a towel. Conn took it, held it tightly to the wound.

"What has happened?" Lavena asked, her voice shaking. She knelt beside Ellis, smoothing his pale brow, and everyone listened to his shallow breathing.

"We don't know," Conn said curtly. "We just found him near the barns."

"Is he badly wounded?" Agnes asked from behind.

"I don't know," Conn said again. "We must get the bleeding stopped." He lifted the towel, which was fast turning red with blood, then pressed it once more against the wound.

"Who would do something like this?" Lavena asked. "Who would shoot my lad?"

Her voice was rising. Hayley knew hysteria wasn't far behind.

Jilly had finished nursing and fallen asleep. Hayley lifted her away, fastened her gown and handed the babe to Agnes.

Agnes retreated to a chair with her precious charge, her face drawn and white.

Hayley grasped Lavena's shoulder in a reassuring grip. "It will be all right," she soothed, hoping she spoke the truth.

"Another towel," Conn said, glancing at Hayley. Concern for Ellis was in his eyes . . . and something else. Love and . . . a tiny bit of reserve of his own.

Because of her, Hayley knew, her lips tightening. She hastened to the kitchen for the towel. She handed it to Conn, and he quickly removed the first towel and slid the fresh one against the wound.

The first towel was sodden with blood. Hayley's stomach turned over as she took it back to the kitchen and put it in a tub of water by the hearth.

"Get the smelling salts," Agnes called from the parlor.

Of course! Hayley hastened to the shelf, found the salts, hurried back to the parlor. Relieved, she saw the new towel didn't seem to be filling with blood as fast. She waved the salts under Ellis's nose.

At first he didn't respond. Then he coughed and turned his head, coughing again.

"Let me do that," Lavena said, her voice more normal-sounding now. She took the salts from Hayley and stuck them close to her son's nose again.

Again Ellis coughed. "Get that away," he protested, opening his eyes and struggling to sit up.

Gustav held him firmly down. "None of that just yet, young man. You've been hurt."

Ellis's dark brows drew together. "Hurt? What do you mean?" Again he tried to sit up.

"Stop that," Conn commanded. "You're starting the bleeding up again."

"Bleeding?" Ellis turned his head and saw the bloody towel wrapping his arm and shoulder.

"Someone shot you," Conn said, his voice clipped. "Do you have any idea who?"

Shock came into Ellis's eyes. His face paled even more. He struggled wildly against the hands restraining him. "Let me up! I have to go after them."

Conn and Gustav kept their grips firm. "Calm down and stop that," Conn said between his teeth. "After who? What are you talking about?"

"That bastard took Darryl," Ellis said. "I heard her screaming and when I got there, he'd done something to her and put her into his carriage. She wasn't moving. Then he shot me."

Ellis's head slumped. "I couldn't stop him."

Hayley moved forward. "Who?" she asked, but a cold feeling already grew between her shoulder blades.

"That bastard Pritt," Ellis said. "I've worried about him since he didn't want to sell her bond and the way he looked at her that day he was here. I knew he wasn't finished with her."

"Damnation," Conn said, his voice tight. "How long ago was this? Do you know?"

Ellis shook his head. "Not long after sunrise. The men hadn't gotten to the barns yet. I'd gone out early because Darryl was working in the gardens. I wanted to see her."

Conn's urgent glance shot to Gustav. He nodded at him.

Gustav nodded back, then hurried out of the room. A few moments later, Hayley heard the kitchen door open, then close.

He'd gone to get Tristan ready for Conn, Hayley guessed. So that Conn could soon be on his way.

Conn cautiously lifted the towel. The wound had almost stopped bleeding. He glanced at Lavena. "It's clean. The ball went through. Can you take care of the wound?"

Lavena drew herself up, got her emotions under control. "Of course I can. I've handled many injuries over the years. You go on."

He nodded. Then his gaze sought out Hayley. He gave her a forced smile. "Don't worry. We'll find Darryl."

Hayley swallowed and stepped forward. "I'm going, too."

He gave her a shocked stare. "Don't be absurd."

She firmed her mouth. "I'm not. Darryl's my sister. I'm going with you to find her."

"Of course you can't go. It's too dangerous."

She tilted her chin up. "Have you forgotten that Darryl and I faced and survived many dangers before we came here?"

"I haven't time to argue," he said, abruptly. "You will stay here."

He turned on his heel and left the room and the house.

Hayley stared after him, then began untying her apron.

Lavena half-turned from her station by Ellis, holding the towel to his wound. "What are you doing?"

"I'm going to help find my sister," Hayley said, her voice every bit as firm as Conn's had been.

Lavena turned back around. "It's a good thing we have the wet nurse. Mrs. Bailey has milk enough for her own and your two with some to spare."

"Yes, that's fortunate," Agnes agreed. "But how are you going to manage, child? Conn won't let you go with him."

Hayley put the apron down on a chair. "I'm not going with him. I'll give him a head start."

"Take Perdita," Lavena advised. "She's gentle and you're used to riding her."

"That's what I planned," Hayley said.

"Give him a half hour's start," Lavena advised. "And he'll probably take the Derryville road."

"I'll give him fifteen minutes," Hayley said, and hurried out of the room.

"Don't forget to squeeze your breasts to keep the milk from drying up," Lavena called after her.

Blast and damn. Why did the horse have to become lame now?

Probably because you've ridden him too hard, Conn answered himself.

He glanced at the sky. The sun hung low in the west. Only another hour or two of daylight. He swore again.

And he was only gambling that Pritt had taken this road, since it was the main one. But he could have taken the lesser one. And he was also guessing Pritt was heading back to his plantation.

He'd inquired of everyone he encountered thus far, to no avail. No one had seen a small carriage, carrying either a man and a woman, or only a man. All had looked at him strangely when he'd phrased his questions thusly.

But if Pritt had any sense, he'd of course keep Darryl hidden.

Conn's face darkened. He probably had her bound and gagged, concealed under blankets . . . or worse. By this time he might have thought better of his foolish, rash move and dumped her . . . or her body . . . somewhere deep in the woods.

No, he wouldn't think like that. The man wanted her. As Ellis had said, that was obvious when he'd balked at selling her bond and given her that lecherous look that day at Holly View.

But only a fool would do such a thing as this, and Pritt hadn't seemed a fool.

Thank God he was near the White Horse Tavern. He'd leave Tristan there and pick up a fresh mount. As it was, Tristan's sudden lameness had cost him a good half hour of lost time.

He reached the tavern with relief, gave Tristan a quick examination, then handed him to the stable attendant

"He picked up a stone, but he'll be all right by tomorrow," Conn told the lad. "Do you have a fresh horse for hire?"

"Only one," the boy said.

"Is he fast?" Conn asked, not able to keep the urgency out of his voice.

"Yes. He'll get you where you want to go."

And where is that? Conn asked himself. "All right. Saddle him and I'll be back in a moment."

He strode to the inn, where George greeted him, saw his urgency and quickly called to Freda to pack him some food.

"Has a dark, heavy-built man driving a carriage passed by

here today?'' Conn asked, wincing at his description. ''He may have had a young woman in the carriage, also.''

George, ever the tactful tavern-keeper, showed no surprise at his question. He pulled at his chin and frowned. ''Can't recall seeing anyone like that. Wait a minute and I'll ask Freda.''

He left, returning in a moment with his wife beside him. She gave him her pinched smile. ''Yes, a gentleman fitting that description did stop here a few hours ago.''

She turned to her husband. ''You remember Mr. Pritt. He owns a prosperous plantation farther north.''

Conn's pulse quickened. ''Was he alone?''

Freda nodded. ''Oh, yes. He came in to water his horses and have a brandy.'' She stopped and shrugged. ''He had two brandies to be exact, and bought a bottle to take with him.''

So the bastard was drunk. Or at least drinking enough to be stupid and reckless. That explained a lot.

The thought of Darryl lying bound and covered in the carriage seat sent fury racing through Conn's veins.

A maid hurried toward them with a wrapped food bundle.

Conn took it, found the coins to pay for it and his fresh mount, then thanked them for their help.

He hurried back toward the stable. Halfway there he stopped short at the sight of a figure in earnest conversation with the stable lad.

A very familiar figure.

His wife. Whom he loved to distraction. Did she love him? Had his withdrawal from her during her pregnancy ruined their relationship?

Conn swore and picked up his pace.

''What are you doing here?'' he asked, reaching her side. ''Didn't I say you couldn't come with me?''

Hayley gave him a level look. ''I didn't come with you. I came by myself.''

Conn swore again. ''Go on inside and wait for me. I'll pick you up on my way back.''

The stable boy moved discreetly away.

She tilted her chin up. "I have to go with you."

Conn ground his teeth together. No use wasting time telling her it was too dangerous. "You'll slow me down."

"No, I won't. I can keep up with you on a fresh mount."

Conn narrowed his eyes. "I hired the last one."

She blinked, then straightened. "All right, then, I'll ride with you."

"Damn it, woman, will you be reasonable? You can't come. I won't take you."

The thought of Hayley behind him, clinging to him while they rode through the night, was unnerving.

He loved her so much. What could he do to make her realize he'd never again treat her as he had during her pregnancy?

Loving her with his body hadn't given her that reassurance. Promising her with words hadn't, either.

How much longer could their marriage stand the strain? Would they end as most married couples did? Sharing their bodies, having more children, but never having that complete union they both longed for?

A sharing of heart and soul.

Hayley folded her arms. "Then I'll run along beside you."

Five minutes later, Conn rode out of the yard, Hayley seated behind him, holding onto his waist.

"Have these people seen them?" she asked.

"Yes. Freda knows Pritt. He stopped here."

"He?"

He'd known she'd pick up on that.

"Pritt appeared to be alone."

"He has her tied and hidden," Hayley said, her voice very firm. Obviously, she was allowing no doubts to creep in.

"Yes," Conn agreed. He would hang on to that hope, too.

They rode in silence for a while, while the sun sank lower in the western sky. The August evening was very warm.

There would be an almost-full moon tonight, he thought gratefully as he kept the horse moving at a steady pace.

And Pritt was apparently still driving his tired horses. How much longer could they keep going?

Conn tried not to think of what he and Hayley might discover at the end of their quest.

CHAPTER THIRTY-ONE

The sun had long since set in a blaze of fire that promised a fine, fair day tomorrow.

As if she cared about that, Hayley thought.

The moon had risen, giving an eerie light to the countryside they traveled along.

The inn's mount had a hard and bony back. Hayley clung to Conn's sides, her rump so sore she didn't even bother to shift her position anymore. Each way she turned was equal torture.

That didn't matter, either.

We'll find you, she promised her sister silently. *We'll find you and all will be well.*

She sent her thoughts out on the still night air, hoping Darryl could somehow hear, be comforted by them.

If she was still able to be comforted by anything.

If she was still alive.

Hayley forced those dark thoughts deep into her mind.

She is, she is, she told herself doggedly. The two of them had gone through too much together. They would both have a long and happy life.

You have problems of your own to solve before that can come about, her mind said.

She ignored it. She could concentrate on nothing more than finding Darryl now.

Her weariness caught up with her and she dozed, her head falling forward against Conn's straight, strong back.

Hayley awoke with a jerk as Conn let out an exclamation of surprise.

Ahead of them on the deserted road was a carriage.

Hayley's arms tightened around Conn. "Oh, is it Oscar's?"

"I'd lay odds it is, but we can't be sure until we overtake it."

Conn pressed his legs against his mount. The horse picked up speed and they gained on the carriage for a few minutes. Then, the carriage pulled ahead again.

"There, that proves it, I think," Conn said grimly. "No reason for an innocent man to try to escape us. No highwaymen in this country."

"No," Hayley agreed, her teeth clenched, fearing what the next few minutes might bring.

"Hang on tight," he told Hayley. He pressed his mount for more speed, and for a few more minutes they kept the same distance, Conn not gaining, the carriage not pulling ahead.

A sharp curve loomed in front of them. Hayley drew in her breath as the carriage horses kept up their breakneck pace, not slowing a bit. As they came into the curve, the carriage wobbled alarmingly.

"Goddammit, the fool's going to overturn!"

Hayley held her breath, fear filling her. The carriage wobbled even more. A wheel came off and rolled across the road. A figure fell into the road.

Its two horses screaming in fear, the carriage tumbled onto its side.

Directly on top of the fallen figure.

Hayley's heart stopped. "Oh, God, was that Darryl?"

"I can't tell," Conn's grim voice said.

The horses were still screaming, struggling to get up, get out of their tangled harness.

"Hurry, hurry!" Hayley begged.

"I am," Conn clipped out. "We're almost there."

In a few more moments, he reined in the horse beside the overturned carriage and jumped down. Hayley slid down beside him.

They both ran to the side of the carriage. Hayley gasped. Two legs and feet protruded from underneath.

Very still legs and feet.

Stout legs covered in bloodstained breeches and feet wearing slippers with large silver buckles.

Relief so great she nearly swooned hit Hayley. She ran to the other side of the carriage. It was too high for her to see inside.

"Darryl," she called, her fear returning.

What if only silence answered her? "Are you in there? Are you all right?"

"Yes!" Darryl's voice said from the depths of the carriage. "I'm fine. But I'm tied. I can't get loose."

Conn was suddenly there beside Hayley. "Don't be scared," he said, his voice firm and reassuring. "We'll get you out."

"I said I'm fine. But is Ellis badly hurt? He's not dead, is he?" Her voice changed into a sob on the last words.

"No, no," Hayley said quickly. "It's only his shoulder."

"Thank God, thank God!"

Conn unfastened the horses's reins, and the frightened beasts struggled to their feet. Then, before Conn could restrain them, they took off down the road at a gallop.

Conn shook his head. "Damn. We needed one of them." He climbed up the side of the carriage and disappeared inside.

In a few minutes, he carefully lowered Darryl, cut ropes still dangling from her hands, onto the ground. Her gown was torn and stained, and a dark bruise marred one cheek.

Hayley enfolded Darryl in her arms, and both sisters sobbed out their relief.

"I was so afraid," Darryl said, giving Hayley a watery smile. "I tried to stop Oscar from shooting Ellis, and he hit me, knocked me out. When I came to, I was bound and gagged, hidden under a blanket on the carriage floor."

"Are you sure you're all right?" Conn asked. "Did the bastard hurt you?"

Hayley knew what he meant, and her heart lurched. Had her sister been forced again?

Darryl knew what Conn meant, too. Her face paled. "No! He was waiting until he got me back to his plantation. He told me in great detail what he planned to do to me then. By the end, he was so drunk he could scarcely talk."

Conn smacked a fist into his other hand. "Good riddance to bad rubbish. If he wasn't dead, I'd kill him."

Darryl swallowed. "I know it's wicked of me, but I'm glad he's dead!"

Hayley nodded. "So am I. He was an evil man."

"I'm going to see if I can find one of the horses," Conn said. He looked at them. "Will you be all right for a few minutes?"

Hayley and Darryl looked at each other. Both of them nodded. "We'll be fine," Darryl said.

"I won't be long," Conn promised. He headed down the road in the direction the horses had taken.

The two women moved farther away from the carriage.

"Why didn't I tell Ellis I loved him?" Darryl said, her voice wobbling. "What if he'd died and he'd never have known?"

Hayley smiled at her. "But he isn't going to die and you have the rest of your lives to tell him you love him."

"But look at all the time I wasted when we could have been together!"

A shock went through Hayley at her sister's words.

Look at all the time she'd wasted when she and Conn could have been together in that complete, deep union she so wanted.

What was she waiting for? The moon to fall? A miraculous

sign to appear in the heavens telling her she needn't ever worry about Conn deserting her again?

Or someone to shoot Conn so that she'd see she mustn't waste any more precious time?

Hayley drew in her breath at that shocking thought.

Anything could happen to either of them at any time. She could be dead tomorrow. So could Conn.

No one could know what life would bring.

She managed a smile for Darryl. "Yes, but now you know how much you love him. You won't waste any more time."

"No!" Darryl said, fervently. "The moment we get back to Holly View, I'll tell him. I'm ready to make him a good wife. To trust him in every way and never fear for the future."

And so will I tell Conn, Hayley echoed, silently. *Sooner, if that's possible.*

Hayley smiled at her. "Well said, sister. Your words are my words, too."

"So things are finally right between you and Conn?" Darryl asked.

Hayley gave her a rueful smile. "Not yet. But when he returns . . . I think I can make them so."

A noise came from down the road. Both Darryl and Hayley glanced that way. It was the sound of horses' hooves.

Soon, Conn came into view, leading one horse.

Hayley's heart turned over at the sight of him.

When he reached them, she stepped forward and looked up at him. "I love you," Hayley said.

She hoped the moonlight was bright enough for him to see what was in her eyes. Her heart.

He looked down at her. A slow smile lit his face.

"I love you, wife."

Their gazes held for a long moment. Then Conn dismounted. "We have two horses between us. There is no way I can get the carriage repaired. Can we make it back to the tavern?"

"Yes," Hayley and Darryl said, in unison.

Hayley wanted to tell him they could make it all the way

back to Holly View. How she longed to see her babies. She knew Darryl equally yearned to see Ellis.

But that would have to wait for tomorrow.

She could wait now that everything was finally right between her and Conn.

CHAPTER THIRTY-TWO

Dawn was breaking as they rode into Holly View. Hayley and Darryl had stayed at the tavern while Conn and other men from there went back and dealt with Oscar Pritt.

Then they'd all slept for a few hours.

No place on earth had ever looked so beautiful to Hayley. The soft, weathered gray of the old shingles welcomed her. The diamond-paned windows glistened in the early morning rays of the sun.

They were finally home!

Home.

She tasted the word in her mind. For the first time it sounded completely right.

Darryl squeezed her waist hard.

The moment Hayley reined the horse, she tumbled off, running toward the house.

The kitchen door opened. Lavena hurried out, holding Ben, her face wreathed in smiles.

"Darryl! Hayley! Thank God all of you are safely home." Somehow, Lavena managed to hug Darryl without losing her grip on the baby.

Darryl returned the hug, then stood back. "How is Ellis?" Her voice and face were taut with worry.

"He won't be able to use that arm for a while, but otherwise, he's doing fine."

The worry lines on Darryl's face dissolved into a smile. She hurried on inside, pausing to hug Agnes, who was right behind Lavena, holding Jilly.

"Thank God you're all home," Agnes said. "These children have sorely missed their parents."

Hayley reached for Jilly, looking down at the sleeping baby. "She seems well content."

Conn, now dismounted, reached for Ben. "So does this one," he said, smiling at Hayley.

She returned the smile, their glances holding, promising. . . .

"Tell me what happened," Lavena said.

Conn did, making short work of the tale.

When he was finished, Lavena reached for Ben. "Here, let me take him and you two get yourselves up to bed before you fall on your feet."

Agnes held out her arms for Jilly. "Upstairs with the both of you," she said.

She and Conn handed the babies back.

Now that they were safely home, Hayley realized she was shaking with weariness, her knees trembling.

Conn took her arm. "Come," he told her. "Let us get you up to bed."

They went inside, walked across the familiar, lovely kitchen, out the door to the back passage.

Dolly, her kittens long dispatched to the barn, except for Darryl's Mischief, meowed in welcome. Hayley stooped to rub her hand down the cat's back.

She straightened. "I love this place," she told Conn. "And I love you. With all my heart."

His answering glance was probing, unsmiling. She held her breath. Would the miracle of true love at last find them?

Or had she waited too long?

A slow smile, full of tenderness and love, lit his face. He reached for her and enfolded her in his arms.

"I have loved you since the moment you tumbled out of the wood that day, and near fell under my horse's feet. I will love you until I die."

Her heart near to bursting with happiness, Hayley lifted her face to his. Their lips met, in a long, soul-satisfying kiss that promised more.

That promised everything.

Finally, breathless, they drew apart.

Hayley lifted her hand, caressed the strong line of his jaw.

"We are both home at last."

"Yes," Conn agreed.

And kissed her again.

EPILOGUE

Hayley glanced skyward at the huge golden globe of the moon. "It's such a lovely night."

Conn, standing beside her on the grassy banks of the pond, nodded. "It is that."

But he was more interested in gazing at his wife than at the mild late fall evening. She was so beautiful with the moon's silvery rays lending mysterious shadows.

"I miss Darryl," Hayley said in a moment. "We've always been so close. But I know it's best that she have her own household to run. And Aunt Agnes seems so content now that she's back in her own house most of the time."

"Aunt Agnes's suggestion that Ellis take over Cedarwood was inspired," Conn said.

"Yes. He and Darryl are so happy. And their child will be close enough to the twins in age they can be playmates. Thank goodness Cedarwood isn't far from Holly View, or Lavena wouldn't be able to stand it. She's going to be the most doting grandmother who ever lived."

"Yes." Conn ran his hand down her flaxen hair.

She smiled at him. "Now that our families are growing, it will be a good thing to have an extra bedchamber or two, also."

He widened his eyes. "What? Are you telling me that our own family will soon be added to again?"

Hayley shook her head. "Not yet. My goodness, give me a little time to enjoy our two scamps!"

"Does that mean you want me to stop sharing your bed?" he asked teasingly.

Hayley gave him a mock frown. "Of course not."

She glanced up at the night sky. "Just look at that moon. Isn't it wonderful with the clouds scudding in front of it like that?"

"Not as wonderful as our life is now," Conn said, huskily.

He bent and touched his lips to hers. Lightly at first. Then, as she warmly responded, he deepened the kiss.

"I'm so glad I found you," he whispered, his arms sliding around her slim form.

"No happier than I, to have found you," she returned.

"We're an extremely lucky couple."

Hayley drew back a little, giving him an impish look.

"Luck had nothing to do with it. It was written in the stars that we would meet." Despite her expression, her words were heartfelt.

"You really believe that."

"Of course. Don't you?"

"Yes," he answered in a moment. "I guess I do. It would have been so easy for me to have missed you. If I'd waited another day, or come a day earlier, we'd never have met."

"But you didn't. It was meant for us to meet. To fall in love. To marry."

She smiled, reaching up a hand to stroke down his face, trace around his lips.

He drew in his breath, pulling her closer. "If you don't stop that, I won't be responsible for what happens."

"Is that a promise, Mr. Merritt?"

"Yes," he growled against her lips.

"Then it's fortunate I brought a blanket along."

"Very fortunate. Let us be using it."

Hayley handed it to him. Conn spread it on the soft grass beneath the tree.

With a sigh of satisfaction, Hayley lay down upon it and held out her arms.

"Come to me, my darling," she whispered.

Her soft words echoed in his mind. He'd said this to her the first night they were together.

On their wedding night, too.

Both those times, shadows had marred their joy.

Now there was nothing except love and the promise of delight.

He settled down beside her, drawing her into his embrace.

"I love you more than life itself," he told her.

"As I love you. May we have many more years of life and love together."

"Together," Conn repeated.

Then his lips took hers, and the moon-kissed night and all else except their hearts beating as one was forgotten.

Dear Reader:

Thank you for reading *Hayley's Heart.* I hope you've enjoyed it.

I'm very excited about my next historical romance from Zebra, *Sarah's Christmas,* which will be published in December, 1999.

Sarah Calder lost Hunter Winslow to a rival seven years ago. Now Hunter, a widower, is back in Little Bethlehem, Missouri, with his young son, and wants Sarah to forgive and forget. But Sarah feels she can never trust Hunter again after what he's done.

With the help of the Christmas season and a newcomer to town named Angela, Sarah strives to find love and happiness with the only man she's ever loved.

I love to hear from readers. Write me at P.O. Box 63021, Pensacola, FL 32526. If you'd like bookmarks and a newsletter, please include a self-addressed, stamped envelope.